D0901962

ALSO BY ANNE RENWICK

The Tin Rose

The Golden Spider

The Silver Skull

A Trace of Copper

Kraken and Canals

The Iron Fin

The Elemental Web Chronicles — Book Three

Anne Renwick

www.annerenwick.com

Publisher's Note: This is a work of fiction. Names, characters, places, and incidents are a product of the author's imagination. Locales and public names are sometimes used for atmospheric purposes. Any resemblance to actual people, living or dead, or to businesses, companies, events, institutions, or locales is completely coincidental.

Book Layout ©2015 BookDesignTemplates.com

The Iron Fin/ Anne Renwick. -- 1st ed.
ISBN 978-1-948359-05-4

Cover design by James T. Egan of Bookfly Design.

Edited by Sandra Sookoo.

To Kristan, Shaunee, Jennifer and the cold, windy weekend that brought this story to life.

THANK YOU TO...

The Plotmonkeys—Kristan Higgins, Shaunee Cole, Jennifer Iszkiewicz, Stacia Bjarnason and Huntley Fitzpatrick—who almost never blink at my bizzare plots.

Jacqueline for answering my questions about the Royal Navy. All mistakes are my own.

Sandra Sookoo, my brilliant editor who mercilessly ferrets out weaknesses and sets my work on a better course.

My husband and my two boys.

My mom and dad.

Mr. Fox and his red pen.

Chapter One

December 1884

Alec McCullough bit back a slew of curse words. Not a damn thing was wrong, but he couldn't shake a feeling of impending doom. He ran a complete systems check for the third time, but couldn't find any reason to scrub the mission.

Everything inside the escape hatch was in perfect working order. Every last dial, gauge and meter indicated that all systems functioned within normal limits. Outside the submersible, saltwater density held constant. Speed was at a minimum, and they drifted silently at neutral buoyancy, holding at periscope depth.

"Something wrong?" Moray's voice—tense and clipped—echoed in the metal tube. He too hoped for a reason to abort.

Davis, the only teammate enthused about this assignment, gave Alec a sharp glance and tapped the face of the countdown timer. "Five minutes until exit. Time to call it, Mac."

"Nothing's wrong," he answered, his neck tight. Any and all objections had been dutifully noted yesterday—and dismissed. He pulled his dive goggles into place. "We're a go."

Cleared for a stealthy exit into the frigid, Scottish sea loch. Ready to rise upward through the dark waters to board an unsuspecting vessel where—sources indicated—Icelandic spies floated, posing as fishermen.

Barring the unlikely appearance of an irate loch kraken, nothing should go awry.

The team's mission was sneak and peek. Find out what information the men on the boat were after. Avoid confrontation and discovery. Employing a submersible turned a simple, low-priority operation into an elaborate, risky maneuver. Why not slip quietly into the loch from the shore? Why employ such a high-risk technique that would stress the limits of their aquaspira breathers?

This was only the first of two red flags.

He glanced again at Davis. Yesterday, his teammate had stumbled. Over nothing. If Alec hadn't been looking in his direction, he would never have caught the awkward sidestep. Minor, yes, but the BURR—Benthic Underwater Reconnaissance and Rescue—team required each man to be in perfect form. A slight imbalance on shore might translate underwater into complete vestibular disorientation.

Irrational orders and a man with a balance disorder. *That* was what had Alec on pins and needles. Despite their reputation in the Navy, BURR men were not indestructible.

As head of his team, he'd expressed such misgivings to his OC. Though Fernsby dismissed his concerns about Davis, his jaw had tightened in unhappy agreement with Alec's objection to the planned submersible depth. But someone high above both their pay grades wanted this exit technique tested. Yesterday.

The operation proceeded as planned. Three fully-outfitted BURR men crammed in a narrow steel tube—some twenty-five feet below the wind-whipped waves of Loch Broom—were about to attempt the first covert exit of a fully submerged O-class submersible. Fifteen feet below established safety standards.

Thirty seconds left. At the surface, Shaw and Rowen would be in position, staging an exercise on the water's surface designed to draw the attention of the so-called fishermen, while Alec and his men emerged from beneath, undetected.

Davis looked at him through the thick glass of his diving goggles and spoke around his mouthpiece, "Ready?"

Alec glanced again at the indicator lights. Still green. Time to move. He nodded and spoke the required command. "Open the seawater valve." There would be no more verbal communication until they reached the surface.

Moray took point, cranking it open.

Water streamed around the outer pressure door and flooded the chamber—ankles, knees, waist. He clamped his lips around the mouthpiece of his aquaspira breather. The loch's water was cold. Though BURR members were used to cold and wet, hypothermia made for a deadly enemy. Hence the black, vulcanized rubber dry suits they wore. They were heavy, awkward, and required constant maintenance. Still, no one complained. The insulation was essential for the long hours they spent submerged in temperatures often below fifty degrees. As the water pressure increased, the dry suit squeezed tightly against his body, and the swirling currents slowed. Time to leave.

Lifting a large, metal wrench from the hatch floor, he banged out a message for those still inside, announcing their imminent departure. Moray twisted the hatch's exit wheel, pushed it outward, and began to kick, finning upward and outward.

Davis followed, then Alec. But halfway through the circular opening, Alec slammed into him. The red light from his phosphorescent headlamp illuminated a man, suspended motionless in the dark waters.

Bloody hell. Aquaspira scrubber failure. Hypoxic blackout. Exactly what he'd feared. Returning to the submersible was impossible. Davis had minutes to live, and the water would not drain from the tube fast enough. His only chance was to reach the surface.

Alec punched the sounder beacon attached to Davis's dive belt, then slapped the UP bag. Millions of methanogenic bacteria entered a rapid growth phase releasing an ever-increasing amount of gas that shot his teammate to the surface. So much for a slow and safe ascent.

Mission failure. There'd be no covert observation or boarding of any ship today. They'd be lucky not to lose a man.

Alec activated his own beacon and began to kick his way free of the submersible door when there was a horrible metallic groan and a loud bang. The rim of the hatch smashed into his right knee, scraping along the side of his calf, catching his ankle, dragging him downward.

An excursion. Freshwater from the hills and rivers feeding into the loch had amassed and run smack up against a mass of salt water from the ocean, forming a kind of wall. One they had unexpectedly crossed. The sudden decrease in water density sent the vessel into an abrupt dive, not unlike a raft going over an unanticipated waterfall.

Excruciating pain radiated through his leg as the hatch door ripped the flipper from his foot and frigid water trickled into his dry suit. A tear. Alec punched his own UP bag and began to kick furiously as ice-cold water crept upward, reaching his waist. He glanced at his depth gauge. *Fuck.*

Despite his efforts, he'd been dragged downward a good ten feet, maybe more. The rip in his dry suit had compromised his ascent. No matter how hard he kicked, he wasn't rising any closer to the surface. Not even the UP bag could compensate.

Negative buoyancy—the point at which he would sink instead of float—threatened. White and black spots flashed before his eyes in warning as he ripped the weighted belt from his waist. He kicked. A pause in his strokes. A glance at the gauge. He'd only managed to maintain position. Water slipped over his chest to his armpits, inching its way toward his neck.

Cold.

So cold.

What would kill him first as he sank to the bottom of the loch? The increasing water pressure or hypothermia?

Shit. This was the end. A watery grave because some politician didn't care if he pushed BURR to their technical limits. His family would be notified that he'd succumbed to an "unfortunate accident" during a mission. Mother would be distraught. His sister would be left wondering. At least his brothers would know what happened.

Small comfort that.

Alec fought to keep his breathing from growing shallow, fought to keep his arms and legs moving and redoubled his efforts even though it felt as if he was swimming through honey. Muscle contraction generated heat. He would quit when he was dead and not a moment before.

Something slammed into his shoulder, a claw of some sort gripped his dry suit and tugged him upward. Though the lights in his eyes continued to dance, a new color joined them. Red. The same eerie phosphorescent glow his own headlamp emitted.

Could it be? No. He'd sunk too far. He was hallucinating. There was no way Moray could have reached him, not at this depth.

Except his depth gauge told him otherwise. He blinked. Twenty-five feet and rising. His heart gave a thud of hope. Perhaps today was not his last.

They stopped for decompression. Alec stared through the hazy glow of two combined underwater headlamps. It *was* Moray. The best swimmer on the crew. But how the hell had he managed to follow him when the submersible took a dive? Or drop to almost forty feet, recover Alec, and head for the surface—all while fighting the negative pull of gravity?

Moray hauled him upward again. Alec kicked, but a fiery pain burst through his right knee. The injury screamed an objection that not even the icy water could quell. He struggled to keep his breathing steady, but the dancing lights returned followed by oblivion.

~~~

Pain erupted, and Alec drew in a ragged breath. Atmospheric air. His eyes registered a blur of white clouds overhead. A face swam into focus above his. Shaw, close friend and teammate, bent over him as he slapped two sticks on either side of his damaged leg.

"Hell of a way to land yourself on desk duty." Shaw's voice was cheerful. That alone was suspicious. Combined with a blank face, it meant everything had
~~~

gone pear-shaped. "Better you than me, though. The way that Icelandic fishing vessel rocketed out of here?" He shook his head. "Paperwork on this disaster is going to be endless."

Beneath him, the floor rocked. The deck of a ship. "Davis?" His speech was slurred, and he focused on the clouds overhead as if willpower alone could stop him from passing out again.

Shaw wound a length of canvas about the brace so tightly that Alec nearly bit off his tongue trying not to howl. "Rowan caught him on his way up."

"Alive?" Alec gritted through his teeth.

"Hold tight." Shaw sidestepped the question. "I'm going to give you something for the pain."

A needle jabbed into his thigh. Blessed numbness began to spread down his leg. But it also crept upward to his hip. Soon the drug would pull him under, and he needed to know if Davis had made it.

"Tell me," Alec demanded. How much damage had some politician's grand plan done?

"Mostly. Rowan dragged him from the water and put him on an oxygen mask."

"Aquaspira failure?" They malfunctioned with alarming regularity, despite efforts to fix problems with the CO_2 scrubber. Add to that the technicians' decree to not use the breathers below the established limit of ten feet, and it was a likely statistical probability. A fact the higher-ups always attempted to overlook, much to their irritation.

"Our first assumption," Shaw said. "But he presented with acute pulmonary edema and symptoms pointing to an acute cerebrovascular event. It doesn't look good, but we're doing all we can. Dirigible transport already has him in the air."

A stroke? A sick feeling compressed Alec's gut. Had he witnessed a warning sign yesterday when Davis stumbled?

"You're next. Hear that whirring? That's ancillary transport coming for you. Next stop, Glaister Institute, section five. We'll find the prettiest nurse we can for your sponge bath."

Airlifting him to the hospital. Never a good sign. A kind of numbness fogged his brain as the painkiller worked its way through his veins. Soon he would drop into a drugged sleep. "My knee?"

Shaw sat back on his heels and gave him a twisted grin. "Nothing that threatens your ability to contribute to the next generation."

Alec barked a laugh. "Well thank aether for that. A reason to live." He should welcome the banter, let it distract him. But he just couldn't leave it alone. "Tell me. The truth, not some fairy tale."

"Truth?" Shaw whistled through his teeth and shook his head. "Your knee's pretty messed up. It crunched when I moved it. I'm not sure the Queen's men can put it together again."

Shit. Worse than he'd thought. Cold sweat broke out across his body and he shivered. If they took his leg, they took his freedom. Life behind a desk, at a laboratory bench, or—worse—attending patients would be intolerable.

He grabbed Shaw's wrist. "Fly with me. Don't let them take my leg."

"I'm coming. But, McCullough, it's bad." Pain floated in his eyes.

"I want to wiggle the toes I was born with when I wake up." He tightened his grip on Shaw's arm. "Find Dr. Morgan. Promise."

Of late, Navy surgeons were all too eager to install the latest prosthetics rather than undertake the extensive work of surgery to repair, or simply replace, a limb. Dr. Morgan took a more conservative approach.

"You know I don't make promises." Shaw's face was tight. "Not even to pretty girls. And you're far too ugly. But I'll find this Dr. Morgan. Make him exhaust every other option first."

He might hate the answer, but he could trust a teammate's word. And Dr. Morgan. Alec exhaled and let the drug take him under.

~~~

He blinked up at the blue of an overhead low-pressure mercury vapor light. Cold, hard steel met his fingertips. A rubber mask pressed to his face exhaled with a faint hiss and a hint of ether. He began to float toward the ceiling.
~~~

Above him, an oval coalesced into a familiar face, and Shaw's voice drifted in. "Good news, Mac. The doc found a solution. Bumped you ahead of another patient. Guess he likes you."

Alec tried to lift a hand to the mask.

"Easy now," Shaw said. "Leave it be. We've got this. When you wake up, it'll all be better."

The lights grew brighter for a moment. Then, with a flash, darkness descended.

~~~

A swish of skirts, leather heels tapped a rhythm against linoleum, both coming to a rest beside him. A pen nib scratched across paper, and two soft fingers pressed against the pulse point of his wrist. He must be in the Fifth Ward, hidden away in the basement of Glaister Institute.

"Water." His voice scratched.

"You're awake," the nurse gasped, turning for the door. "I'll find the doctor."

Her footfalls faded as someone at his side released a long-suffering sigh. "Scaring away the nurses already with your incessant demands."

Alec peeled open desert-dry eyelids as the hulking form that was Rowan unfolded himself from a nearby chair. "You on guard duty?"

"Keeping an eye on things," Rowan answered, pouring a glass of water and pressing it into his hand.
~~~

"This doc of yours seems trustworthy, but the rest?" He shook his head. "You want me to leave you—drugged into unconsciousness—with bored surgeons roaming the halls? They have as many sharp blades as we do, not to mention other torture devices."

A grin cracked Alec's dry lips but fell away when his eyes focused on a square lump beneath the scratchy wool blankets. His heart slammed against his sternum, beating wildly. Forcing words past his lips, he asked a question he wasn't certain he wished answered. "Is it all still there, my knee? Leg?"

"Took the doc nine hours to piece you back together, Humpty Dumpty. Said the only other options were to fuse the joint or take the leg."

Hand trembling, Alec took a sip before setting the glass down and reaching for the blanket. Sweat beaded on his forehead as he yanked the blanket aside. Linen. Yards and yards of it wrapped about his knee. All of this surrounded by a square, metal cage from which rods extended into—and possibly through—his knee.

He looked to his toes. Still there. He wiggled them. Still functioning. He flexed his ankle and felt the starched sheet beneath his heel. But all sensation to the knee was gone.

Dr. Morgan appeared in his doorway, a wide-eyed nurse behind him. "Good to see you awake, Dr. McCullough." He glanced at Rowen, amused. "You have a most protective group of large friends. I can't say I've ever operated under such... close observation."

"He means threats," Rowen clarified. "Shaw promised to remove the Doc's own leg if he mucked up the installation. He posted me here to ensure your exceptional care continues."

"Installation?" Alec felt numb.

The doctor cleared his throat. "The cage is temporary. Do not attempt to bend your knee yet. The soft tissue I managed to save needs time to heal. Two weeks at a minimum." The surgeon's next words dropped a giant soul-crushing weight upon his chest. "Unfortunately, the bone and cartilage of the knee joint itself was beyond repair. I've replaced it with the arthroflex, an experimental artificial knee joint."

Artificial? Experimental? *Fuck.* They'd never let him dive again.

Chapter Two

January 1885

"Your toes as well?" Frowning, Isa McQuiston looked up from her young patient's hand, hoping she'd heard wrong.

Nearly all Finn moving to the cities chose to remove the webbing between their fingers. Why? Horrified stares. Ridicule. Outright contempt for a physical deformity that was deemed clear evidence of personal failing. Scars were easier to explain away. She herself had made the exact same choice.

But toes?

Avra slid her hand from Isa's grasp and looked over her shoulder at the small group of family members gathered about the warm peat fire that burned in the center of the blackhouse. A man—the young woman's father—gave her a nod of encouragement. "Everything." Avra swallowed hard. "All at once. Today."

"You do realize you're facing several long hours of surgery and a painful recovery?" Isa warned. "Fingers and toes—and even the tips of ears—are densely populated with nerve endings." She kept her back rigid, resisting the impulse to turn and glare at the man. "If your family is pressuring you—"

"You don't understand," Avra objected, her voice petulant. "I'm doing this for myself. I'm sixteen, and I've never left this village because my mum refused to go. I miss her dreadfully, I do. But I want to see more, do more. I sent samples to a seamstress in Glasgow, and I've been offered a position. My da found a job building ships. And my aunt contacted a matchmaker." A delighted gleam lit her silver eyes as she announced, "She already has eight men who wish to meet me!"

Isa fought an urge to wince. Ten years ago *she* had been Avra, determined to abandon the Isle of Lewis for the mainland, to marry well, to make her mark on medical science. One item on her list had been accomplished. Many would argue she'd managed the second. But the third had proved impossible. Her heart shrank a bit. All too easy to place a finger on the very date life had forced her to set aside her own hopes and dreams.

"None of your goals require perfectly shaped toes," Isa pointed out, eyeing the tightly laced leather boots Avra wore with great skepticism. "You will find it painful—or impossible—to walk for quite some time. It may delay your departure."

Aether, she hated being the voice of good sense and reason. Hated her drab, woolen skirts, how her hair was scraped into a tight knot. Hated how she needed to constrain even her physical movements so as to convey both competency and respectability. But her acceptance as a healer was hard-won, and she could not afford to alienate a single individual among her people. If she lost an essential source of income, her uncle would win. Again.

She'd rather walk ten miles barefoot upon barnacles.

"Yes, but..." A flush rose to Avra's face as she leaned forward. Her voice emerged as a whisper, "What if I contract a marriage with a progressive? He might find defective toes repulsive."

Caught between the urge to laugh and scold—for Finn features were a gift, not an abnormality—Isa choked.

In her experience, a husband rarely cared what was at the end of his wife's legs, being more interested in what was between them. Besides, any Finn man trying so very hard to assimilate to such a degree should skip the matchmaker altogether and marry a Scottish woman. But she didn't dare voice such an opinion.

"It's but a small flap of skin," Avra continued. "In Glasgow, it serves no purpose and can only cause trouble."

In the city, what good is being Finn?

She'd heard that question asked far too frequently, and had yet to find a satisfactory answer. In recent years, more and more Finn were tempted away from their traditional fishing villages to seek their fortunes in cities where technology breakthroughs promised a life of wealth and luxury. Many returned, broken, but the rare story of success was an unrelenting siren's song.

To fit in, to be fully accepted in the city, a Finn must appear to be no different from Scots. To look "other" was to invite comment, to solicit derision. Nothing could be done about their odd, gray eyes. But ears, fingers and—yes—even toes could be altered.

Once, extra skin stretching between the fingers and toes was celebrated—the more the better—among the Finn as proof of a pure heritage, of their descent from the gods and goddesses of the sea. Those days were long past.

Conform? Or stand proudly apart? Both had merit. But a nail that stuck out was almost certain to be hammered down. Avra must reach her own decision.

Item by item, Isa unpacked her surgical equipment. Gleaming scalpels, clamps, needles and scissors. Lengths of fine ophthalmic catgut and silver wire for sutures. Balls of lint to mop up the blood and flannel to bandage the incisions.

"You understand that the operations require general anesthesia," she said, presenting the dangers bare and unvarnished. A moment of truth that turned many a Finn away from the surgery. "You'll feel no pain, but there is a risk the narcotic might trigger the diving reflex and drop your heart rate dangerously low."

And sometimes a heart beating too slow might simply... stop. It was an outcome that had been all too common in the past, and one of many reasons Finn gave surgeons a wide birth, calling upon them only when truly necessary.

The girl pressed a trembling hand to her throat. "I thought..." She gulped as Isa placed a leather and rubber mask upon the table between them, studying the embedded brass gauges that allowed her to monitor various respiratory gas levels. "I thought you'd solved that particular problem."

"Not entirely," Isa disclosed, her chest tight with the memory of every time she'd lost a patient. "I have a specially formulated mixture of volatile anesthetic agents for Finn and rarely encounter complications now. But the longer you're asleep, the higher the risk. Are you certain you wish for me to operate upon your feet?"

The young woman's eyebrows drew together as this new worry carved a groove in her forehead. Isa gave her time to weigh her options, but continued to position her paraphernalia upon the bleached canvas she'd spread over the kitchen table. As the only flat surface available in the small cottage, it would serve as an operating table.

"I do," Avra replied, setting her jaw. "I do not wish a small flap of skin to keep me from my goals."

Isa could refuse to proceed, of course. But this procedure was part and parcel of the profession she'd adopted. If she refused to alter Finn, they would take matters into their own hands. She'd seen the results.

Without anesthesia or sterile procedures, the unlucky developed infections that festered, oftentimes ending in blood poisoning. The lucky merely bore angry, disfiguring scars.

But—they rationalized—at least they wouldn't be ogled as a quaint curiosity—or worse—be called a selkie. A tiresome and irritating piece of fiction.

The selkie was a mythological creature. Imaginary. Though the sea called to each of them, not a single Finn—man or woman—had ever shape-shifted into the form of a gray seal to slide into the surf beneath the moon.

"All three," she agreed with some reluctance. "Provided you promise me the choice is your own."

"I swear it upon the sea and the moon that turns the tides."

Her fingers tightened around the bottle of ethanol she held. It was uncanny to hear a Finn oath sworn upon the intent to sever ties with that very community.

Avra held a trembling hand out above the white cloth, and called to her grandmother. "*Mummo*?"

"You wish the first cut ceremony?" Isa asked, blinking in amazement.

"No. But my grandmother requested it," her voice softened, "and I've broken her heart enough."

An old woman rose from the gathering of relatives and crossed the room to stand beside her granddaughter. Tradition—one most Finn largely ignored—required the eldest family member to mark the moment a Finn renounced any future right to lead the community as an elder. "It is decided?" Her grandmother's voice was weak and thin, as if watered down by a deep sadness.

"Yes, *mummo*." Avra's voice was as resolute as granite. "It needs to be."

With a faint nod, the old woman placed a hand—wrinkled and webbed—upon her granddaughter's head. Drawing herself up straight and proud, she began to speak in the old language, "I stand as witness—"

The throaty consonants catapulted Isa back in time, to the first day she herself had broken with Finn convention. A vat of dull, brown dye had boiled upon the stovetop, a monthly ritual, ready to conceal the coppery roots that sprung from her head. Defiant, she'd crossed her arms and refused. "The chemicals burn," she'd protested, then, knowing she was about to unleash a thousand furies, continued, "And why bother? My Scottish ancestry is an open secret."

Her refusal had sent the household into an uproar. Eyes wide, her brother and sister gaped. Mother cried. Uncle Gregor frowned. Grandmother had all but disowned her. But Isa had stood firm, forever altering the course of her future.

Though her stomach knotted at the memory, any regret was directed at the events that unfolded afterward. Naïve of her to think her relatives would ever understand her viewpoint. She'd become a problem to be solved, her future a situation to be manipulated.

A certain melancholy washed over her as the matriarch spoke the final words of the invocation. "The waves have surged and cast you adrift. But the moon's pull is unceasing, and the sea endures. When the tide turns, may you find the current that carries you safely home."

With a shake of her head, she knocked aside the unwelcome emotions, consigning them to a distant corner of her consciousness. She needed to focus. Reflecting upon the implications of this surgery could wait.

Isa uttered the response in the old tongue. "Until then may you find the tranquility of deep waters within your heart." Swabbing the skin that stretched between the third and fourth finger of Avra's right hand, she lifted the scalpel and made the first cut. Blood welled along the incision, and she waited for the matriarch to pronounce the final words.

But they did not come. Instead, the old woman stared at Isa, her gaze razor sharp. "Once I called your grandmother friend," she said, continuing in the same old tongue. "For her, I make you this offer. Decline to finish. Leave my granddaughter intact, and I myself will play matchmaker on your behalf."

Irritation pricked her skin. Every Finn woman wished to see her safely marriage-bound, but she'd come to value her freedom far too much. She enjoyed this new career, traveling about in her houseboat from community to community, attending to various medical complaints, many of which were Finn specific. How many Scottish physicians knew to warn a Finn not to dive with a spleen infection? To treat digestive complaints with Epsom salts and oil of thyme to rid them of parasites? "Thank you, but I do not seek a new husband."

The matriarch's mouth opened once more, but Isa was spared her reply as the door to the blackhouse swung open. A frigid blast of air blew inward, and the flames leapt at the sudden flood of oxygen. All eyes, however, fixed upon the man who staggered inward, his clothes sodden and dripping from the storm that raged outside. He dragged a woolen cap from his head. "I need the healer. It's happened again."

"Who?" Avra's grandmother demanded.

"Abel. We found him on the beach. Alive, but he's lost much blood."

Those were the only words Isa needed to hear. This surgery could wait. Thrusting items back into her doctor's bag, she turned to find the old woman holding out her cloak. "He is a good man," the matriarch said, hustling Isa toward the door. "A father, with many mouths to fill."

Outside, the howling wind hurtled shards of icy rain into her face as she followed the man down a footpath that snaked its way toward a blackhouse crouching beside a bluff. A weighted net fought to keep its thatched roof atop windowless stone walls. Anemic wisps of peat smoke escaped the central hole only to be yanked away by the wind. Just beyond, the surf crashed and boomed against the rocky coast.

They hurried across the threshold and into a smoky room. A single oil lamp hung from the rafters casting a weak, yellow light. Three young children quietly playing with marbles at the far end of the house stopped to stare. A hugely pregnant woman—presumably their mother—rose from her seat beside a bed whose sole occupant lay motionless, his face pale and drawn.

Though her eyes were red and puffy, she blocked Isa's approach, giving the man who had delivered her a pointed stare. "Are you certain she can be trusted?"

He shifted on his feet. "She *is* Finn."

And Finn avoided sharing anything that might be considered an eccentricity with outsiders. What could be so amiss that denying her husband treatment was even an option?

"My practice focuses upon Finn," she said, drawing the woman's intense and anxious gaze. "Whatever his complaint, the details will not leave this room."

Hand upon her abdomen, the woman nodded, then stepped aside.

Isa pressed the back of her hand to the man's forehead. Cold and clammy and unresponsive to her touch. His breath was shallow and his face slack. When she pointed the light of a decilamp into his vacant eyes, they danced. A nystagmus. Not good. "Was he conscious when you found him? Has he spoken?"

His wife shook her head. "He woke up once, but his words were garbled and made no sense. I spooned broth into his mouth, but he barely managed to swallow."

Facial hypesthesia with dysphagia. Dysarthria. The evidence mounted in favor of diagnosing an apoplexy.

Drawing a stethoscope from her bag, she slid it beneath the blanket to listen to his heart—a regular rhythm, but too slow—and continued gathering a history. "You said this is the second time this has happened?"

"No," the man spoke. "He is the second fisherman to be attacked."

"I'm sorry." Isa's head jerked up as her eyebrows drew together. "Did you say attacked?"

"He left on his fishing boat," the wife said, "and was gone for weeks. Today, my son found him on the beach like this." She tugged down the blanket covering her husband's form.

Isa's mouth fell open and her eyes grew wide. She struggled to regain a professional demeanor. And failed. "*What* in the seven seas..." This was far, far outside her experience.

A pale, flesh-like cylinder—tube?—of about three inches in length protruded from his stomach. Someone had tied the end off with rough twine. It appeared to have been severed from... from...

"That is what we hoped you could tell us," the man volunteered. "We found him like this, with blood oozing from the tentacle."

"Tentacle," she repeated, as if pronouncing the word aloud might help her make sense of what her eyes observed. Gingerly, she reached out with a probe, half expecting the rubbery mass to move of its own accord. It didn't. Flipping it across the man's abdomen, however, revealed rows of tiny suckers. "Not sea kraken." Not only was the tentacle not squid-like, but sea kraken of such size had claws embedded in their suckers and rarely ventured this far north into the cold Atlantic.

"No," he agreed.

"Then it must be..." Her face twisted in confusion. Octopuses were not known for attacking men. Not in such a manner. Provoked, they might bite with their sharp beaks or wrap an arm about a man's arm, leg or neck. But to pierce the abdomen with a tentacle? Unheard of. "How can it be...?"

He nodded. "Octopus."

Knees weak, she resisted an impulse to drop into the unoccupied chair. "Impossible."

And yet the evidence lay before her.

"Can you save him?" his wife asked, her voice a whisper of hopelessness.

Closing her eyes for a moment, Isa took a deep breath and spoke her thoughts aloud. "This is far, far outside my experience. On the surface, it appears to be a case of apoplexy, bleeding in the brain. With care and time, he might recover. But the presence of the tentacle complicates matters."

"Can it be removed?" the man prompted.

"Certainly." Isa ran damp palms over her skirts. There was no other course of action, even though it would stretch her skills to their limit. "It *must* be removed. If not, infection will set in when the octopus flesh begins to decay." The patient's wife winced. "However, removing the tentacle is also risky. It might be a simple procedure. Or it could cause further bleeding." Depending upon what had been pierced, he could easily die. She opened her black bag and began to prepare for an entirely different surgery. Placing the anesthesia mask upon the bedside table, she looked into his wife's eyes. "I *can* promise you he will feel no pain during the surgery. The decision is yours to make."

A desperate and horrible sound came from the afflicted man. All flinched as they turned toward the bed. His chest expanded drawing a deep and labored breath, a gasping, rattling, endless inhalation.

And then it stopped.

But there was no exhalation.

"I'm so sorry." Isa grabbed his wife's hand. "He's gone."

Chapter Three

February 1885

Alec clenched his fists. Punching his brother in the eye would be immensely satisfying but would solve nothing. “My knee is fine,” he growled. Again.

“It’s fine for a civilian. Excellent, really,” Logan agreed. “But not even I can pull enough strings to send you back to your team. How many times do you need to hear it? Until Dr. Morgan produces the appropriate paperwork documenting that the artificial joint meets BURR specifications, you cannot be reinstated. Given it’s experimental, that might be never.”

He clenched his jaw. "Well I'm not staying here."

He glared at the windowless laboratory buried beneath the Glaister Institute in the heart of Glasgow. A temporary assignment, he'd been promised, but months had passed in this humid, saline pit of despair, and no end was in sight. The artificial light and stagnant air ate at his soul. No matter how many immense saltwater tanks it held or the number of bizarre sea creatures that swam in their depths, it didn't—couldn't—hold a decilamp to the exhilaration of working on the open ocean.

"Casting aspersions upon Lord Roideach's facility?" Logan's eyebrows rose. "BURR teams have benefitted from multiple innovations that emerged from this very laboratory." Across the room a technician, one Miss Lourney, puffed with pride as his brother ticked off item after item upon his fingers. "You yourself reverse-engineered that Russian nematocyst weapon in under two hours."

"After Roideach's people spent a month studying it, unable to reproduce the coiled thread." Alec scoffed. "Every other item on your list was developed when the lord was in his prime, some five years past. Now?" He shook his head. "The man himself is never present and has no idea that his laboratory technicians are incompetent. They insisted upon using the Volterra equation when the viscoelastic material was clearly nonlinear. He ought to dismiss them all."

"I beg your pardon," Miss Lourney snapped. She planted a fist on her hip. "That was an oversight that would not have happened had we been informed the trigger material was silicon-based. A fact you kept close to your chest."

Tipping his head back, Alec focused on an overhead network of pipes covered in a sheen of condensation.

"Which you would have deduced for yourselves if any of you bothered to keep abreast of the latest internal reports." He missed his team, where everyone went above and beyond to perform to the best of their abilities and no one was allowed to rest upon their laurels.

Though even among the military elite, it was possible to overreach. Over a month had passed, but anger, guilt and sorrow still swirled together in his gut. That unwarranted enthusiasm of Davis for their last dive mission? Explained by the drug vial found in his sea chest. Striving to increase the ability of his red blood cells to carry oxygen, Davis had used an intravenous blood thickener of dubious origins and had, according to the autopsy report, thrown a clot to his brain.

If the man wasn't already dead, Alec would strangle him. Davis had put the entire team at risk. Still, he'd called the man friend, and his death left an empty, hollow space inside Alec's chest. Would his teammate still be alive if he'd forced Major Fernsby to address his concerns?

His brother clasped his shoulder. *That* had Alec's instant attention. Logan avoided casual touch. Always had, even amongst family. Which meant he wanted something, and when Logan Black wanted something, there were few screws he wouldn't turn.

Alec braced himself.

"Nonetheless," his brother said with deceptive good humor, "your prompt grasp of the problem and instantaneous solution has convinced the Glaister Institute to offer you your own laboratory." He slapped a sheet of thick, letterhead paper onto the workbench before him. "Congratulations! You'll answer to no one but yourself. Except, of course, the Institute's Board."

Slowly, deliberately, Alec lifted the paper, touching its corner to the flame of a Bunsen burner. "No. Not for all the treasure of a sultan's palace."

Logan's lips twitched. "What if I threw in the harem too?"

With huff of disgust and a glare that threatened to incinerate them both, Miss Russel stormed from the room. Miss Lourney, Roideach's other laboratory assistant, frowned at him.

"My apologies," he offered. "My brother can be an insensitive oaf."

With a roll of her eyes, Miss Lourney turned back to her work.

"You have a way of burning bridges." Alec tossed the charred offer into a sink and crossed his arms, waiting. His brother always had more than one option up his sleeve.

"It was worth a try. You're certain you never witnessed Roideach's people acting... suspicious?"

"Unless you count a certain shifty-eyed glance at the great man's empty office before making excuses and slinking out the door for an exceptionally early tea?" He shook his head. "No. Now what is it that you *really* want from me?"

A crooked smile broke out across Logan's face. "Follow me."

Though his knee ached with the first few steps, it settled down to a low, manageable throb as they walked down a long hall, then turned off into a narrow corridor. Several flights of stairs—connected by cobweb-strewn passages and doorways—at last led them to a corroded iron door.

His brother produced a rusty punch key, a previous generation's concept of security. Whatever lay inside, it was certain to be unpleasant. Even as a child, Logan was more likely to present a frog rather than a flower. He and his brother had been treated to many "gifts"—various reptiles, rodents and stinging insects—quite often left for them beneath the bedsheets. With a scrape and a hard twist, the door creaked open admitting them to—

"An air shaft?" Dust swirled, and Alec coughed. "When was it last used? During King William's rule?"

"Possibly. More importantly, it's long forgotten." Logan closed the door before crossing the room to a stack of wooden crates upon which a silver refrigeration case rested. His fingers hovered above the latches. "A perfect location to unofficially store questionable items."

"And you want me to...?"

"Work for me. For the Duke of Avesbury on behalf of the Queen."

"As a spy." Alec shook his head. "No thank you. If I wanted to sneak about on my own, I wouldn't have joined the Navy." Still, since Logan had breached the subject, he had to ask. "How is Quinn?"

Theirs was a family with interesting branches grown from an unhappy marriage. Only Alec and Quinn were full, legitimate siblings. Though all four children had been raised beneath the same roof, Logan and his sister, Cait, were the products of illicit affairs. Midst the constant squabbling, they'd formed a solid alliance, each developing unorthodox skill sets to discourage excessive parental intrusion.

And old habits die hard. Today, all four of them pursued unique careers incompatible with polite conversation.

Like Logan, Quinn was a Queen's agent, but spent most of his time abroad. Or so Quinn led all to believe. No point in asking *where* he was or *when* he might return. Logan would die before giving up the slightest of secrets.

"Alive and fit, if perhaps uncomfortable." Logan drew a deep breath. "I need your help. And you need mine. Commodore Drummond has issued papers for your discharge based on medical grounds."

Every muscle in Alec's body clenched, bracing for a fight he could not hope to win. He cursed. If the man wanted him out, there was little he could do.

"Wait." Logan held up a hand. "I pulled on strings, ropes, leashes and lanyards to make those papers go missing. Then I called in several personal favors. Fernsby is in line for a promotion. In the event your knee never passes muster, I can't reinstate you onto the BURR team, but I can see you installed as Fernsby's replacement."

His gut twisted at the thought of no more missions, no more deployments. Desk duty. But the alternative—discharge—was unthinkable. "I accept." Though he'd expected to work for several more years—perhaps grow a few gray hairs—before such a position became inevitable.

His brother laughed, then shook his head. "It's not that easy, not when the duke is involved. There is a task you must accomplish first."

He should have known. Nothing with his brother was ever straightforward. He sighed. "What's in the case?"

"A mystery."

Logan waggled his eyebrows, and Alec rolled his eyes. Such drama. But as the lid lifted and a cold fog flowed out of the refrigerated case, a piece of ragged flesh torn from some creature of the sea became visible. White with interlacing streaks of red, it glistened.

Interest sparked, and he stepped closer. "May I touch it?"

"Of course."

Alec lifted the scrap of rubbery integument and turned it over in his hands. "Kraken?"

"That's what Professor Corwin thought at first." Logan lifted a lid off one of the crates to reveal a small, portable aetheroscope. "Look closer."

Though he was no cryptozoologist, the last few weeks studying predatory mollusks proved useful. Columnar epithelia, gland cells, neuronal fibers, connective tissue, striated musculature. Everything one would expect to find upon histological examination of cephalopod tissue. And yet...

He adjusted the focus as baffling details revealed themselves beneath the lens.

Strange.

A thin lattice-work of what appeared to be charred carbon fibers formed a kind of internal network around which the various cellular strata grouped. It was—or had been—a living tissue with a fabricated core. Neither artificial nor natural, but both at once.

In a heartbeat, Alec was caught in Logan's net.

Straightening, he regarded his brother with a frown. "A wire mesh. Upon which cephalopod tissue has been grown. How is this possible?"

"Exactly what we'd like to know," Logan replied. "Particularly as the man who collected this sample—along with a number of odd reports of deaths that may or may not be related—has gone missing."

"Missing. From where?"

His brother tipped his head and lifted an eyebrow. "Do you accept the commission of the Queen's agents?"

Arrogant bastard.

Alec rubbed the back of his neck. There would be a steep price to pay—of that he was certain—for allowing himself to become entangled in Logan's web of intrigue. But what else awaited him in Glasgow? He could work as a general surgeon, take a wife, produce offspring. A perfectly ordinary life. Absolutely nothing wrong with that. Except... to be cut off from the inner circles of the Navy and the innovations emerging from Glaister Institute? He wasn't ready to let go of that. "I do."

"Took you long enough," Logan said. "Professor Corwin, chasing rumors of selkies near the Orkney Islands—"

Alec sniggered.

"You laugh, but Icelandic agents have approached our shores, why not disguised as mythological creatures? Recall why your failed mission was launched."

Good point. Alec sobered. "Continue."

"It has recently been brought to the attention of the Queen's agents that there are shadow committees within our biological research facilities, ones that seek to investigate certain human... oddities. They call themselves CEAP, the Committee for the Exploration of Anthropomorphic Peculiarities. Speculations regarding the existence of selkies would certainly pique their curiosity. We believe the professor may have run afoul of one such committee."

"Go on."

"Though rumors proved false, an underlying pattern emerged. Inquiries led Corwin to the Outer Hebrides. Near a beach on the Isle of Lewis where this particular tissue fragment washed up, there was a curious incident involving a fisherman. A man found half-dead upon his boat was carried ashore. The local physician offered assistance, but the family waved him away. Instead, they brought in an itinerant, self-styled healer. The man died shortly after her arrival." Logan tapped a finger upon a crate. "This put the good doctor's nose out of joint, and he adjourned, grumbling, to the local tavern where our man, Corwin, overheard a most bizarre claim." Eyes gleaming, his brother paused for effect.

"Don't make me beat it out of you," Alec warned. He stopped himself from leaning in. Not a chance he'd give his brother the satisfaction of seeing him dangling on a hook. "It's a bad habit of yours."

"Much as I'd like to see you try," Logan snorted, "I need you intact." His eyes flashed with pleasure. A grand reveal was imminent. Alec held his tongue. "As the doctor drank himself under the table, a snippet of conversation filtered through the general chaos. Corwin heard a man mutter about this not being the first time someone was killed by an octopus attack."

"An octopus—not a kraken—attack?" That far north, both species rarely reached a substantial size, but only the kraken were given to attacking humans unprovoked. "How old is this Professor Corwin? Perhaps he's gone hard of hearing?"

"He was entirely fit for duty, unlike some." Logan threw a withering glance at his knee.

Was. Alec narrowed his eyes. "Go on."

"The octopus is reported to have stabbed a tentacle into the fisherman's stomach."

"Stabbed?" Alec repeated. He glanced at the aetheroscope, scratched his jaw, but didn't question his brother's words again. "Strangled is at least a remote physical possibility—indigenous octopuses of sufficient size can survive off the northern coastlines—but the only sharp portion of an octopus's anatomy is its beak."

"Yet there is this." Logan waved his hand. "An unexplained scrap of flesh, not easily dismissed. Moreover, my agent has gone missing."

"And who better to act as an interim operative then your wounded, BURR-trained brother?" He gave a bark of laughter as it struck him. "The laboratory assignment was no mistake, was it? Orchestrated by none other than you, designed to drive me slightly insane while forcing me to study mollusk biology."

Logan smirked. “I’d offer you a TTX pistol, but—”

“I’ve far, far better in my BURR locker,” he said, dismissing the weapon. “Assuming I’m permitted access?”

“Of course. You have full clearance and are authorized for independent shore duty. You report *only* to me. You share your findings *only* with me. Investigate the tissue’s origins and collect, if possible, a larger sample of the material. Blend with the locals and find out more about these rumors. Keep your eyes and ears open for news of Corwin. I want to know what’s going on.”

Chapter Four

April 1885
Stornoway, Scotland, the Isle of Lewis

Weeks of biting cold, lashing wind and endless rain had turned up nothing. No strange scraps of skin, no whispers of octopus attacks and no dead bodies—human *or* cephalopod.

All he'd managed to do was relax his grooming standards. He resembled a slightly insane Scottish fisherman inclined to pass his evenings in the local pubs. Yesterday, he'd caught a passing glance in a salt-crusted window and barely recognized himself.

Wind-bitten skin. Shaggy hair. A bushy beard. Wool sweaters and oilcloth outerwear. And though it wasn't visible, a hint of rancid fish prompted the more finely dressed to step away with a wrinkled nose and a sidelong glance.

Temporary work on a fishing boat, hauling in nets of herring, had won him a cautious acceptance in town. He'd even dropped in on the local physician with complaints of knee pain—which was, alas, not a complete fiction—prompting the doctor with a fish tale of a kraken injury sustained at the London docks, but the man refused to bite. Alec's direct inquiry about dangerous local squid had earned him an odd look, but he'd left with no more than an overpriced bottle of laudanum.

Only yesterday had a ray of sunshine finally broken through the clouds. His ears had pricked at talk of a wedding. Not because generous amounts of libations would flow—this town frowned upon alcohol consumption in all its forms, negating a valuable source of information that often sprang from loose tongues—but because the bride was sister to a healer. A *female* healer named Mrs. McQuiston.

The very woman he watched now.

She'd arrived on a houseboat, one impossible to miss as it was painted a bright, turquoise blue, and docked next to the fishing boats. The somber and simple clothing she wore did nothing to hide her slender figure or its gentle curves and served only to highlight the brilliant shine of her copper hair bundled into a mass at the base of her neck. The black leather bag she clutched while preparing to disembark set his heart pounding. At last. This *had* to be the woman he sought.

As she turned, luminous silver-gray eyes caught what little light filtered through the clouds and every molecule of oxygen rushed from his lungs. She was stunning. Not a classic beauty—society would disqualify her due to her freckles and strong chin—but he could not tear his eyes away.

"You made it!" a second woman exclaimed, who rushed down to the quay to throw her arms around the first. The bride?

"Of course, Nina," the red-haired woman said, kissing her cheek. "I wouldn't miss your day for the world."

"Mum would never forgive you."

They linked arms and set off down the rutted street, heads bent together. He followed at a discreet distance, snatching snippets of conversation that drifted back to him on the wind.

"Traditional... at the turning of the tide."

"Really?" The redhead frowned. "Mum agreed?"

Nina nodded. "...blessing... full immersion."

Did they discuss the wedding? Or did the two sisters plan to dance in the light of the full moon before taking a dip in the sea? Either way, he was intrigued. He closed the gap.

The redhead's jaw dropped. "Someone offered up their child? In April?"

"Pushed for it," Nina replied. "Mrs. Carr is fit to be tied. Insists it's 'unseemly' in this day and age. But Uncle Gregor and Maren managed to convinced the grandmums to allow it. He wants his daughter consecrated in the time-honored manner."

The presumed healer stiffened. "Uncle Gregor is here?" A few steps more and she stopped in front of a curiosity store, The Dragon and the Flea. "Let Mum know I've arrived, that I'll be along in a bit. There are a few supplies I wish to purchase."

"He *is* family," Nina insisted, glancing nervously at the ghoulish displays in the window. "As is Maren. Twice over once I marry her brother." Her sister paused. "She explained everything to me."

"Did she? Everything?"

"Her husband was abusive, a philanderer. She had no choice but to leave the child with his father. Should she live her life forever alone? Besides, she and Uncle Gregor married according to the old ways. No laws have been broken. Is there no way to mend things?"

"Their marriage is their business, but they trespassed on mine. I want nothing more to do with them."

The sisters parted, with Nina continuing down the road and the redhead pushing open the shop's door.

Alec needed an excuse to follow. He fumbled open the neck of his oilcloth jacket and reached into a deep, interior pocket, fishing out a singular device. With a ragged fingernail, he flicked a pin loose from a brass hinge, letting the liquid microlens fall free. Even with that classified piece of material removed, Logan would kill him for what he was about to expose.

A blast of welcome warmth rolled over him as he stepped into The Dragon and the Flea. At the far end of the room, the proprietor waited on his latest customer. "How can I help you today, Mrs. McQuiston?"

As easy as that, he had confirmation of her name.

Glass-fronted counters defined a narrow pathway into the store. Behind the counters were more shelves, every available inch stacked with obscure items threatening a landslide. A customer might be buried alive and never discovered missing in a place such as this. It was impossible to rest the eyes upon a single object for more than a second. Taxidermied animals abounded, including a goat with two heads and a four-legged chicken. A mummified hand. A shrunken head with yellow teeth. Papier-mâché anatomical models detailing hideous skin diseases.

His eyes dropped lower, and he realized he'd stepped into what was—underneath all the trappings of a side-show—a medical supplies store. Brass microscopes, a trepanning drill, amputation kits, bandages, syringes, a birthing chair. Bottles and jars and paper packets full of powders and potions. A few fascinating items defied classification. Hours could be lost exploring this store's wonders.

"I require fine suture materials," Mrs. McQuiston informed the proprietor as she set her black bag upon the counter. "A jar of skin salve. And three needles, size eight, nine, and ten."

A finger lifted. "A moment." He crossed to a multi-drawered wooden chest and returned with a selection of fine, curved surgical needles to spread them out upon a blue-velvet cloth. "You might also find this useful," he said, adding a paper packet. "A new suture material. Sharksilk. Absorbable. Finer than any catgut I can provide and likely to work well with the number ten."

"I'll take them all," she said, counting out several coins as the man wrapped everything in brown paper.

Alec coughed and stepped forward from behind a stuffed... dodo?

The shopkeeper looked up sharply, his lips pulling downward as he took in Alec's shipwrecked appearance. "May I help you... sir?"

Time to cast a lure to see if she would bite. He pulled the surgical eyeglasses from his pocket and set them upon the counter directly within the woman's view. "I'm looking for a replacement lens, a catadioptric dialyte."

She inhaled, a soft gasp of air rushing past her parted lips. Her hands fluttered, flashing a network of unusual scars, before she tucked them into the folds of her skirts. Still, caught on his hook, she didn't collect her purchases and depart.

Eyes wide and fingers twitching, the proprietor took in the details of the deceptively simple eyeglasses. He all but drooled. "Might I, sir?"

Logan would strangle Alec for allowing a civilian to see, much less examine, this particular prototype, but to produce a more interesting object from one of his many pockets would violate military law. "Of course," Alec said, waving a casual hand at the device as if dismissing its value.

Mrs. McQuiston eyed him with obvious suspicion. Did she think him a thief, pawning stolen goods? "That would be the wrong kind of lens, Mister...?"

"Dr. McCullough." He gave a brief bow.

Her mouth pursed, unconvinced. "If that device is in your possession, *legally*, you ought to know it requires a microlens filled with an electroreactive fluid that remains viscous at room temperature."

Curious. An electric thrill ran over his skin. Not only did her words indicate extensive training, but she knew something of the research conducted behind the locked doors of Glaister Institute. Moreover, she sought to challenge him with a condescending recitation of obscure details. His opinion of her soared. This woman was no self-styled healer, yet somehow she'd escaped the facility's notice.

They would have to become better acquainted.

He drank in every detail of her appearance, hunting for clues as to how he might accomplish just that, for there was no doubt in his mind that she knew something.

Her dress and her cloak were of wool in demure shades of gray, unadorned by fripperies such as ribbons or lace. But resting upon the counter were bright blue fingerless gloves knitted with an intricate pattern. A woman who took pains not to attract attention, allowing herself only the smallest of indulgences. What other personal extravagance of color might all the gray conceal? Red silk stockings beneath practical petticoats padded for warmth?

He shoved such inappropriate speculation aside. He ought not be toying with such thoughts about another man's wife. There were some lines he wouldn't cross.

Instead, he would have to appeal to her mind. But how?

Alec grinned. "I rather thought my odds of finding such a lens on this island were low."

"So low as to be negligible."

"Which is why I asked for a catadioptric dialyte lens." Leaning an elbow onto the counter, he waved a hand in the air. "They find their way into establishments such as these all over Britain. But you are correct, it is less than ideal. Can you think of an attainable yet suitable replacement?"

"A Meikine lens might serve." She tipped her head, her eyes bright with intelligence beneath arching brows. Her gaze skimmed over his unwashed form, reevaluating first impressions. "If one cannot be found here, the ferry travels to Ullapool daily. How desperate are you?"

"Growing more so by the day." He winked, unable to turn off the charm despite his appearance. "Without the lens, it's next to impossible to discern the fine mesh beneath a cephalopod skin graft. Not that the fishing nets have lifted much of particular interest thus far."

She blinked, confused. "What kind of doctor did you say you were?"

"I didn't." His lips twitched. "The usual kind. My patients are almost always human."

"Wouldn't both squid and octopus tissue be incompatible with human flesh?"

"Yes, I would expect just that. Yet eight-legged creatures can stir up quite a bit of trouble."

"Can they?" A question, yet her voice grew rigid, informing him their exchange was at an end. Telling, for he'd expected her to press him for more information.

"Er." The proprietor's eyes bounced between them. "If that's all, Mrs. McQuiston, I'll have a look in the back for that lens mentioned."

"Of course." Slipping on her gloves, she lifted her parcels and directed a parting question at the shopkeeper. "Will you and your wife be present at the wedding tonight?"

"We wouldn't dream of missing such an event," the man replied. "We'll be there to witness your sister's vows."

With a sharp nod aimed in Alec's direction, Mrs. McQuiston took her leave.

In a moment, he would make his excuses. Time to dig his razor and a bar of soap from the depths of his rucksack. He had a wedding to crash.

A safe distance from the gently lapping waves, Isa placed one worn black slipper beside another. Darkness approached as the Finn community gathered upon the sand. Among them Maren and Uncle Gregor stood, holding a small child. She let her gaze skim past the family without acknowledgement. It wasn't their marriage or the fifteen-year age gap between them that set Isa's teeth on edge, but rather the manner in which both had betrayed her.

Ignoring the first twinges of a headache, she tugged and pulled at the lacing that ran through the eyelets of her skirt, lifting the hemline so that its ruffled edge fluttered about her knees. Scandalously high by British standards, but a perfect length for standing in the surf. She tied a secure knot, then straightened to take a deep breath as salt spray misted her face.

Beside her, Nina stood, barefoot, her hands clasped tightly about a beautiful seashell-studded bouquet. "Thank goodness." Her sister exhaled a sigh of relief. "I wasn't certain Mrs. Carr would come."

"Truly? She'd miss her own son's wedding?"

Nina frowned and looked down at the sand. "She objects to the public venue and worries her grandchildren might be born with red hair."

Ah. Now she understood. Their family was not Finn enough and no amount of tradition or ceremony could repair the tainted blood that flowed through the veins of their mother and her offspring.

The Carr children had all been surgically altered at the earliest possible age, the better to blend with others here in Stornoway, the island's largest town where the ferry connected them with Ullapool on the mainland and Scottish strangers walked among them daily. But that didn't mean Mrs. Carr wanted Scottish blood to enter her family's bloodline.

The Finn people struggled to maintain their tight-knit community while adjusting to the demands and temptations of modern life. Over time, a number of local traditions—particularly those that took place in a more public arena—had faded. This particular stretch of sand hadn't held a traditional Finn wedding ceremony since she was knee-high to a gull.

Jona's decision to marry Isa's sister in a public ceremony was tantamount to open rebellion.

"Just look at her heavy, full-length skirts and ankle boots," Nina said. "Her pinched face. Who knows what threat Jona held over her, but at least she came. Oh! I almost forgot." Isa's sister caught her wrist in a quick grip and her eyes flashed. "Be warned, she's of a mind to throw you and Elias together."

Involuntarily, her gaze flicked across the beach. There, hovering on the edge of the gathering, slouched Elias and, indeed, his eyes were trained upon her. She quickly looked away.

A solid, dependable fisherman, he was neither old nor young, ugly nor handsome. After a lingering illness, his wife had passed away. As Mrs. Carr had made her disapproval of Isa's lifestyle, traveling from Finn community to community while living alone on her houseboat, well known, she would be keen to match Elias and her, anchoring her firmly back into their community. In this particular case, Isa's mother would do everything to assist Mrs. Carr.

Her mother stood behind her brother, Danel, as he touched a torch to a pile of driftwood. Growing flames threw sparks into the air, and an elder raised her hands to the sky, chanting in the ancient language. Letting the awe of tradition wash over her, Isa followed her sister to stand as her attendant beside the bonfire.

A wide smile spread across Nina's face as Jona stepped forward to place a crown of seaweed upon his bride's head. Beneath the ethereal light of the moon, they made their vows. Any worry Isa might have had for her sister melted away when she saw how Jona looked at her. As if she'd hung the stars. This was a love match.

Her smile faltered.

Had Anton ever looked at her in such a way? Their courtship had been brief. Only three meetings before he'd presented her with a ring. She'd accepted his proposal the very minute he agreed to allow her to become his assistant, to pursue further medical education in Glasgow. As the most senior member of the family, Uncle Gregor had overseen all the legal paperwork prior to their marriage, arranging a brief ceremony held in a church before a stern minister.

Would she ever marry again? Possibly. Somehow she didn't think it very likely.

She blinked and realized the ceremony drew to a close.

Her heart twisted as Maren stepped forward, handing the elder her three-month-old daughter wrapped in a seal skin. The old woman carried the crying infant into the surf. Wet skirts swirled about her legs as she lifted the baby above the waves and began to chant.

A consecration to the sea. Gods whose names were all but forgotten were thanked. For peaking ears and joining fingers and toes. For slowing the breath and warming the skin. For transforming the Finnfolk so that they might harvest the bounty beyond the water's edge. The child was dipped into the cold waters, then lifted once more to be named—Emma—and declared a daughter of the seal.

Isa wasn't the only one who dashed away a tear or two. The old ways were beautiful, but dying, and this might be a sight never witnessed again.

"Oddest baptism I've ever observed," a deep, male voice rumbled.

Startled from her thoughts, Isa spun on her toes and found herself eye to chest—*Mother of Pearl*, he was tall!—with the unkempt man from The Dragon and the Flea. Except the stained oilskins were gone, he'd shaved, and he no longer smelled like rancid fish. She caught herself leaning forward to find out if he smelled as pleasant now as he looked.

She stopped herself and presented him with a tight smile. "Do you always appear uninvited?" Dr. McCullough might be appropriately dressed, but he was certainly no Finn.

"Regularly." His grin hitched up the corners of his lips, and he rocked backward on his heels, flicking a glance at her bare feet. "With such lovely bare ankles, what man could stay away?"

"It's a private ceremony." Her tone was clear: *go away*. Yet a traitorous heat sank into her cheeks.

Intelligent, blue eyes stared down at her, glinting as they reflected the light of the bonfire. A gust ruffled his overlong hair and a curving strand fell across his forehead. But for the jagged scar that ran from the corner of one eye across his cheekbone, he was uncommonly handsome. A fact she refused to acknowledge. "So I gathered," he said. Not so much as a foot shifted.

The man was impossible. Behind her, voices rose offering their congratulations to the couple, to the parents.

Sighing heavily, she said, "It's my sister's wedding, and I need to join my family." Whether she wished to or not. She glanced over her shoulder, relieved to find the happy couple at the center of attention. For once, no one took notice of her. If she wanted it to stay that way, Dr. McCullough needed to leave before Mrs. Carr turned her beady eyes in their direction. "You followed me. To the shop, and now you've followed me here. What is it you want?"

His smile faltered. "A conversation. No more."

"I doubt that." She turned away.

"Please." He caught her elbow, the calloused pads of his fingertips catching on the raw silk of her sleeve.

Every nerve ending in her arm stood at attention. He was strong. That she could appreciate. But—considering they'd scarcely met—far, far too bold. Isa scowled.

He set her arm free, but made no apology. "Two deaths of an unusual nature—two that I am aware of so far—have been attributed to octopuses on this isle. Though dismissed by most as a gruesome yarn to which Scottish fishermen are prone, the tales are not entirely unsubstantiated. I have been charged with separating fact from fiction."

All the blood drained from her face as various pieces began to fall into place. The picture forming in her mind was bone-chilling. Had there been more such deaths? Flitting from one community to the next, it was entirely possible she'd missed talk of other incidents.

He stepped closer. Too close. But she refused to cede her ground. "Ah, you *do* know something." His voice dropped. "What must I do to convince you to speak with me?"

She couldn't. To do so would be to expose the Finn to outside scrutiny. That hadn't ended well for her husband, and she certainly would not invite Dr. McCullough, with clear ties to the Glaister Institute, into their midst. "I have nothing to share," she insisted, backing away.

A scream tore across the beach, slicing through the wind, freezing her where she stood. Words and phrases rippled through the gathering. "Larsa dead... washed ashore... attacked... happened again." One word in particular made her blood run cold. *Tentacle.*

In that moment, choice was taken from her. Either she assisted this man or, given the look upon his face, he would insert himself—forcibly—into the Finn community. As a guide she could smooth the path and perhaps contain any resulting damage.

Dr. McCullough cleared his throat, his eyes searching through the crowd, as if deciding who else he might approach. "A third?"

"Fine," she hissed. He had to be stopped from approaching the knot of people gathering about what must be Larsa's corpse. "I will speak with you. But not here. Not now. Trust me, overt interference will cause more trouble than it's worth." She pushed at his arm, surprisingly muscular beneath his sleeve, urging him to hurry away. "You must go. Meet me by the quay at midnight."

Chapter Five

Long before the midnight hour arrived, Isa stood quayside, listening to the waves churn as the wind blew clouds across the moon, bringing a light rain that—with the late hour—kept those inclined to wander inside. The hooded, woolen cloak she wore provided a comforting measure of anonymity, concealing her rigid posture and her hands that tightly clasped the handle of her medical bag before her. Waiting, she stared out at the horizon to where cobalt sky met black water.

Unwise, meeting a strange man alone on a dark beach. She ought to have informed the elders of Dr. McCullough's presence, of his interest in Larsa's death. But Finn detested the scrutiny of outsiders and, with such a warning, they would have closed ranks, refusing to speak to him.

She'd seen Larsa's body, albeit from a distance. The bite mark upon his shoulder, the hole in his chest, the tentacle, the lack of blood—all called to mind the man who had died before she could operate. And then there were the rumors. She'd questioned her brother who admitted to hearing whispers of Finn men disappearing from boats, only to be found weeks later washed up on beaches without a drop of blood left in their bodies.

A larger pattern was emerging and, given that it had attracted the attention of at least one Scottish physician, it was one she couldn't ignore. At the store, he'd mentioned octopus skin grafts and fine mesh. Acid swirled in her stomach. What dreadful facts would he impart? How much should she share without revealing their unique physiology to an outsider? How would the Finn community react if—when—they realized she assisted a Scot?

"You think very loudly, Mrs. McQuiston."

Dr. McCullough. The very tenor of his voice sent a tremor across her skin, an exceedingly unprofessional reaction to a fellow medical professional. Particularly in light of the topic they met to discuss.

"And what am I thinking?" she asked, taking a deep, steadying breath before turning around.

How long had he been standing there, watching her? A tremor ran through her. His hands were tucked into two of the many patch-like pockets sewn atop dark, loose-fitting trousers. The cut of his wool coat was loose, allowing for the unrestricted movement of his wide shoulders and muscular arms. A rucksack lay at his feet. Despite his casual stance, he was not a man to be trifled with.

A corner of his mouth hitched upward. "You are clearly contemplating how to take advantage of me."

Was he *flirting* with her? Her mind rapped her knuckles as an unfamiliar warmth flooded her chest. She pursed her lips, refusing to allow his charm to worm its way past her good sense. "Is such a thing possible?"

He laughed. *Laughed!* "Perhaps. But only a few have dared to try." He lifted his rucksack and slung it over his shoulder before holding out his elbow, as a gentleman did for a lady. "Allow me to escort you to the body. The more time that passes, the fewer answers it will provide us. After our examination, we shall discuss the findings."

"Such inclusive words." Isa narrowed her eyes at his elbow and took not one step. "But I have little confidence that you—a man—will treat me as an equal." Allowing him access to Larsa's remains was a risk. Should they be discovered, any repercussions would fall upon her head, while he could easily depart without sharing so much as a single piece of unique information. She scanned his many pockets. "Perhaps if you provide me with an item of collateral. Your surgical eyeglasses will suffice."

With or without a lens, they were valuable. If he left without them in his possession, his superior at the Glaister Institute would have his head. How badly did he want her help? A faint wince, a slight hesitation, then he reached into a pocket upon his chest and drew them forth.

"Take care," he warned. "You know their value."

Her mouth fell open as he placed the surgical eyeglasses upon her outstretched palm. The liquid microlens was intact! She lifted an eyebrow. "You have much to explain."

His lips twisted. "As do you."

~~~

With her small, strong hand upon his arm, Mrs. McQuiston steered him away from the beach and onto the main road.

He'd tipped his cards, turning over those surgical glasses in one piece, but somehow he had to win her trust, or he'd return to Glasgow emptyhanded and unpromotable.

For the umpteenth time that day, Alec wondered at her connection to the Glaister Institute. How had such a stunning woman gone unnoticed in its corridors? Very few women worked within its walls—at least in a scientific capacity—and none had ever been allowed to enroll in the University of Glasgow School of Medicine, from whence the institute recruited bright minds. A shame to arbitrarily dismiss fifty percent of the population from consideration.

As they walked, the man he'd spotted earlier watching her from a distance followed for a while, then peeled away to enter a brick building. Would trouble emerge to stalk them? He expected so. But by the time their silent walk along a dirt road ended before a blackhouse with a single candle burning in its window, there was no sign of anyone trailing in their wake.
~~~

"Wait here while I convince the watcher to grant us entry." She indicated a location distant enough that he would not be able to overhear—or interject—any words into a conversation at the house's threshold.

He eased himself onto a low, stone wall. Walking barefoot upon the sand earlier this evening, he'd felt something inside his artificial knee shift. Ever since, something felt "off" with each step he took. He'd braced his knee, wrapping a long strip of linen tightly about it, but he would need to visit Dr. Morgan to have him fix whatever was amiss.

With luck, he'd not head back to Glasgow emptyhanded. If Mrs. McQuiston could secure them entry, at the very least he would be able to describe a victim's injuries.

He was dismayed to again find himself admiring her slender frame and its pleasant female curves. With her feet once more in shoes and stockings, his imagination wandered upward and, unbidden, contemplated the color of her corset. Not that he would ever see such a garment laced about her form. She was another man's wife. But the mental exercise served to keep him alert. And warm.

Too warm.

An old woman opened the door and peered up at her. Words were exchanged in low voices. Doubt pressed the woman's lips into a thin line, but then she relented and swung the door wide. Mrs. McQuiston turned to beckon him into a dim, smoky room.

The body, bloated and bruised, lay upon a plank stretched between two chairs. On the floor, a dry rag was draped over the edge of a bucket of water. A bright lantern hung overhead. A pile of clean, folded clothes rested upon a nearby table.

Their arrival was perfectly timed: only one person was in the house, and the body was not yet prepared for burial. Still, from the tension in Mrs. McQuiston's shoulders, he gathered circumstances could alter in a heartbeat.

Alec bowed. "I'm sorry for your loss. Thank you for allowing us to view him."

The old woman stared back at him in unblinking silence, then moved to stand beside a wall clock that ticked loudly.

"She has granted us a quarter of an hour," Mrs. McQuiston said, her voice tight. Already she'd placed her medical bag upon the floor and extracted a rolled cloth of dissection tools, selecting a blunt probe. "Our postmortem is restricted—no cutting is permitted. We need to hurry."

"Not a problem." Working under pressure was his specialty, and he'd not argue for the right to wield a scalpel, not unless they located cephalopod tissue that needed to be carefully excised. Setting down his rucksack, he began with an external examination. Dark bands wrapped about an upper arm and marred its surface. "Bruised tissue possibly attributable to an octopus," he said in a low voice.

"Agreed."

As he turned the arm over, he noticed jagged scars running down the inside edges of the fingers. Scars much like the ones he'd noted on Mrs. McQuiston's hands. Not relevant to the current investigation, but intriguing nonetheless. He caught the hitch of her breath when he studied them and decided to save his questions for later.

More bruises disfigured the torso, but it was a ragged hole in the man's chest, located just below the left clavicle, that drew his focus.

"Did I not hear the word *tentacle* spoken aloud when his body was discovered?" He directed his question at the old woman.

"I ripped that abomination out with my bare hands and saw it destroyed," she said, pointing her chin at the peat fire that burned in the center of the room.

He lunged, grabbing a stick to knock a narrow tube of metallic wire from the flames. "Let it cool. I'll remove it from the premises." He smothered a curse at losing such important evidence and turned his attention back to the body.

Mrs. McQuiston had donned *his* surgical eyeglasses and was peering into the wound. "There's something resting inside." Without looking away, she held out her hand. "If you'll pass me a blunt probe and forceps."

He blinked, then dropped the requested tools into her palm. Years had passed since he deferred to another in the field when medical matters arose. Save, of course, when he himself was the wounded. "If you'll describe what you see..."

"Yes, of course." She glanced up, looking contrite. "My apologies. Most do not wish to hear spoken details."

Using the blunt probe, she moved aside the damaged tissue. "Something has pierced a blood vessel."

"An artery?"

"Yes. The subclavian artery." She slid the forceps in and attempted to pull the object forth. "It's lodged rather tightly." Leaning back, she offered him—with only the slightest hesitation—his own captive surgical glasses. "Perhaps you should take a look before we wrench it free."

Bending close, Alec slid the forceps into the hole and immediately felt metal grind against metal. A close look confirmed her observation. The object was firmly lodged in the artery just past where the subclavian artery branched from the aortic arch. He took a firm grip and pulled out half an inch of...

"Finely braided wire." Rotating the outer ring of a lens a notch, he brought it into sharp focus. "Seven wires, their tips fused into a sharp, triangular point. A barb points backward." He passed her the surgical glasses and their discovery, letting her gape at it while he dug a glass vial from his chest pocket.

"The hole was manmade," Isa whispered, looking up from the wire, her eyes made enormous by the magnification effects of the lenses. "*Deliberately* manmade." With a shake of her head, she dropped the wire into the collection vial.

Together they scanned the corpse, passing the surgical glasses back and forth as they identified and studied more bruises, scrapes, and cuts. All to be expected when a body spent hours rolling and pitching in the surf of a rugged coastline. Except...

"Another hole," he said, pointing at another half inch perforation bored into the skin of the ankle. No octopus he'd ever heard of attacked its prey in such a manner. He leaned closer. "It decreases in size, tapering to a fine point. I don't detect any wire. Without dissection, it's difficult to be certain, but it appears to penetrate either the anterior tibial artery or vein."

Mrs. McQuiston took the surgical eyeglasses from his hand. "Curious." She leaned closer. "And most disturbing."

Balancing a glass vial upon the plank, he extracted a syringe from his pocket. The old woman standing quietly in the shadows of the blackhouse squeaked in protest.

He glanced in question at Mrs. McQuiston who wore a pained expression. She shook her head. "We can't. I promised we wouldn't remove anything from the body."

"We removed the wire. Why not a small sample of whatever blood remains?"

"There's a world of a difference between the foreign object and the tissue of the deceased. Local tradition dictates he be buried intact."

Her pointed stare declared he ought to know better. Indeed, he did, but concrete evidence to support the rumors lay before him. Not a chance he was leaving without samples.

He lifted a cotton-tipped swab. "There may yet be foreign tissue in the wounds that could prove instrumental to understanding what happened and why. Octopus blood is copper-based—unlike our own iron-based blood. Would you throw away the chance to confirm the rumors?"

Her forehead wrinkled. "All valid points." She turned and addressed the old woman. Words were muttered in the strange tongue he'd heard earlier, one that only bore the faintest of resemblance to Gaelic.

Heaving a great sigh of forbearance, the old woman crossed her arms, frowned and tipped her head at the clock. "Take your samples. You have seven minutes."

While Mrs. McQuiston's capable hands drew blood, Alec swabbed both puncture wounds and an odd-shaped, deep wound on the man's shoulder. Straightening, he dropped the samples into vials and screwed on the caps. "Will you help me roll him over? We ought to examine his—"

The door slammed open. His head jerked up. Two red-faced individuals stormed into the dwelling. He recognized them from the oceanside wedding where their disapproving frowns had cut deep grooves into their stern faces. Yet they'd been the ones to take control when the body was found, organizing transport and comforting weeping family members. He pegged them for community leaders who disapproved of the marriage.

Mrs. McQuiston—all five and a half feet of her—stepped in front of Alec. "Mr. and Mrs. Carr, allow me to introduce—"

"Shame on you," the red-faced woman interrupted, planting her hands on her hips. "To think I encouraged

Elias to consider you as a potential wife. Thank goodness he followed you. Do you think a young woman can wander along the quay at midnight and not be observed?"

His body tensed as a question darted through his mind. Was Mrs. McQuiston a widow? He brushed it aside. Not the time.

A vein throbbed at Mr. Carr's temple. "You have no right, allowing a stranger—a Scot!—to examine one of our own." Mr. Carr threw a nasty glance at the old woman who cowered in the shadows. "No one here has the authority to grant anyone such liberties."

"Direct your anger where it belongs, Mr. Carr," Alec said, grasping Mrs. McQuiston by the shoulders. She stiffened at the contact, freezing as he leaned close to quietly breathe the words, "Secure the samples and the surgical glasses."

She gave a slight nod.

He released her shoulders and stepped sideways, drawing away Mr. Carr's ire. "I insisted. Mrs. McQuiston and I merely conducted a cursory examination."

Behind him was the faint clink of glass vials being collected.

"City life has made her forget who she is, where she belongs." Eyes narrowing to flinty slits, Mrs. Carr peered at him. "I've seen you about town. What kind of doctor pretends to be a fisherman? And why?"

"One who's up to no good," Mr. Carr answered.

The man's nostrils flared as he cracked his knuckles. Spoiling for a fight, he'd found his target. Though the man appeared strong, Alec could take him down with a single, well-placed punch. But he did not wish to make enemies in a community where potential informants lived. Civil discourse, however, wasn't looking promising.

"As you wish." Alec held up his palms. "I'm leaving."

"Not on your own two feet, you're not." Mr. Carr's hands balled into fists.

He sighed. A fight it would be. He ducked the first swing with ease. As the man lashed out again, Alec caught the man's wrist, twisting it behind his back. The man howled his displeasure at finding himself immobilized. "Best if you depart without me, Mrs. McQuiston. I'll settle this." He jerked his head toward the door.

To her credit, she didn't hesitate. Snatching up her medical bag, she was out the door in a heartbeat.

"You let him go!" Mrs. Carr ordered.

Loath to injure Mr. Carr—it would only further complicate the situation—he shoved the man against the stone wall and eased the pressure on his elbow joint. "I'd be happy to, for I'm only here to help. Might we discuss, like civilized men, the steps that need to be taken to discover what creature hunts your people and why?"

"We want no help from the likes of you." From the corner of his eye, he saw Mrs. Carr approaching, hoisting a heavy, cast iron frying pan over her head. So much for reason.

Enough. He'd disarm her and make his departure. Perhaps Mrs. McQuiston could shed light on this unreasonable behavior and propose a better approach.

Then again, she was the one who had suggested a clandestine, midnight meeting.

He stepped and twisted, reaching... Snap! Deep inside his artificial knee some unknown internal mechanism shattered. Metal grated against metal making a most disturbing sound. Muscles and tendons struggled and strained to hold him steady, but he wobbled.

A moment of weakness that was his undoing.

Mr. Carr shoved him to the floor, and his wife wasted no time. Stars exploded in his head, and he pitched into a dark abyss.

~~~

He woke to the familiar sound of waves lapping at the hull, to the clang of ropes and metal in the wind, to the ringing of... No. That was his head. He touched a few fingers to the back of his skull, and they came away bloody. Wincing, he sat up. He—and his rucksack—were aboard a fishing boat.

"We're bound for Harris," a callous voice informed him. "Mr. Carr ordered you off the island."

"Not fed to the fish? Or the octopuses?"

"Aye, that was suggested," the fisherman said. "Luckily they thought someone might miss you."

In the distance was a small cluster of lights. He dug through his bag. Good. Nothing classified lay within. Everything he needed was stowed in his pockets.
~~~

"How far out are we?" He pulled off his boots with regret and stood, testing his knee. It hurt, but it still functioned. Mostly.

"Almost a mile. But don't you be getting ideas. Water's cold. And you're not a—"

Whatever the fisherman compared Alec to was lost as the cold water of the Atlantic Ocean closed over his head. He'd swum longer distances in worse conditions. And he certainly wasn't going to leave behind the clues he'd unearthed just to avoid a short stretch of unpleasantness. Besides, there was a beautiful, young widow he'd abandoned. He needed to be certain she was safe.

As to the mechanics of his knee… that could be fixed. Later. Once he'd retrieved the samples and his surgical glasses.

He was in luck; the tide was with him. The storm had passed, the waves were minimal and the cold water soon numbed the pain. Sometime later, he treaded water beside the rusty hull of her houseboat. Pulling himself out of the water and onto a small ledge beside the door, he raised a fist and knocked.

A minute passed before a small door opened and a faint light threw a female form wearing nothing but a pale blue, ruffled dressing gown into relief. Wide, silver eyes stared down at him as if he were a merman intent on dragging her to a watery grave.

"Apologies for the delay." He grinned his reassurance. "Our business is unfinished. May I come in?"

"You're bleeding," she gasped. Her hand darted out and touched his head. "Badly." She waved him inside. "Sit and tell me what happened."

It boded well that she cared about his health, given the earlier events of the night. He hauled himself upright and limped inside. Water streamed off his clothing. "Mrs. Carr took advantage of a... weakness. Hit me with a frying pan." *Aether, it hurt to admit to one.* "The Carrs dumped me aboard an outward-bound fishing boat." The boat rocked, and his rump landed on a chair with a *thunk.*

"You swam here?" Her voice rose with incredulity. She wrapped a warm, woolen blanket around his shoulders and threw linen towels at his feet to sop up the seawater. "From a boat?"

"A mere mile or so." A casual reply, but his knee was beginning to throb again. He rubbed a hand over its surface, all too aware nothing could be done to set it right, not here in the Outer Hebrides.

Her living space was tiny, its furnishings minimal. A small table and two chairs. An iron cookstove. A sea chest. A raised bunk with a thick feather mattress partially shielded by curtains. All illuminated by canning jars hung from hooks, their swirling contents emitting the blueish-white light of phosphorescence. Lucifer lamps.

Her medical bag landed on the small table in front of him as she began to dig out suture materials. Was he about to trial the sharksilk? Cold ethanol followed by the sharp bite of a needle through the skin of his scalp made him flinch, but he held still.

Well, almost. For he leaned ever so slightly backward, soaking in the delicious body heat she radiated. For a female, she ran unusually hot and her dressing gown, now damp, had clung to her form as she circled behind him, revealing far more than he had a right to look at. A pleasant distraction, nonetheless.

"I should collect my samples and depart," he offered. Given her community's response to a simple postmortem, he hated to think how they'd respond to learning she'd taken up with him. Next time he'd end up tossed overboard with a bucket of chum.

"Oh no you don't," she said, tugging a knot into place. "I want far more from you than that."

Chapter Six

Her face grew hot. How on earth had she uttered such words? It wasn't like her to be so moved by the sight of wet fabric stretched across well-formed, broad shoulders.

Dr. McCullough twisted, looking at her over his shoulder, eyebrows raised. She met his gaze, refusing to acknowledge any embarrassment as she took in the stubble of whiskers upon a square jaw, a teasing half-grin and dark eyes. His gaze flicked to her lips, and her pulse jumped, setting something fluttering deep in her belly.

Bandage. She needed to bandage his head injury. Threading her fingers through the tangles of his dark hair and tugging his mouth to hers was not an option.

Isa swallowed. It had been a long time since she'd felt such stirrings of desire. Not that she intended to act upon them. Such behavior would be entirely inappropriate. She barely knew him. She picked up a bit of lint and some flannel. "You'll need to keep this dressing dry. Eyes forward."

Bloody and beaten, he'd returned. By water. He might not be Finn, but he was more than a simple doctor. What else did he know about the attacks? She was at a loss as to how to proceed, but he clearly had resources at his fingertips. It remained to be seen if he would share them.

"There," she said, tucking in the edge of the bandage. "You're going to have a nasty lump, but your head should be fine. About your knee—"

He held up a hand. "Nothing to be done about it, I'm afraid." He paused. "Unless you have whisky?"

Perhaps, given inevitable topics, introducing spirits into the mix wasn't the wisest idea, but it would take the edge off his pain and perhaps loosen his lips. Uncertain, she tucked a lock of hair behind her ear. He'd seen her bare hands and now her feet, why not her ears? Let him wonder.

Anton had left behind a half-full bottle on their boat. Fetching it from a sea chest, she splashed a finger of golden liquid into a glass and set it upon the table. As he reached for it, she placed her hand over the top, and their fingers brushed, sending a faint tremor through her body.

It was a struggle to keep her voice steady as she bargained, "Only if you let me examine your leg."

He wanted to pry into her secrets? Let him share a few of his own first.

"It's not a pretty sight." He hesitated. The worry in his eyes only heightened her curiosity.

"Please." She rolled her eyes to lighten the mood. "I'm a medical professional. I'm certain I've seen worse. Pull up your trousers, let me have a look."

"Insulting my appearance without even a glance?" His eyebrows lifted, and the corner of his mouth hitched into a smile. "If a woman's ankles can inflame desire, what might the sight of my calf do?"

Her own laugh surprised her. After months of strain and recent events, surrendering to a bit of inanity felt... marvelous. "How well you seem to know me." She grinned, then lifted her hand from the glass and pushed a low footstool toward him. "Kneecaps are my greatest weakness."

"Then you are quite safe. My run-in with a heavy, iron door made quite a bit of reconstruction necessary." He tossed back the whisky in one gulp. "Very well. You were warned."

Foot on the stool, he pulled the hem of his wet trousers above his knee. She unwound a length of linen, and her smile faded. His kneecap was... gone. She winced. Beneath a significant amount of scar tissue—still a raw pink—was a vaguely hexagonal shape, impossible to confuse with a natural patella.

"A complete knee replacement," he said, answering her unspoken question. "Experimental and—apparently—not without its flaws."

He'd sustained quite an injury if such a device had been installed. Moreover, he must be a person of note to have benefited from such uncommon and unheard-of technology. Most surgeons would have amputated in favor of an entirely artificial limb.

She crouched beside his knee, staring as her hands fluttered. "May I?"

He nodded, and she lowered her hands gently onto his leg, palpating the unusual shape beneath the skin. With one hand on his muscular thigh and the other beneath his calf, she extended his leg. A faint grating sound emanated.

She cringed. "How badly does it hurt?"

"Despite the sound, the joint doesn't hurt. No nerves run to it anymore. But something is loose and catching on a tendon. I'll visit my surgeon when I return to Glasgow."

"Glasgow—and the Glaister Institute—is far away." Straightening, she retrieved a roll of linen from her supplies. "I'll replace the binding, but a brace would give your knee more stability."

"What do you know of the Glaister Institute?" Dr. McCullough still slouched in his chair, but the weary look upon his face had vanished, replaced by one of intense interest.

Much. But she didn't wish to share the details of her dead husband's career with him. She'd set aside old regrets—or was trying to—and carved out a new and different life. Still, when she returned to Glasgow herself, the only way forward would involve confronting her past. She'd let matters drift long enough.

"I know you work there," she said, avoiding eye contact as she wrapped the cloth about his knee. A faint twinge of jealousy pricked at her heart. Though life had slammed door after door in her face, she'd never managed to entirely let go of her childhood dream of becoming a physician. For now, her place was here with her people, where she could make an immediate difference in their lives.

She finished binding his knee and took the chair opposite him, placing the table safely between them. It was time for deeper, more pressing questions. What kind of physician investigated the strange and unusual deaths of rural Finn? Few cared much for them, except to enjoy the usefulness of hard-to-kill sailors and fishermen.

Watching his face closely, she took a deep breath and asked. "So tell me, Dr. McCullough, why are you here, risking your knee to work as a fisherman while investigating strange tales?"

"Mention was made of a beautiful, traveling healer." His eyes sparkled, and he leaned closer. "They neglected to mention that you were a widow." He glanced at her lips. "Please tell me you're not keen to remarry."

"Stop." She lifted a hand, palm out, willing her pulse to slow. There was no denying that the chemistry between them could easily reach a flashpoint, but she would not allow him to use it to extract information from her. "Flattery is all very well, but I believe we have a situation to discuss? What evidence arrived at the Glaister Institute to bring you to our windblown shores?"

"Very well." His voice grew serious, clinical, and she lamented that lightheartedness must be set aside. "A piece of skin, by all appearances that of an unknown octopus species. Except microscopic analysis revealed that within the expected layers of epidermal and dermal tissues lay a carbon fiber latticework."

"Both manmade and natural. A tentacle containing a braided and barbed wire." She bit her lip. "You've no idea why someone would wish to... construct or grow such a creature?" *Or target the Finn?* But she kept that thought to herself.

He shook his head. "None. But I doubt it's for good."

Tilting her head to the side, Isa considered the man before her, setting aside her inexplicable attraction to his rough-hewn looks to analyze the facts. Intelligent and highly educated. Persistent and determined. Scarred, muscled, capable of swimming a mile in frigid water while seriously injured. "You're more than a physician," she said, resting an elbow upon the table and propping her chin on her fist to stare. "Far more. But what? You don't look like a professor..."

Something approaching alarm flashed across his face, but it was gone in an instant, replaced by that flirtatious half-smile of his. "I do not teach or see patients. I'm currently assigned to a research laboratory where we study the byssal threads of mussels—"

Lies. No man developed such an impressive physique working in a windowless laboratory. He might be attached to a research program, but she doubted very much that he spent much time devising and executing experiments.

"Spare me," she interrupted, leaning back to cross her arms. Her voice brooked no nonsense. "What kind of scientist investigates mysterious deaths at the hands, no, tentacles of vicious attack octopuses?"

His smile widened. "Or is it octopi? I'm never quite certain." When she lifted her eyebrows, he sighed and sobered. "I'm afraid that's classified."

"Well, that's better than spinning me falsehoods," Isa said. "I rather prefer the direct approach. Try asking me for what you want."

Her heart gave a great thud as Dr. McCullough's hand tightened upon the glass. He cleared his throat and raised his eyes to hers. Heat shimmered in the air between them. What would it feel like to have his hand wrapped gently about her neck, the pad of his thumb brushing the edge of her chin?

She closed her eyes, pressing a finger and thumb against her eyelids. How dare she let her mind take this beyond a harmless flirtation? She needed to focus. Men were dying. Finn men. "About the attacks," she added far too late.

His warm hand closed about hers, and her eyes flew open, her heart nearly leaping from her chest. But his words weren't ones of romance. Not even seduction.

"The scars between your fingers, on the tips of your ears." His voice was cautious as he tugged her hand closer, studying the space between her fingers. "I saw the same on the dead man, on the woman attending him. A handful of others present at the wedding..."

"Syndactyly is the proper term." Rough callouses upon his palm scraped hers as she pulled her hand away, sending a shiver across her skin. "It's a familial trait in the area, but nothing more than a bit of extra skin between the fingers and entirely irrelevant to the attacks."

She hoped. Two Finn fishermen did not a pattern make. There were likely Scottish fishermen who had suffered a similar fate. *Aether*, how awful of her to hope that was so.

He tapped a finger on the table. "Your ears?"

Hitching a shoulder, she said nothing. He had his secrets, and she had hers. It seemed they'd reached an impasse.

"Fine. Tell me about the other man," he stated simply. "The one you were unable to save."

Careful to include every detail, she recounted the event. Recalling the awful sound of his final breaths sent a shard of ice sliding down her spine. "He died from an apoplexy brought on by the sudden and severe loss of blood via a severed octopus tentacle that had somehow inserted into his abdomen."

"A tentacle," he restated. "Just one?"

"Only one. The piece that remained was some three inches in length, complete with suckers. The only reason he died in his bed was because someone tied the end with twine to stop the bleeding. I saw no evidence of wire."

"Dare I hope you collected a sample?"

She shook her head. "The shock sent his wife into labor, and I became otherwise occupied. His body was removed and later, I have to admit, research was not at the forefront of my mind."

"Of course not," Dr. McCullough agreed. "Can you recall the exact location the tentacle appeared to insert?"

"Near the path of the abdominal aorta." Closing her eyes, she tried to recall any other evidence of an attack. "He was bruised and battered, but I can't say that any marks upon his body were specifically caused by tentacles gripping its prey."

For a moment, they sat in silence, each contemplating implications.

Isa spoke first, voicing the obvious. "Why? To what end? Not that it matters. Whoever is orchestrating these vile attacks has to be stopped."

"I intend to get to the bottom of this." Regret filled his eyes. "I'm afraid I can't ask you to weigh anchor and accompany me."

"Of course not." She stood. Reaching for a nearby canister, Isa pulled out a tin punch card and placed it on the table before him. "I expect to return to Glasgow in the near future. If you hear about more attacks, I'd appreciate it if you contact me by skeet pigeon."

Dr. McCullough tapped his finger on the card, studying it. As if allowing such a connection to stretch between them—even if the link was nothing more than the tenuous flight of a mechanical bird—held grave consequences. With a nod, he tucked the card into one of his many pockets, then swung his foot to the ground and stood. "I'll take the samples and be on my way then."

With twinges of regret, for she'd enjoyed his company, she set the glass vials upon the table. But as Dr. McCullough peeled the damp, woolen blanket from his shoulders, he swayed.

"Your head. Your leg." She placed a hand on his shoulder, pushing him back onto the chair. "You cannot go. The next ferry doesn't leave until morning." She opened a drawer and pulled out Anton's old, worn dressing gown and thrust it into his arms, her stomach fluttering. "Take the hammock." Turning away, she lifted the canvas sling from a chest and clipped its ends to bolts.

"I shouldn't," he objected. "The Carrs. Your reputation in the morning..."

She spun about and planted her hands on her hips. "I am a widow, Dr. McCullough. People will assume I've taken a lover. That is all."

Not that she ever had. A few tentative offers had been made, but she'd been grateful to be free of matrimonial demands. Not that they'd been frequent in their last year of marriage and, since Anton's death, not a single man had set her blood on fire. Until now.

"A lover." An appraising gleam flared in his eyes.

This man was a dangerous temptation. Every nerve ending tingled, urging her to misbehave. Just this once.

He would be gone by morning and who would know? She would. But to have those calloused hands moving across her soft skin... all that intensity focused entirely upon their mutual pleasure. Her face flushed hot. Such thoughts. She'd leapt blindly into marriage and, although this certainly didn't compare, such decisions ought to be made with a clear head.

Sensing weakness, he lifted an eyebrow.

Laughing, she waved a finger. "No." Lowering her defenses and inviting a stranger into her bed was out of the question. At least tonight. "Besides, you'll be gone at first light." With steel in her spine, she turned and climbed into her bed, tossing a dry blanket into his hands before drawing the curtains closed. "Do try to get some sleep."

It would be a miracle if she managed any.

Chapter Seven

It took Alec an entire day to reach Glasgow. Three hours by ferry to Ullapool on the Scottish mainland, followed by a short trip to Adaroche Park, where he conscripted a sparrow class dirigible from a hunting lodge. The steward grumbled mightily, but in the end relented.

Ten minutes into the flight, Alec rather wished he'd borrowed a horse instead. Harrowing conditions were one thing—he was used to that—but poorly maintained equipment was another. Improperly housed, the bird had been exposed to wind, rain and salt for far too long and had a tendency to buck against a stiff wind before plunging into an adrenaline-inducing nose dive.

Never before had he been so happy to land on the rooftop of his family's Glasgow home. Leaving the aircraft in the capable hands of Munro, their steam butler, he snuck down the stairs to his room where he peeled off his salt-crusted clothes, stashed the samples, and sank into a hot bath. Warm for the first time in weeks, he finally allowed a most persistent thought to occupy the forefront of his brain.

Mrs. McQuiston.

Hard with desire, he'd barely slept at all last night. Nor had she, for he'd noted the exact moment her breathing had changed, when she'd drifted away. A gentleman would have refused the hammock and departed, but he was no more the top hat-wearing sort than she was likely to hold a lace-trimmed parasol above her head, and so he'd selfishly stayed, waiting, hoping.

That she'd answered the question he hadn't asked meant the attraction was mutual. He wanted to see her again badly enough that it was almost a need. And he didn't even know her given name.

The dull, gray gown she'd worn that day had been neatly folded and laid upon a nearby sea chest. Peeking from beneath was the fine silk of her undergarments. A corset, embroidered with swirls that brought to mind a stormy sea, was edged with a ruffled ribbon. As he'd suspected, her plain clothing concealed hidden, vibrant layers.

Lust flared again, and he took himself in his hand, recalling the deep V of her dressing gown and the glimpse of small but perfectly formed breasts as she'd bent to examine the inside of his knee.

He groaned. Time to get past this absurd longing, this wondering of what her deft fingers would feel like in place of his, fingers that managed to be elegant despite their scars.

A fist banged on the bathroom door. "Alec!"

Shit. His sister. "Go away, Cait."

"You missed my birthday, you big dolt. You owe me. Are you decent? I'm coming in."

"No!" he yelled, his voice rough with frustration of an altogether different kind. Why hadn't he locked the door? Reaching for a towel, he pulled it into the water, covering his arousal. Just in the nick of time.

The door cracked. An eyeball appeared. "Aether, you're a hairy coo! When was the last time your hair met scissors?"

He threw a bar of soap at her—and would have hit his mark had she not ducked.

"Don't be difficult," she said, laughing. "You've little time to waste. People will be arriving for the dinner party soon. The minute Munro informed Mother of your presence, she began rearranging the seating." She gave him an evil grin. "Perfect Patsy will be in attendance."

Miss Patricia Thompson. Daughter of his mother's best friend. Remembering the parson's mousetrap she'd tried to spring upon him the last time they met, he swore. "Hasn't she married yet?"

Once, years ago as a young man home from school, Alec had made a terrible, horrible, awful mistake. He'd plucked a yellow rose from the garden and handed it to Perfect Patsy. Her pursuit of him had since been relentless, no matter the discouragement. A lesson that taught him to be very clear with women from the start that they had no future together, only the present.

"Ha! She's waiting for *you.* She asked after you yesterday at tea." An evil grin cracked Cait's face. "Sadly, I had to inform her that you had yet to find yourself a bride."

He closed his eyes. "Have I told you lately how much I hate you?"

"You have not. *That* is the problem. You simply disappear for weeks at a time. But no worries, I hate you too." She pointed a finger at him. "Clean up, suit up, and present yourself in the parlor. Invent a fiancée. Anything to break her heart irreparably."

"I can't," he said, pleading. "I need to go to the laboratory."

"*Won't* is more like it," she said, planting a hand on her hip. "All this social nonsense keeps me from my own laboratory as well."

"Anything but a dinner party. Not tonight." He closed his eyes, prepared to be exploited. "Name your price."

He could *hear* her grin stretching from ear to ear. "I want a chance to study that Russian nematocyst weapon you reverse engineered."

He sat up straight in the tub, sloshing water onto the floor. "That's classified! How—" He narrowed his eyes. "Never mind. I don't want to know."

"Logan said much the same thing." Cait tipped her head. "Except he's as slippery as an eel and even that didn't keep me from studying his weapon."

There had been yelling the morning his brother awoke to find his government issued TTX pistol missing. No one would soon forget the roar of fury that echoed through the house when he found its parts and pieces spread across a countertop in her basement laboratory.

"Well?" Cait said. "Do we have a deal?"

"Absolutely not!" Alec said. "Your proficiency with vertebrate poisons is disturbing enough."

"It's your funeral." The bathroom door slammed.

So much for a brief respite upon a feather mattress. He shaved with such haste he narrowly missed slitting his own throat. A few rough hacks at the ends of his hair shortened it to a respectable length. Minutes later, he was dressed—punch key and samples in his pockets—and sliding down the drainpipe outside his window, ignoring the screaming protests made by his knee.

For the first time the Glaister laboratories felt like a refuge rather than a prison. He stepped into the air shaft, closed the iron door behind him and exhaled a great sigh of relief. Not only was he safe from swooning females, but a quick survey told him that Logan had met his demands. The wooden countertops groaned beneath equipment and supplies, including an Ichor machine, an inordinately expensive device. It was a measure of his brother's clout that it rested here in such a room.

Alec set the samples on a wooden crate, then lifted a vial to peer at the blood collected within. As expected, it had clotted. No matter. Octopuses had neither blood cells nor hemoglobin; histological examination would accomplish little. What the creatures did have was hemocyanin, a copper-containing protein, to transport oxygen. And if that was present, he'd find it in the supernatant.

Using a rubber-bulbed glass pipette, he transferred a measure of the yellow serum into a capillary tube, then inserted it into the Ichor machine. He rifled through a number of punch cards until he located a Cu Quantitator program. Plucking it out, he slid it into the cipher cartridge.

A quick check of reagent levels, tubing connections and the battery power source revealed everything to be in working order, so he keyed in a command and flipped a switch. A small internal motor began to hum.

Turning his attention to the swabs, Alec prepped a number of glass slides, stains and fixatives. Locating the aetheroscope, he primed the gas chamber and slid in the first slide. An hour or so later, he had proof positive that foreign tissue had, at some point, been inserted into the dead man's leg wound: non-mammalian tissue containing chromatophores. Octopuses employed these cells to undergo a physiological color change to adapt to their environmental background.

He was on the last slide when Logan walked through the door carrying a metal case.

"Did I trip an alarm?" Alec asked.

Logan grinned. "Did you find the healer?"

"I did. Mrs. McQuiston can now be linked to *two* dead men attacked by octopus." He paused, attempting to frame a description of a hypothetical creature that would defy biological classification.

"McQuiston?" Logan tipped his head. "Mmm. I know that name."

"She knew quite a lot about Glaister Institute considering her supposed lack of training." Distance had done nothing to alleviate a growing curiosity about the beautiful, interesting widow. "Spit it out. It's clear you know something."

"Her husband worked here. Hematological research." Logan lifted his chin at the Ichor machine. "That was his device."

"Really?" A thought flitted past just beyond his grasp. "His findings?"

Logan shrugged. "Unreported at the time of his death."

He leaned forward. "And how—exactly—did he die?"

"I'm told he was working to improve the efficacy and safety of blood transfusions." Logan paused. "Autopsy indicated multiple ischemic events. Severe damage to his kidneys was noted."

"That is an all too frequent outcome." Alec's brow furrowed. Reaching for the punch cards that accompanied the Ichor machine, he tugged out a handful and passed them to Logan. "Then this set of cards might be his design. They're unlabeled and make no sense. Not to me. Can you have them analyzed?"

"Yes." Mischief flashed in his brother's eyes. "Lady Rathsburn will be delighted to help. Nonetheless, I see you have already found use for the device." He bent to examine the Ichor machine's progress, then slid his gaze sideways at Alec. "Interesting program choice." His voice was wry.

"I know. It reads as if I'm analyzing blue Cornish pixie blood." Logan's sideways glance made Alec bark a laugh. "So there's truth to that rumor. Dare I hope they've been caught dancing around a dolman?"

"I couldn't say. Yet." Logan's eyes warmed. "But there has certainly been mischief."

"Quinn?"

"That would be telling." His brother leaned against the stone wall of the airshaft. "Now, before I bestow good news, a bit of bad first. Your return to Glasgow has been noted, and the price of your unprecedented freedom comes due. A pair of unwelcome eyes caught sight of your paperwork for advancement. Lord Roideach complained to the head of Glaister Institute who let slip that you are in possession of an Ichor machine. The board meets in two days' time. Discussion of who should have custody is an item on their agenda. You're to attend."

The Glaister Institute's board. Alec would instruct Munro to drag forth his formal military uniform for a thorough brushing. He hoped the balding, white-haired men would be impressed by the multitude of hardware pinned to his chest. If they weren't, Lord Roideach's lineage would reign supreme.

Alec had spent weeks in Roideach's laboratory and barely set eyes on the man. Since his father's death, the vast amount of his attention was focused upon the restoration of the family's ruinous castle. When he *did* condescend to appear, not once had he lifted a single finger of his own to directly participate in an experiment. He'd swoop in, demand progress reports, shuffle papers in his office and yell at his secretary. In less than an hour, he would be out the door. Roideach had no business directing research when not one discovery or invention had emerged from this laboratory in five years.

"He wants it for himself," Alec stated flatly. "But why? Mollusk blood doesn't warrant exclusive use of such equipment."

Logan raised an eyebrow.

"Yes, but I'm at least investigating human attacks." Alec narrowed his eyes. "Is this why you're in Glasgow? Does it have something to do with that case you're clutching?"

"Politics," his brother complained, "I've been caught in a net and dragged under." Pain washed over his face. "My name was put forth as a guest for the royal wedding, and they want me to wear a kilt."

Laughing so hard he almost broke a rib, Alec wheezed, gasping for air. "Why would they want to put *your* hairy knees on view?"

"Someone let slip that my father was—or is—the second son of a Scottish laird." Logan gave him a dead-eyed stare. "They asked me if I could play the bagpipes."

He nearly choked on laughter once more, but finally managed to shove aside the comical image. Logan considered himself Gypsy, not Scot. Alec dragged in a deep breath. "The one between some Icelandic prince and a Danish princess?"

Iceland had demanded freedom. But Denmark was too reliant upon Iceland's natural resources to let the country cede. Rather than take up arms, a compromise had been reached.

To keep both the rebellious Icelanders under control and strengthen political ties, the King of Denmark had offered one of his daughters, an alliance to be cemented with the spectacle of a royal wedding. Any resultant children would be eligible for the Danish line of succession. A palliative gesture that might calm the majority of the population for a dozen or so years. Until they realized nothing had changed.

"The very one." He rolled his eyes and sighed. "The Queen seems to think granting me an invitation is some kind of reward. What with the political outcry surrounding the wedding negotiations, she wants me to keep an insider's eye on the situation. But enough of that," he lifted the case, "I've brought you something... enlightening."

"Another skin sample?" Alec stood, a twinge of jealousy erasing any lingering laughter. Weeks of searching and he couldn't locate one. Then again, Logan was always one step ahead.

A nod. "This was found among Professor Corwin's belongings at a nearby inn." Logan thumbed the clasps, lifting the lid to reveal a misshapen ceramic lump and an attached flap of the odd skin.

"Where, exactly, did they find this?" Alec asked. "Near what town?"

"Tarbert on Harris."

The main ferry port of another western Scottish Isle. Curious and yet not surprising.

Together, they moved the ceramic fragment—roughly the size of a hen's egg—onto a rubber sheet, careful not to damage it, the scrap of hybrid skin, or the thin, tough filaments that connected the two. The loud mechanical buzz of a vibration knife filled the air and moments later, Alec placed a sliver of the ceramic into the aetheroscope.

He bent to the eyepiece. "Tiny pores." Alec made a quick calculation. "None smaller than eight micrometers in size, which is the upper size range of a red blood cell. A ceramic blood filter?" He straightened and locked eyes with Logan. "The dead man's blood vessels were pierced." He quickly described the hooked, braided wire to his brother. "Not a coincidence."

"Unlikely." Logan frowned. "Professor Corwin's body was drained of blood."

Hairs on the back of his neck rose to attention. "Why must I drag everything from you?" Alec swore. "What more is there?"

Logan waved a hand, dismissing his question. "What connects the skin to the ceramic?"

Biting back annoyance—for nothing short of torture could force his brother to share information—he turned back to the specimen. More slides were prepared, more chemical reagents mustered forth, this time to study the filaments that bound the octopus hybrid skin to the ceramic filter.

"Byssal threads," Alec announced. "Manmade components combined with octopus skin and attached to a ceramic filter using the keratin-polyphenolic proteins produced by clams and mussels."

"I'm a spy. Not a scientist. Summarize."

"Someone has undertaken a ground-breaking biotechnological project to create a very strange chimera." He rubbed the back of his neck. "If I were to guess, I would say someone is trying to extract—and filter—the blood of these fishermen."

They stared at each other for a long minute.

"There's more to this." Alec stood. "Much more." His thoughts jumped straight to Mrs. McQuiston. Perhaps she could share details about her husband's work. He didn't believe in coincidences. "I need to go back into the field."

"Not before you present yourself before the board," Logan insisted. "And have that knee examined. You've gone crooked."

Alec sighed. Dr. Morgan would want to explore the internal mechanisms and that meant more surgery. Perhaps he could entice the lovely Mrs. McQuiston to come to him.

Time to locate a skeet pigeon.

Chapter Eight

Standing on the deck of her houseboat, moored at yet another quay, Isa inhaled deeply. Tension melted from her shoulders. Nothing surpassed the salty, fresh smell of the ocean at dawn. The first rays of sunlight glinted on the horizon, reflecting off the waves. Overhead seabirds called, some swooping low to skim the water's surface. The world felt at peace.

It had been a demanding night, attending a long and complicated delivery. A breech birth. There were hours when she thought the woman might not survive but, in the end, her baby was born healthy. The mother was exhausted—and rightly so—but Isa saw no further cause for concern.

She'd held the swaddled infant, a warm, soft bundle of joy, and stared down into his bright, blue eyes and kissed his soft, downy forehead. In a few years, his parents might call her back to remove the webbing between his fingers, but they had also murmured to each other about seeing their son baptized in the sea. That gave her hope that the Finn people might find a way to preserve at least a few of their ancient traditions.

A year spent adrift, loosely connected to all the Finn communities, had revealed a pressing need for better medical care. But there was only so much a single woman could accomplish, particularly when her own medical education had stagnated.

It was time to return to Glasgow, to resubmit her application to medical school. She could be as good a physician as Anton ever was, if only the University of Glasgow would allow her to matriculate so that she might broaden her studies. With an official degree in hand, she hoped to convince more Finn—particularly women—to train as healers.

Glasgow.

A flush crept up her neck. If she were honest with herself, she missed Dr. McCullough. Missed—despite the morbid task he pursued—how he managed to swat away the gloom with flashing eyes and an easy smile. And teasing words. She'd spent the better part of that night awake, telling herself that his flirtations were empty and meaningless, akin to listening to the lure of sirens. To listen was to crash upon the rocks...

Isa snorted at her musings. Crash she might, but she certainly wouldn't drown.

He'd left her a note, pinned to the table beneath a rock. He'd thanked her for her hospitality and care and promised to keep her abreast of any developments. A perfectly proper note, yet she'd run her finger over his scrawling script.

What was it she felt? Regret?

Three years of marriage. Three years of watching her vibrant dreams fade to a dull sepia. A year of widowhood, wearing black and gray, an itinerant healer at the beck and call of others. Not that she regretted providing remote Finn communities with quality medical services, but somewhere along the line, she'd lost herself.

But in Dr. McCullough's presence, she felt a renewed sense of purpose. She grinned. Along with a renewed interest in functional male anatomy.

Isa refused to let recent events—fear of what might lurk beneath the water's surface—keep her from a short swim near the shore. Setting the linen towel she held upon the deck, she removed her dressing gown. Such a perfect April morning ought not be wasted. She was no fool, however. Her dive knife was strapped to her thigh, its blade sharp enough to cut through any octopus tentacle, whether or not it contained a braided wire at its core.

Naked, she leapt into the water.

The water was cool, but not cold. Not to her. One of many physiological advantages all Finn shared.

Again her thoughts strayed to the well-muscled Dr. McCullough and his swimming abilities. He'd climbed onto her boat, water sluicing down his body... Could there be Finn heritage in his family tree? Blood. The lint she'd used to blot the blood from his head wound might hold a clue. But only if she could analyze it using Anton's equipment. In Glasgow.

She shouldn't. To do so without his knowledge or consent crossed a certain boundary. But perhaps if he called upon her once more, she might find a way to breach such a topic. Cautiously.

As she bobbed at the surface, the salt spray misting her face, a gull landed upon the railing of her boat. A living creature, but it reminded her of the punch card she'd handed Dr. McCullough, its address programmed to send a skeet pigeon to her Glasgow home. Glasgow, because when next she saw him, she wished to wear a gown more appealing than the dull, gray wool suited to her role as an itinerant healer. How long since she'd last felt an urge to preen?

If she left now, she could dock there this very evening. She took a stroke back toward her boat, then paused. Forever at another's beck and call, it had been too long since she'd allowed herself to swim in the sea, and she'd missed it. With a reputation to protect, Isa had denied herself this pleasure—too many pleasures—all in the name of professional dignity.

No more. The world could wait a few more minutes. Then she would attend to duty. Or—she smiled—Dr. McCullough.

Taking a deep breath, Isa flattened her nostrils and dove.

~~~

The metal brace about his knee caught at the inside of his formal uniform trousers as he limped down the hallway to the board meeting.
~~~

"A relatively simple repair," Dr. Morgan had said, then fixed Alec with a narrow-eyed glare before sewing up the inch-long incision. "But no more pivoting. As I stated before, you no longer have an anterior cruciate ligament, and this artificial joint cannot take that kind of sheer strain. Next time you might not be so lucky. I'd hate to have to install an entirely new joint."

"Is there a model capable of pivoting yet?" he'd responded, contemplating if he'd be willing to endure another six weeks of rehabilitation to replace this joint with a better model.

Dr. Morgan's scowl informed him there was not. "Are you keeping up with the exercises? Swimming laps in the BURR training pool?"

Swimming, certainly, though he imagined the doctor would blow an artery if he knew Alec had been in the ocean. And he thought it best not to mention the work he'd been performing aboard fishing vessels. It wasn't at all what the man had in mind.

"A brace," the surgeon insisted with a sigh. "Until your muscles are capable of compensating."

There was one more unpleasant task to wade through before he could return to the field on a hunt for the elusive biomech octopus. Meanwhile, he checked the rookery daily, hoping for a return skeet pigeon from Mrs. McQuiston. So far, nothing. Was she not back yet? Avoiding him?

He rubbed the back of his neck as he paced down the hallway. The Ichor machine had failed to indicate high levels of copper. It had, however, spit out a long strip of white paper, informing him of the presence of hirudin in the swab he'd taken from the man's neck wound. Hirudin—an anticoagulant produced in the saliva of leeches—was most definitely a biological peptide that did not belong in human blood. It would, however, prevent human blood from clotting.

A vampiric octopus?

Except this thing was not alive. Not exactly. Neither was it machine. The fragments he'd examined contained living tissue, yet incorporated artificial elements.

Octopus. Mollusk. Leech. Ceramics. Carbon mesh.

This was... biomech.

Alec was used to evaluating foreign biotechnological devices, but so far those had been mechanical in nature, interacting with living systems, but not incorporating them to the point where they were almost indistinguishable. The cube jellyfish gun he'd reverse engineered had integrated a nematocyst and its poison, but it was still ninety-percent mechanical and incapable of sustaining the nematocyst for more than a month's time. After that, the biological material would degrade.

Could the same be said of this octopus-ceramic-wire mesh thing? Or was it more alive than he wished to contemplate? And what was the end game?

Five punch cards of tests remained to be run. If there were any more serum abnormalities, he'd find them. Not to mention the cards that Logan had carried away for analysis. Perhaps those might prove enlightening? Not that he'd heard from his brother since. Irritating, how Logan chose to ration out bits of information only at his own convenience.

Once this meeting was over and the final programs run, he could escape the laboratory and return to the field. No reason to stay. He had no interest in establishing an actual research project, a path that would doom him to a windowless laboratory and a staid existence. Neither did he wish to return home, where Mother lurked, eager to marry off her second son.

"Sir!"

Alec blinked and found a young man saluting him. Weary, he returned the courtesy. "Do I know you?"

"Jasper Sinclair, sir. Your replacement, sir."

Already they'd replaced him. Alec suddenly felt old. At thirty. It struck him how young the new guy looked, his face still smooth, as yet unweathered by years of exposure to the elements, by exposure to the pressures of the job.

"You're here for the board meeting?" Alec asked, striving for civility.

A nod. "Yes, sir. The entire BURR team was ordered to attend the inquiry, sir. About the aquaspira. Isn't that why you're here?"

A knot formed in his gut. Davis's death was on the board's agenda. They were convening to discuss his teammate's death. Today. Now. "It was ruled an apoplexy," Alec said. "Have new findings come to light?"

Sinclair kept his expression carefully neutral. "You've been hard to locate, sir."

Once, he'd been inseparable from his crew. Now he was no more than a peripheral satellite hugging the edges, drifting further away with each circuit. His fault. It was time to correct such behavior. To start acting like the leader he hoped to become.

If he couldn't operate at full capacity in the field, he could at least pass on all his hard-won knowledge. He could drill new operatives, organize and oversee training missions. He grimaced. And there was always paperwork.

No. He wasn't ready to concede the winning point to his knee. Not yet. Not even if it meant more time on shore to pursue a certain widow.

Sinclair cleared his throat. "No. No new findings. But there are those on the board who wish us to declare otherwise."

Glowering, Alec followed the young man into the room, watching as he strode to the front, passing the file he held to Fernsby.

At the front of the room, five men sat side by side behind a long table, grumbling at each other and the papers that rested in front of them. Three men, including Fernsby and Commodore Drummond, who wished to see Alec removed from service, were dressed in military splendor. The other two wore fine wool suits. All of them politicians to one degree or another. Occupying the chairs before them were a number of other military types and more politicians, including one Lord Roideach. BURR team members occupied the shadowed corners of the rooms.

Lord Roideach turned, fixing Alec with a glare. He pointed to his chest and mouthed, "Mine."

Alec ignored him and slid into an empty chair in the back corner of the room beside Shaw. "Bring me up to speed," he muttered under his breath.

"Glad you finally made it back because something fishy is going on," Shaw said, dropping a hand on Alec's shoulder. "Heard you scored an Ichor. Take this sample of Davis's blood." The palm of Shaw's hand concealed a glass vial. "Analyze it. There must be more to the blood thickening drug he took than we know, or someone wouldn't be so keen to have his death deemed an aquaspira breather failure."

Alec took the vial and slid it in his pocket. "Who's the man next to Drummond?"

"Commander Norgrove, the Navy commander who gave the orders for our mission to proceed."

His opinion unvoiceable, Alec narrowed his eyes.

"The aquaspira breathers were all thoroughly examined prior to the mission," Fernsby said, passing pages from the file to the row of men. "The barium hydroxide carbon dioxide scrubber shows no evidence of failure, though sudden blackouts are not unheard of even at shallow depths."

A uniformed steam maid appeared at one end of the table, accompanied by a heavily loaded roving table. The old men on the board perked up, anxious for their afternoon tea. A switch was flipped, and the conveyor belt built into the long table began to move.

Working quickly, the steambot poured tea—occasionally adding sugar and cream—and placed teacups upon the belt alongside individual plates of biscuits, sending the fine china rattling across the table. The conveyor belt came to a stuttering halt, and the privileged availed themselves of a nibble and a sip.

Alec resisted an impulse to roll his eyes. *Aether forbid his* superiors *missed a meal.*

Commander Norgrove cleared his throat. "I recommend we discontinue working with the aquaspira breathers at depths greater than nine feet. Submersible approaches in open water are ill-advised."

Alec nodded. *Yes.* Too late to save Davis, but at least the man would not put the BURR men at further risk.

"I must object again," Lord Dankworth said, nibbling upon a biscuit before continuing. "With the upcoming Icelandic-Danish wedding, we must be prepared to stop the radicals who object to the new alliance. That involves policing our offshore waters."

Alec's jaw tightened. Shaw hissed a curse. Rowan leaned forward. Moray rumbled.

They'd lost Davis over a royal wedding?

Shaking his head, Commander Norgrove said, "It is a mistake to become involved in such foreign affairs. It's a wedding, for aether's sake."

Exactly. Picking a side offered Britain no gain, only loss. The best course was to remain neutral.

Lord Dankworth pressed a hand to his head and swayed. "I disagree. The riot..." he swayed again, "in Reykjavik, last week... our waters..." He lifted a trembling hand before his eyes, then pressed it to his chest. "I'm afraid—" He collapsed, boneless, to the floor.

The BURR men leapt to their feet, shoving past rows of seated onlookers that far outranked them, in a mad rush to Lord Dankworth's side. Alec half-knelt on the floor as the man convulsed, while he checked his vital signs. Shortness of breath. Slow pulse. In minutes, he was dead.

"Do you smell that?" Alec asked Shaw, who nodded.

He lifted the gentleman's tea to his nose. Nothing. His biscuits. There it was, a faint scent of bitter almond. He passed the plate to Shaw. "Poison."

Shaw sniffed, then nodded. "Cyanide."

Lord Dankworth had received the first plate of biscuits, a planned poisoning that had permanently silenced him.

"Find the steam maid!"

Chaos broke loose.

Chapter Nine

As dusk gathered its arms about the streets of Glasgow, Isa stepped inside her terraced house and dropped her bag on the floor. Dark and musty, the walls seemed to smirk, reminding her of all the dreams she'd brought to the city with her as a new bride, nearly every one of them thwarted or outright denied.

The townhouse was hers alone now. Located on a street near the docks, nearly all her neighbors were Finn—including her brother's family—and most were tied in one way or another to the nearby boatyard. Finn had comprised the majority of her practice during her time in Glasgow, knocking on her door at all hours, a small room in the back of the house serving as an examination room.

She'd abandoned it all when Anton died, taking her practice onto her boat and out to sea.

Now that she was back, word would spread quickly. Though she wouldn't turn away patients, she dreaded the arrival of the matchmakers with their lists. To date, every last man fit one of two categories. Either he needed a wife to care for existing children, or he was convinced he could give her children. All turned a blind eye to her career, all pretending—or perhaps believing—that it was something she would be happy to jettison.

Could she stand to live within these walls again? Possibly, but that would depend upon the answer to another question: would the University of Glasgow School of Medicine grant her admittance? To date, not one woman had matriculated. Odds were against her.

A written response to her last application had pointed out that the expectations placed upon their students were high. That the conflicts of a husband along with the possibility of children were distracting influences they couldn't ignore.

Application denied.

Now that such circumstances no longer pertained—the required mourning period had passed—would her chances improve? Unlikely. But unless she wished to leave Scotland, her options were limited.

There was nothing to do but apply once more.

First things first. She would begin by tending the lights and dispelling the gloom. Setting down the Lucifer lamp she'd brought from the boat, Isa drew an eyedropper from the drawer of the hallway table. With a tug on the pulley rope, the overhead light fixture lowered.

Peering into its basin, she was relieved to find the gel matrix still adequately hydrated, though the bioluminescent bacteria had long since died. She transferred a measure of bacteria from her boat's light into the hall lamp, adding a sprinkle of powdered agar and other nutrients. Hoisting it aloft, she wound the rocking mechanism and stood back. The gel oozed from one end of the long cylinder to the other, slowly mixing bacteria with food and oxygen, rewarding her with a few tiny, faint blue sparks.

Isa whisked through the house, rekindling Lucifer lamps and yanking dust sheets from furniture. In the cellar, she fed coal to the black, hulking iron beast of a furnace and set fire to its innards. Hauling the steam cook from her closet, she oiled joints, filled the water reservoir, and shoved a few lumps of coal into the burner. She inserted a simple punch card—tea and biscuits that could be made with the available stale supplies—and tossed in a match. With the flip of a switch, the steam cook creaked to life.

From the kitchen window, the metal-ringed eyes of a skeet pigeon blinked at her, and her heart leapt. The mechanical birds were forever dropping by with messages of medical emergencies, but no one—save Dr. McCullough—knew of her plans to return to Glasgow.

Throwing open the sash, she retrieved the message and read his note with wide-eyed interest, dismayed that it held so little detail. And not the slightest flirtatious remark. He merely requested permission to call upon her when she returned. She huffed in frustration and dropped the message on the table. What had she expected, another offer of a non-matrimonial dalliance?

She'd been unable to stop thinking about him. About that word he'd used. *Lover.* She'd barely slept a wink ever since. Then again, she *had* discouraged him, and if he'd learned something of import, it hardly belonged on a scrap of paper bound to the ankle of a skeet pigeon.

She turned on her heel. Time to decide. To test—or not to test—Dr. McCullough's blood?

He had no knowledge of the Finn people and didn't exhibit any Finn physical features. But, injured, he'd swum back to her boat though extremely cold waters. It was possible an unknown Finn ancestor lurked in his family tree, that—like her—he was both Finn *and* Scot.

She slid her hand into the deep pocket of her wool skirt and pulled forth the bloody cloth she'd used to dab at his head wound. She couldn't. It was unethical and immoral to study his blood without his consent. What right did she have to pry into his ancestry merely to satisfy her own curiosity? She tossed the scrap into the waste and turned away.

Her steps slowed as she walked toward the study. Once she and Anton had worked side by side, studying Finn blood, documenting an unusual trait they termed factor Q. Those Finn possessing this—greater than ninety-five percent of the population—were especially sensitive to traditional anesthesia, a trigger that could induce the dive reflex.

Ignoring her protests, Anton had taken a number of Finn blood samples with him to work, to the Glaister Institute, insisting that factor Q could be better analyzed in his laboratory using a device he called an Ichor machine. She'd asked to accompany him, to study the results generated by the instrument. He'd refused both requests, always ready with an excuse, growing ever more secretive during the last few months of his life. Then her husband had died, severing the fragile connection she had to the Glaister Institute. If any documentation of his discoveries existed, it was tightly locked inside the bowls of the research facility.

One to which Dr. McCullough had access—a thought to contemplate later.

Before she would allow herself to anticipate his arrival on her doorstep, she had a task to accomplish: reapply to the School of Medicine. Forcing herself into the room, she reignited one last Lucifer lamp and, as it slowly rocked itself back to life, tugged away one more dust cloth, uncovering a massive oak desk.

Perching upon its chair, she sat down before a keyboard that resembled a mechanical sea urchin with round, lettered discs mounted upon its spines. A Malling-Hansen Writing Ball. Manipulating the spiked creature, she mounted a fresh sheet of paper upon its curved, semi-cylindrical paper frame before raising shaking hands above the alphabet.

What would she do if they denied her entrance?

What if they did? She'd simply apply again. And again. Schools in London and Paris had accepted women. Perhaps the tide would turn in Scotland.

With that, her fingers began to strike the keys...

~~~

They found the steam maid in a closet, her cipher cartridge charred and burned, the paper punch cards within incinerated. The whispers "murder by steambot" could be heard throughout the institute's halls. Terror had overtaken the kitchens as the BURR team searched for tainted supplies.

With the board meeting at a macabre end, all submersible exit aquaspira exercises were ordered to cease... and Lord Roideach's petition to claim the Ichor machine was indefinitely postponed. Despite the death of a board member, Alec couldn't suppress a spiteful smile when Roideach cast a narrow-eyed gaze in his direction.

Patting his pocket to ensure Davis's blood sample was secure, Alec jabbed an elbow into Shaw's ribcage and jerked his head in the direction of the door. Together, they took advantage of the confusion to slip away.

"You have your lock picks?" Alec asked, relieved Dr. Morgan's adjustment—and the brace—allowed his bad leg to match Shaw's stride.

"Always. What are we breaking into?"

"Records room," Alec said.
~~~

If Dr. McQuiston had left behind any research notes, that's where they would be stored. He'd yet to hear back from Logan about the unmarked punch cards. Between Lord Roideach's rabid interest in the Ichor machine and a need to analyze Davis's blood, Alec felt his actions justified. If there were any connections, he'd find them.

Perhaps because of the commotion, perhaps because of the intricate lock, not a soul guarded the door to the Records Room. Shaw had them inside in less than five seconds.

"Barely a challenge," Shaw commented. "Might want to tip your brother to the fact. The security here needs a serious upgrade."

If or when Logan bothered to reappear. Alec had tossed repeated skeet pigeons in the air and not heard a peep in return. His mistake. He should have found his own programming specialist. Shoving irritation aside, he scanned the room until he located the shelving labeled "L-N".

Shaw followed. "Who are we looking for?"

"McQuiston," Alec answered. "Former owner of the Ichor machine and hematopathologist. Anything Roideach takes an inordinate interest in is suspect. The man hasn't had an original scientific thought in years. As such, I want to know what McQuiston was studying and how—exactly—he died."

Was it wrong of him to hope he found something unpleasant? He blew out a breath. Ridiculous of him to feel jealous of a man who had been dead for an entire year. But there it was. True, she'd turned him down despite her obvious interest. So unless she crooked her finger, he would play the gentleman.

Not that he could mention the man's stunning widow to his friend without inviting ribbing. And questions. Questions he wasn't supposed to answer even if he knew *what* was going on. If he could find a single connection, one solid lead...

"Something about Davis's blood isn't right." Shaw's musing reminded him there was another mystery to solve.

"Not right?" Alec flicked a glance at his friend as they walked down a long aisle. Heavy wooden boxes filled with laboratory notebooks bowed the tall racks of shelving looming on either side of them. *There.* A box labeled "McQuiston." Alec dragged the crate from the shelf and looked inside.

It was nearly empty. A lone personnel file lay within. His jaw clenched. Telling, this lack of laboratory notebooks. *Someone* didn't want the dead man's research exposed.

"Chemistry took a look at a sample and commented that not only did his blood have too many red blood cells, it seemed... stickier. They were going to isolate components, but that night, all biopsies and samples—even Davis's body—were confiscated."

His head jerked up. "Confiscated? Why am I just hearing about this now?"

"Please." Shaw rolled his eyes upward. "You were in no condition to handle anything other than yourself. The team thought it better to leave well enough alone."

"Except now the board wants to deny anything went wrong beyond standard aquaspira failure. And I have private and controlled access to an Ichor machine." Davis might have been a fool to act as a lab rat, and there was no denying that he'd put his team at risk, but he had been their friend. "If we let them get away with this, there's no telling what kind of experimental liberties they'll think they can take with the BURR team."

"Exactly." Shaw nodded. "Someone here did something they shouldn't and has powerful friends willing to help hide it. He needs to be stopped." He crossed his arms and gave Alec a pointed stare. "Glaister Institute is too fond of its secrets."

Of which Alec was one. He pinched his lips together, but nodded. Much as he hated keeping information from his friend, he'd promised Logan. "I'll do everything I can to figure it out."

"Good." Shaw pointed his chin at the file Alec held. "On with it then."

Opening the file, Alec quickly scanned basic information, flipping through the pages. "Born in Stornoway. Graduated medical school with honors. Married shortly thereafter. Nothing particularly interesting... wait..." Fingers tight on the file, he looked up and met Shaw's gaze. "Mentored by one Lord Roideach prior to receiving his own laboratory."

He could wait no longer for Mrs. McQuiston's return. It was time to visit the widow's home.

Chapter Ten

A loud knock woke her.

Though the house was warm, Isa uncurled stiffly from her position upon the not-so-comfortable sitting room settee and staggered onto her stocking-clad feet.

When her letter was finished and posted, tea and biscuits consumed, she had stared at the narrow flight of wooden steps leading upward. Deep inside her chest, her heart recoiled and her lungs rebelled. Every heartbeat pounded against her ribcage, and every breath scraped the inside of her throat. The only available bed in this house was the one she'd shared with Anton, and she refused to ever sleep there again.

More knocking. A glance at the hall clock informed her it was five past seven o'clock in the morning. Any number of neighbors might have seen a light in her window last night and come calling to confirm. With luck, it was Mrs. Wilson with a loaf of fresh-baked bread and a pot of jam. Her stomach growled.

She crept to the front window and twitched the curtain aside. Dr. McCullough stood upon her doorstep in the bright morning sunlight where anyone in the neighborhood might see and remark upon his visit. Her pulse jumped. She'd sent the skeet pigeon back, inviting him to tea, not breakfast. Was there dire news? Had another man died?

Or was he here for another reason? After all, he didn't look worried. He *looked* every inch a gentleman, not merely a lightly-groomed drifter. A dark coat. Waistcoat and cravat. Pressed trousers. She smiled. But no top hat. His dark hair was tousled and windblown, and *that* sent a shiver across her skin.

But sleep-tousled was not how a woman wished to answer a door. Particularly when she was considering taking the man on the other side of it as her lover. Sensing her gaze, he turned his head and looked directly into her eyes. His lips twitched, then spread into a smile that formed crinkles at the corners of his eyes, as if he found the locks of hair that tumbled about her shoulders amusing.

She dropped the curtain and pressed a hand against her stomach, a futile attempt to calm the butterflies she seemed to have swallowed. Combing her fingers through her hair, she twisted it into an acceptable knot at the base of her neck and pinned it in place before glancing down with despair at her hopelessly wrinkled bodice and skirts.

A proper lady would ignore him, refuse to answer the door, but he'd seen her before in nothing but a dressing gown, a memory that made her heart beat even faster.

Taking a deep breath, she pulled the door open and tipped her face upward to meet his assessing gaze. "Might these surprise visits be the start of a trend, Dr. McCullough?"

His smile fell away as he held her gaze. "They might, Mrs. McQuiston, were I to receive the slightest encouragement."

Her breath caught, and her tongue darted out to moisten her lips. "Then consider yourself encouraged. Do come in."

With a glint in his blue eyes, he stepped inside, filling the entryway. He closed the door, and the noise of a waking city disappeared, leaving nothing but the two of them in the faintly illuminated hallway. "I must admit, there's a certain appeal to catching you in various stages of dishabille."

His voice curled around her like a tendril of smoke, leaving her breathless. His gaze fell on her lips, and heat settled low in her belly, igniting a slow burn. But instead of kissing her, he tucked a loose strand of hair behind her ear. Slowly. The tips of his fingers traced the outer shell of her ear, his touch sweet torture.

Her eyes fluttered closed, her entire body quivering with anticipation. "Please," she whispered, done suppressing her inexplicable desire for this man's touch. "Kiss me."

Low rumbling laughter echoed from his chest as his hand slid down the back of her neck. His fingers pushed into her hair to cup the base of her head and drew her closer still. Soft full lips pressed against her own, gently exploring.

Too gently.

Ignoring a certain weakness in her knees, she rose up onto her toes and—gripping his shoulders to hold herself upright—boldly parted her lips in invitation. With a growl, he caught at her rib cage, pulling her up against him as his tongue plundered her mouth. But all too soon, he drew back, but not before catching her lower lip between his teeth with a nip.

She gasped. What sort of kiss was this? Nothing she'd ever experienced had set her skin aflame in such a manner. Her body swayed forward pleading for more.

"Later." His voice was low and husky, but his hands fell away. "There is news."

"Is there." She dropped heavily onto her heels. Perhaps it was best she took a moment to focus on something other than the thought of unwinding his cravat and pressing her lips to the skin of his neck. Men were dying. That sobered her. "Another fisherman?"

"No," he answered, his face growing serious. "A colleague. When his belongings were located, more evidence came to light. We need to talk."

Her mood deflated. Such words never preceded anything good. "Tea?" she asked, needing something to do.

"Please."

In the kitchen she stirred the fire inside the cast iron stove to life, then put the kettle on to boil. No point in activating the steam cook until she'd been to market. Bracing herself for unpleasant news, she turned and asked, "So what brings you here at such an early hour?"

"I've run tests on Larsa's blood. While I found nothing to indicate the presence of octopus tissue or blood, I did find evidence of hirudin."

"An anticoagulent produced by leeches." She dropped heavily onto a chair, staring at him with eyebrows drawn together trying—and failing—to sort the purpose of such a creature.

"There's more." Lowering himself onto a chair opposite her, he went on to describe a ceramic—what might be a kind of blood filter—attached to another scrap of the odd skin by way of some strange kind of mollusk filament.

She shook her head in bewilderment. "Manmade, yet living." She shuddered at the horrible depiction he'd painted. "A chimeric vampire octopus with fabricated features attacking fishermen to drain them of their blood. But... why would that involve a filter?"

"That is the question to be answered. But until we can find an intact creature, or a man in possession of one—"

"We won't know it's full purpose," she finished his thought, rising as the tea kettle whistled. Pouring hot water over tea leaves, she set the teapot upon the rough wooden table to brew and collected two tea cups, spoons and a sugar bowl. "Apologies for the lack of cream. I've only just returned."

He waved away her concern, instead launching their conversation in an entirely different direction. "Have you heard of an Ichor machine?"

"Ichor machine," she repeated tonelessly. Her feet froze to the floor, and her grip upon the sugar bowl threatened to shatter the delicate bone china. That was the very name of the device Anton had spoken of when he justified the transportation of Finn blood samples to the Glaister Institute.

Mother of Pearl, what had Anton left behind for others to discover? If the Institute learned of the Finn people... Could this possibly be related to the octopus attacks? Anton had been studying their blood... and she'd let Dr. McCullough carry away a sample of Larsa's blood. If he had access to the machine...

Dr. McCullough rose and took the sugar bowl from her shaking hand to set it gently upon the table. Twisting her hand into her skirts, she looked into his searching eyes. Could she trust him with her people's secret?

"I see you have," he said, then cupped a hand at her elbow as if afraid she might tumble to the floor. "You're looking rather pale. Please. Sit."

Knees shaking and her mind racing, she sat. If Dr. McCullough had access to Anton's Ichor machine, to his punch cards, he might well know already. If he didn't, and it was somehow related to the attacks, not informing him would direct his attention away from the Finn people, leaving them vulnerable.

He needed to know.

"My husband and I worked together for some time, studying the blood of those individuals with syndactyly." She struggled to find a way to explain their findings without naming the Finn people specifically. "We found that many of them possess a unique feature of the blood that we designated factor Q. When the serum of a normal person," and by that she meant full-blooded Scot, "is mixed with their blood, clumps form."

There were outliers, results that didn't fit their proposed model, that Isa was at a loss to explain. Once, she had tested the blood of a man presenting with strong Finn features and received a negative result. No clumping. A pair of siblings with not a single Finn feature—the pride of their progressive, city-dwelling mother—had tested positive, clumping. Anton interpreted it as a clear sign of Finn ancestry.

Hence her temptation to test Dr. McCullough's blood. Would it have made it easier to confide in him, had she proceeded and found he tested positive? No. Possessing Finn ancestry changed nothing. In the end, it was a person's inclination toward prejudice—whether Finn or Scot—that mattered. Though disposed to trust him, she would proceed with care.

"Agglutination." Eyes bright and alert, he leaned closer, fascinated. Tea was the last thing on his mind. "Have you determined what, exactly, factor Q is?"

"No." Her hands fisted in her lap as she struggled to control the anger she felt toward a dead man. "That was why he removed the samples to the Glaister Institute."

She took a deep breath. “Shortly before his death, Anton started spending long hours in his laboratory. I requested he submit a petition to allow me to work alongside him, but he demurred and refused even to share his results with me.” Demands made by females were never well-received, and so she bit back her bitterness as she prepared to press her right to know. “Might I take a look at his laboratory notebooks?"

“I’d be happy to share them with you, but someone else has confiscated them.”

Her blood ran cold. “Who?”

“I wish I knew...” He fell back in his chair and tipped his head. “Once, your husband studied under Lord Roideach.”

She shook her head. "I've no idea who he is." Did he suspect this gentleman? If so, what could this lord plan to do with the results of such an obscure research project? Then again, without examining Anton’s results, who knew *what* he’d discovered?

Dr. McCullough’s lips pinched together. “The dead man I examined had scars much like yours. Was the other man who died in a related manner also afflicted with syndactyly?”

Her body tensed. Afflicted. Impaired. Damaged. She hated applying such terms to Finn features. But it was the medical viewpoint of such a condition. Until and unless she was ready to reveal all... “Yes,” she replied. “You think this is somehow related to the unusual blood characteristics?”

He raised his hands in the air. "Evidence is extremely limited. But the biomech octopus seems to be out for blood. Your husband was a hematopathologist. And a gentleman I do not trust has an extreme and unwarranted interest in the Ichor machine that I find suspicious." He thumbed his earlobe. "Is there any chance—"

"That my husband brought any data home?" she finished. "None. But you are welcome to examine our early research findings." Syndactyly status had been noted beside a positive or negative result, nothing more. Besides, if something or someone was hunting her people, there was no choice but to allow him access. She rose, abandoning the tea that sat cooling upon the table. "Permit me a few minutes to freshen up, and we'll get started."

An insistent knock came from the front of the house. "Isa!" a voice called. "I know you're in there. Open up!"

She cringed, and Dr. McCullough's eyebrows rose. "My overprotective brother lives nearby." And was forever intruding. "Not only will he have glimpsed you at the seaside wedding, the Carrs will have subjected him to a tirade condemning my—our—actions. When he sees my appearance, he will..." Her face grew hot.

Dr. McCullough's lips twitched. "Assume a torrid affair."

"He will." A possibility she wished to revisit.

The banging continued.

He stood, catching her hand in his. The pad of his thumb traced a slow path over her knuckles, and every nerve ending woke, shivering in anticipation. His lips curved into a knowing smile. "Is that what you want, a torrid affair?"

"Are you offering me one?" She turned her hand over, and his thumb slid upward, beneath the cuff of her sleeve to trace small circles on the inside of her wrist. Every rational thought flew from her mind...

His answering laugh was low and rough. "I am. For as long as we both desire it. No promises, no commitments."

Isa could barely breathe. She certainly couldn't speak. How could she, a respectable widow, be considering such a thing? She bit her lower lip.

"But only if it's what you want." He frowned, and his thumb stopped moving. "It's not a condition of us working together. If you don't—"

"It's what I want," she whispered, her entire body trembling in anticipation. "I've simply no experience in such... matters."

"I'll try not to rush."

"No." *Absolutely not.*

"No?" His eyebrows rose.

She'd promised herself to chase after what she desired, and she wanted this. Badly. Time to be bold. "Do not wrap me in cotton batting as if I were fine china that might break. I'm stronger than that." With a deep breath, she forced words a respectable woman wouldn't speak past her lips. "I don't want a careful, gentle lover. I want passion. If that's not what you intend to deliver—"

He pulled her against his chest, and his lips descended upon hers. A hard and fast kiss that threatened to melt every bone in her body. As quickly as it began, it ended. A whimper slipped from her mouth as he stepped away, taking his heat and hunger with him. A catlike grin spread across his face as she gaped. "Answer the door," he prompted. "The sooner we're alone..."

Head still spinning, she nodded, then stomped to the front of the house and yanked open the door. "Someone had better be bleeding."

Danel might own his own shipyard and command hundreds of men, but once he'd been a snot-nosed brat that followed her everywhere, throwing seaweed and snails in her hair.

"Why so long to answer the door, Isa?" He crossed his arms and stared at her, unsmiling. "And why did you not let me know you had returned? I had to hear it from a neighbor that you were home. That, unchaperoned, you welcomed a strange man into your house."

Because her mind had been on other things. Because with a new baby in the house, her sister-in-law didn't need unexpected company. And because the older women in the neighborhood would materialize with lists of eligible Finn men looking for a wife.

"It was late." She squared her shoulders. Absolutely under no circumstances was she going to allow *anyone* to manage her. Not anymore. "And it's no business of yours whom I do or do not grant admittance."

Danel bristled, and that was all the warning she received before she felt Dr. McCullough's powerful presence beside her. Cats stomped louder than him. She'd expected him to remain in the kitchen, avoiding the troublesome complications of relatives. He'd offered an affair, not a courtship. Then again, he'd also agreed to a partnership in which they investigated the odd deaths together. And it appeared he meant to do so publicly. Her chin lifted with pride.

"Is everything all right, Mrs. McQuiston?"

His voice held a dark note. Would he forcibly evict Danel at her word? A thrill ran down her spine. Tempting, but her brother only had her best wishes at heart.

"Everything is fine, Dr. McCullough. Allow me to introduce my brother, Mr. Danel Guthrie."

Danel glowered.

Dr. McCullough inclined his head, every inch the gentleman. "Apologies for monopolizing her, but your sister's medical expertise has made her an indispensable asset to an ongoing investigation of mine."

"Expertise? Investigation?" Her brother rubbed his chin as he looked between them, uncertain.

Served him right for listening to the Carrs.

"A string of odd deaths. Mostly fishermen. All of them suffering severe blood loss." Dr. McCullough tipped his head. "Might you be the Mr. Guthrie of Guthrie Shipyards? Inventor of Guthrie Vibration Dampening Tubes?"

"None other." Danel's chest puffed. His shipyard was second in his heart only to his wife and family.

A disarming smile stretched across Dr. McCullough's face as he chose all the right words. "As a fan of emerging marine technologies, I've followed your career in the papers. When do you think there might be practical application of the tubes?"

"They're already installed in a Navy vessel being retrofitted in my shipyard," her brother said. "The last one is due to be injected with crystalizing fluid today."

Dr. McCullough leaned forward and dropped his voice to conspiratorial levels. "Any chance I might beg a tour?" Danel hesitated, and he pressed. "I must ask a favor of you as well, Mr. Guthrie. Who better to ask than a man who works beside the ocean, who built his shipyard from the ground up? Have any rumors reached your ears of reliable seamen disappearing without warning?"

Danel looked at her and frowned.

She pursed her lips. "You may disapprove of us working together, but men are dying. If you know something..."

Her brother jerked a nod. "Very well. A tour, then. I've a man at the boatyard who's been known to tell a strange tale or two." He glanced at her with a frown. "If you'd care to freshen up, Isa, then we'll go directly."

Chapter Eleven

It was a miserable spring day. Gray clouds produced a constant drizzle and blotted out the sun, dropping the temperature enough to give the occasional gust of air an icy bite. If not for her brother's presence in the crank hack, Alec would have tugged Isa close and done his best to warm them both.

Isa. A name made for soft whispers. The first moment they were alone, he'd brush away that artful twist of bright hair that grazed her cheek and suggest something naughty. Something that would bring a flush to her cheeks. If he nipped her earlobe, would he unleash her inner vixen? *Aether, he hoped so.*

The carriage clattered along the road, her brother rattling on about a proposed propulsion engine based on cephalopod physiology and his good fortune in winning a number of naval contracts, thereby allowing him to work with cutting-edge marine technology. Alec asked a few probing questions, but held back, preferring not to reveal the depth of his naval training. Let the man boast of his achievements while Alec stared boldly at his sister, who cast him occasional heated glances from beneath long lashes.

"The problem lies in our fluid dynamics calculations," Mr. Guthrie expounded, oblivious to the swirling undercurrents. "Using the Bernoulli equation fails to properly account for intramantle pressure during the propulsion phase. However, when we apply the Froude equation..."

He tried to focus on the reason he'd forced this tour.

Both Isa and her brother knew something about the two dead fishermen that they weren't sharing. Not hiding, exactly, but a careful reserve entered their manner whenever the topic was broached. How it pertained to his—their—investigation, he wasn't certain. Not yet. He intended to find out, but for now, he was enjoying this other version of Isa.

Gone was the gray and sensible widow. In her place, an urban woman with an upsweep of hair pinned beneath a teardrop hat, her capable fingers hidden by long, satin gloves that disappeared beneath elbow-length sleeves edged with a waterfall of black lace. The sea-green garment hugged her form as the lapels of the jacket dipped into a deep, suggestive plunge to her navel. A shame about the blouse she wore beneath.

For a moment, their eyes locked and—as if she read his mind—her cheeks colored. With a knowing smile, he let his gaze drift downward to another departure from conservative attire. The ruffled skirts she wore were fashionably cut a few inches shorter to reveal patent leather boots that—dare he hope?—laced to her knees.

He looked up to find Isa biting her lower lip as she studied his cravat. Something she did when she wanted something, but struggled to admit it even to herself. His groin stirred to life as he wondered if he could convince her to whisper her own desires in his ear. Teasing forth such confessions would take top priority the very next moment they found themselves alone.

Isa's brother cleared his throat as the carriage came to a halt. "We'll need to walk from here."

The door of the crank hack swung wide, and Alec tore his gaze away from Isa, in favor of gaping at the scrapyard before him. "Impressive. I remember reading that your enterprise began as a salvage business. I had no idea you continued to maintain that aspect of your occupation."

Pride gleamed in his eyes as Mr. Guthrie surveyed the heaps of scrap that stretched out before them and completely surrounded a warehouse and dry docks. "Started with the rusty old fishing boats that ran aground out on Lewis. Learning to fix what others deemed hopeless. No formal schooling can beat getting your hands dirty. Look there." He lifted a finger to point. A number of young men were paired with steambots wrenching loose bolts, cutting through metal plates, pulling apart rusty, old vessels. Other steambots rolled through the yard, sorting the various pieces into functional piles. "If they show promise and interest, I send them to the tinker's shed where we learn just what those boys have between their ears. Found my best men that way."

They climbed from the crank hack, and Alec opened an umbrella, beckoning Isa to his side. She stepped close resting her gloved hand upon his elbow, bringing with her a sweet, floral scent that teased his senses as it wrapped around him. "Retrofitting and repair is my brother's stock in trade."

"And I see no reason to give it up," Mr. Guthrie said. "Salvaging old vessels saves time and money." He waved his hand. "Now, careful where you step."

They wound their way through the heaps of scrap past two ships that sat in dry dock, barely visible behind the layers of scaffolding that covered their every inch. At the end of a pier stretching out over the water, a third vessel floated low in the water, almost out of view.

Alec let out a low whistle. "An S-126 Class Water Skimmer." These vessels monitored Britain's shoreline, keeping a close eye on foreign and domestic vessels. They also employed a number of marine cryptobiologists to study kraken and other unusual sea creatures that had begun to emerge from the ocean's depths in recent decades. "How did your brother manage such a lucrative Navy contract?"

For the slightest of seconds, her hand clenched. When she answered, her voice was tight and controlled. "We've an uncle in the Royal Navy. He's advanced quite far."

A spot of nepotism from Uncle Gregor, he surmised. The man otherwise known as Commodore Drummond. The uncle Isa strongly disliked. Were there deep, dark family secrets Alec ought to let lie? Probably. But he found himself unable to keep from asking. "What did he do to you?"

She tripped, and he stole the opportunity to wrap an arm about her waist, drawing her yet closer and denying her any escape. "That bad?"

"Yes. No." She stepped over a long rotor, falling silent for a number of steps. Then, with a glance at him she gave a long, resigned sigh. "You're not going to leave this alone, are you?"

"Not much chance of that. An irritating familial trait, I'm afraid." He smiled as he spoke, hoping to wipe some of the pain—or was it fear? —from her face. That failing, he let his voice grow rough. "You intrigue me, Isa. I've an itch to pull back every layer."

"And if you don't like what you see?" She sounded worried.

"We all have secrets. You show me yours, and I'll show you mine."

She laughed. "Fine. My uncle arranged my marriage, making grand promises he did not keep. Then he married Mr. and Mrs. Carr's only daughter, a spoiled brat. You witnessed the baptism of their child."

He nodded. "At the wedding of your sister Nina to their son Jona." Sympathy bloomed. "Bound to the Carrs by marriage twice over. I can only surmise what it must be like to attend a family gathering." Miserable. Much like those of his own.

"It's utter torment. The pressure to remarry, to produce offspring is all but unbearable."

Panic raised its head and blinked awake.

"Wipe away that look, Dr. McCullough." Back stiff, she came to a sudden stop and turned to face him. "I agreed to an affair. Not every woman is looking for a husband or a family. Some of us have our eyes on a career."

His eyebrows drew together. He'd assumed—incorrectly—that she was content to be an itinerant healer. "A medical degree? But—"

Doubt must have shown on his face, for she grabbed his hand and slid it beneath her jacket lapel to her upper arm. His fingertips grazed over the fine linen and felt a narrow ridge. He shook his head in confusion.

"A contraceptive device," Isa said, releasing him, and he pulled his hand back before her brother took notice. "Experimental, but effective. Before I married, four years past, my uncle arranged for me to visit the Glaister Institute as a test subject. I was promised five years without children. Five years to pursue a degree in medicine."

Relief came with the price of knowing a bright mind had been stifled, a battle his sister currently waged against their mother. "But?"

This time her laugh was bitter. "Three applications, three rejections. My married status used against me.

Though I am now a widow who has submitted a fourth application, I surmise my sex is unwelcome in the hallowed halls of the University of Glasgow."

He expected she was right. Could his brother pull a string or two upon her behalf? Possibly, assuming she had the proper academic credentials. But Logan would demand a favor first. Which circled them back to why they stood in this shipyard to begin with.

"My given name is Alec," he said. "No need for formality between friends, lovers or co-investigators who are not on a path to the altar. Trust me, I know all about family members and their matrimonial schemes. We shall dodge them all." He cocked his elbow. "Come now, we've a murderous octopus to locate."

A faint smile returned to her face, and together they hurried toward her brother who stood upon the pier, wearing a frown. "Something I ought to know?"

"Dr. McCullough had a question about our uncle." Isa's chin lifted in challenge, as if she expected her brother to scold her.

"Yes, well," Mr. Guthrie cleared his throat. "Family connections have, at times, been of assistance." He glanced nervously at his sister. "If—"

"Say no more." Alec held up a hand. "I've no interest in naval politics, only in saving lives. And," he presented his most disarming smile, "a chance to see those Vibration Dampening Tubes."

Wariness was replaced with a conspiratorial grin. "She'll slip around our coasts silently now," Isa's brother bragged. "You might be able to see her coming, but you won't hear her. This way, then." They crossed a narrow plank onto the ship's deck, then descended into the bowels of the ship, passing through hallways and over bilge doors. They turned a corner, following the noise of several crewmen and—

"Beautiful," Alec said, crossing the space to stand before the tubes in awe. All the activity on the ship was concentrated here, on this new technology. A hand's breath in diameter, the cylinders stretched upward, pressed against the ship's hull like glistening ribs. "It's a permanent installation?"

"It is." Mr. Guthrie rocked back on his heels. "We begin by using a cotton webbing that resembles a stocking more than it does a tube. As the gel is injected, my men press them into their grooves, holding them in place as the gel polymerizes to form..."

~~~

While Dr. McCullough—Alec—peppered her brother with questions, Isa wandered away from the crowd, stepping over the materials and tools strewn about, her eyes drawn to the cavernous furnace of the ship's engines. Flames licked at the glowing coals, throwing heat as it consumed everything in its path.

Beside her, filtration pipes hummed as they siphoned and filtered sea water, pumping it into enormous water tanks. She placed a hand upon the cool pipe and drew
~~~

a deep breath. There would be no keeping the truth about the Finn people from Alec. She'd seen him glance at her brother's scarred fingers. If this biomech octopus specifically attacked those with factor Q flowing through their veins, then there was a chance the creature was after more than mere blood.

Finn were highly susceptible to an induced dive reflex under the influence of standard anesthesia, a trait she suspected—but had yet to confirm—was linked to their ability to dive deeply into the sea, remaining underwater far longer than most humans were capable. But what could someone want with such Finn blood?

A transfusion? A violation of a man's body in search of the ability to confer unusual abilities? Her stomach curdled. Could a transfer of blood provide a Scot with the ability to dive like a Finn? Impossible. Or was it?

She needed to speak to Alec, alone and uninterrupted. Not here, not aboard this vessel. But soon. She grew warm, thinking about what might also come to pass once they finally managed to spend time together. Alone. Aether, she wanted this affair, wanted to experience his definition of the word *torrid.*

"Vibration dampeners don't interest you, Isa?" Alec materialized beside her, so close his warm breath brushed the edge of her ear.

A shiver ran down her spine. "Though I am proud of my brother, I find discussion of all this machinery decidedly dull. My hearing fades and my vision blurs." She glanced sideways. "Where is he?"

"Called away." His eyes sparked as he caught her gloved hand in his, tugging her behind a large boiler. "Presenting me with an opportunity to demonstrate the romantic opportunities that hulking equipment aboard a Navy ship presents." His gaze fell on her mouth.

Her breath caught. Would he kiss her now? Here? Where anyone might discover them at any moment? The only kiss she could remember that didn't end with a perfunctory and unsatisfying tumble upon a feather mattress was the one Anton had placed gently upon her lips when the minister pronounced them man and wife.

Nothing about Alec seemed gentle or unsatisfying. Lust flared and her heart pounded with anticipation. Curling her lips into a coy smile, she teased, "Are you implying that activities in its shadows can be... stimulating?"

"I see you take my meaning." The boat rocked and tipped her upward onto her toes, and he used the momentum to tug her against his chest. His very hard chest. "Has your hearing faded?"

"Not at all, Dr. McCullough." The flat of her palm was pressed against his firm abdomen, she was eye level with the topmost button of his waistcoat. "Alec. But my field of vision is suddenly very limited."

His head dipped, and he brushed his mouth along the edge of her jaw. "Perhaps with a little creative manual dexterity, that view might... expand." His hands fell on either side of her waist and spun her about, lifting her to set her feet upon a raised conduit at eye level.

"Allow me to demonstrate." He popped the large button of her jacket free, then placed his fingers upon the top button of her blouse. "All torrid affairs ought to begin with stolen moments. May I?"

Her lungs could manage nothing but shallow breaths. "I certainly don't want you to stop."

He loosed the top button, the second and a third, baring her throat. "One advantage of boiler technology is the heat it provides when one exposes bare skin." He pressed warm lips against the hollow of her throat, her neck, exploring the shape of her clavicle. "I sense you're new to this."

"Yes," she breathed. "To boilers, to affairs..."

"To...?" He lifted dark eyes to hers in question.

Did she dare admit it? Three years of marriage, and she barely knew anything of pleasure. "To bare skin."

For the briefest of moments, shock rippled over his face. "Then wrap your hands about my neck, Isa," he murmured, popping one button after another free, exposing the swell of her breasts. His fingertip traced the path of one of the many decorative spiral whorls embroidered upon her corset. "I am reminded of waves, water, of rocking on that boat of yours unable to sleep." His eyes flashed. "Now, hold tight, and bite that plump lip of yours."

She anchored her hands about his neck as he tugged at the edge of her corset, sending a sudden rush of air across her bare breast, pebbling her nipple.

"So perfect." He palmed the weight, then bent, closing his mouth over its peaked tip, sucking hard.

Arching against the cold metal of the hull behind her, she cried out as hot, delirious pleasure, sent lines of fire racing over her skin, that met and fused at the apex of her thighs. Never before... not even... who knew that a man's lips could bring such pleasure?

"Isa, shh." His lips pressed now against her breastbone in admonishment, but she could feel him laughing against her skin. "The hum of shipboard technology can mask only so much."

"More," she gasped. "Again."

"No," he said, quickly tugging her corset into place and popping one pearly button after another back through its slot. "Not here."

He gripped her waist, swinging her onto the floor where her unsteady knees threatened to buckle. She caught at his arm. "That was most informative, but perhaps you ought to have initiated your exploration in a more private location."

His sultry laugh promised that there was much more to come. "And leave you thinking ship technology dull?"

Heavy footsteps echoed in the room. "Dr. McCullough? Isa?"

~~~

Alec was certain Mr. Guthrie wished to toss him overboard. Truth was, the cold water would have done him good, but he couldn't bring himself to regret his actions, not a bit. When she'd shrieked in pleasure, the
~~~

surprise of her unexpected innocence had thrown him off balance, sending rampant need rushing through his veins.

But she was right, they needed a private location. Perhaps aboard a small, turquoise houseboat moored far from civilization. He pushed aside the thought for later as Mr. Guthrie led them to the ship's wardroom, his back stiff.

Isa's brother stepped aside, waving his sister inside. He caught Alec's arm. "She is not for you. Do I make myself clear?"

His affair with Isa was no one's business but their own. But as Alec didn't intend to propose marriage, he nodded. Satisfied, Mr. Guthrie released him, then led him into what was—when under Naval command—the officer's wardroom.

The young man inside took one look at him and snapped his heels together and saluted. "Captain McCullough."

Alec suppressed a sigh. "Lieutenant Dunnet." Though he had hoped he wouldn't be recognized, he'd known it was a possibility.

"You know each other?" Isa's mouth fell open. "You're a Naval surgeon?"

Dunnet cleared his throat. "Royal Marines, ma'am."

"I am," Alec said. *Close enough.* Dunnet gave him slight nod, acknowledging that the details of their time spent along the Irish coast were confidential. "Lieutenant Dunnet is an exceptional engineer."

Lieutenant Dunnet stood a bit taller. “Thank you, Captain McCullough.”

Isa’s brother narrowed his eyes. “*Captain* McCullough and my sister, Mrs. McQuiston, are investigating a handful of unexplained deaths. Though they specifically asked about disappearances of reliable seamen, their question brought to mind the experience you had when visiting your family this past winter in Ullapool. I wonder if you’d mind sharing?”

“Not at all, sir.” He looked to Alec. “I was out at sea with my father and his men, helping to bring in the daily catch when we spotted a shark's fin. Common enough except for its size and for the way the sun glinted off its dorsal fin. It circled the boat a few times. We turned for home, but a deckhand jumped into the water."

"Jumped?" Alec asked, incredulous. To do so in the North Atlantic in the winter months without preparation and equipment was to court death.

Mr. Guthrie gave a curt shake of his head, and Isa dropped her gaze to the floor. Interesting. There was that feeling again. That there was something more she—her brother and now Dunnet—concealed from him.

"Fell, I mean." Dunnet swallowed, doing his best not to break eye contact. "Caught in the trawling net. We pulled him out, but the experience... unhinged him. Took a couple of fingers of whisky before we could get anything intelligible out of him, and even then he was raving about how the face of a man looked straight out at him from inside the shark’s eye.”

"Inside," Alec repeated. "As if from a window?"

Dunnet nodded. "I reported the incident to the Department of Cryptobiology. They promised to look into it, but I'm afraid no one took me seriously, sir."

"I'd like to talk to this man. His name?" Ullapool could be reached by airship within the day.

"I'm afraid you can't, sir. That night he went missing."

"Missing?"

"Not just him, but his whole family. Wife and a young daughter. Left everything they owned behind and... disappeared without a trace."

Chapter Twelve

When it became clear Mr. Guthrie had no intention of letting Isa leave the shipyard unchaperoned, Alec had taken his leave, promising to call on her later. From the look on her brother's face, he half-expected the man to post a guard outside the front door of her townhome.

He stopped briefly at home. Long enough to snag a few papers from his brother's not-so-secret stash, launch another skeet pigeon in his assumed direction and drop in on the tea his mother served her guests. His mistake. Perfect Patsy was among them, her eyelashes batting fast enough to circulate a light breeze about the parlor.

"Are you available this evening?" his mother asked without preamble, looking quite irritated. “There’s a small matter concerning your brother I’d like to discuss.”

Pressing a quick kiss to his mother's cheek, he snagged a scone. “Quinn?” Had the apple of her eye finally done something to earn her displeasure?

“No, the other one.”

Ah. *The other one.* Telling, that phrase. Mother only spoke of Logan when it became absolutely unavoidable.

Cait shifted, her back rigid.

Wonderful. That decided it. A conspiracy orchestrated by Cait and Logan was the last thing he wished to become involved in.

He took a step backward. "I’m afraid I’ve a prior commitment.”

"Might I speak with you a moment, brother dearest?” Cait rose from her chair, her eyes narrow. “I've been reading the most fascinating monograph about how nematocyst venom degrades the cellular membrane. I have questions."

The room froze in horror. A woman discussing science. How dare she? It wasn't the science that bothered Alec, but rather the bloodthirsty methods his sister devised for its use.

"Must run. Meeting with Shaw. But I'll be certain to answer all of them later."

Cait's stare burned twin holes in his back as he made his escape. Was it any wonder he worked such long hours when his home life was fraught with matrimonial traps, conspiracies and poisons?

When he arrived at the Glaister Institute, Shaw waited outside the Department of Cryptobiology. "What's this about a mysterious fishing expedition you wish to launch?" he asked. "Find something in Davis's blood?"

"Not yet," Alec answered. "But I don't hold all the cards. The minute Logan reappears, I'll run the program."

He'd hoped to find a message waiting for him at home, but Logan still hadn't responded to his many missives. His brother had dragged him into this mess, dropped all kinds of difficulties in his path, then disappeared. As always. It warmed Alec's heart to envision an entire flock of skeet pigeons swarming Logan when he reappeared.

"In the meantime, I've word of a mysterious shark-like creature swimming off our shores." And as this was not officially linked to the biomech octopus creature, it didn't yet fall under the umbrella of confidentiality Logan had imposed.

"A megalodon?"

"Could be." Alec yanked open the door. "At twice the length of a fishing boat, whatever it is could be some two hundred feet long."

Five feet inside the room, a bored-looking woman wearing dark spectacles in the already dim room looked up from the piles of paperwork stacked chin-high upon her desk and sighed. "Authorized personnel only. If you don't have a requisition order—"

Alec slapped down the paperwork. Stolen and forged, but he'd been scrawling his brother's signature for years. "As ordered by Mr. Logan Black."

"Mr. Black?" The corners of her mouth twitched. "I'll be right back."

A certain spring to her step made him wonder— No. He didn't want to know.

Shaw snickered. "And not one of his women ever talk. What *is* his trick?"

Tipping his head backward to study the brick arches that spanned the width of the ceiling, Alec said, "Not a topic we discuss."

"Oh? Maybe you should. That nurse back in the Fifth Ward—"

"Shut it."

Shaw only laughed.

The secretary returned a moment later, holding a thick paper folder. Alec reached for it. "Thank—"

She snatched it away, holding it against her chest, a sly grin upon her face. "Will you let Mr. Black know the item he requested has been located?"

Ignoring the awful sounds Shaw made as he choked back his laughter, Alec pulled a punch card from his pocket. Logan would box his ears for this, but anything to make him surface. "Tell him yourself."

"Thank you," she purred, tucking the card inside her bodice before at last handing over the file he'd requested.

Across the room, out of earshot, he flipped open the folder and thumbed through a dull record of shark sightings off the western coast. Dull until January. There, it was, an unusual sighting buried among the standard notations.

A large shark-like creature totaling approximately one hundred fifty feet in length, not inconsistent with a hypothetical megalodon. Displays many features suggesting a classification among the elasmobranchii. Unable to determine order. First observation noted 16 January 1885, since spotted repeatedly off the western coast of Scotland. Retreats when approached, making any unique markings impossible to observe. As yet unable to confirm number of individual members of this new species. Investigation ongoing.

He flipped through more pages. The small handful of sightings—none of which contributed additional information—had been made along the western coast of Scotland—from Portree to Ullapool. But Water Skimmers rarely patrolled the outer Hebridean islands.

"You think they finally found a megalodon?" Shaw asked, reading over Alec's shoulder. He scratched his jaw. "Seems like overexcited cryptozoologists to me. They can't even decide if the fish is male or female."

"What if it's neither?"

"Neither?" Shaw tipped his head. "Explain."

"Remember the Irish coast and Lieutenant Dunnet?"

"Impossible to forget." Shaw grinned. "A good man, keen to work with us, but couldn't handle dirigible work worth a damn."

"True." The man had spent the better part of the mission bent over a bucket. "Our paths crossed again today. He sighted the dorsal fin himself and reports another man went overboard. This individual, when fished out of the drink, claims a man was staring out of the creature's eye." He snapped the folder shut. "The next day, this man disappears along with his entire family. Rather convenient, is it not, that the only witness can't tell his tale?"

Shaw stroked his chin, then nodded. "You think there's only one creature because it's a submersible, not a living beast, that someone from its crew was sent ashore to kidnap this man?"

"I do."

"You're right. I don't like it," Shaw said. "But it's rather thin evidence to launch a fishing expedition."

Alec ran his fingers through his hair and swore. Was it a long shot, connecting this megalodon with the biomech octopus? A group of people with scars upon their fingers, unique blood characteristics, members of their community disappearing... one returning anemic, with most of the blood drained from his body. Isa was hiding something, and gut instinct told him this was tied to her husband's research, Roideach and maybe even Davis's death.

"Going to share, Mac?" Shaw stood with his arms crossed, giving him a look of growing annoyance.

He needed help. Professional, trustworthy help. And he could trust Shaw, trust his team. "What I'm going to tell you goes no further than the team. I've been commissioned by the Queen's agents."

Hours later, they left Fernsby's office. It had been a difficult task, convincing Fernsby to bypass standard protocol, especially given Dr. Morgan had yet to clear Alec's return to the team. In the end, the tenuous link to Davis's death tipped the argument in their favor. They stepped into the BURR operations room and the team, bent over a nautical chart, looked up with interest.

"Drop everything and pay close attention. I've got a fish tale to tell."

~~~

Loyal to the Finn people but clearly unwilling to elaborate on his connection with a captain in the Royal Marines, Lieutenant Dunnet made himself scarce the moment *Captain* McCullough left the wardroom.

"He is not a man you should involve yourself with, Isa." Her brother tugged at his collar. "A Scot investigating Finn deaths brings nothing but trouble."

"Trouble is already here," she countered, planting her hands on her hips. "You met him. Do you think he'll drop this investigation? Not a chance. Better that I'm at his side to inform and guide him, lest he reach absurd conclusions." He was a man of science, not one to believe humans could alter their form at will.

"You can't, Isa." He frowned. "No one knows about us."

"Please," she huffed. "They only just pretend."

"Perhaps on the islands," he said. "Here in Glasgow, Scottish men are happy to work for me and among our people. Here skill counts above all. Scars are ignored,
~~~

and it's a rare Finn who would invite commentary by *falling* into the water. We're happy here. We've won a place here. But shove our people into the limelight, Isa, and we're sure to suffer repercussions."

"Better to let Finn fishermen disappear?" she shot back. "To wash up on shore, their blood drained by some kind of vampiric octopus?" She held back the details, as she'd promised. "You would ignore that to save your business?"

"I would let the elders of our community handle it as they see fit." His eyes narrowed. "Time to go. My wife is preparing a noon meal to celebrate your return, and you'll not miss it."

Danel employed the entire duration of the carriage ride to fill her ears with ominous predictions should she continue her liaison with Captain McCullough.

As if she could so easily walk away from either the burning pleasures of his touch or the fascinating mysteries he presented, both on a personal and academic level. All she wanted to do was to hurry back to her townhome to scour Anton's study, to hunt for the missing laboratory notebooks. But until she made an appearance among the Finnfolk of the Glasgow community, she would know no peace.

Passing the afternoon with her sister-in-law Livli was not at all a trial for it had been too long. But even as she laughed at the antics of her adorable nieces and nephews as they attempted to keep a feather aloft with puffs of air, an unwelcome knock came at her brother's door.

Matchmakers. Three of them.

"It's been too long," one woman said, shaking her head. "All this nonsense about mourning an entire year. Three months is sufficient, particularly when you've yet to fulfill your obligation to have children." Tongues clucking, they presented Isa with lists and schedules and instructions as to how she must appear and behave when introduced to the next man she would marry.

Livli beamed at Isa, as if she did her widowed sister-in-law a great favor. Most Finn women would have been grateful, and Isa did her best to swallow her ire, if only for Livli's sake, but she soon made her excuses.

Isa slammed the door behind her and fell backward against it, looking up at the glow of the gently rocking Lucifer lamp. Aether, they'd have her married by next Friday. This was why she'd fled Glasgow. Without a husband, would she be able to reestablish a medical practice here among the Finn? Certainly not while conducting an affair right beneath their very noses. It was becoming harder and harder to imagine a future in Scotland, at least one in which she controlled her own fate. If the University of Glasgow denied her admission once more, she might need to travel to London—or abroad—to train as a physician. Could she bring herself to take such a step?

Closing her eyes, she let her mind drift to thoughts of Alec. In less than five minutes behind the boiler, he'd managed to bring her to an intense state of arousal. She flushed at the memory. Keening at a man's touch? A few days ago she'd have rolled her eyes at such a suggestion. What could he manage with no interruptions?

Anton had not been an unkind man, but never had their lovemaking—conducted quickly beneath the covers in the dark—ever elicited more than a warm satisfaction. If that. Over time, they'd drifted ever farther apart, his absences from home growing longer, until—their marriage in tatters—she'd finally confronted him. About her failed applications to medical school, his refusal to confide his research discoveries, and her assumption that he'd taken a mistress. Like an exploding boiler, he'd vented what must have been a long-simmering anger.

"Three years!" he'd ranted. "And not the slightest hope of a child." He'd paced back and forth, stabbing his hands into his hair, tugging at the roots. "I should have followed my instincts. All that garish red hair proclaims your ancestry. Finn and Scot aren't meant to mix. Damn your uncle and his promises." Amidst tears and further accusations, he'd stormed from their home.

All that time Isa had believed her husband knew there was no possibility of children, that—during marriage negotiations with her uncle—he had agreed to the temporary use of contraceptives while the newlyweds established their careers. Lies had been told to them both.

The very next day he was dead, his words left behind to forever echo in her mind.

A cold shiver ran down her spine. Anton's death had been unexpected, but she'd never suspected it was anything but an unfortunate incident. Not until now. Alec had mentioned missing laboratory notebooks, assuming someone at the Glaister Institute had stolen them from his laboratory. Because of Anton's refusal to share his findings with her, she'd also assumed he kept his notes there. But if he were worried about a colleague stealing his work, might he have brought them home? If his work—their work—was linked to the recent rash of Finn deaths, she needed to know.

Where would he have secreted his laboratory notebooks? Somewhere his wife was unlikely to look but, charged with nearly all the domestic duties, where could that possibly be? The basement. He'd been in charge of maintaining the coal supply, shoveling deliveries from the coal chute into the furnace.

Isa launched into action, tossing off her jacket onto a chair and rolling up her sleeves. Grabbing a Lucifer lamp, she hurried down the narrow stairs. There, in the underground gloom, a small stack of boxes covered by a dusty tarp shoved between outmoded and broken equipment, saved for parts. She tossed aside the tarp and pried off the topmost lid.

A circulator, an agitator, a hand-cranked fuge. One by one, she set them all aside, digging to the bottom and pulling forth a single cloth-wrapped notebook. Muscles quivering with barely suppressed anger, she investigated the other boxes, but found nothing more.

Hours passed as she sat in the study, paging through academic scribblings of hypotheses tested, rejected, refined and repeated. Her eyes grew bleary as the afternoon light faded into darkness, but she kept reading. Anton had indeed been studying the blood of Finn patients without their consent. Unethical, yet seemingly innocuous.

But as relief began to replace suspicion, one particular notation leapt from the page: *secretory glycoprotein.* Her pulse jumped. Secretory? Her eyes raced down the page of experimental data. Not only had Anton managed to isolate factor Q, he'd discovered it was not a glycolipid as expected, but rather a glycoprotein, comprised of both carbohydrates and protein.

At this point, his handwriting grew increasingly illegible as he wrote of a series of inoculated blood cultures. But there, among his fevered jottings, a single telling phrase: *hypoxic conditions release factor Q into the blood's serum.*

Hypoxic. Low oxygen levels.

An unladylike string of curses worthy of a hardened sailor tore from her lips. How could he have kept such discoveries from her? Hypoxia was directly relevant to her own investigations into the effects of different surgical anesthetics upon their people. A large part of supplying a patient with anesthesia centered around ensuring that oxygen levels did not fall too low. He'd kept this from her knowing that further studies might elucidate why most Finn reacted poorly to a standard anesthesia mixture while others did not.

She shoved her fingers into her hair. Without a medical degree, without access to sufficient funds or the research facilities of the Glaister Institute, her work could proceed no further.

~~~

Cut off from the light of day and working under bright argon lights, Alec lost track of the hour. The coded brief had to be flawless. Everything rested on his shoulders. He would be breaking chain of command on two fronts—Naval and Queen's agents—by sending a message directly to the Duke of Avesbury in London, requesting permission to engage the BURR team for a secret reconnaissance mission. If anything went wrong, it was his neck on the block.

By the time he was finally satisfied, the clock face on the far wall of the operations room informed him that it was twenty past midnight. He stretched out his aching leg, aware he'd sat for far longer than Dr. Morgan would approve.

Too late to visit Isa?

Yes, too late. He ran his fingers through his hair in frustration.

"Done yet?" Moray pushed back from his own deck, stretching. "When are we going fishing?"

Alec grinned. "Soon as Shaw figures out where to dangle the hook."

The *HMS Beta Water Skimmer*—responsible for the sightings—had been messaged for updates, and the Alpha and Gamma Skimmers contacted to see if they'd noticed
~~~

anything unusually large about the fish population this winter. By the time approval came back from London—if it came—they needed to have the mission ready to execute.

The door to the operations room swung open and Shaw strode in, dropping a stack of paper on Alec's desk. "This just in from *HMS Alpha Skimmer*. You need to take a look."

Sightings. Depth readings and speed recordings. There was no way Alec was leaving the operations room, not even long enough to knock on Isa's door for an overdue goodnight kiss.

He rubbed the back of his neck and grumbled at the piss-poor timing. Perhaps it was just as well. For the moment, there was too much he couldn't share with her. He'd send a skeet pigeon with a note of apology and plead for her forgiveness.

~~~

Unable to sleep, Isa threw open a window to see what messages had come to roost. Outside in the dark, wee hours, five skeet pigeons perched on her window sill. Not many knew she had returned to Glasgow but, with only a handful of Finn working in the medical fields, word would spread quickly among them.

She plucked the canisters from the birds, unfurling the messages they carried. Three alone were from her mother, one message chiding her for involving herself in Larsa's death, a second complaining about the Carrs, and a third praising Mrs. Carr's efforts on Isa's behalf and imploring her to return home to marry Elias.
~~~

Rolling her eyes, she unfurled the fourth message.

Rigid with frustration, but unable to leave work. Know my every stray thought lingers behind a boiler, behind a button. Or ten. May not be free for hours or days.

Heat curled low in her belly at Alec's words. Perhaps it was just as well. She needed time to process the data in Anton's laboratory notes. There was too much she wasn't ready to share.

The fifth bird hailed from Achiltibuie, a tiny village north of Ullapool, and the words scrawled upon the paper raised every hair on the back of her neck.

Help. Husband found on boat, clinging to life. A tentacle is lodged in his neck. Fear blood poisoning is about to set in. Cannot call the local doctor. Please come immediately.

Gathering the pigeons, she stuffed them into a canvas bag and slammed the window shut. Correspondence could be attended to from her boat. Weather permitting, at full throttle she might reach his bedside before midnight. En route, she would pen a reply to Alec assuring him that her recently altered opinion of shipboard machinery still held, that she would write again when she'd returned from attending the bedside of a patient whose condition was relevant to their investigation.

Chapter Thirteen

"Grab your gear, we're a go." Shaw strode into the operations room. "*HMS Beta Skimmer* spotted the megalodon not far from the Summer Isles. They've wired an exact position. A Cormorant class dirigible is standing by on the strip. Time to get a bird in the air and hunt for shark."

All five men—Alec, Rip, Moray, Rowan and Sinclair—straightened and grinned. They'd spent the better part of the last two days bent over a table littered with nautical charts and various sheets of paper, attempting to predict where the megalodon might surface next. They were beyond ready.

Shaw pointed a finger at Alec. "Observational status only. You're not cleared to dive with that knee."

He opened his mouth to object.

"Don't even try." Shaw's eyes narrowed. "That's an order straight from Mr. Black, who is pissed as hell you broke confidentiality and went over his head."

Alec grinned. About time his brother surfaced. "Got his attention, didn't it?"

~~~

Orange and brilliant, the sun dipped ever closer to the horizon, but for once the comforts of her houseboat failed to beckon. Ignoring the path leading to the shore, Isa turned toward the small cluster of buildings that lined a street and—after the slightest of hesitations—yanked upon the heavy wooden door of an unofficial tavern where Finnfolk gathered. She breathed in the smoky scent of the peat fire that burned on the grate and let the dark warmth of the room wrap around her. Scots might wander in, but they weren't welcome and rarely stayed long. Women were barely tolerated either, but there was nowhere else in town to go, and she didn't want to be alone with the thoughts swirling through her head.

Ignoring the pointed stares of three men who gathered in a far corner, she placed her medical bag on the floor and sank onto a stool to bury her face in her hands. She'd arrived too late.

The publican set a pint of ale onto the table before her.

She raised her head and met his sad eyes. "Thank you."
~~~

"On the house, Mrs. McQuiston," he said, his face long. "Heard what happened."

By the time Isa dropped anchor and arrived at the cottage, septicemia had already sent the man into shock. There hadn't been much left of the tentacle—his wife had cut it down to a mere stub before she arrived—but its path was easily traced.

The biomech creature had pierced the man's neck, stabbing at it twice before tunneling into his external jugular vein and causing significant blood loss. Isa had anesthetized the man and removed the narrow, braided wire with its hooked tip, carefully storing it and the remaining cephalopod tissue in a vial of ethanol. Alec would wish to study it. A distant corner of her mind pointed out that she'd rushed here as much for Alec as for the poor fisherman, hoping to impress him by gathering a fact or two that would shed light on the strange attacks.

Performed earlier, the surgery might have saved the fisherman, but his body temperature had continued to climb, sending the man into feverish convulsions. When death finally arrived, when his teary-eyed wife had looked to Isa for an explanation, she was at a loss. Word of the octopus attacks was spreading, and all she could say was that the incidents were being investigated.

Wishing to leave the family to their mourning rituals, she'd not conducted a full postmortem, only taking note that the fisherman did indeed bear scars between his fingers, indicating a high probability that factor Q had flowed through his veins and arteries.

Hypoxic conditions release factor Q into the blood's serum. The phrase from Anton's notations kept running through her mind. Could this biomech octopus somehow detect factor Q? She pressed her palms to her eyes. Worse, did it drag its victims overboard first, the better to deprive them of oxygen—to induce hypoxia—before burrowing toward a man's blood vessels?

She shuddered at the thought.

"Grateful you came, even if..." He waved his hand, unable to finish. "Well, there's not too many Finn left in town, what with so many families packing up and heading north. Two more families left earlier today."

"North?" Her head jerked up.

"Heading to the Shetland islands to build a community of Finn. Something about returning to their roots." He tipped his head at a line of skeet pigeons that sat on a shelf. "So many have gone that I'm running more of a postal service than a pub."

Spread thin about the western shores of Scotland, Isa could see the appeal of gathering together Finn who yearned to return to the old ways. But in doing so, they cut themselves off from the outside world, including medical care and education. And how long could they hope to live apart with technological advances of all kinds making distant corners of the globe ever more accessible?

"Ah, there's one now," he said. A skeet pigeon had landed outside a small window propped open with a stick. Ducking through the opening, it shuffled forward and held out its metal-jointed leg. The publican tugged off the brass canister and pulled out the paper, peering beneath his glasses to read the words. His face paled.

"Nikko!" he called to one of the men, waving the paper. "It's the boat. The one to Lerwick. The Brown and Lovitt families are requesting a rescue. Their propeller malfunctioned and a giant shark is circling."

The megalodon. Which might or might not be alive.

Adrenaline flooded Isa's system, and her heart began to pound. A shark. Circling a boat of traveling Finn. Her people were under attack. This was all connected. It had to be.

"My boat," Nikko called as he strode for the door.

Everyone moved to follow him. Including Isa. The publican cast her a look and opened his mouth, ready to set her aside like a fine piece of china, pretty but not particularly useful. But she was done letting others assign her value.

She held up a hand. "I'm coming. What if you need a healer? I could have saved that man, if I'd only been able to reach him sooner."

He hesitated, then nodded.

Clutching her medical bag, she hurried after the rough-hewn fishermen. Some frowned, some ignored her, but not one stepped in her way to prevent her from boarding.

A cold wind lashed at them as the boat churned through the water, rising and falling with the waves, its helm pointed at a darkening horizon. Nonetheless, the men stripped down to their undergarments, providing access to the knives strapped to ankles and wrists. If danger lurked in the ocean, they would dive overboard to fight the creature and save those they could.

As would she.

She tossed aside her own cloak and pulled off her bodice. Her hands shook as she unhooked the clasps that held her skirt in place. Did she go too far? Would they stop her now? All wore tight-lipped frowns, but one man stepped sideways, waving her forward.

In nothing but her linen shift, her own dive knife strapped to her thigh, Isa stood beside the railing with the men, her hair whipping in the wind, as they searched for a boat in distress.

~~~

"An overlarge dorsal fin at ten o'clock." Alec stared through the eyepiece of the inverted periscope. "Circling a large boat with a distress flag. Another smaller vessel is on course to intercept it. A probable rescue."

The cryptobiologists aboard the *HMS Beta Skimmer* had called in a final sighting of the megalodon, and then veered out to sea while the pilot of the R14X Cormorant class dirigible maneuvered into position above the cloud cover.

Beside him, all the BURR men—Shaw, Rowan, Sinclair, Moray and Rip—were ready to drop in for a peek at this oversized shark. Dive masks and hoses hung
~~~

around their necks, breathing bags and tanks on their backs. Harpoon guns were strapped to their legs. Self-defense only. Alec was similarly attired, prepared for things to go pear-shaped.

"You're not to leave this dirigible," Shaw had protested when Alec geared up, reading intent on his face.

"I won't go down unless it's safe," he had promised, shrugging off Shaw's concerns as he shoved an acousticocept into his ear canal. "I'm prepared to stand here receiving transmissions. But when the all clear comes, I need to get a look at this thing with my own two eyes."

Shaw had scoffed. "I'm tempted to toss you in first as bait."

Alec grinned.

The men ran a final check of their equipment along with a last test of the newfangled acousticotrans system. The Duke of Avesbury had given him clearance to run this mission, with the caveat that it would be billed as an exercise to test an experimental communications method. Proven on land, it had yet to be used in the water—though the devices were safe beneath thick layers of vulcanized rubber. Alec had his doubts about the transmission system but, as he pointed at each man in turn, he couldn't help grinning at the profanities that cracked back at him.

"Ready?"

Thumbs went up.

Satisfied that everything was as it should be, Alec leaned into the cockpit. "Good to go. Hover and hold."

"Yes, sir." The pilot flipped switches and punched buttons. A moment later, the dirigible slowed, floating motionless.

Alec pulled a lever, sliding open the great door in the gondola's side. He threw out five thick ropes secured to the dirigible's undercarriage, ones calculated to end some two feet above the water's surface and fifty feet away from the distressed boat. There, the team would drop into the water. If all went well, the megalodon would never notice them.

"Don't belly flop," he ordered and stepped back.

Lifting middle fingers as they passed him, each man grabbed hold of a ratchet handle, slid a booted foot into a ratchet stirrup, then jumped out, making a swift, but steady, descent.

Seconds later, noise crackled over the acousticocept as each crew member reported in.

"Shit," Rowan barked. "Bodies in the water. Draw your weapons."

"Same on port," Moray said. "I've got a severed head. What the hell happened here?"

"I've got a partial torso," Sinclair added. "With an attached tentacle."

"I need that," Alec yelled into the acousticotransmitter, pacing in the confined space of the dirigible. "Do not let go! Gather any other remains that appear to have an octopus or fragments of an octopus attached to it in any manner."

"Bagged it," Moray reassured him. "Anyone got eyes on the fish that did this?"

"There," Rip spoke. "Behind the stern of the boat. Twenty feet down."

"Oh, hell," said Shaw. "Its eyes glow. And its mouth is open. Sharp teeth, glinting... in a flood lamp?"

"It's covered with standard shark skin," reported Moray. "But has hinges on the tail, and I can see rivets anchoring the pectoral fins in place."

"Portals on the sides. Aw, hell, they're opening!"

Shaw swore. "They're expelling hyena fish!"

"Back away!" Alec yelled. "Get out of the blood zone."

Hailing from the South Atlantic off the western coast of Africa, hyena fish were bad news. Vicious, they swarmed carrion, stripping them to the bone in minutes. The human remains in the water would whip them into a feeding frenzy. Collateral damage was likely.

"The megalodon is diving," Rip reported.

"I'm bit," Shaw said. "Bleeding. Not impaired, but exiting the zone."

"Time to leave." Moray's voice was deadly calm over the acousticocept. "The rescue vessel is attempting to pull alongside the first."

Alec stared through the inverted periscope, straining to make out details. There appeared to be a single figure in distress, curled into a ball upon the deck of the original boat. Though that individual would have quite the tale to tell, now was not the time to demand it.

"Do not surface," Alec ordered. "Allow the rescuers to assist any survivors." If the BURR team were to board either boat dressed as they were, they would be met with fear and resistance. "Rowan, assist Shaw. Moray, survey the scene and estimate how many individuals are—were—in the water. Sinclair, collect samples. Rip, keep an eye on the rescuers. I'll hover and monitor for further trouble. Prepare to retreat to rendezvous alternate point and await pickup."

"On our way."

A figure—a woman—dressed in nothing more than a shift stood at the railing of the rescue boat, hair whipping about her face. A familiar face. He spun a dial, increasing magnification. Quicksilver eyes, copper hair and a quiet, determined bravery. The stance of a woman willing to face the unsettling and unknown. What the hell was Isa doing here? Had she any idea of the danger that circled below? He bet she did, that she'd purposefully inserted herself into this situation.

He'd promised—been ordered—not to interfere. Any risk to her was low. The megalodon had disappeared, and there was no reason for her not to attend to any survivors. He could ask her for a report later. Time to order the dirigible about, retrieve his team. But his feet were frozen to the floor.

~~~

When the distressed boat came into sight, its white flag flapping in the wind, not a soul stood on deck, yet around the hull, seawater churned, dark with... blood. An eerie keening sound rose from the water as fish with
~~~

whip-like tails and mouths filled with long, sharp teeth shredded scraps of human flesh.

She shuddered.

"Hyena fish," the man beside her hissed. "We're too late."

A sour taste rose to the back of her throat. This was far, far worse than an individual octopus attack. Who would do such a thing to a family and why? The Brown and Lovitt families—six adults and nine children wanting nothing more than a peaceful life—gone.

On the wind, Isa caught a different kind of cry.

"There!" She pointed. "A woman. Bring the boat around."

The minute they drew aside, Isa leapt over a small stretch of water where the horrible fish still swarmed, landing on the other ship's deck. She ran to the woman who huddled against the railing. Arms around her legs, she rocked, wailing her misery into the wind.

"What happened?" Isa wrapped her own arms about the woman's shoulders, offering comfort. Behind her, the Finn men thundered onto the boat, glancing in her direction with a nod, they ran down into the hull, searching for other survivors.

"OctoFinn came." The woman spoke in a monotone, her eyes vacant. "We fought, killed two. Lost. There was a culling. Blood was taken. Some were worthy, and those they took into the mouth of the shark. Those who weren't..." Her pale face tipped upward. "They threw my baby overboard."

No. No it couldn't be. Condemned or saved by a blood test? "Did they mention factor Q?" Guilt—already grasping her by the throat—tightened its grip as she waited.

But the woman didn't answer, she only rocked, her lips moving without sound.

"Come," Isa said. "Let's get you away from the water."

"Don't touch me!" the woman screamed, exploding to her feet, shoving her hands outward.

And pushing Isa over the railing and into the water.

She broke the surface gasping for air and kicking.

Pain shot through her leg. Bloody hyena fish. Rotten little chum chewer had bitten down on her calf, its inch-long fangs tearing a gash through her skin. Blood swirled around her. Bits of flesh, mostly unidentifiable, churned in the waves. The salt water burned as she stroked away from the shrieking fish, away from both boats. Had—with the horror and chaos that surrounded them—anyone noticed she'd gone overboard?

Something bumped the back of her head. She spun and screamed. A severed leg, cleanly cut with as if with a large, sharp blade. Megalodon teeth? Coughing up the bloody salt water she'd inhaled, she started to kick away until she noticed something else. A tentacle protruded from the knee. Treading water, she spun around again. The hyena fish surrounded both boats, blocking her return. Drawing her dive knife would do no good; slashing at such small, darting creatures would accomplish nothing but to drain her of energy.

The shore was two miles away, and the water not unreasonably cold. Not for a Finn. Swimming for shore would take time and—given the attacks—was ill-advised. Besides, the survivors might require medical assistance. Aether, she hoped there were more aboard that boat than a single woman. She bobbed in the water, waiting. When they discovered her missing, the men would set up a search.

Sharp teeth pierced her ankle. With an abrupt intake of breath came water. A second bite at the arch of her foot. The hyena fish had found her, but still no one was on deck. Kicking, she moved away, away from the boats. Another bite. If she waited for the men to remember her, to begin a search, she might have no toes left. *Horrid fish.*

Cringing in distaste, she wrapped her fingers about the ankle of the tentacle-impaled, disarticulated leg. If need be, she could save herself.

Chapter Fourteen

Never again would she underestimate the damage hyena fish could do to a live human. Several more attacked before she broke away. Dragging a severed leg through the water hadn't helped. It was like waving bread crusts in front of a gull, a game she and her sister had played as children. Except gulls didn't have long, needle-sharp teeth. She'd make it—and with the bloody leg—but it was going to take a Herculean effort.

Splash!

Isa spun in the water, strands of wet hair whipping about as she searched the choppy waves, finding nothing but a ring of ripples. Overhead the frayed end of a rope dangled as if hanging from the cloud above. Impossible. But so were octopus attacks and giant shark-like submersibles.

Abandoning the leg, she dragged in a breath, filling her lungs in preparation for a deep dive, praying that whatever had fallen from the sky wouldn't—couldn't—follow. Bending at the waist, she dove. Deeper and deeper.

Until a thick and rubbery band wrapped about her waist and jerked her to a halt, dragging her upward toward the surface. In one sharp motion, she connected her elbow with—a head? The arm loosened, and she twisted in the unwanted embrace of a masked man encased in a rubber suit. Clutching at his shoulders, she brought her knee upward hitting hard between his legs.

He let go.

If his face contorted in pain, it was impossible to tell through the haze of scattered underwater light. Air escaped her mouth in great bubbles as she lashed out with her feet, kicking at his knees, at muscular thighs and hard shins. Drawing her knife, she slashed at the many tubes protruding from his mask, ripping it from his face, before stroking for the surface in desperate need of more air.

She broke the surface. Gasping. Kicking. Reaching. Heart pounding in preparation to swim as she'd never had to before.

"Isa!"

Alec? Again she spun, gaping. Familiar blue eyes stared back at her, pleading for understanding.

How was it possible? A Navy doctor who dropped from the sky? She looked upward. There, if she squinted, she could make out flashes of silver—a dirigible balloon hiding beyond the clouds. Rational thought trickled back.

A physician. A Naval officer curious about advanced ship technologies who was comfortable above, in and under the water. There was only one classification for such a man: BURR.

Finn men dreamed of achieving such a position in the British Navy. Powerful, intelligent and chosen only after much trial, few men managed it.

"I promise to explain," he called. "If you'll only let me help!"

Blood loss and their underwater struggle had drained her of all the fight she had left. "How?" she yelled back.

"Watch!" He pried something free from the harness buckled over his chest—a strange rubber item attached to a cord. With a yank of the cord, air hissed and the item exploded, unfurling into a long, narrow inflatable raft. “Get in!”

She struggled into the odd craft, gaping at Alec as he clambered in behind her. With the twist of his wrist, he activated a canister, releasing a compressed gas to power a propeller that sent them rocketing toward shore. She ripped the hem of her shift, tearing free a strip of linen and binding the worst of the hyena fish lacerations, as he expertly steered the craft over the waves, his dark hair whipping in the wind.

Alec had shed a kind of breathing apparatus and peeled back a thick, vulcanized rubber suit to his waist before taking hold of the rudimentary helm. Saltwater sprayed across muscles that rippled over his arms and shoulders, strength she'd gripped behind a boiler. The scars that marked his skin, his damaged knee, a focused determination on a task set before him. She saw them all in a new light, as if the colors of the spectrum had shifted. If BURR was investigating the octopus attacks, then that meant the British government was involved. Something beyond the deaths of mere fishermen was at play. A worrisome development.

The raft slowed, pulling alongside her houseboat, and the wind and noise died down. After lashing a rope to her boat, he turned, extending his hand.

It was hard to stand on the pliant and shifting rubber, particularly given the deep lacerations that covered her calves and feet. She struggled onto the deck of her boat and stood, her wet shift stuck to her body, blood running in rivulets down her leg, staring uncertainly at the man she'd agreed to take as her lover.

So much was different between them now. She ought to be in shock, after the tragedy she'd witnessed. That poor woman, her family... gone. Fear should hold her in its grip. Instead, a kind of peace stole over her. Beneath the waves, they'd glimpsed each other's essence. Him as warrior. Her as Finn. Whatever happened between them from this point forward, there need be no more half-truths. Would there be acceptance, or would it drive a wedge between them?

With a leap, Alec landed on the deck before her and pulled her into his arms. The bites throbbed. Her hair was a tangled mess of sea snakes. And still he looked at her as if she were Aphrodite risen from the sea. Shoving stands of wet hair from her face, he dragged her mouth to his. Lifting up on her toes, she met him halfway. Warm and demanding and desperate, their lips fused, and she had her answer.

Too soon, their kiss was over.

"I'm sorry I dropped in on you like that," he said. "But my men reported such carnage in the water. When you went overboard..." He took a deep breath and pressed his forehead to hers as the boat rocked beneath them. "You scared me to death."

Her hands had landed on his chest—his bare chest—which rose and fell softly beneath her palms. A swirl of emotions she couldn't define warmed her. He'd jumped into the ocean to rescue her. *Me.* Not strictly necessary, but welcome all the same.

"Thank you," she breathed. "You'll have questions. As do I." Uncertain what to do with the flutter in her stomach, she looked past him out to sea. Perhaps they could start with the easy ones. "Men? I didn't see anyone else in the water." Not alive. "We left—"

"I would never leave a man behind, not like that. They're fine. And will be here soon." He scooped her off her feet and carried her inside. Limping. "So we'll start by seeing to those nasty lacerations."

"Your knee? I—"

"Kicked it?" He grimaced. "Yes, rather hard, but there's nothing to be done about it here." He deposited her on a chair before wrapping a blanket about her shoulders—a reversal of roles. Reaching to his ear, he pulled away a small blinking device—its light fading away with the flick of a tiny switch—and tucked it into a pocket above the harpoon gun strapped to his thigh. She opened her mouth, then shut it again. Answers to other questions mattered more.

"Communication device," he said, answering her unspoken question.

"Someone's been listening?"

"Not anymore," he said. "Drink this. All of it." A glass clinked against the surface of the table as he placed a generous pour of whisky beside her. The bottle landed beside it. He gave the Lucifer lamp a shake and began to lay out suture materials.

"Is it that bad?" She took a deep breath and stretched her leg out onto the stool, bending forward to unwrap linen bandages and examine the state of her lower leg. A mistake. The bacteria in the lamp brightened, casting a white-blue glow over torn skin and muscle, over a wound that was deep and some four inches long. The boat spun about her, as if it were being sucked into a whirlpool. She tossed back the whisky. Those blasted hyena fish. This was going to hurt.

Alec pulled her calf across his knees, a makeshift operating table. Not encouraging, the way his eyebrows drew together. "I'm estimating twenty-four stitches. Want something stronger than whisky?"

"No," she said, but poured more of the spirits into her glass. "I just want this over." She closed her eyes. "I tried to... bring a leg—"

He nodded. "I saw. It had a tentacle attached." He slid suture thread through the eye of a curved needle. "I saw. My team collected samples. They also spotted the megalodon. As suspected, it's a submersible. Like the biomech octopus, there are biological components." He paused to look up at her. "I would have told you all this. There was no need to follow me, though I'm interested to know how you managed."

"I didn't follow you. I was summoned."

His eyebrows lifted.

"To a patient's bedside. I did mention that in my note." Isa narrowed her eyes. "Which, apparently, never reached you. Is this to be an interrogation?"

"It doesn't need to be." His face was tight. And not just with concentration. With the rush of adrenaline behind them, the gears of his mind were turning again, and her presence at the scene was being logged as more than mere happenstance.

She sighed. "A skeet pigeon arrived with a note begging me to help a fisherman, one who had a tentacle embedded in his throat, attached to his external jugular. It seemed relevant to *our* case. He died, but I saved you the specimen." Though the vial was in her medical bag, aboard the rescue vessel. "I happened to be nearby when the distress call came and insisted upon going with the rescue boat."

He blotted away blood. "What were you thinking, jumping into the water?"

"Jumping? I was pushed!" She hissed as he poured a good measure of rubbing alcohol over the cut, then clenched her teeth at the first bite of her curved surgical needle pierced flesh, drawing sharksilk through her skin. "By a woman raving about OctoFinn."

"OctoFinn," he repeated. His eyes flashed a stormy blue, and his hands stilled. "You know something more. Tell me."

"I found my husband's laboratory notebook." Well hidden. But from whom? From her, certainly, but someone else as well, or he would have left it in his laboratory. "Anton discovered that hypoxic conditions release factor Q into the blood's serum." No more holding back. She'd tell him everything, but the more private details about the Finn people would have to wait until she wasn't expecting a number of BURR men to board her boat at any moment. "People like me, with a certain kind of syndactyly also possess an uncommon ability to hold their breath underwater. That can, at times, induce hypoxia."

"You refer to your uncanny swimming ability," he said, tugging another stitch into place. "And your seeming resistance to cold temperatures?"

There were too many myths to dispel. Only one needed to be addressed at the moment. "What if someone is targeting people like me? Not to simply drain us of blood, but for some other reason." She shuddered.

"The ceramic blood filter." He nodded. "It's certainly something to consider."

The needle rose and as it fell, her fingers tightened on the glass. "Your turn to share," she said through clenched teeth.

"By now you've guessed." The needle rose and fell, piecing her back together inch by inch.

She drained the glass of whisky and let it land on the table with a smack. "That you're more than a doctor? Or even a Naval officer? Dropping from the sky was a dead giveaway." She crossed her arms. "You're BURR."

"You've heard of us, then." The skin around his eyes crinkled as he smiled. "Tasks deemed too wet, too dangerous, or too impossible." The needle dove again. "My knee injury pulled me from active duty and—as I possess a particular talent with bioengineered devices—when a scrap of peculiar cephalopod skin surfaced and fish tales began to spread, they sent me. And I found you." He tied a final knot, then washed his hands. She leaned forward, impressed that such large hands could make such tiny, orderly stitches. "But you're hiding something."

Her mouth fell open to object, but he held up a finger.

"Don't bother denying it," he said. "And a megalodon is a bit much to hunt solo. I enlisted the help of my team. Five men entered the water, but they were too late to stop whatever attacked those people. They've confirmed the submersible's existence and collected the remains of these so-called OctoFinn."

Her head spun at the sudden onslaught of information. Or was it the whisky? "The leg." She'd been making off with evidence. So much for contributing to the effort.

He nodded. "When the rescue boat arrived, I ordered my team away. We prefer to remain unnoticed. Which is another way of saying I'm good at keeping secrets." He wrapped a bandage about her calf, tucking in its ends. "How is it, Isa, that you can hold your breath for over five minutes and swim in water a bracing fifty-four degrees Fahrenheit wearing nothing but a thin shift? What are you, a selkie?"

Was that admiration she saw in his eyes? It was. He envied her. The thought settled deep inside her. *That* was a first. His gaze flicked to the dive knife strapped to her thigh. Not just envy, desire. Warmth shot through her.

"Yes." She dragged a teasing hand down her front, over her translucent, wet shift. His eyes followed, growing a touch hungry. "I am clearly part seal." She flapped her hand at a sea trunk. "Dig a little deeper, and you'll find my other skin."

His lips twisted. "Too much whisky?"

"Yes," she said. The pain only nagged in the background. "And a bit too much suspicion."

He rose from the chair, wincing as his damaged knee straightened, and she caught his glance at her trunk. Was he actually going to look? Of course he was. Alec wasn't one to leave a stone unturned.

She caught his hand in hers. "I'm not a selkie." Time to tell the truth before she lost his trust, his respect. "There's no such thing. But I am Finn. Mostly."

"Finn?"

"There's a thread of truth to every myth." She twisted a finger about a strand of her hair. Red hair.

Scottish hair. "But if you tug at it hard enough, it all unravels. No one can shape shift, turn into a seal. Such ridiculousness."

Wearing a half-smile, he lifted an eyebrow. "Is your liver overwhelmed, or is there a point to—" All trace of amusement vanished. Alec's head snapped around, his free hand falling to the knife at his belt.

"Sorry to interrupt." A man—a familiar man dressed much the same as Alec—stood at her door.

Alec relaxed. "One of my team," he explained. "Mrs. McQuiston, meet—"

"Aron?" Isa stumbled to her feet, grinning. "Is that you?"

Chapter Fifteen

Alec slid his knife back into its sheath and tried to dial down the glare he threw at Moray. A better man would be pleased that backup had arrived so swiftly. He ought to be grateful as well. Ten minutes later and Alec would have been caught taking advantage of a tipsy, wounded woman. "You know each other?" His question was more of a demand.

"We grew up together on Lewis." Isa's smile fell away. "My uncle's wife, Maren, is his cousin."

Curious. Moray was related—in a roundabout way—to Commodore Drummond. Isa's uncle. The one who had dropped her into an unhappy marriage. Or was there more to it? He was beginning to suspect the latter.

"I'm so sorry," Moray began, dive mask shoved onto his forehead, dripping swim fins in hand. "Leave was denied, or I'd have been at Anton's funeral."

With a bouquet of flowers clutched in his hand, no doubt. Alec didn't like the daft look that had overtaken his friend's face. Had Isa not tugged the wool blanket tighter about her shoulders, Alec might have growled. Jealousy was an ugly beast, and its arrival completely unexpected.

"Four years, is it?" Alec drawled. "Since you joined BURR?"

Easy enough to do the math. Three years of marriage, a year of mourning. If Moray had wanted to stake a claim, he'd missed his chance. Alec wasn't stepping aside.

Moray sliced a sharp look at him. "About."

"Mrs. McQuiston and I have been working together." He moved to stand beside her, wrapping an arm about her shoulder to steady her when she swayed. "Her medical practice brought her into contact with two, now three, victims of this biomech octopus." The acousticotrans system would have alerted Moray to Alec's rescue mission. "She's aware of the megalodon."

With a nod, Moray acknowledged the unspoken message. Straightening, he gave his report. "Shaw circled back to watch the rescuers. The woman—the sole survivor—is safe in their hands. They did note Mrs. McQuiston's unusual rescue."

"There were fourteen people on that boat, Aron." Face pale, she lowered herself back onto her chair. "Children."

Moray's voice softened. "My survey, though cursory at best, indicates there were significantly less remains in the water than those numbers would indicate, even accounting for the hyena fish."

"Men were taken aboard the megalodon," Alec said.

"Possibly women." Moray cleared his throat. "We need to leave. The higher ups back on base are certain to have noticed our absence and will be asking questions. And the—er—evidence ought to be placed on ice. The pilot has offered to hurtle us home using the afterburners."

"Come with me, Mrs. McQuiston." The formal name felt odd on his tongue. Dangers lurked beneath the water's surface. She was tipsy. And he wanted to know what—exactly—a Finn was. He dangled before her the one thing she could not resist. "Between the samples collected today and other information that has recently come to light, your laboratory expertise is required. "

He fully expected Logan to be waiting, steam billowing from his ears as he devised any number of ways to make his brother suffer for going over his head. Logan could yell at Alec all he wanted, provided he granted Isa security clearance and handed over those damned punch cards.

"Inside the Glaister Institute?" Her face brightened, then paled. "I can't."

Silently he cursed her husband. Why refuse such a brilliant woman entrance? What had he done to make her think... wait. She was shaking in his arms. He tipped her face upward with a single finger and frowned. Again she held something back. "Why not?"

"Someone needs to interview the survivor. I can't abandon my boat." Her voice shook. "And air travel makes me ill. Severely ill."

Moray snorted, and Alec gave him a quelling look. "What happened to the brave woman who swam through hyena fish dragging a severed leg? Who nearly unmanned me while underwater during my misguided rescue attempt?"

She scoffed. "You would regret putting me on a dirigible."

“I’ve dealt with airsick passengers before. It’s only three hours.”

"If you're willing to go with him, Isa, I'll handle the situation here." Moray made the offer through gritted teeth, grudgingly ceding the win to Alec. "The elders will respond better to me."

“Elders?” He'd heard that term before, applied to the Carrs. Finn, she'd said. A community of some sort that shared a number of biological traits. His gaze slid to Moray's fingers. A few scars, but nothing that would indicate a past surgery to correct syndactyly.

Isa and Moray shared a look, the same one he'd seen Lieutenant Dunnet give her brother, Mr. Guthrie. Moray was also in on the secret. Good. If necessary, he could beat it out of him.

"Go," Moray said to Isa. "Apply your expertise where it's needed. I’ll leave the boat with your brother." The corner of his mouth hitched as he turned toward Alec. "You'd better hope there's a bucket on board."

While Isa dressed, Alec stood on the deck outside the cabin beside Moray, signaling for a lift line to the dirigible hovering overhead.

As a rope unfurled, Moray cleared his throat. "She deserves to be more than another notch carved into your bedpost."

"She's a grown woman, Moray. And widowed. Not some innocent, young virgin with stars in her eyes. She can decide for herself what she wants." Alec caught the rope, checking the equipment tied to its end—stirrups, the handles, and the gears of the clockwork winch mechanisms that would haul Isa and himself skyward.

"What if she wants marriage? Children?"

Alec barked a laugh. "Then she won't choose me."

Moray looked away.

Alec swore. "You're in love with her."

"Once."

Isa stepped out onto the deck, her auburn hair tightly bound, dark wool covering her from neck to ankle. Puritanical and self-effacing once more. Was it only he who could see a certain wildness bubbling beneath the surface?

Perhaps not. A wash of regret darkened Moray's face, but he said nothing, silently clipping her valise to a transport winch. With a flip of a switch, an internal spring uncoiled, turning a multitude of interconnected gears to send her bag—twisting and spinning upon the wind—into the clouds.

If Moray was a rejected suitor, Isa gave no sign as she tipped an anxious face upward and pressed a hand to her stomach. "A rope, dangling from the sky. I can't believe I've agreed to this."

"You'll be fine. I've done this a time or two." Isa might be petite, but she was tough. "Hold tight, and we'll be aboard in seconds."

Alec slid her right foot into a stirrup and passed her a handgrip, then adjusted his own transport winch so that he could keep a tight arm about her waist as they ascended. Isa buried her face in his chest, clutching at the rubber of his dive suit with a white-knuckled fist.

"Send a report ASAP," he said.

"Will do," Moray answered. "Bon voyage." He flipped their levers, sending them rocketing into the clouds.

~~~

Gagging, Isa staggered onto the floor of the airship's gondola. "Bucket," she gasped, slapping at Alec's hands as he tried to escort her to a nearby seat.

He refused to let go.

She clamped her lips together, but there was no stopping the involuntary contractions of her stomach. Every last ounce of whisky not already running through her arteries spewed forth, running down his chest and dripping onto the floor.

From somewhere in the vessel, she heard the deep rumble of men laughing.

"Bet you've never been so grateful for a rubber suit," one snorted.

"Shut it, Rowan," Alec growled as he lowered her into a rough metal chair that was bolted to the wall. He
~~~

dragged wide canvas straps across her shoulders, across her lap, fastening them tight.

"Bucket," she repeated. The floor beneath her feet swayed, and waves of nausea rolled over her. And the dirigible had yet to move.

"Here."

A man pressed a blessedly cold metal bucket into her hands. She clutched it to her chest, emptying what little was left in her stomach. When she finally looked up, Alec was crouched beside her, his eyebrows drawn together.

"Is there anything I can do?" he asked.

The concern in his voice made her wish she could reassure him, but Finn belonged in the water, not in the air. She shook her head. "How long?" she whispered.

"Three hours."

Too ill to cry, she groaned. Then fell forward, gagging once more above the bucket.

"Buckle in, McCullough," a man barked. "Wouldn't want your knee to snap in half. Again."

Alec dropped into the seat beside her. Somewhere deep beneath her feet, an engine rumbled. The entire dirigible seemed to shudder. A second later, she was thrown backward into her seat as they lurched forward.

The laugh of a madwoman escaped her lips moments before the dry heaving began. Though Alec murmured words, and the damp cloth he pressed to her forehead was welcome, true relief arrived in the form of a swift and sudden loss of consciousness.

~~~

The entire trip back to Glasgow, Alec held Isa as she drifted in and out of consciousness, rousing long enough only to heave bile into the metal bucket. Nothing he did seemed to help, and she swatted away his water flask no matter how many times he held it to her lips.

Shaw gave a shake of his head. "And we thought Moray turned green around the gills."

Alec was never so grateful to land. Dehydration was becoming a serious concern. He ought to take her directly home. Locate her brother and pass her into his care. But as he scooped her limp form from the chair and leapt from the gondola onto the gravel of the airstrip, her skirts flew upward.

With bandages wrapped about her calves, she'd not donned stockings, and there was nothing to obstruct any remaining bare skin. A web-like net of blueish streaks radiated from beneath the wrappings. Icy needles crystalized in his stomach. An infection? If it was, it was like nothing he'd seen before. Cursing, he pressed a hand to her forehead. No doubt about it, she was running a fever. Focused on easing her airsickness, he'd failed to note the rise of her body temperature. He needed to take her to the Fifth Ward, immediately.

Alec drew breath to holler to his teammates for assistance, when he spotted more trouble already among them. Five military guards dressed in black uniforms and holding prominently displayed weapons were
~~~

arguing with Shaw and Rowan, waving at the canvas-wrapped body parts they carried. Pressing Isa against his shoulder, he lengthened his stride. As instigator of their mission, he couldn't abandon his team.

"Our orders come directly from Commodore Drummond," the guard barked, holding out an official document.

Isa's uncle was involved? He frowned, recalling her ramblings about selkies and fins. Commodore Drummond was a member of her community, why would he obstruct the BURR team? Were their communal secrets valued above those of individual lives?

"What the hell?" Rowan yelled at the guard, his hands lifting into the air. "Civilians on that boat were brutally murdered. We need to get to the bottom of this."

"Stand aside," the guard ordered. "Your mission was unauthorized. All materials collected are to be confiscated and destroyed. We are to take you and your team into custody if necessary."

The guard's voice held a slight tremor as he knew damn well that his men were no physical match against a BURR team. But to disregard a superior's orders was career suicide. Possibly a prison term. The only way to combat this was through official channels. Or to make his brother call in a number of favors. He needed to find Logan posthaste.

"I intend to challenge those orders," Alec said to the guard, glaring daggers. "Store our *materials* on ice. Fill out the paperwork with precision, then stand watch over them while I find out what the hell is going on."

Turning, he strode away. Isa stirred against his shoulder, her forehead damp with sweat, reminding him he had a more critical situation to address. A sinking feeling overtook him. Whatever infection spread rapidly across—through? —her skin had likely originated from the mouths of the hyena fish. Hyena fish that had emerged from the mouth of a biomech megalodon. Chances the infectious agent could be easily controlled were slim.

He picked up his pace.

Chapter Sixteen

"Shaw!" Alec yelled as he jogged to his friend's side, ignoring the slight crunching sound his knee made. "Your bite, did the hyena fish infect you?" He flipped up the edge of her skirt.

Swearing, Shaw yanked up his sleeve. A nasty bite on the side of his hand was swollen and bloody, but not blue. "What the hell?"

"Help me get her to the Fifth Ward."

Leaning on the horn of a conscripted Armored Navy Steam Demon, Shaw careened down the city streets at breakneck speed, weaving wildly through any pedestrians or vehicles unfortunate enough to be in his path. Alec held Isa tight, clasping her limp form against him during an interminable ride through Glasgow. The Demon screeched to a halt beside a small, obscure sandstone building—a back entrance to the Glaister Institute. The guard snapped to attention, flinging the door wide. A spiral staircase led down three stories to an iron door. Shifting Isa against his shoulder, Alec pressed his finger into the identification slot, praying for the pectin coagulator to recognize his signature and respond.

The light blinked green, gears turned, and a thick iron bolt retracted.

He strode down its tunnels, shoving doors open with his shoulders as he barreled into the research ward where doctors and nurses confronted the unknown on a daily basis. "Find Dr. Grant!" Alec bellowed.

A nurse stepped into his path, blocking his access. "Sir! This is not standard procedure."

"My name is Dr. McCullough, and this isn't a standard ward," Alec replied, again flipping up her skirt. The nurse gasped. "Her infection is cryptic and spreading by the minute." He tempered his voice. "Please, find Dr. Grant."

Eyes wide, the nurse sprang into action. "Follow me." She held open the door to an isolation chamber. "Stay here. I'll bring him directly."

He carried Isa inside, laying her gently upon the bed. Her head lolled to the side, her breaths shallow, face pale. He brushed aside stands of hair to press a palm to her forehead, noting an elevated temperature. Would she chastise him for the guilt that tightened his chest? She'd insisted on being a part of his investigation, insisted she not be left out. His team always had his back, but a woman? The only woman he knew who ran toward, rather than away, from trouble was his sister, and his feelings for Isa were anything but sisterly. Would he lose her before he had the chance to know her? Worry clogged his throat.

Determined to exhaust every possibility to save her, he threw open the doors of a supply cabinet and grabbed a pair of scissors. Dragging up her skirts, he cut away the linen strips that bandaged her wounds. Red and swollen with inflammation, a blue tinge overlaid the jagged bite marks, converging into bluish tendrils to form a fine web-like mesh beneath her skin, a gossamer net that crept proximally, edging toward her thigh.

His stomach clenched. In the time spent traveling from airstrip to hospital, the blue streaks had gained an inch.

Several excruciatingly long minutes passed—spent cleaning Isa's wounds with a more potent antiseptic—before the door opened again. A stooped man entered, peering at Alec through thick glass lenses perched upon his hooked nose. Dr. Grant might appear feeble, but his mind was razor-sharp. Years ago, his discourse on infectious water-borne organisms had made an impression upon Alec as a student—impossible to forget the gruesome images projected by the magic lantern upon the lecture hall's screen.

Dr. Grant's mouth opened—perhaps in greeting, perhaps in reprimand—but closed again as he caught sight of Isa's bare leg. "Aether, what happened?"

"Approximately four hours ago, she was bitten by hyena fish. I cleaned and disinfected the wounds, suturing the deepest one. En route to Glasgow by dirigible, she vomited repeatedly before passing into unconsciousness. Though ascribed to airsickness, upon landing, I discovered this. The streaking pattern brought to mind your research into filamentous mycobacteria infections."

"It does," Dr. Grant said, dragging an overhead argon light directly over the wound site, bending close. "You were right to bring her to me. Fortunately for the lady, the creatures did not enter her body via the central nervous system nor do they appear interested in her blood vessels or lymphatic pathways."

Alec nodded, forcing his mind to focus on the infection and not the patient as he fought to speak despite the lump in his throat. "They appear to be moving beneath the epidermis." A surgeon by training, sterile procedure was second nature, but he knew little about infectious disease beyond those that were common to field work.

"Agreed. Though it's not moving in a manner consistent with flagellated organic-walled plankton. However, the color is suggestive of blue scintillans, similar to those I've observed in dinoflagellates. Therefore, we'll start with an application of Cyprus Metal Acetate. It's quickly applied and might purchase us some time." Dr. Grant passed Alec two gas masks. "One for you, one for her."

"How can I help?" Alec asked, his voice reverberating inside the mask.

Dr. Grant selected a paper packet from the drawer. He tore the paper and dumped the contents into a shallow bowl, added three centiliters of solvent and stirred. He handed Alec the resultant paste and a flat wooden stick. "Apply this to the wound and affected skin one inch past the margin of streaks." His voice was muffled from the heavy rubber mask. "The mixture should slow lamellipodial protrusion. Do not touch her skin with your bare hands again. I'll prepare a skin biopsy for the aetheroscope."

Neither the sharp bite of a scalpel nor the cold wet paste caused Isa to stir. And when Dr. Grant beckoned him to the aetheroscope, his heart plunged into his stomach.

"I've never seen the like," Dr. Grant said, shoving his stool back so that Alec might peer through the eyepiece. "It appears to be a kind of chimera, sharing features of both marine ameboid trophozoites and fluorescent organic-walled plankton."

The aetheric gas permeating the chamber ought to have killed the tiny creeping amoebae, but somehow those in the sample survived, meandering across the microscope slide, glowing a faint bioluminescent blue.

Swearing, Alec dragged a hand through his hair. Those bloody hyena fish. Another hybrid organism. Everywhere he turned, chimeras. Somewhere a most bizarre marine laboratory existed and within it was an extremely prolific mad scientist. He intended to locate both and put an end to these malicious creations.

The moment Isa was cured. He glanced at her face and ran a jerky hand through his hair.

The doctor scratched his head. "What confuses me is that the amoebas infected her at all. Both such species are free-living. Neither of them infectious, not to humans."

Finn. Not selkie, she'd said. Was it possible? Was Isa not completely human? And what could that possibly mean? Not that he'd be getting answers to any such questions if she died. "Would salt of propamidine with isethionic acid kill them?" he asked.

"Perhaps." Dr. Grant tapped his chin. "Is there any chance of locating ipecacuanha? It's a drug made from the dried root of *Cephaelis ipecacuanha*, originating from the tropical forests of Brazil. A pharmacobotonist by the name of Tredegar published something about using the alkaloid to cure amoebic dysentery."

"If it's in this building, I'll find it." Even if it meant digging into the forgotten corners of every single storage closet, cabinet and cupboard. He stood, and his knee popped. Audibly. Dr. Grant's eyebrows lifted. But Alec waved it away. "It's nothing." But it wasn't. Something inside the joint had again been knocked ajar. If Dr. Morgan learned he had fast-roped from a dirigible into the ocean, he would probably wish to see him spitted and roasted over hot coals. "I'll be back within the hour."

Teeth clenched against the pain, Alec burst from the Fifth Ward into the tunnel and came to an abrupt halt. Arms crossed and a foul look upon his face, Logan leaned against the door that led to the research wing, blocking his exit.

"What the hell have you done?" Logan growled. "Going over my head. Involving the BURR team. Not to mention the bevy of birds hovering above my various lodgings. The arrival of one particular skeet pigeon nearly compromised a mission in progress."

When did his brother *not* have a mission in progress? Alec rolled his eyes. "A new lead arose, I followed it."

Logan slapped a handful of punch cards against Alec's stomach. "Here. All labeled by Lady Rathsburn to the best of her ability."

"Finally." He pocketed them. "I need you to locate and secure the anatomical evidence we retrieved from the mission. See it carefully stored on ice until I can examine it." He paused. "And find out everything you can about Commodore Drummond." Potential friend or foe?

The answers might provide enough information to formulate a strategy for approaching Isa's uncle. She might dislike him, but perhaps they could meet, face to face, and set aside their differences so that they might work together rather than at cross purposes. Given Commodore Drummond's actions and because he far outranked him, Alec would proceed with caution, making it clear he respected the man's wish to conceal his relationship to the Finn community.

"I'll make it my very next order of business," Logan said. "But no more working outside the boundaries I have set. Do you have any idea of the political ramifications your actions have caused?"

"No. And at the moment, I don't particularly care. Now step aside. I've not the time for a political debate."

He shoved past his brother. Newly published, ipecacuanha was an obscure drug that might not yet have attracted the attention of an Institute scientist. With luck, it would still be in specimen storage facilities.

Logan followed, spouting nonsense about security preparations for the upcoming Icelandic-Danish wedding and how Alec had forced him to excuse himself from planning procedures. When he began to spout the names of politicians, Alec let his brother's voice fade into the background like the buzz of an annoying insect one could never quite manage to swat. Logan loved his snarled web of intrigue.

Limping, he threw open a door and turned a corner. Holding tight to a railing, he made his way down three flights of stairs into the bowels of the Institute. Right, then left, then down a hall.

"You need to have that knee looked at," Logan snapped. "You're a fool to push yourself so hard after such an injury. None of us will ever measure up to Quinn, and Father isn't even around to take note if we did. It's long past time you stopped trying to prove you're as skillful and as brilliant as he."

"I'm aware, and I'm not trying to prove anything." Alec had dropped that burden from his shoulders long ago. He stopped before a plain door—marked with only the number 549 painted upon it—and dialed in the entrance code. The lock clicked open, and he pushed, stepping inside a vast, dark chamber.

Upon the wall to the right was a switch. He flipped it, releasing the catch on a tightly wound spring and setting the lighting mechanism into motion. Overhead, long glass tubes began to rock gently, slowly stirring the bioluminescent bacteria within to life and casting a faint blue-white light throughout the chamber.

Rows and rows and rows of metal shelving filled the space, all of them stacked with a variety of items. At the front of the room were boxes and bottles and paper packets—supplies of commonly used drugs and reagents—and commonly used medical supplies. Further back, outdated equipment. And in the dark shadows, obscure specimens of all kinds lurked in bottles, bags and boxes, each sent to the Institute in hopes of precipitating medical breakthrough. Some sat forgotten. Others awaited discovery. Or funding.

"Why are we in here?" Logan demanded. "Does this have something to do with the civilian woman you returned with from your *unauthorized* mission?"

"I had the Duke of Avesbury's approval." Pulling a decilamp from his pocket, Alec began by raiding the drug supplies, pocketing a vial of isethionic acid and one of propamidine.

Out of the corner of his eye, he saw his brother vibrate with anger as he followed. "You gave the duke the impression that I approved. Do you have any idea how many Naval officers would like to see me keelhauled? Don't you ever dare go over my head again."

"Don't ignore me and I won't need to." Stalking deeper into the room, he scanned hastily scrawled labels tied to paper-wrapped packages. There. *Cephaelis ipecacuanha*, contributed by one Mr. Evan Tredegar. He pulled the parcel from the shelf and tugged loose the twine that bound it. One dry and shriveled root. It needed to be processed, but finding it gave him hope. He closed his eyes a moment in gratitude, hoping the strange plant would enact a miracle.

Time to return to Isa. With luck the disinfectant and antimicrobial paste had slowed the advance of amoebae. Tucking the packet in his pocket, he pivoted.

And nearly toppled to the floor. A grunt of plain slid past his lips, but he managed to bite down on the foul words that threatened.

"Alec," his brother muttered in a dire tone.

"Later." He made his way back to the stairs and hauled himself up, one painful step at a time, returning to the Fifth Ward. "I've a critical medical emergency on my hands involving an unheard of, lab-created, parasitic amoeba. The woman infected is rather important to me." That gave him pause, but now was not the time to examine his growing affection. "To our case."

"She must be, to risk your knee in such a manner." Logan tipped his head, a light sparking in his eyes. "Important to you how, exactly?"

He slid his eyes sideways as he pushed open the door. "Not your concern."

"He's back!" a nurse called.

The entire room froze as Dr. Grant rushed forward, eyes wild, gas mask shoved onto the top of his head, hair sticking out in all directions. "They took her."

"What!" He'd been gone all of fifteen minutes. "Who took her and where? She needs to be kept in strict isolation. She needs treatment."

"I'm so sorry," a nurse said, placing a hand on his arm. "We couldn't stop them."

"Masked men in canvas overalls stormed the room and refused to identify themselves." Dr. Grant swallowed hard. "One pointed a weapon at me while the others rolled your woman onto a canvas stretcher. The handles were wooden."

Canvas and wood, easily burned. The perfect way to contain infectious disease, once a patient had—

"Alive?" His heart thrashed wildly inside his rib cage.

Dr. Grant nodded, but his eyes predicted a grim future, for no place was better equipped to handle such a patient than the Fifth Ward.

Alec pinned his brother with a stare. "We need to find her. Now."

Chapter Seventeen

Cold. *So very cold.* Isa woke up shivering, her arms er head.

She pried open her sticky, swollen eyes. But even with them open, her field of vision was dark and hazy. She couldn't open her mouth and the air smelled faintly of rubber. An oxygen mask? The faintest memory of Alec carrying her against his chest surfaced. Never before had she felt so sick. Even now the bites to her legs throbbed. Had they become infected? Was she in a hospital?

Consciousness trickled back. This was no bed. Water lapped at her face, and her wrists were bound together. Somehow she was suspended, half-floating, in water. Something was terribly wrong.

Fighting a rising nausea, she pressed her face against her bare arm. A tube sprouted from the inside of her arm, the insertion painful and both covered and secured by a tight bandage. A saline drip? From the mask covering her mouth and nose, a hose extended, providing a source of oxygen. And goggles covered her eyes, most likely to protect them from the water. But why the smoky and distorting obfuscation lenses?

Heart racing, she yanked on whatever bound her wrists—and found them tied to the edge of... what? She kicked, her bare foot connecting with a smooth surface. She listened to what she could not quite see. Ripples of water sloshed against a wall some two feet away.

A tank? She was immersed—naked—in a tank of ice-cold water? Had she been so febrile, so feverish they'd needed to take such extreme measures to lower her core body temperature? How much time had passed? Hours? Days?

Isa kicked again, thrusting herself upward in an attempt to reach her face, to rip free the mask and call for help, but she couldn't curl her fingers beneath the edge of the mask.

There was a scratchy sound of something sliding over the rim of a tin bucket, then a series of tiny splashes—sand or salt—as it hit the water's surface.

Did they think her unconscious? Is that why no one addressed her, made an attempt to speak to her? She cried for help, but her chin was strapped tight, preventing her from opening her mouth, the sound that emerged more the squeal of a wild animal than a distressed woman.

"She's awake!" a boy's voice called from above.

At last. Trembling—from cold, fear and the unknown—Isa tipped her face upward toward the child, squinting through the smoky glass. A pale, unfocused oval bent over her.

Stiff leather soles tapped across the floor, approaching her. "So she is." An unfamiliar man's voice, one that seemed to come from beside the tank. His voice held no sympathy. No acknowledgment. Nothing but cold indifference. "A point that is relevant only in that it indicates she's still alive. Add all the salt as instructed. The hydrometer indicates the salt water density is only halfway to the prescribed levels."

Fear skittered down her spine, and her breaths grew shallow. From Alec's careful care to a cold, dark tank of water. The man she'd become acquainted with wouldn't have abandoned her to such a fate. Had something happened to him? What had gone wrong?

"Yes, sir," the boy answered deferentially. More salt splashed into her tank.

Struck with an overwhelming need to know who held her captive, Isa submerged as far as the bindings on her wrists allowed, opening her eyes wide. Between the goggles and the thick glass that comprised the water tank, she could only make out a pale oval of a face, a vague form garbed in a white coat.

Isa kicked back to the surface with all her might, yanking on her wrists, gaining enough thrust to glance over the tank's edge. But again the lenses of the goggles made it impossible. She sank back into the water and kicked the tank wall.

"Stop struggling!" the man barked. "You'll dislodge the breathing apparatus. Or your goggles. Even a Finn can drown. Besides, the salinity is being raised to twice that of sea water. I assure you, even *your* eyes will burn."

Isa froze. *Finn.* The man knew she was Finn. With her jaw strapped in place, she couldn't even ask the most basic of questions.

"I'm trying to help you," he continued, his voice harsh with annoyance. "You are infected with a particularly nasty protozoa, the *caeruleus* amoeba. The only other Finn to try escaping after the bite of our hyena fish died within hours. You, we might be able to save."

The bites were infected? It would explain her fever, if not the callous treatment. Where was Alec? She tried to scream, but only a muted whimper reverberated through the mask.

"You have every reason to worry, Mrs. McQuiston." *He knows my name.* There wasn't enough oxygen flowing through the tube for her brain to process the implications. "You are quite the experimental patient. But I assure you, I have every intention of curing you. This time."

Isa twisted about, willing her eyes to focus through the distorting lenses. There were more Finn? Here? In other tanks?

The man sighed, his voice heavy with irritation. "I'm told you are a healer with considerable medical experience. If you'll calm down, I'll explain."

Gulping deep breaths of air, Isa held still. But she was anything but calm. Terrified and, with each passing second, more and more furious.

"This procedure is the only hope of curing your infection," the man continued. "Extremely cold temperatures slow the amoeba's advance. Extremely high salinity will kill it. Eventually. But perhaps not before eating a good portion of your leg. The tube inserted into your arm is not just supplying you with much needed hydration, it's raising your internal sodium chloride levels to the edge of that compatible with life. As the drip progresses, you can expect to feel thirsty, weak and fatigued. Your heart rate will increase. Along with life-saving saline, you are also being administered a drug, the specifics of which are proprietary."

There was a loud thud and a slosh, the sound of another heavily laden bucket landing upon the platform beside the tank. Isa snapped her head about, trying to make out the features of the new, third pale oval to peer at the curiosity in the tank.

"My lord." A woman spoke for the first time, her voice cautious and deferential. "You might wish to step away. It's time to release the corpse fish."

Corpse fish? Isa's heart rate spiked.

"One at time," the man instructed her. "Thomas, sit beside the tank. Fish them out with the net every fifteen minutes. The salinity is too high for them to last any longer."

"Yes, sir," he replied. "See? I have the net ready."

"No!" Isa screamed into the mask. "Please, stop!"

"Maggots of the sea, Mrs. McQuiston," the man said. "The fish are our assistants, here only to remove the dead flesh from your leg, to allow the saline to better reach the phagocytic amoeba which managed quite a lot of damage before you arrived at my facility. They will nibble upon your legs. Provided you float motionless. Kick them, and they'll shy away, leaving necrotic tissue to accumulate. Live or die, the choice is yours."

Tears welled in her eyes, and she blinked furiously behind the mask. Though she refused to believe that she was under the care of a physician at the Glaister Institute, neither could she discount the man's words. As he spoke, the painful itching had crept its way up her legs.

Plop.

When the first soft nibble touched her flesh, Isa held still.

~~~

Alec hunted for Isa until he collapsed, but not from pain or exhaustion. Shaw had stabbed him in the back. With a tranquilizer syringe. "Traitor," he whispered as he sunk to the ground.

"It's been five hours." His friend had dogged Alec's every step, helping to search every last inch of the Glaister Institute. "We've looked everywhere, spoken to everyone. She's not here." After ditching the armored vehicle, Shaw
~~~

had returned, replacing Logan as chaperone while his brother attempted to locate Isa via more official channels.

"Not quitting," Alec gurgled.

"You are for now." Shaw groaned as he hefted Alec's weight into a creaky, old wooden wheelchair. "I've been listening to that knee of yours grind for over four hours, watching you limp. Don't pretend you didn't hear that loud crunch, the one that nearly threw you down a flight of stairs. That brace isn't helping. If we don't get you fixed, you might not walk again for weeks. How will that help your search?"

"Time... first twenty-four hours... most important." His words were slurred, but Shaw had heard them all before.

"Which leaves us with nineteen." Shaw shoved the chair into motion. "While you were stomping all over, I contacted the doc. He cleared his schedule. You're getting an upgrade to titanium. It'll take him four hours to change out the gears."

"Roideach." Missing—as always—from his laboratory, but at the moment he was the only suspect. "Keep. Searching."

"Never surrender, never give up," Shaw said, swinging the chair around to back through a door. "We won't, not until we find out where Lord Roideach is and what he's been up to while you take a nap. Let that subconscious of yours ponder the question."

Alec bobbed his head in agreement as the white room swam. He eyelids grew heavy and slammed shut. "Marine scientist. Only possibility."

Shaw spun the chair, backing them through the swinging door of the operating room. "By the time the tranq wears off, the doc will be done with repairs, and we'll storm Roideach's laboratory."

"Promising my patient miracles, Mr. Shaw?" Hands lifted Alec onto a steel table and cut away the heavy cotton of his combat trousers. "A bit heavy-handed on the medication..."

"Gotta up the dose when you're dealing with a man who's lost his love, when he needs to rescue a damsel in distress."

"Love?" Alec slurred, flapping a hand. "Just met. She's..." What was Isa to him, anyway? More than an affair, yet still not his lover.

"I told you no more jumping out of dirigibles. You've stripped the teeth off the hypoid gear. You'll have your knee working in four hours, but it's going to hurt." Steel tools clanged on a metal tray. A bright light shone through his eyelids.

"No ether," Alec begged.

"Sorry," doc said. "But I can't have you moving."

A mask fell upon his face, the strong, pungent smell spinning him away into a deep abyss where he hoped he might dream of Isa.

~~~

"Wake up!" A hand slapped her face, but Isa could barely bring herself to care. The cold had carried away all her aches and pains, and the shivering had finally stopped. Sleep beckoned, offering a welcome release.
~~~

"Too many have died." A man's voice boomed, echoing off distant walls hidden in shadow. "If we lose this one, it will not matter that we have eradicated the *caeruleus* amoeba."

"The sensor indicates her body temperature has fallen to thirty degrees Centigrade," the woman, his assistant, stated. "We might have pushed her too far." Her voice suggested that the next time Isa was stretched out horizontally, it would be in a coffin.

"Discovering the temperature limit of a Finn isn't enough," the man said. "We need solid proof that the attachment procedure will work consistently. We can't lose her. Besides, do you not realize who she is?"

"I'm well aware, my lord." A hint of insolence laced her voice.

"Then make it happen. Bring her back."

Isa started to float away. Calm waters beckoned. So peaceful.

Fingers wrapped about Isa's wrist. Another set of fingers gripped her chin. "Blue lips. Pulse of twenty-five beats per minute. She's barely breathing. Three breaths a minute."

"Increase the percentage of oxygen through the line, Miss Russel," the man ordered. "And it's time to begin raising her core temperature." A pause. "Thomas, shovel more coal into the boiler."

"Yes, sir."

Gas began to hiss through the hose attached to Isa's mouth. Some distance away, there was a loud clang. The sound of metal scraping over stones. Another clang. A snap. And then the sound of flames roaring to life as the boy stoked a boiler.

Isa slipped back into dreams of Alec's strong arms.

Only to be yanked awake once more. A current, tugging, pulling, sucking her toward the bottom of the tank, but her bound wrists refused to let her follow the draining water. Then warm water trickled over her hair, ran down the length of her body and dripped from her toes, slowly refilling the tank. Disappointment washed over her. So much for a peaceful death.

~~~

He dreamed of Isa. Of her long, red hair streaming down her back as she stood, hip deep in the sea. Of her bare skin shimmering in the moonlight as she glanced at him over her shoulder, a smile playing at the corners of her lips.

Fog rolled in from the ocean, reaching out with misty tendrils, engulfing everything but a long, curved tentacle that lifted into the air, water dripping from its many suckers. It snaked around Isa's neck, cutting off her screams as it dragged her beneath the waves. Screams that continued to echo off the rocks of a nearby castle. Stones tumbled from the weed-infested fortress, crashing downward onto—

Alec bolted upright, blinking at the sudden change of scenery. Bright lights. A lingering chemical smell. Dr.
~~~

Morgan and a bevy of nurses stared back at him. He was in the operating room. Falling backward onto his elbows, he dragged in a deep, ragged breath.

"Welcome back," Dr. Morgan said, his voiced laced with sarcasm. "Unpleasant dreams? Knee's fixed, a full hour ahead of schedule. You're welcome."

Alec stared down at his knee. After three surgeries, it was a railroad of stitches. Five new stitches adding to the pre-existing twenty-two, the scars beneath still pink and somewhat raw. "What, no bandage?" he rasped.

Dr. Morgan pushed a glass of water into his hand. "Figured you'd want to inspect the work. It'll hurt, but only superficially this time. You're lucky. I didn't need to fiddle the bone attachments, but no more jumping from dirigibles."

"Yes, sir. I'll try." *Had Isa been found yet? Safe?*

"Try." Dr. Morgan sighed and passed Alec a sheet of paper. "Take a look at that while we bandage your knee. Shaw dropped it off while you were still under."

Alec's eyes widened at the list of names dating back some ten years.

Fifteen minutes later—ignoring stitches that tugged and burned, Alec banged on Roideach's laboratory door for the third time.

The door cracked open. "Go away," Miss Lourney said. "How many times do you need to be reminded. Your clearance was revoked. I can't let you in."

"I don't need to come in." He held out the paper Shaw had obtained from human resources. "Roideach makes a habit of hiring female laboratory technicians. Mine is the only male name to ever appear."

"You really have no idea?" She stared at him for a long minute. "It's why I tolerated you, Dr. McCullough." Miss Lourney's laugh was brittle. "For the first time, Roideach stopped standing too close, stopped measuring the span of my waist with his hands, stopped pinching my arse. For the first time *invitations* to his bed ceased."

Alec's jaw hung open. "Why didn't you say something?" His irritation with Roideach grew every time he learned something more about the man. "Why keep working here?"

"Oh, please." She rolled her eyes. "How many marine research laboratories will employ a female technician? Exactly none. There are two choices for us, endure or quit." She reached out and snatched the list from Alec. "Let me see. Most of these are from before my time. I knew Bridget Stewart. She didn't last long. One grope and she screamed. Erica Thompson won herself a promotion to Lister Institute in London. Flora Murray." Amanda's face twisted with pain. "Suicide by arsenic. Plenty of poisons to choose from when you work in a laboratory."

Bringing a lord to justice was a near impossibility, though he could try. Alec was silent a moment, contemplating all his sister faced should she continue to pursue a career in chemical research. They would need to talk. Soon.

"Miss Russel," Alec prompted. Isa was extremely ill, all else needed to wait.

"Has grand ambitions." Miss Lourney met his gaze directly. "And fell into his lap a bit too quickly, not realizing that he can't marry her or that her duties would include nursemaid."

Alec raised an eyebrow. His understanding was that most gentry handed their children over to staff within minutes of their birth.

Miss Lourney threw her hands in the air. "I've no idea why he doesn't hire one. In any case, her willingness to care for the child in exchange for the opportunity to work with Lord Roideach on some cherished and secret project funded by CEAP reflects that."

"CEAP?" he nudged.

She shrugged. "Secret."

"You must know *something* more about this project," he pressed.

Miss Lourney stared at him a moment, then heaved a great, long sigh, handing him back the paper. "Most of their work is done off site, though they make free use of Institute resources. A few hours ago, Miss Russel was here, loading a satchel with supplies and gloating about a promotion. Better her than me."

Chapter Eighteen

A mark of true desperation it was, entering his family's home through the front door in the full light of day, an open invitation for his mother to drag him into the midst of eligible young women. But she—and her friends—were the fastest way to learn about Lord Roideach's Scottish property holdings, in particular, the location of one possessing a castle in disrepair.

"Sir!" Munro blinked.

The steam butler rocked backward on his wheels and nearly toppled over when Alec strode past him to peer into the parlor. Into an *empty* parlor.

"Is this not Mother's day at home?" Irritation crept into his voice. Of all the days for her to break protocol. "Where is she?"

"She's in bed with a malevolent megrim," Cait's disembodied voice called from the speaking tube. "Social disaster has struck."

Any other day and Alec would have been amused, but with Isa missing, he wasn't in the mood for showmanship or games. Despite her earlier request, a headache meant Mother would refuse to speak with him, that left his sister. He crossed to the speaking tube. "What do you know about Lord Roideach?"

"So, so much," Cait answered, her voice crackling. "Descend and I will impart *all* the gossip."

Resigned, he yanked open the door and descended a flight of stairs, ducking beneath a curtain of dusty cotton thread spun to resemble a spider's web. The deterrent contained no less than nine hairy spiders constructed from lint and wire. Not a real threat, perhaps, but enough to have kept their parents and the servants from ever entering the basement laboratory.

Cait held up a finger as he reached the bottom of the stairs. He waited silently while a rotor slowed, as his sister pulled the test tubes free, nestling them each into a bucket of ice shavings with extreme care.

He squinted at her scrawled notes, then took a quick step back. "Tell me you are *not* culturing *Corynebacterium diphtheriae.*"

"How else is one supposed to collect the toxin of a nasty pathogenic bacteria for study?" Cait asked, her voice pure innocence.

Swearing loudly, he jammed his fingers into his hair. One kidnapped woman was enough to worry about. He didn't need his sister challenging her immune system with a potentially lethal exotoxin. Not that he could stop her. She'd just find something else to experiment with.

His sister turned toward him with a mischievous glint in her eyes. He narrowed his. "You mentioned social disaster."

"Of the best kind." A sudden grin split her face. "I finally did it, Alec. I discovered the best way to stop a man from weighing down our parlor cushions in pursuit of my hand. All it took to chase away Mr. Morrison was one, simple phrase whispered in his ear!"

"What was that?" He braced himself for the answer.

"I'm not my father's daughter."

He groaned.

"Oh, but it worked like a charm. Most gentlemen don't need such a blatant push toward the truth." Cait waved a dramatic hand beside her face. Her eye color and complexion were far darker than his pale, blue-eyed parents could ever have produced. "Who could have known he was such a shameless gossip? And now Mother has taken to her bed, freeing my time even further."

His father's absence had cleared the way for Mother, frustrated by her inability to marry off her sons, to hunt for a husband for Cait among the upper crust of Glasgow society. Most men, able to read her family tree—or lack thereof—upon her face, politely refused to engage. If Cait wanted to chase away a man, well, it was her life, her decision. He rubbed the back of his neck. But to grab the truth by the scruff of its neck and drag it from the back of the closet into the light? Well, there would be a backlash that might negatively affect her future.

"We'll have to table this topic for later, Cait. I'm here for information about a pressing and serious matter."

"What's wrong?" She rolled the papers from her workbench and held them tightly against her chest.

"It's nothing to do with you." He narrowed his eyes. "But don't think I don't know what you're up to down here. Promise you won't do anything stupid."

"I promise."

She blinked a few too many times, but short of setting a guard on her, there was little to do. "Lord Roideach. He's been rebuilding some ancestral castle. Do you know where?"

"Of course," she said. "Allanach Castle on Asgog Loch. Such fussing over castles lately. Did you hear about the one they've built out of iron and steel for the future Queen of Iceland?"

Alec stared at her. "Even you've been sucked into this wedding nonsense?"

"It's all society talks about," Cait huffed and bugged out her eyes at him. "No one seems interested in discussing the latest monograph on poison dart frogs and the lipophilic alkaloid toxins they secrete. Imagine that."

"Probably not the best topic to introduce over tea," he admitted with a grin. "Thank you." Then, with a wary glance at her ice bucket, he gave his sister a quick hug. "Be safe." He started for the stairs, but Cait's next words brought him to a sudden halt.

"Don't you want to hear the rumors?" Her voice teased.

"Rumors?" He turned. "About the royal wedding?"

"No, idiot, about Lord Roideach and his medieval castle."

Alec crooked his fingers. "Spill, Cait. I've not time for games." Isa's life might hang in the balance.

"Fine. Six, maybe seven years ago—or so the story begins, Lord Roideach was collecting mussels on the shore when he came upon a gray-eyed lass taking a dip in the sea. Besotted, he pursued and married her. She made quite the splash in society. Bore him a son. Then simply... disappeared." His sister's matter-of-fact voice took on a lilt as the story turned into a fairytale. "Some say she's a selkie, that Lord Roideach stole her seal pelt, trapping her in human form and forcing her to wed him."

"Nonsense," Alec said. "Shapeshifting is a physical impossibility." But he couldn't entirely discredit the myth, not after Isa had all but claimed to be one. Every time he uncovered new information, it tied back to her and her so-called people. Finn, she'd called them, and they clearly possessed physiological characteristics not found among the general Scottish population.

Cait shrugged. "Agreed, but it makes a good story. Do you want to hear the rest?"

"There's more?"

"No one has seen his wife in years, though he is sometimes seen with the child. He refuses to speak of her and there's speculation that childbirth unhinged her mind. Shortly after her disappearance, Lord Roideach set about restoring Allanach Castle. Some say she's there now, locked away in a tower, but calmed by the view of open water and the Scottish Highlands."

Alec rolled his eyes. "Perhaps he returned her pelt."

"What?" Cait widened her eyes in mock horror. "Allow his love to change forms and disappear back into the ocean? Never." She sobered. "Any man who would steal such a thing to force a woman into his bed would be disinclined to return it."

"That's not love." Alec might not know exactly what love was, but it didn't involve force or captivity. But he wasn't here for a philosophical discussion or to debate the existence of mythological creatures. "No one has visited this castle?"

"Only those involved in its restoration. Lord Roideach claims it too dangerous for tours. But yet another rumor, no doubt perpetuated by said workmen, claims it's haunted, that screams echo from the dungeons."

"Haunted." Alec doubted that anything supernatural loitered in its halls, but expected to find at least one tortured soul within its walls.

"The moment it's finished, Lord Roideach will have all kinds of visitors keen to wander about in the dark pushing at locked doors and listening for nighttime disturbances."

"He'll have one tonight." No mistaking the growl in his voice

"You," Cait surmised. "Who has he kidnapped? Another selkie?"

Alec swore.

"Really? A selkie?"

"There's no such thing," he insisted. "Now, not a word about my mission." He pointed at her ice bucket. "Or I'm sending in a biohazard team."

"Oh please. I've held my tongue for years. If you're not 'eliminating a threat', you're rescuing some poor hapless individual." Cait tipped her head. "But there's something different about this rescue." She slapped him on his shoulder with the rolled-up papers, laughing. "There's a woman involved. And you *care*. Have you gone and fallen in love?"

Why did everyone keep accusing him of that? "Me? Of course not."

~~~

Rough fingers pried open Isa's eyes. A bright light blinded her, and she tried to turn away—a futile attempt as a leather strap bound her head to a hard metal surface. She clenched every muscle—arms, legs, back—but moved not an inch. Straps bound her tightly in place upon a metal gurney. But for the rough wool blanket that covered her, she was naked.

"The corneal epithelium is highly keratinized."

The features of the man bent over her were indistinct, obscured not by the decilamp he held, but by the bright argon lamps above them. There was a soft scratching sound. Miss Russel taking dictation?
~~~

"The sclera is thick," he continued. "Excellent for withstanding the pressures of diving. But there is only a hint of a nictitating membrane."

"She's awake," the boy announced in a small voice. "Is she cured?"

"Yes. Now hush, Thomas," Miss Russel said. The sound of her pencil moving never stopped.

The light blinked off, and Isa caught an unfocused glimpse of a pale, emotionless face before the smoky and distorting goggle lenses were pulled over her eyes again.

"Water, please," she whispered. Her lips were dry and cracked, and a chin strap left her barely able to form the words. Though her stomach growled, she didn't dare ask for anything more. How long had she been in captivity? What had happened to Alec? Had he come to harm? Or was he even now wondering what had become of her?

"I think she's hungry too," Thomas spoke up once more. "Isn't possible to feed a person by sticking a tube in their arm."

"All that is necessary to sustain the creature has been done," Miss Russel hissed.

"She's a woman," the boy objected. "And pretty. Why are you being so mean?"

"Thomas," the man's voice was stern. "I've explained the need to collect information. Do you recall what is at stake?"

"Yes, sir," the boy said, contrite.

"Now not another word, or there will be no sweets after supper." The man cleared his throat. "To resume.

Dry body temperature elevated one degree above that of human core temperature." Cold metal probes touched against the sides of her nose. "Initiating nostril exam."

A bolt of electricity ran through and across Isa's nose, spreading outward. Her back arched, and she squealed in agony as the voltage contracted a number of facial muscles to their limits.

"Subject possesses musculature to close the nostrils, most likely the nasalis muscle," he noted while Isa panted in pain, unable to wipe the tears that ran downward from the corner of her eyes. "Closure is sufficient to prevent water entry during submersion."

"That hurt her!" the boy objected.

"Thomas!"

"Recorded," said Miss Russel. "Lung capacity is next on the list."

"Now, Mrs. McQuiston," the man said. "We need to record the full amount of air you are able to inhale and exhale in preparation for a dive. It's a simple matter of breathing—as deeply and as strongly as possible—though a spirometer. I am going to remove the chin strap. Cooperate and Miss Russel will provide you with oral nourishment."

The buckle fell free, but before Isa could ask any questions or make any demands, rubber tubing was forced between her teeth. Two fingers pinched her nose closed.

"Exhale first. Then seal your lips and inhale as deeply as possible," the man commanded.

With no real choice but to breathe through the tube, she did her best to reduce the volume of air moving into and out of her lungs. Isa refused to allow them to collect accurate data on the lung capacity of a Finn. They knew too much already.

"Mmm," he said. "Rather low. Perhaps because she's still recovering from the amoeba infection."

A bell clanged in a distant corner of the room. The man and Miss Russel exchanged silent glances, then set down their instruments and hurried off to investigate.

A small hand shoved wet strands of hair away from her face. "Sorry," the boy said, leaning close. "I can try to slip you one of my biscuits later." He paused. "Unless it's true what he says, that you would prefer raw fish?"

"No fish," Isa rasped. Sensing a potential ally, she added, "But tea would be lovely."

"I knew it!" the boy exclaimed. "You *are* human."

Miss Russel stomped back, yanking Thomas by the arm. "Do not speak to the creature, Thomas."

"But she wants tea!" he whined.

"Go. Now. You have a math assignment to complete."

"But—"

"Now, Thomas!"

Isa's small friend ran away.

"There will be no forthcoming tea," Miss Russel snapped, pushing a rubber tube between Isa's lips. "Drink."

Isa sucked. And nearly gagged as the nasty taste of fermented cod liver oil met her tongue. This was what the woman imagined the Finn people consumed in lieu of tea? But fat was a substance unavailable to her via an intravenous line. She drank every last drop. The moment she was done, the woman yanked the chin strap back into place, snapping Isa's teeth together, buckling it more tightly than before.

"Well, well, well," the man said. His footsteps came to a stop beside her. "Now that I have managed to secure an Ichor machine and a proper program card, I can definitively say that this woman's husband was brilliant. If only he'd shared his work earlier, there would have been no reason to see his *work* so abruptly terminated."

Isa inhaled sharply, the leather straps digging into the skin of her chest. Had this man seen Anton killed? She squinted, trying to make out his features through the lenses. Miss Russel had called him "my lord" and he knew—had known—her husband. Could it be Lord Roideach? Not that she would know; she'd never been introduced.

"The Ichor machine has provided us with fascinating data." Paper rustled in his hands. "As suspected, in hypoxic conditions, she strongly expresses factor Q. The protein allows her blood to bind oxygen at twice that of human blood and explains why a Finn can stay submerged for up to twenty minutes at a time. That makes her a most excellent candidate for our project."

Factor Q. Project. This had to be Lord Roideach. Fear clawed at her skin like sea lice. Not only did it sound as if he'd played a role in Anton's death, but he didn't consider her—a Finn—to be human. A state of mind that would make it all that much easier for him to conduct experiments upon her and her people.

"Do you think the data will convince the committee to continue their funding?" Miss Russel asked.

"CEAP is to receive only the basic physiological data. As our private sponsor procured the Ichor machine, the Q status of our test subjects is to be considered among the proprietary information. Never forget he holds the trump card, Miss Russel."

"Of course not, my lord." Was she mistaken, or did Isa detect a hint of acid in the assistant's voice? "Are there any further tests you wish to run before we return her to the tank?"

"I need fine needle biopsies of her liver and spleen to examine potential location of blood reservoirs." Steel instruments rattled upon a metal tray as he searched for the right tool. "Perhaps a lung biopsy as well."

What? "No! Please!" But only a strangled, feral cry emerged from Isa's throat. One to which they paid no heed.

Chapter Nineteen

By the time dusk fell, Alec stood amidst a copse of trees, studying Allanach Castle. Reports of its reconstruction were greatly exaggerated. It was inhabitable, but just barely. The roof of the keep had been restored, though the same consideration had not been extended to the watchtower which rose above the loch at the end of the curtain wall, some distance from the main structure. Scaffolding climbed one side of the keep where it appeared glaziers were at work during the daylight hours, installing windows.

If any significant sum had been poured into this building, he was willing to bet he'd find the investment concentrated in the lower portion of the castle, in the dungeons, where screams were muffled and small, high-set barred windows discouraged prying eyes.

Once, before succumbing to mediocrity, Lord Roideach's laboratory at the Institute was a source of groundbreaking marine biotechnology. Though his skirt-chasing tendencies and sudden, intense interest in his family history could explain the behaviors of many spoiled gentlemen, Alec was now convinced something more underlay the man's long absences from his laboratory.

What if Roideach had found compelling hypotheses that fell outside acceptable ethical parameters? Where better to pursue interests of the gray—or even black—variety than inside the walls of his very own ruinous, isolated castle? Like so many of the gentry, however, his funds were stretched thin. Which, if Alec's supposition was correct, begged the subsequent question: who provided funding?

Alec already knew the why. Selkies.

In times past, the possibility of their existence would have been ignored by academia, lumped with the faerie, the stuff of myth and legends. But with the arrival of kraken and pteryforms, creatures so common now in London's rivers and skies that they posed a nuisance, should he be surprised at such possibilities? Cryptozoologists were forever discovering new and strange animals—such as hyena fish. Why not, then, odd human variants?

Which circled Alec back to the conclusion that Isa was a selkie. Or that Roideach believed her to be one.

Not that it mattered. Experimentation upon unwilling human participants was not to be tolerated. Isa and her people were most definitely human, though they did appear to possess some extraordinary aquatic talents that might cause people to think otherwise. Such skills only strengthened the pull of her attraction upon him.

In the time he'd stood watch, Alec had detected no obvious guards, save the gardener and the shepherd who—given the late hour—showed a suspicious dedication to their assigned tasks. But they were obstacles easily eliminated. More worrisome was the fact that light only flickered behind three windows. Had instinct led him astray?

He'd find out as soon as the sun finished slipping over the horizon.

His primary goal was to rescue a damsel in distress. What happened next would depend upon what he found after breaching the castle walls. Or—he adjusted the focus of the sight upon his rifle—after scaling the scaffolding to slip through one particular low-set window secured by heavily oxidized iron bars.

How they would exit would depend upon Isa's medical condition. With luck, they'd leave on the backs of the two black, clockwork horses that stood behind him, oiled and fine-tuned, their drive springs tightly wound. Given the proximity of the loch, he was also prepared for a wet exit. Alec might be on his own, but the fact that he had options at all was courtesy of his superior's willful blindness.

Nearly an entire day had passed since he'd left Glasgow.

Preparing for his trek into the highlands to save one Mrs. Isa McQuiston, Alec had returned to the BURR operations room to acquire a few specialty items. The room had been dark, all men elsewhere.

"Is that you, Captain McCullough?" Fernsby asked, stepping from his office.

Hands on an air rifle and a box of tranquilizer darts, Alec froze. The timing couldn't have been worse. "Pursuing a lead, sir," he said, slowly turning to face his commanding officer.

"I regret to inform you that Mr. Black was unable to recover the samples recovered during your last mission. Commodore Drummond has declined an explanation and remains unapologetic." Fernsby's lips pressed together in displeasure. "However, I understand a woman—quite alive—rescued during this same mission has also gone missing?"

"Yes, sir."

Fernsby lifted a sheet of paper and peered through spectacles perched upon the end of his nose. "According to Rip's report, at least one individual appeared to have been attacked by an octopus while the rest of the human remains had been severed by the 'razor-edged teeth of a biomechanical megalodon and fed upon by hundreds if not thousands of hyena fish'."

"Accurate, sir."

Eyebrows raised, Fernsby looked at Alec. "Quite a bloody scene, I imagine."

"It was, sir."

"While you were under the knife—*again,*" Fernsby's eyebrow lifted, informing Alec that his continuing disability was noted and categorized as worrisome, "the rest of your team was called to Edinburgh. Seems we're to be involved with providing security for the Iceland-Demark wedding as Queen Victoria's personal gift to the bride and groom." He shook his head. "Ridiculous, building a floating castle."

"A *floating* castle?" Alec blinked, recalling his sister's words. "Built of iron and steel?"

"And of copper and brass and about any alloy they could think to bolt, rivet or weld to the structure." Fernsby waved a hand. "But it's not your concern. Mr. Black made it clear that you are attached to the Queen's agents until the situation surrounding this megalodon is resolved."

"Yes, sir." A moment's stirring of regret—the mechanics of a floating castle aroused his curiosity—was quickly replaced by relief. No one would be ordering him to step away from his mission to discover and stop the biomech octopus attacks.

"Good. Fold any actions taken within the next forty-eight hours into the reports of this most recent mission." Fernsby turned, calling over his shoulder as he disappeared back into his office. "I expect any equipment and munitions expended to be accounted for." He fixed Alec with a look. "I've a promotion pending. As do you. Proceed accordingly." His office door slammed.

Tacit permission received, Alec had wasted no time, dragging a large rucksack into the middle of the floor. Keeping in mind the very real possibility that he might be carrying Isa along with all his gear, he gathered the bare minimum of equipment and headed for the highlands. Several hours later, he'd arrived at Allanach Castle on horseback.

A gust of wind snapped his mind back to the present.

Night had fallen. Time to act. Alec lifted the air rifle's sight to his eye, surveilling the castle and grounds once more. With a muffled pop, he dropped the shepherd amidst his flock with one dart. The TTX poison injected into his system would wear off in a few hours with no residual effects. The gardener fell next.

Slinging the rifle over his back and clipping his gear into place, Alec froze. There, in the distance, a figure rose from the water at the edge of the loch.

He yanked a spyglass from his pocket and lifted it to his eye. An icy chill took hold of his core. Dripping wet and wearing nothing but a simple pair of trousers, the man walked to the castle door—and was granted admittance. What the hell was Commodore Drummond doing here?

~~~

Isa woke with a start, heart pounding. Again she floated in the tank. The obfuscation goggles were in place, her wrists tightly bound. This time the water wasn't ice cold, but rather pleasantly cool, like the sea in late summer. A gentle current circulated through the
~~~

water. None of it calmed her in the slightest. They'd been far too interested in her blood.

She could make out Thomas sitting beside the tank, holding some kind of stick. But for the stick, the sight of the boy would have brought a certain measure of relief.

"If you promise not to scream, I'll unbuckle the chin strap."

Though her stomach churned, she nodded. What choice did she have? Screaming would only bring back Miss Russel or, worse, Lord Roideach. Waterlogged leather loosened from her chin, and the oxygen tube dropped away. "Why are you here?" she rasped, her voice rusty with disuse.

"Me?" He blinked, as if no one had ever asked. "Lord Roideach is my father. My mother is a selkie, like you."

Her breath caught. Thomas was half Finn? Never before had Isa ever heard mention of Finn gentry, though this child might be exactly that. "Is your mother... here?" Had they married? Either way, Isa prayed Lord Roideach wouldn't experiment upon his child's mother.

Thomas jabbed at something in the water, then shook his head. "No. She found her seal skin and left when I was a baby." His voice held a note of longing. Imagine that, heir to a viscounty, yet he wished himself something else entirely. "But sometimes she visits. Soon I'm going to the ocean to get my own seal skin."

"We don't have skins," Isa said. Not in the sense he believed. Gray seal pelts were purely ceremonial, traditionally given to children at the dipping ceremony when an elder presented them to the ancient sea gods. Perhaps he meant that? "Nor do we shape shift. But we *are* really good swimmers. Have you never been to the seaside?"

His head shook. "Father won't allow it. I'm too valuable."

"As the next viscount, of course," she said.

"No. In the laboratory. He needs my blood. I have webbing between my fingers and everything." His voice held a note of pride.

Something pliable touched her hip, the merest brush across her skin. Thomas jabbed his stick into the water again.

"What was that?" Isa cried, twisting on the rope that bound her wrists, her eyes struggling to focus on whatever swam through the water beside her. Ice crystallized in her veins and arteries.

Thomas ignored her. "But your blood is better even if your hair *is* red. Father says full-blooded selkies are better."

"Better?" Her voice rose an octave as something rubbery curled about her thigh. When Thomas didn't lift his stick, she kicked it away. "Thomas, what—exactly—is in the tank with me?"

"The tentacles," he answered, as if she ought to know. "You shouldn't have kicked that one away. That's exactly where it needs to be. You're lucky. It's only been an hour and the tentacle has tried to stick to you seven times already."

"What!" Her pulse thrashed in her ears as realization struck her with the force of a tidal wave. The tentacle was probing her leg, searching for a blood vessel. Like all the fishermen before her, she was about to become the biomech octopus's newest victim.

"You promised you wouldn't scream." The boy reached toward her chin, toward the leather strap.

Isa yanked her face away. "Please, make it stop."

"I'm sorry," Thomas said. "I don't want to. But Father says if it works, he'll take me to the seaside. I'll get my own skin and then I can be with my mother. I'm tired of living in this castle. The loch is freshwater, and my mother doesn't like that."

Panic rose in her throat, threatening to drown her. "Who is your mother?"

"A real selkie, of course," he said with exasperation. "She looks like me. Father says we have the same eyes." A tentacle was back, probing her ankle. The boy swatted it away with his stick. "Eight times now. Don't worry, I'll make sure it sticks in the right place."

"Show me your face," Isa demanded, grasping at straws. "Perhaps I know her."

After a long moment of silence, Thomas reached out and pushed the obfuscation goggles onto her forehead. Isa gasped. Maren's child stared down at her. She'd know those gray eyes, that expression anywhere. Maren had married a Scottish *lord.*

"Do you?" The boy's eyes were wide. "Can you take me to her?"

"I do. But—" A tentacle slid across the skin of Isa's thigh, and she swallowed a gasp. The soft tip tapped gently, as if searching for something. It paused.

"You won't. Won't help." He crossed his arms. "None of the others would either."

"Swat it away," she pleaded, kicking.

"No," Thomas pouted. "That's exactly where it's supposed to go. If you hold really still, it hurts less."

"Please," she begged. "I don't want this. Let me out of this tank."

The soft, muscular tube slithered around her leg, tightening its grip as its suckers attached themselves to her skin, directly above her femoral vein.

Tears welled in her eyes. *Sea to sand*, she was going to end as a corpse, washed up on some distant shore. Isa opened her mouth to beg again, but all words were cut off by a sharp, stabbing pain. She kicked, fighting against the creature that had her in its grips, but the beast merely gripped her thigh more tightly. The tip of the tentacle twisted and turned and it bore downward and inward, burrowing into her skin.

Isa screamed.

Chapter Twenty

Making as little noise as possible, Alec hoisted himself onto the scaffolding, climbing until he clung to the poles beside an illuminated castle window where the traitorous silhouette of Commodore Drummond loomed over that of Roideach's.

"I'm sorry, sir," Roideach said. "I assumed—"

"You take unwarranted risks and continue to pander to CEAP," the commodore interrupted. The glaziers had yet to fully repair the rotten lead of the window and numerous glass panes were missing. Enough so that Alec was able to catch their words. "First the incident with the blood thickener, now this."

"I was only following your orders, sir, attempting to prepare a highly trained Naval officer to receive the tentacle attachment, so that you might spare your people."

Alec had never heard Lord Roideach so deferential and obsequious. He leaned closer, curious about the power Isa's uncle, a Navy officer, held over a gentleman.

"But it didn't work. Fool that you are, you chose a BURR team member and look where that's led us. A death. An investigation. Hell, I had to dispose of a difficult board member to save your arse. The next thing I know, the BURR team is dropping out of the air beside my submersible." The commodore's hand sliced through the air. "Now this."

Alec ground his teeth together. That explained much. Davis, lured by the promise of an ability to dive deeper and longer, had willingly submitted to treatment. Except the experimental blood thickener had killed him, a fact Roideach had attempted to conceal. No wonder the lord had avoided Alec, opposing his access to an Ichor machine. A situation Commodore Drummond had resolved by poisoning a board member, permanently ending any investigation.

His nostrils flared, and he grabbed the weapon at his hip. Too many lives treated as no more than the inconvenient price of scientific progress. Designated a Queen's agent, did he have to right to terminate them both now? Or was he limited to those lightweight TTX darts his brother had pushed upon him? He loosened his grip. Tempting though it might be, he had no concrete proof, and Logan would want to interrogate them both.

"Your technician is a fool," the commodore growled. "Snatching a Finn woman directly from the Fifth Ward of the Glaister Institute? Miss Russel *knew* the patient was attached to Captain McCullough, a man who worked in your laboratory. He's a BURR team member, for aether's sake. She might as well have scattered bread crumbs the whole way here. The man is a threat. If CEAP discovers my people, our entire operation is at risk."

"Miss Russel was attempting to manage the situation. Your niece was on death's doorstep—"

"And should have been left there!" Isa's uncle threw his hands in the air. "She's of no further use to us. She's nothing but trouble, and her death would have solved many problems."

A faint scream echoed through the night, and ice shot down his spine.

Isa.

Alec would bet his life on it.

"I'm sorry, sir, but she's in the tank now. Her blood tested positive for factor Q, and the boy is overseeing the attachment procedure as we speak."

Shit. He needed to find Isa, now, while they argued. Bringing a superior officer and a gentleman to justice would have to wait. Gripping the crumbling stone of the castle wall, he stepped off the scaffolding, moving in the direction of the sound, angling his head, listening for another cry.

Commodore Drummond cursed. "I trusted you. You promised not to draw the attention of CEAP to me or mine. In return, I agreed to leave the child with you."

"Please, sir," he begged. "I'll make this right."

Hand by hand, foot by foot, Alec climbed over the stones. The faint sound of a child trying to hush Isa met his ears, even as her uncle pronounced a death sentence.

"No more mistakes. There's not a chance she'll cooperate. Glean what information you can, then see her terminated. Transport our operations to the sea cave. Be certain you sever all links."

Roideach's reply was lost to the howl of the wind that whipped past him as he rounded a corner, steadily moving toward a lower window—barred, of course—from which a faint glow emanated.

"Hold still," a boy pleaded. "It needs to grip your leg just so, or it won't work."

"Please." Isa's voice was tearful but, thankfully, both conscious and coherent. "Don't do this."

Alec channeled all the anger—fear and betrayal—into reaching her. Grabbing the iron that proposed to bar him from her, he yanked. Metal groaned, then the bolt that held it to the stone crumbled. The iron had turned to brittle rust. He yanked and tugged and twisted, throwing each iron bar to the ground below.

"Get it off! Get it off!"

Alec lowered himself through the window, dropping silently to the floor, taking aim with his weapon.

Isa floated—naked—in an enormous, glass aquarium. Blood tinted the water pink. Wrists bound, she thrashed, twisting her torso back and forth as she kicked. A boy stood upon a platform holding a long, wooden dowel that he used to direct the movements of two tentacles.

One curled and undulated about Isa's thigh, tapping on her skin. The other explored her shoulder and neck.

But the tentacles were not connected to a body of any kind. Rather to a machine. A contraption with a panel of knobs and switches and dials and gauges. Tubes and wires ran from the device seamlessly fusing and merging with the wet, gleaming flesh of two octopus arms. Arms that plunged into the water, reaching for Isa.

"Drop it," Alec commanded as he stepped forward. The only thing that stayed his hand was the child's age. He was only six, perhaps seven years. He could not hurt a child. Would not. Though the boy need not know that.

The boy's mouth fell open, and the stick clattered to the ground. "Father!" he yelled, leaping to the floor and running away.

Alec climbed the metal ladder attached to the platform. Holstering his weapon, he tugged his dive knife free and sliced through the writhing, soft flesh and tough wire of one tentacle. The other tentacle thrashed, yanking Isa beneath the water's surface. With a vicious strike he cut it free from the machine. Opalescent fluids pulsed forward from the severed ends of the tentacles, but the monstrous things fell limp. He cut the ropes that bound Isa's wrists, then ripped away the goggles and a harness strapped to her head.

"Alec?" she gasped through a tangle of wet, dripping hair as she reached for him.

"It's me." Relief washed over him. Thank aether she was alive and relatively unharmed. He lifted her onto the platform, quickly taking stock of the puncture wounds to her thigh. Blood seeped, but slowly. He didn't think any blood vessels had been compromised. He ran his palm over the raw gash in her calf. Good. No sign of infection, amoeba or otherwise.

"A long and miserable story," she said.

Overhead, shouts erupted. Time was running out.

"We need to go." He wrapped a blanket about her body, scooped her into his arms and carried her to the window. Tying a rope to the tank's ladder, he threw the loose end out the window. "It's a bit of a drop. Wrap your arms around my neck. Hold tight."

She complied, and he lowered them to the ground. Eyes wide, she looked up at him for direction while blood seeped from her legs in tiny rivulets. Wrapping his arm about her waist, Alec was about to steer her toward the trees where the clockwork horses waited when dirt kicked up at their feet and a loud crack tore through the air.

"Stop right there, Dr. McCullough!"

Alec swung Isa around behind him, lifting his rifle to his shoulder as he turned to face a very determined woman pointing a rifle in his direction.

Standing on the rubble of what was once the castle's curtain wall, stood one Miss Russel looking not at all like a victim, but rather like a mad scientist attempting to stop the theft of her creation.

They'd never make the horses. He fired a dart into Miss Russel's shoulder, and perhaps felt a bit too much satisfaction when she crumpled onto the stones. Enough so that he almost missed the rising shadow of Commodore Drummond behind her. Isa gasped as recognition took hold, as Alec used a second dart to drop her uncle before he could take aim.

Another weapon fired. The gardener had recovered from the effects of the TTX dart and taken a defensible position behind a pile of rubble. Alec didn't dare risk the few seconds it would take them to cross the open clearing into the woods.

"This way."

He slung the gun about his shoulder and grabbed Isa's hand, steadying her shaky legs as she stumbled down the rocky slope toward the loch, splashing into the water. He inflated the neutral buoyancy float on his wet bag, setting it to suspend the equipment four to five feet below the water's surface then tethered it to his hip. The metal brace about his knee might suffer, but it could be replaced.

"Across the loch is the most direct and safe route. Given your rough treatment, I have to ask. Is it too cold? Too far?"

Another shot rang out in the dark.

"Not in the slightest," she answered, throwing aside the wool blanket and wading into the water. "I want nothing more than to swim away from this nightmare."

Ignoring as best he could the glorious sight of her naked form standing waist-deep in the moonlight, Alec pointed across the loch, to the faint glimmer of lamplit windows. "Aim for that small village. Stay close to the surface, close to me."

Isa nodded, and Alec stared in amazement as she inhaled deeply, closed her nose—*closed*—then dove into the water and disappeared beneath its surface.

Chapter Twenty-One

As a gray dawn broke outside, Isa stood in the hallway of her Glasgow town home, a hand pressed to her chest, and stared in shock while Alec scoured the house, searching behind every stick of furniture—broken or not—and peering into every dark corner.

Though she'd been unconscious for the vast majority of the past few days, she felt like she'd not slept in weeks. A megalodon attack, a stomach-turning journey in an airship, an exotic, Finn-targeted amoebic infestation compounded by imprisonment as a mad scientist's test subject? And still there was to be no rest.

Her eyes swept over the reckless damage. A chair had been overturned, a lamp shattered, but most of the chaos concentrated about the study's large oak desk. From the papers strewn about the floor at its base, it wasn't much of a leap to conclude that the burglars had been looking for Anton's laboratory notes and grown infuriated when they'd been unable to locate what they sought. She'd hidden them where no one would think to look.

All of this because of her traitorous uncle. Fiercely loyal to the Finn people, he had joined the British Navy and risen to a high rank, inspiring a number of Finn, including Aron, who had set his sight upon—and won—a position on the BURR team. No matter how she despised her uncle, not once would she ever have thought him capable of such atrocities. How many lives had he stolen?

Pieces were falling in place, but gaping holes remained. Why would her uncle encourage experimentation upon his own people? Why would Maren allow her eldest child to remain in the hands of a mad scientist, gentry though he was? What did either of them stand to gain from such actions?

Isa had dedicated her entire life to helping the Finn people, doing all that tradition demanded to earn—prove—her place among them. The depth of her family's betrayal cut to the quick. Promises made and broken, shattering her life upon the sharp rocks of their own agendas, beginning with the lie that had been her marriage.

Her mother had cared only that her daughter found a Finn husband so as not to bring further shame upon the family. Her uncle had abused his half-sister's wishes, arranging Isa's marriage to suit himself, to exploit her medical knowledge, intelligence and drive. Maren had arrived as an emissary, urging Isa to accept Anton's proposal all the while handing her own child over to Isa's uncle as a bargaining piece to further whatever bizarre agenda was afoot. She found it hard to dredge up much sympathy for Anton or Lord Roideach, who were both participants and pawns. To think of all the suffering they'd caused! And would cause, unless stopped.

Since their first meeting, Alec—a man who barely knew her—had *repeatedly* put himself in harm's way to keep her safe. He'd earned her loyalty, proving himself worthy again and again. Him, a Scot, she could trust.

She had so much to tell him, so much to ask, but they had been unable to speak privately the entire trip home. Between his combat clothing, a rifle-shaped bag slung over his shoulder, and her bedraggled appearance—tangled hair, no corset and stolen skirts that were several inches too long—they'd drawn far too much attention. But the farmer had let them onto his steamcart for a fee and, though he'd raised eyebrows and warned them not to cause trouble, the conductor on the train hadn't thrown them off.

Through the entire journey, Alec had kept her by his side, wrapping his strong arms about her to draw her close whenever the memories of the tank—of how close she'd come to being a victim of those horrible, groping tentacles—surfaced. She didn't feel safe—not remotely—but for the first time she didn't feel alone.

She jumped when a loud clang echoed from the cellar. Why was Alec firing the furnace when they wouldn't be staying long? Glasgow was no longer safe for them, not with the influence and power a Naval officer and a gentleman would soon bring to bear. Running wasn't a long-term solution, but she had no better plan. Perhaps Alec did. She briefly closed her eyes as a gentle heat wafted up through the floor registers about her feet, cutting the chill from the air and bringing with it a measure of relief and comfort.

"All clear." Alec strode back into the hallway, filling its space with his wide shoulders and his grim expression, every inch a fierce warrior.

Her heart jumped to attention, beating faster. What was it about this side of him that called to her, made her want to wrap her hands around the base of his skull and drag those full lips down to hers? She swallowed hard, fighting the sudden upwelling of lust, and forced her mind back to the situation at hand.

Stopping some feet away, he holstered his weapon. "You understand we cannot let your family—or any members of your community—know we're here?"

"Of course." Her family adored Uncle Gregor. She doubted they'd believe her story and, even if they did, there was nothing they could do to stop him, not without risking their own lives.

"Don't activate any lights. Don't answer the door. Don't send them any messages via skeet pigeon." His lips twisted. "Though there's an entire flock perched on your kitchen window sill. We'll collect the messages and set the birds aside." He shifted on his feet. "I do need to send one message. To my brother. He's a government... official with some influence."

A cautious hope fluttered in her chest. "And now that we have names, he can arrange for their arrest?"

"I sincerely hope so. But he can be difficult to contact." His steely blue eyes softened as he looked at her, then grew warm as his gaze traveled over the wreck of her attire. "While we wait, we'll have a few hours to rest and regroup. To talk." A smile flashed. "But first I thought you might like a hot bath."

A chance to wash away the soot and dirt that clung to her skin and the bits of hay lodged in her hair? She hadn't dared to hope for such a luxury. Yet curiosity nailed her feet to the floorboards. This was the first time he'd offered her a personal glimpse into his life and, suddenly, she wanted to know more.

"Just one brother?"

He glanced at her, stabbed his fingers into his unkempt hair. "I've two. A full brother and a half-brother. And a half-sister." Arriving at some internal decision, he took a deep breath and peeled back a layer. "Not via the acceptable route of death and remarriage, however. My father doesn't subscribe to the concept of faithfulness, hence my half-brother. My mother retaliated, producing my sister. My parents fight like cats and dogs. I can't recall a single childhood moment of household harmony."

"I've some experience with that," Isa said, offering a confidence in return. She lifted a lock of her hair. "Red hair is unusual among the Finn. My grandmother took a

Scottish lover after her husband's death. My mother was the result. I am a constant reminder of that indiscretion, a fact held against me and my siblings by an entire community."

In a small town, blood purity meant much, and Finn were conditioned to think of Finn and Scot as two separate entities never-to-be-intertwined. Here in Glasgow where Finn and Scot worked side by side and occasionally intermarried, the stigma lessened. Separation benefited no one; together they were stronger.

Except when one sought to take advantage of the other. She took a deep breath. "About the boy, Thomas. He's the son—legitimate—of my former friend, Maren. I questioned him, when I was able, and from the child's words I suspect he's being used to ensure Lord Roideach's cooperation. Not that the gentleman in question had any hesitation performing tests upon me." Her hands curled into fists. He'd treated her as if she were no better than a laboratory rat.

"Maren." A groove formed between Alec's eyebrows. "Your uncle's wife, mother of the child whose seaside baptism I witnessed?"

"Yes. There was a scandal when she returned from Glasgow. Someone let slip that she'd abandoned a husband and child. I objected when my uncle began to court her." A vast understatement. "When their intent to marry was announced, I spoke with Mrs. Carr."

"Bigamy," he said simply.

She nodded. "But not, I was told, in the eyes of the Finn people. Lord Roideach is Scottish and by leaving the child with him, their marriage was dissolved."

Alec's eyebrow rose. "About that term, Finn..."

"Finnfolk. The origins of my people go back so many generations that they're lost." She almost sagged with the relief of turning to a more familiar—and therefore more comfortable—topic. "I can't turn into a seal. But I can hold my breath for up to twenty minutes and swim in the cold sea for hours."

"How deep?"

"Perhaps one hundred feet?"

"On one breath alone?" He stepped closer, bringing with him a raw fascination that stole the air from her lungs. Her blood started to hum again, and all she could manage was a nod. He lifted her hand, tracing the scars between her fingers with his thumb. "And these?"

"Syndactyly," she said. "Webbing on our fingers and toes. A common and once highly valued feature among my people, said to aid in swimming, though we do well enough without. Most choose to remove the extra skin, the better to fit in among the Scots."

He pushed the hair from the side of her face and skimmed the tip of his finger over the top of her ear. "And cut away the points?"

She shivered at his touch. "Yes."

"What else?" He stared at her intently, hanging on her every word.

"Gray eyes, ancient traditions, a language most can no longer speak." She turned her face into the warmth of his palm, indulging herself for a fleeting moment. But Alec needed to contact his brother, needed to read with his own eyes the notes Anton had scribbled. Whatever her uncle and Lord Roideach were up to, it involved factor Q. "Come."

She caught at his hand and pulled him down the hall and into the kitchen, intent on retrieving the notebook from its hiding place on a ledge inside the chimney, one she'd discovered when the cast iron cookstove had been retrofitted to fill the space of the kitchen's fireplace.

"Here," she said, handing the details of their research—of Anton's discoveries—to him. "Factor Q is linked to Finn syndactyly. The tentacles are able to sense the glycoprotein in our blood. How or why, I don't know."

"We'll sort this out and stop them, one way or the other." He held her gaze. "But you realize we might not be able to keep all this information secret, though I *will* try."

"I understand." She believed him. Trusted him. But though he took the notebook from her hand, he set it aside. "What—"

"A moment, Isa." Eyes smoldering, Alec caught her waist, lifting her with his two large hands and depositing her onto the end of the kitchen table. "I wanted to do exactly this the last time we were in this room. Alas, there was an interruption." His voice dropped to a low pitch. "A woman who can swim better than me?" The corner of his mouth hitched into that smile that melted her insides. "Have you any idea what that does to me?"

From the pulse that jumped at his throat, she had a very good idea indeed. A man aroused at her prowess?

And not just any man. Alec, a man among the Navy's elite. Desire flooded her with warmth, then settled hot and wet at her core. Given how events kept conspiring to keep them apart, the notes could wait. Time to put theory into practice and take advantage of the heat simmering in his eyes.

"I do." She lifted her fingers to the topmost button of his shirt and popped it free. Alec unleashed a boldness she'd never known she possessed. No more waiting, no more wishing. Leaning forward, she pressed a soft kiss to the base of his neck. "But I've not seen much evidence of your desire to conduct that torrid romance you promised."

"I've been a bit busy." His hands slid to her knees, parting them as he stepped closer. "Rescuing you. It's hard to romance an injured, bleeding woman."

True. But his intense concentration on her shoved away recent memories. She couldn't bear it if he stopped. "Minor injuries."

His fingers brushed the skin near the nasty gash the hyena fish had left. "Have you any recollection of how ill you were, of how they managed to cure the amoeba infection?"

"They called it the *caeruleus* amoeba." As Isa recounted her time in the freezing water, Alec's fingers curled into fists, as she systematically listed every treatment, every comment, every horror.

"Maggot fish," Alec said. "It's a wonder you survived. A wonder none of my team were infected. Shaw himself was bitten by the hyena fish."

"I was delirious and confused, but something they said made me think this particular amoeba was altered with the specific intent to infect Finn alone."

"And seeded inside the mouths of hyena fish," Alec mused. "Any Finn attempting to escape a megalodon attack would either be shredded alive by hyena fish, or die shortly thereafter, consumed by amoeba one cell at a time. Horrible."

"It is. It was." But she didn't want to think about it anymore. Not right now. "Stop delaying and kiss me."

With a rumbling laugh, his lips came down on hers. Softly. The kind of kiss a man might give an injured woman. She wanted none of that. He'd shown her mad passion before on the ship, against a wall. *That* was what she wanted.

Skimming her fingers over the rough beard on the edge of his jaw and into the dark, silky hair at the base of his neck, she opened her mouth, tugging, urging him to sink into her deep and hard. With a growl, he accepted, his tongue plunging and plundering as his hands swept behind her, cupping the swell of her arse and yanking her core tight against his thick, hard column of flesh.

She moaned and flexed her hips in encouragement. Her mistake for not inviting him into her bed that very first night, but how could she have known?

His lips left hers. "We have to wait." Cold air shocked her back to reality as Alec released her, his chest heaving. "If we're to have any hope of stopping your uncle and Lord Roideach, I must send a letter to my brother. Now."

His finger trailed down her face as his hot gaze scorched her skin. "Point me to your skeet pigeons. I'll scratch out a message while you bathe. Then we'll continue our... discussion."

~~~

Isa stared at the tub, her clammy hands wrapped about a towel as memories of those dark hours in the tank swelled, nearly engulfing her. Perhaps she would use the ewer and basin instead. She took a step backward.

No. No, she would not let Lord Roideach or her uncle—a man who ought to have done everything he could to see to her safety, health and happiness—steal the many pleasures of water from her.

She turned on the hot water tap. Steam rose as the tub filled. Gripping its enameled sides, she climbed in, wincing as intense heat triggered brief, sharp pains where the tentacles had punctured the skin of her legs. She grabbed a cloth and a bar of castile soap and scrubbed her skin pink before attending to her hair. With a yank, she pulled the plug and sat there, watching the water swirl down the drain, carrying away all the dirt and blood of the past few days.

But memories of that horrible tank hadn't washed away. The time she'd spent in it had left both mental and physical scars, a stark reminder of the value placed on her life by the men who sought to control it because of who she was, what she was.
~~~

Not entirely Finn. Yet certainly not Scottish. She'd spent her entire life moving about the edges of both societies, making tentative bids at acceptance, waiting for some stamp of approval that would never be awarded.

Enough. She was both.

Finn by birth, upbringing and mindset, she could not—would not—turn her back on her people by allowing her uncle to experiment on those Finn he deemed "inferior" by blood or by birth. Neither would she dismiss her growing feelings for Alec—admiration, friendship and most certainly lust—simply because he was Scot. Again and again he'd demonstrated that he would stand by her side. As unaccustomed as she was to such assistance, if she had any hope of stopping her uncle, a traitor who had risen from the depths of their own and moved among the Scots as a powerful officer in the British Navy, she needed Alec's help.

She refilled the tub and sank into its warmth, focusing on the glorious buoyancy within the delightful warmth that the miracles of modern plumbing provided. As the knots in her muscles began to untwist, her thoughts drifted down a more pleasant pathway to Alec. To his kiss. To his promise of finishing what they'd started in the kitchen. Her hand skimmed over her skin.

He'd developed a habit of plucking her from the water, but perhaps this time she could convince him to join her in the tub? For all that she was Finn, she'd yet to experience that kind of pleasure in the water and, aether, she wanted Alec to be the one she shared it with.

Closing her eyes, she rested her head against the tub's edge. She'd wait right here for him to find her. A few inked words on a scrap of paper tied to a skeet pigeon's ankle. A twist of a key to wind its clockwork. A quick launch from a window. Then all that was left between them was a single flight of stairs and an unlocked door. She smiled, feeling both wanton and resourceful.

Chapter Twenty-Two

Floating. *Unable to move her hands. Unable to see. A man with gray, sandpaper-like skin stood above her holding a harpoon-gun in his hand. He smirked, revealing a mouth filled with sharp, triangular teeth.*

With a gasp, Isa woke, her heart pounding. She blinked, and the nightmarish images washed away. Bright afternoon rays of sun slanted through a window, highlighting the edges of a familiar jagged crack in the plaster ceiling overhead. Nestled deeply into a feather mattress and swaddled in soft blankets, she was safe in her bed. She hated that crack, one she'd first noticed on her wedding night, years ago, then watched spread, slowly, inexorably toward the wall. She'd vowed never to sleep again in this room, in this bed. Why, then, was she staring at that blasted crack?

Memories of the recent past flooded back.

A faint snore drew her attention, and she turned her head. Her breath caught and the rhythm of her heart took up a different beat. An arm's length away, Alec slept, sprawled in an armchair that he'd dragged from the corner of the room to her bedside. Bare-chested and bare-legged, he wore nothing but a damp, linen towel wrapped about his waist.

She must have fallen asleep in the tub from exhaustion and missed his entrance. Disappointing. Yet touching, for he'd carried her to bed, leaving her to rest.

A shiver of delight skittered across her skin as she rolled onto her side, brazenly cataloguing the features of a man that she'd only seen awake and alert. And fully dressed. His dark hair was rumpled, his eyes and cheekbones shadowed. The beginnings of a beard roughened his jawline. All evidence of the effort he'd expended—much of it on her behalf—these past few days.

Sunlight highlighted the cut edges of muscles hewn by countless field exercises and missions—and a number of scars she imagined he had also collected in the line of work. She wondered at the story behind each. The slight pucker of an elliptical mark atop his shoulder. A thin white line stretched across the curve of his biceps. A still-raw gash upon his chest concealed by a sprinkle of coarse hair. A few faint lines scattered upon the sculpted ridges of his rectus abdominis. But it was the creases leading from each hip downward, diving beneath the towel that made the tips of her fingers tingle with a growing need to touch.

How long had they slept? Could they steal a bit more time for themselves, for each other? She bit her lip, but only for a second. Yes. But not in this bed. The chair, on the other hand, held no memories.

Pushing back her blankets and swinging both legs over the edge of the mattress, Isa touched bare feet to the cool floor. A froth of white ruffles collected about her ankles. Ruffles encircled her wrists and cascaded from her neck. She smiled. He'd dressed her in her finest—and thinnest—nightgown. One she'd purchased, but never worn. Why bother, if a man only wished a quick coupling beneath a blanket in the dark?

Yet Alec had chosen this one, tucked in the corner of a drawer and still wrapped in tissue paper, a gown that was nothing if not a flirtatious invitation.

She would wake him slowly. Appreciatively. With the sun at her back to make the cotton voile gown all but transparent. Warmth shot through her limbs, then collected low in her core. Who better to appreciate such a garment than the only man to ever set her skin aflame with a single look?

Lifting the hem of her nightgown, Isa slid one knee onto the seat beside his hip, then straddled him, lowering her bare bottom onto his towel-wrapped thighs. Nervous anticipation fluttered in her stomach. To be so bold...

She bent forward and placed a soft, teasing kiss against the edge of his chin, brushing her lips over the beginnings of a beard. Sitting back, she traced a tiny scar at the corner of his eye, letting her fingertip skate across the angle of his cheekbone.

His lips, the obvious next choice, twitched, and Isa knew he'd woken. Did he keep his eyes closed with hopes she'd continue? Smiling, she played along, stealing a moment to sketch the arch of his clavicle, to skim her palms over the scattering of coarse hair that curled upon a chest that rose and fell slowly, still feigning sleep.

Time to call his bluff. She dragged her finger down the center of his abdomen, following the groove the linea alba cut, hooking her finger beneath the folded edge of the towel. She gave it a slight tug. "I see you availed yourself of my tub."

A smile stretched across his face, but his eyes stayed firmly shut. "I was filthy and almost as exhausted as you were. Not the best way to begin a torrid affair."

Laughing softly, she circled his navel with her fingertip. "Yet here we are now, all alone." She pressed an open-mouthed kiss to the edge of his neck. Beneath the fragrance of her soap, she could smell him. An intoxicating scent that ignited a deep craving inside her that she had every intention of filling. She nipped at his skin. "Rested. Clean. Nothing between us but a scrap of fabric, and you still can't summon the energy to move?"

Strong hands gripped her hips, yanking her closer to pull her tight against his thick length. "Is this what you had in mind?" he growled, thrusting upward.

"To start." She rocked her hips against the hard column and hummed her delight when Alec's fingers dug into her flesh.

Threading hers through the waves of his hair, she dragged his lips to hers, opening her mouth to welcome the invasion of his tongue. Too long they'd been denied this moment, and the hunger of their kiss spoke of a desire not to be denied a single moment longer.

He groaned, uncurled his fingers and shifted his hands upward. Cotton pulled and stretched as his hands ran over her hips, her ribs, until they cupped the weight of her breasts. Her nipples hardened beneath his thumbs and when he pinched them, she cried out, breaking their kiss.

"Aether, you take my breath away," he said. "Molten sunlight for hair and a gown that frames the glory of your breasts." An impish grin formed. "As I'd hoped."

She smiled. "And yet it feels far too thick."

His hips flexed, pressing into the desire that pooled between her thighs. "We'll get to thick in a moment." A laugh rumbled deep in his chest and he closed his hot, wet mouth over the entirety of her nipple, cotton and all, teasing and toying as her fingers fisted in his hair. A low keening sound rose in her throat, and she clamped her lips tightly against its escape.

Alec drew back, a look of extreme self-satisfaction on his face. "A screamer?"

Heat flooded her face. Her? Screaming? Never. Well, never before.

"I see." His grin stretched wider. "This is a first for you. But I promise it won't be your last. What kind of affair would I be offering if I couldn't drag forth screams of pleasure?"

His mouth came down on her other breast, but this time she didn't bite back the sound of her pleasure. Nor did she stay her hands. Lifting up onto her knees, she yanked at the towel about his waist. The damp cloth parted and his hips jerked as she wrapped her fingers about his heavy length, brushing her thumb across the moisture already collected at its tip.

Impressive. As a Finn, she'd *seen* plenty of men, and he was far bigger than she'd expected. And there was no duty, no expectation. The stolen moments of their affair were to be all about pleasure. Only pleasure. Hers. His.

"And what of you?" she asked. "Will you yell? Shout?" She stroked him. Slowly. His hips bucked and he groaned, a guttural sound she wanted to hear as he sank deep inside her.

His hand, rough with callouses, slid beneath ruffles and skimmed upward over the skin of her inner thigh. She held her breath, completely open to him as he explored her damp folds. She gasped as the pad of his thumb passed over the tiny nub of nerves at her core.

"Mmm," he hummed, as if considering the adequacy of her response. "Not nearly loud enough."

The pad of his thumb began to circle, teasing, driving her insane with need. And when he leaned forward, catching her nipple once more between his teeth, she did cry out.

A few moments later, she pushed against his shoulders, and Alec fell backward into the chair. "Enough of this torture. I need you inside me. Now."

"Impossible to deny such a wanton request." All amusement had drained from his face, leaving behind nothing but white, hot lust. "Take what you want." He spoke through gritted teeth, holding perfectly still.

Waiting. For her. To take *him.*

This was a new concept. *To take, rather than be taken.*

She rose onto her knees and moved closer to notch the wide head of his cock against her entrance. Capturing his gaze with her own, she grasped the back of the chair and lowered herself, embedding him within her inch by sweet inch until he was as deep as she could take him. *Full. So deliciously full.*

Alec's fingers flexed against her buttocks, but otherwise he didn't move. Didn't make a sound.

She rocked her hips. A small movement that shifted him inside her. *Yes. There. That.* Again she rocked. Slowly at first. Then faster, until she was rising upon her knees over him, a wonderful pressure building inside her. She moaned, a sound that must have snapped his control, for his hands gripped her buttocks, pulling her to him as his hips shoved upward, embedding himself even deeper.

"Aether." Isa stared into his eyes. "Do that again."

His legs shifted beneath her as he braced his feet on the floor. "Harder?"

"Please."

With each stroke, he drove upward, thrusting into her, plunging ever deeper as she cried out her encouragement and spread her thighs wider. Each thrust heightened and gathered close a dark pleasure that grew inside of her, until it reached an intensity she had never before experienced. A primitive sound that began at the back of her throat struggled to tear free.

"Yes," Alec hissed between clenched teeth. "Like that. Let me hear it, Isa."

Her body clenched about his, and she screamed his name. "Alec!"

He dove into her once, twice more. Then shuddered, his body taunt, as his own release slammed down upon him.

She collapsed against his heaving chest, sliding her palms over the taut muscle of his back as her lungs dragged in deep gulps of air. Never had she thought a joining could ignite such flames. Or create such a feeling of closeness.

He wrapped his arms about her and for a long moment, they held still, their bodies still joined. Isa listened to the sound of his heartbeat as it slowed, felt the rise and fall of his chest beneath her cheek as his own breath steadied. All the while, his fingertips traced patterns on her lower back.

"Such passion," he murmured. Sliding his fingers into her hair, he tipped her face upward. "Would that we had time for more. The nightgown was—is—delightful, but next time, no clothing. So that I might make a proper examination of your many charms."

Her face grew hot. *Embarrassment? Now?* She forced the corners of her lips upward into what she hoped was a coquettish smile. "Expect to find yourself also beneath the microscope."

Best to keep things light, lest she start caring too much, wanting more from him than an affair. Pulling away, she shifted on his lap, and the thin barrier of her nightgown fell between them.

He caught her by the arm, his expression growing serious. "No regrets?"

"None." She smiled her reassurance.

It took only a fraction of a second for Alec's mouth to quirk, to erase a hint of deep contemplation, but he needn't worry. She didn't want a husband, a man with the legal right to control her every action. Taking a lover was the perfect solution. But they had also formed a partnership to catch a pair of criminals. A task toward which they now needed to redirect their attention.

Chapter Twenty-Three

Alec imagined they presented quite the cozy, domestic scene, dressed and seated beside each other at the kitchen table. A pot of tea wrapped in a towel. Two simple teacups. A plate of scones.

But the thoughts that ran through his head were anything but docile. Never before had he woken to such glory. Images flashed through his mind. Ruffles and red hair tumbling over smooth shoulders. Dark shadows of her nipples beneath wet cloth. Her head tipped back in ecstasy as she rose and fell upon his hard length.

His groin grew heavy. He slid his gaze sideways, to where Isa sat, properly dressed, her hair bound primly at the base of her skull, and was unable to think about anything other than nibbling the lobe of her ear to see if he could reignite the flames that had crackled between them. Did his damp clothing—wet from the quick wash he'd given it earlier—steam from the heat of his thoughts?

Like a schoolboy, he'd spent the last half hour working miserably at the task before him: untangling the spiderweb writing Dr. McQuiston had scrawled upon page after page. The work was groundbreaking, but in his current mental state, Alec felt like he was trying to break the code of a cryptographer's fevered musings. Not since he was a boy had he been so distracted by a female.

While they awaited the arrival of one specific skeet pigeon—from his brother—Isa sorted through the mail. Again and again she tossed curls of messages in the direction of a growing stack. He caught the most recent one in his hand. He had to know. "Three piles. One from prospective patients." He'd noted the pain in her eyes for, as the situation stood, she couldn't hurry to their sides. "Another containing notes from family members." That pile made her look weary, a sentiment he fully understood. "But this pile has you snorting and rolling your eyes. Why?"

Her slight hesitation only magnified his curiosity. "Go ahead." Her lips pressed together. "Read it."

The perfect husband has been found. A location and a date was listed. Brow furrowed, he snatched up another strip of paper. And another. All contained similar messages. A certain possessiveness unfurled in his chest, crowding his lungs and making it difficult to breathe. "Why is everyone so desperate to find you a husband? Are you heiress to a fortune?"

"If only," she said with a huff. "Though I have the financial means to remain independent, Finn culture abhors an unmarried woman of childbearing age."

That again. He paled. "But—"

She touched her arm where the contraceptive was lodged and gave him a small smile. "Remember, no worries. I'm quite pleased with the status quo and have no intention of remarrying."

"Only pleased?" He grinned, forcing levity into his voice. "I'll have to do better." *Next time.* He tapped the notebook. He couldn't keep his eyes off her, but reading wasn't the only—or even the most ideal—method to glean its information. "This is going to take me hours to sift through. Perhaps you might run me through an overview, provide any context that might enlighten your uncle's motives. If I understand correctly, your work began as an effort to provide Finn with a better anesthetic?"

She gave a grim nod. "It was my intent to save Finn lives, not make them a target of a madman." She took a deep breath. "With alarmingly high frequency, standard anesthetic agents can plunge a Finn into a dive reflex, dropping heart rate dangerously low to the point where it simply stops. Because lungs take in the volatile gasses, passing them into the blood stream, we hypothesized that Finn blood carried some component that caused the chemicals to be metabolized differently."

He flipped the pages of the notebook backward, to a section containing extensive notes about individuals, their marriages and progeny. "Hence the family pedigrees?"

"Finn and Scots have interbred for generations, but to simplify our work, to discover a blood trait originating among the Finn, we needed to study the blood of a family whose line was pure Finn. Or as close as one might manage. We certainly couldn't use mine."

There was that flash of pain again. He frowned and placed his hand upon hers. "Is blood purity so important to your people?"

"In small communities? Ridiculously so. Not so much here in the city." She closed her eyes. "Though both my head and my heart tell me it doesn't matter, I spent my entire childhood censured for my grandmother's *indiscretion* with a Scotsman." She waved her hand at her hair. "One day, I refused to dye it brown. My decision was treated as an act of open rebellion, and my marriage was quickly arranged to subdue any further defiant tendencies I might express."

"Arranged," he stated, then recalled an earlier conversation. "By your uncle."

"Yes." Isa stood and began to pace. "He orchestrated the entire thing. I was promised a medical education." A bitter laugh escaped her lips. "Naïve fool that I was, I expected to attend the University of Glasgow." Her thumb rubbed against her upper arm, above the contraceptive device. "He told me children would hinder my application when, in fact, he simply wanted to ensure I might work, day and night, upon a project he now exploits for his own gain." Her voice dropped. "Anton was also used. He wasn't told about the device, and my seeming infertility drove us apart." She shook her head at the impossibility of pleasing everyone. "I didn't—don't—want children. Someday, perhaps, but not any time soon."

"You have other aspirations to attend to first." Nothing Alec could say would take away the pain of the years she'd lost to her uncle's manipulations, but stopping him would make a good start. "You're a danger to him now, Isa. You know too much."

"I also know *you*." Her eyes glinted in a way that made him think wicked thoughts. "And *we* will stop him." She dropped back into her chair and reached across him, flipping the pages of the notebook. "While comparing the purest Finn blood to the purest Scottish blood we could obtain, we discovered four blood type variations shared by both populations—factors designated as A, B, C and D—that affected the clotting of blood." She paused to turn the page. "Among the Finn, a fifth variation was discovered, factor Q, a trait tightly linked—but not always—to syndactyly."

"Groundbreaking," Alec said. "Properly documented and published in a journal, this discovery would revolutionize hematological studies."

"Alas, not only would that expose the Finn to unwanted scrutiny, but these notes indicate consent was not always freely given." She pursed her lips. "In any case, factor Q stood out in that it seemed to have no influence upon blood clotting. To dig deeper, Anton took the samples to his laboratory in the Glaister Institute,

"When I was in the tank, the boy—Thomas—wanted me to hold still while the tentacle tapped along the surface of my skin. He kept a close eye on it, knocking the tentacle away whenever it wandered away from my leg and shoulder, away from the location of large blood vessels." She shivered and pressed a hand to her throat, swaying slightly upon her feet.

Alec pulled her into his lap, gathering her against his chest. He rubbed her back, but found himself unable to speak the usual lie. He'd seen the dead fisherman, seen how the tentacle targeted blood vessels. Everything wasn't fine. "Go on."

"He spoke—freely, as a child will—about how the tentacle wouldn't stick to everyone. What if this biomech octopus is trained—engineered—to seek out the blood of people expressing factor Q?"

"Explaining why all victims discovered have been Finn." Except Davis. Though not a victim of a biomech octopus attack, but he was certainly one of Lord Roideach's test subjects. "If this glycoprotein was isolated in large quantities—I hate to think about how—could it be transfused into a Scotsman's blood in order to attract a tentacle?"

Isa lifted her face from his chest to stare into his eyes. "That's a most gruesome question."

Alec closed his eyes. He too had heard things she deserved to know. "Your uncle was there, at the castle."

"Lifting not a finger to save me." Bitterness laced her voice.

A statement he wished he could contradict. “A few months ago, one of my teammates, Davis, died during a dive.” Impossible to keep the anger from his voice. So much had altered in a matter of minutes. A friend lost his life. Alec almost lost his, almost lost his leg. Though he was lucky to have this mechanical knee, it was hard to feel grateful. “Autopsy results found an unidentifiable foreign protein—described as ‘sticky’—in his blood.”

“A glycoprotein could fit such a description.”

“It would,” Alec said. “Questions were raised, conveniently cut off by a man’s murder. And though I suspected Roideach’s involvement, I couldn’t understand why he would be interested in thickening a man’s blood until—while searching for you—I overheard him speaking with your uncle about the failed attempt to improve the diving ability of a BURR man so that he might attach a biomech octopus to a Scot, instead of a Finn.”

Her eyes grew large. “But it didn’t work.”

“He didn’t survive long enough for them to try.” Alec paused, not certain if that was a blessing or a curse. “Instead, they decided to target Finn directly. But to what end?” That was the crucial question.

At the front of the townhouse, someone knocked on the door. Their eyes caught, but Alec slowly shook his head. They couldn’t acknowledge their presence, not before knowing her uncle and Lord Roideach were in custody. Though the ransacked office demonstrated that anyone truly interested in breaching the front door wouldn’t be stopped by something so simple as lock. He glanced at their bags which sat, packed and ready, by the back door should they need to make a fast exit. He held Isa's gaze, waiting for the unwelcome company to depart.

The rapping finally stopped.

"You're rubbing your knee." She caught his hand in hers, and drew it close, pressing it to her chest. "Might this dive have involved a submersible and a collision with a solid, iron door?"

His hand froze. "It did."

He'd not told her about the submersible exit that had gone so horribly, terribly wrong because explaining the why of his knee dragged up thoughts of Davis, thoughts that hadn't yet sunk deep enough beneath the surface. Besides, he'd promised her a torrid affair. Not an emotional quagmire with a man whose career threatened to founder on the rocks.

The nature of the mission was confidential, but not the disaster that had occurred. A second later, he found himself unburdening the events of that fateful day, detailing the stress his team had been under, forced to dive at dangerous depths with aquaspira breathers. The apoplexy that took Davis's life even as Alec attempted to save him. The unexpected dive that plunged the submersible over a halocline, slamming the door onto his knee. Negative buoyancy tugging him ever faster into the inky depths of the sea loch.

Isa's slender fingers stroked the back of his hand as she hung on his every word, transfixed by his story.

Then he stopped cold. Too focused on Davis, on himself, he'd given it not the slightest thought. But

Moray had saved him that day, plucking him from a depth that no normal human—not even a BURR team member—should survive. Yet he'd done exactly that. Alec owed him his life.

"Moray," he said, wrapping his mind around the likelihood. "Aron Moray, your childhood friend, didn't find your presence amidst the hyena fish at all surprising. He's Finn, isn't he? Why didn't you say something?"

Isa looked away. "It was not my place to reveal his heritage. Men have been ostracized for less."

They'd worked together for years and, try as he might, he couldn't think of anything about Moray that struck him as unusual, save a disinclination to air travel and— "There's no scarring between his fingers."

Tap, tap, tap. A skeet pigeon's beady eyes peered through the kitchen window. Isa stood and crossed the room to fetch the clockwork avian.

"Syndactyly is a highly variable trait," she said, holding the bird in her hand. "And as I recall it, his webbing was slight, a minimal stretch between the third and fourth fingers of one hand."

"Would he express factor Q?"

"Almost certainly, to manage the breathtaking rescue you've described." She pried open the small canister and unfurled its contents. All color drained from her cheeks as her eyes scanned the message. "It's from your brother." She handed it to him. "What's CEAP?"

Investigations of unofficial laboratory papers highly suggestive of CEAP, but not actionable. Gathering individuals to make pilgrimage to the castle. You remain an independent agent.

He clenched his jaw. In other words, Commodore Drummond and Lord Roideach were still loose. Queen's agents were on alert, but had—as yet—nothing definitive. But his temporary commission remained in place, authorizing him to pursue the suspects. The hunt continued. "Your uncle spoke of a sea cave," he said.

"The Isle of Lewis is riddled with them." Her shoulders sagged. "It's impossible to search them all, even if we had a navy to assist."

Click.

A key turned in the lock of the front door, and they both froze. Alec moved his hand to his hip, wrapping his fingers around the grip of his weapon. He waved Isa deeper into the kitchen, out of sight, while hurrying to position himself behind the staircase where he had a clear line of sight to the front door without making himself an easy target.

In walked a petite, brown-haired woman holding an infant. "Isa?" her voice trembled as she stepped tentatively into the dim hallway. "I'm so sorry to intrude, but we must speak. I bear terrible news."

Chapter Twenty-Four

A baby let out an air-splitting wail, and Isa rushed from the kitchen, past Alec and down the hallway to where her sister-in-law stood, shaking and clutching her youngest to her chest.

"What's wrong?" Isa asked, laying a hand on Livli's rigid arm.

"Isa," Livli whispered, jiggling Isa's nephew. Red-faced, he stuck his fist in his mouth and sucked in a sloppy breath. "There's a large man behind you holding a gun."

Isa turned about and frowned at Alec as he re-holstered his weapon. With his military bearing and his face devoid of all expression, he cut an intimidating figure. He nodded, politely acknowledging Livli's benign presence, but didn't step forward to force an introduction.

Wise, given the hunted look in Livli's eyes. Something was terribly wrong.

"I'm so sorry. My house was vandalized while I was away. He was taking precautions in the event they had returned."

"Vandalized?" Livli's eyes grew wide, but stayed fixed upon Alec. "No one in the neighborhood saw a thing!"

Which, considering the number of busybodies concentrated within their small neighborhood, spoke to the skill of those who'd entered. Not reassuring. She needed to send her sister-in-law away as quickly as possible. But not without first hearing what she'd come to say. With five young children in her household, Livli often looked drained. Today, she also looked distraught. Two dark circles pooled beneath her eyes as if she'd not slept in days.

"You're scaring me," Isa said, trying to redirect the conversation.

Her sister-in-law was a wonderful woman, but she lived a simple, traditional life. Which included a culture of gossip among the other wives. Tempting though it was to use that network to warn the Glasgow Finn about her uncle, she and Alec were already losing their ability to move about with stealth.

Livli blinked, then tore her eyes away from Alec and frowned. "Aron dropped off your houseboat, then disappeared without explanation, before we could catch him, as he's wont to do these days. With your sister and Jona missing, we've been so worried."

Drawing her next breath was a struggle. "Missing?"

"They were traveling here, to visit those of us who were unable to attend the wedding, but never arrived. Your brother went home to Lewis to help search. They found Nina yesterday." Livli shook her head slightly. "It makes no sense, none at all, but your sister was found at Traigh Ghearadha. Sitting upon the sand, staring out to sea."

Traigh Ghearadha. A beach north of Stornoway and not overly distant from a number of sea caves. *Not missing. Taken.* A band of iron wrapped about her chest and began to ratchet tighter.

"She's injured and won't speak." Livli's voice, though hushed, came out in an insistent rush. "Save one word: your name. Over and over. You need to go home. Now."

"I'll grab my gear." Alec's voice boomed from the end of the hallway. He turned and disappeared into the kitchen.

Livli's eyes grew round. "That man," she hissed. "You can't mean to take him with you. Not to Stornoway. Already there are whispers, Isa. Your good name is being dragged across barnacles."

Reminding herself that her sister-in-law only wanted the best for her, Isa tethered her irritation. "Tradition dictated my first marriage. We were miserable. There's a reason I avoid your table, Livli. You I like. Not so much the matchmakers or strange men constantly pressed upon me. *If* I ever marry again, I will choose. Until that time, my affairs are my own."

Torrid ones and all.

Livli gasped. At Isa's proclamation or the man who now stood beside her, she couldn't tell.

Alec's rucksack was slung across his shoulder and he clasped the handle of her own bag in his hand. "I took the liberty of packing the notebook and a few skeet pigeons. I don't believe there's any reason to remain here."

"None." Save to paint a target on their backs. Better to face her family—her uncle—dead on. She lifted her chin. "To the docks."

~~~

With his team away and his brother unable to throw him a bone, there was no chance of stopping a pair of madmen by remaining in Glasgow.

It was an awful situation, but Isa's sister offered them the best—and only—lead they had to follow. The shreds of his career were flapping in the wind and the only way to earn a new sail was to locate Commodore Drummond's sea cave, collect damning evidence and put an end to his macabre experiments.

Two individuals against a man with enough resources and willpower to build that megalodon, to devise a biomech octopus, to transform a simple amoeba into a creature that would eat away at the flesh of his own people. Isa's uncle, though deranged, was a formidable foe with an as-yet undetermined goal.
~~~

Traveling to meet her family was as much about peeking into Finn psychology as it was locating a sea cave where they might—or might not—find answers. Isa was beautiful, intelligent and possessed of a steadfast loyalty to her people. Some would argue her mother must be of the same mindset, but he need look no further than his own family to know that sometimes the apple fell from the tree, rolled down a hill and sprouted in an entirely different environment.

If he was brutally honest with himself, he was also looking forward to meeting the rest of her family for entirely selfish reasons. Had he lost his mind? Possibly. His sister would call it love. Perhaps it was the same thing. Not that it mattered. They barely knew each other. He had no business contemplating a future with her. Not now.

With daylight fading fast, they navigated the River Clyde heading out into the Firth of Clyde. They wouldn't reach Stornoway until dawn which left plenty of time for conversation.

For the last hour, Isa had stood, her back stiff and straight with worry, clutching the brass and wood steering wheel as she stared at the horizon. If willpower alone could hasten them to their destination, they'd already be past the Isle of Skye.

Enough brooding.

"Both my brothers are spies," he said simply. *That* caught her attention.

She looked at him, the fine arches of her eyebrows lifting. "Secret agents? Ought you be telling me such things?"

He shrugged a shoulder. "It rather feels like we've moved past a superficial friendship as your intimate secrets have been laid bare."

Her cheeks grew pink, and he let his gaze wander over her attire. Oh, yes, he'd definitely been thinking about their morning activities. Especially now. Upon boarding, she'd disappeared into her cabin and emerged looking rather like a pirate. Knee-high boots, bloomers, a lightly boned corset and a bolero jacket spoke to practicality and sailing upon choppy waters—even if a surfeit of ruffles fell from her elbows and cascaded down her backside from the short skirt she'd ruched to her hips. She'd even tied a bright red bandana about her hair. A cutlass would complete the picture with perfection, but the dive knife strapped to her thigh was also rousing.

Not the time. And what better way to tamp down his libido than to talk about his family? "My sister, Cait, has a certain talent with poisons, the more unusual, the better." He tipped his head, contemplating possible outcomes of introducing them to each other. "I rather think you'd like her."

"Poisons and spies." The corner of her mouth quirked upward. "Have your parents any idea of the nest of vipers they spawned?"

"None." He grinned back. "My father spends his life chasing business opportunities and women. He is successful at both, leaving little time for family life. My mother lives her life in denial." He snorted a laugh. "She's set upon marrying Cait to a gentleman. It would take a strong man to take a wife who wears a poison ring and has an inclination to use it. Even so, Cait has no interest in marriage and uses her dark complexion—clearly marking her as another man's daughter—to keep suitors at bay."

"Ah, that I know something about," Isa said. "The flames of my hair forewarned all Finn men of my unsuitability. Go on. Tell me more about your brothers."

"Your hair is beautiful. Their inability to appreciate it is their loss." He paused, pleased to see a smile tug at her lips. "I've not seen hide nor hair of Quinn—eldest and heir—for months. All my other brother will tell me is that Quinn's mission is classified. Logan, known in his circles as Mr. Black, planted me in Roideach's laboratory. He's on a hunt for members of CEAP, the Committee for the Exploration of Anthropomorphic Peculiarities, a group of dishonorable individuals set on studying humans with unusual traits or abilities."

"Like selkies." Her lips pressed together into a thin line. "There's a certain irony to this situation. My uncle, the very kind of individual this committee seeks, infiltrating the membership of such a group before manipulating its knowledge and resources to his own objectives."

Which brought them around to motivation. They were overlooking something important about the man's psyche, and it likely had something to do with the Finn mindset. "Tell me about this community of yours." Leaning against the helm, he pried one slender hand free from the spokes and pressed a kiss against her fingers.

"You're wondering about the scars," she said.

"Of course," he answered, tracing a fingertip over the faint lines that marked the inside edges of her fingers. "But I'm also trying to entice you back into my arms." He tugged on her hand.

Isa's features softened, and she scanned the instrument panel affixed to the helm before her. She set in their course and flipped the lever enabling automated pilot. "Very well. Who can resist such an opportunity to unburden a childhood trauma upon such strong, broad shoulders?"

"I do believe that's the first compliment you've paid me." He led her to the railing. Turning her to face the setting sun, he wrapped his arms about her waist and pulled her close, letting his fingers trace the brocade pattern of her bodice at her waist.

"A man of action wants words?" Teasing incredulity lifted her voice.

He laughed and pressed a kiss to the top of her head, to the bandana that struggled to keep the copper threads of her hair bound, fighting against a salty wind that kept plucking free strand after strand. It was true. He much preferred waking to find her soft and warm upon his lap trailing appreciative fingertips over the contours of his body. She relaxed against him, and his groin stirred to life, but now was not the time.

"From what you tell me, the Finn people are proud of their heritage, if perhaps a bit rigid. Why, then, remove the webbing between fingers?"

"The same reason my mother would have me dye my hair brown. Marriage." She sighed. "Every year introduces another technology that shrinks our world. There's no avoiding interaction with Scots, particularly if a young man wishes to pursue a profitable trade in a town or city. Such progressive Finn don't want to be labeled 'other', nor do they wish to marry a woman who would be shunned for such a deformity. The number of alterations I perform upon fingers is ever-increasing."

"Toes?" he asked.

She turned in his arms, lifting a hand to push aside strands of wind-whipped hair. "And pointed ears."

Alec touched a finger to its scarred surface and shook his head. "Pressured to dye your hair brown."

"Ah," she said, tapping his chest. "Because we are to marry Finn men, and they—and their relatives—know red hair means my bloodline is not pure."

"Pure." Society had a decided tendency to pass judgment on such nonsense. Witness his brother, half Gypsy, and his sister, half Indian. "It would seem your uncle subscribes to this notion both literally and figuratively."

Isa rolled her eyes. "When we were small children, he would gather us all about the peat fire on cold winter nights and tell stories about how we, the Finn people, are descended from a magical Saami shaman who was able to shapeshift into the form of a seal." A glimmer of a smile twitched at her lips. "His adventures beneath the waves were extensive. My favorite involved a sunken Viking ship and a treasure chest full of gold."

"What child wouldn't?" he agreed. "Is that the origin of the selkie myth?"

She shrugged. "Perhaps. Many believe the Finn people originated in Norway, arriving here via the Shetland and Orkney islands. Our language does share some similarity with those of the Sea Saami, but after so many centuries, who can say?" She winced. "The boat attacked by the megalodon?"

He nodded.

"Was filled with members of two Finn families spanning three generations. They were headed to the Shetland Islands with the intent to establish a fishing colony upon its shores where they could speak the old language and follow old traditions."

Two Finn families, their lives shredded. Some killed, some kidnapped. All of it overseen and orchestrated by Commodore Drummond. Who was out for blood. Literally.

"What if your uncle was selectively choosing those Finn who express factor Q?"

Her jaw dropped. "He—or his minions—could screen by looking first for syndactyly. Later, they could perform a more conclusive blood test. But why would he want to drain the blood of those positive for factor Q?"

"I'm not certain," he said. "Before this series of disasters rained down upon us, my brother brought me a curious piece of ceramic that was attached to a fragment of biomech octopus skin. It contained numerous tiny pores, as if it were designed as a filter. Until I saw *two* tentacles reaching for you, until I learned about factor Q, I was at a loss to guess at its function."

"Blood. It's *filtering* blood! Not simply extracting it." She gasped. "Two tentacles. One to extract the blood of a Finn, a ceramic filter, another tentacle to return the blood."

Every brain cell buzzed with activity, drawing connections, synthesizing all evidence with what Isa had just told him. "Octopuses breathe under water by means of gills. Between the natural abilities of the Finn people, the unusual blood that runs in your arteries and veins, attaching a such biomech creature could enhance a Finn's natural ability to dive beneath the water's surface for an extended period of time."

"And stay there indefinitely." A hand flew to her throat. "What a ghastly idea." She shuddered. "But it could work. Integrating the gills of a cephalopod and the abilities of a Finn. So horribly simple."

"Yet complex," Alec pointed out. "The skill, the engineering required to construct—grow—such a creature." He shook his head. "It should be impossible, and yet—"

"All evidence points exactly to that particular goal." She swallowed. "My uncle is utterly amoral. But after the way he's treated me, I really ought not be surprised at all."

"Your *sister* escaped," he pointed out. "A *woman* was overlooked upon that ship bound for the Shetland Islands. Only *men* have washed up following an attempted tentacle attachment. The more information we gather, the more I begin to think Commodore Drummond is building some kind of unusual task force."

"Aether," she whispered. All color drained from her face.

He squeezed her hand. "We'll speak to your sister and locate her husband." For the first time in months, the weight on his chest lifted. The ugliness of the situation was not over, not by a long shot. But at least he could finally wrap his mind around the facts and begin to make plans. He patted a pocket sewn into his jacket. "I've an assortment of punch cards, and the minute we find this sea cave, we'll call in reinforcements. Shutting down this kind of operation is the reason my teammates joined the Navy."

Chapter Twenty-Five

Isa had been certain she wouldn't be able to sleep, but she could scarce remember past the point her cheek touched the pillow. Alec had insisted she rest. Between recent revelations, worries about her sister and the complications of bringing a Scot directly to her mother's doorstep, she hadn't been thinking clearly. Even now, with so many thoughts whirling inside her skull, it took her a moment to realize that her boat no longer sailed on the open water, but was tied alongside the quay. In Stornoway.

Less than two weeks ago, she'd attended her sister's wedding. What had Nina ever done to deserve such treatment from their uncle? She'd married a Finn fisherman, celebrated her vows upon the beach and moved into a small, nearby cottage. How long had her uncle plotted against Nina and her husband? Had he stood beside them at their wedding, contemplating their abduction even as his daughter was dedicated to the sea? The smoldering coals of hate Isa forever carried in her chest burned hotter. Stopping her uncle—permanently—was the only thing that would ever extinguish them.

And Maren. What was her place in all of this? Maren had excitedly pushed Isa to accept Anton's proposal. "It's everything you've ever dreamed." But the ink wasn't dry on her marriage certificate before Maren announced her own engagement to Isa's uncle and refused to answer any of her messages. Now her own brother had disappeared, leaving Isa to wonder what kind of understanding the two shared.

She rubbed at a pain in her stiff jaw, then climbed down from her bunk to dress. Much as she might wish to parade through the streets in a brilliant emerald dress, her bright hair loose and flowing, she needed to hold on to every scrap of respectability left to her. To that end, she donned her usual island uniform of dull gray wool and bound her hair into a tight knot at the base of her neck. Fixing her cape about her shoulders and drawing the hood over her hair, she stepped out onto the deck holding her medical bag.

Once the ever-present ocean winds would have blown her distress away, but today they merely plucked at her ankle-length skirts, snatched at her hood and screeched in her ear as if in league with Mrs. Carr, howling even louder when Alec turned to face her.

He took in her attire with a frown. "Necessary, I assume, to appease the elders?"

"It also helps stem the flow of marriage offers." A flash of color—indicating a complete end to her mourning—would have the matchmakers and their male clients descending upon her and her family like midges on a warm body.

"In which case, I approve. I prefer to be the only man wondering about the color of your corset." He stepped closer, catching her by the waist, and leaned close. He smelled of leather and salt and soap, a toe-curling combination. His lips brushed the shell of her ear. "Might it be blue with a swirl of embroidery?"

"It might." With a faint smile she rocked onto her toes, his gentle tease buoying her despite the tension threatening to turn her every muscle into stone.

"Come." He climbed from the boat onto the quay and held out a hand to help her ashore. "Time to scandalize your mother."

They left the harbor and turned onto a street that led past The Dragon and the Flea. Too early for it to be open, but she needed to restock her supplies. Today if possible. "How long has it been since we arrived?" Given the events surrounding her last visit, news of her boat at the quay would spread quickly, and she did not wish to be drawn into the local drama, particularly as it was the Carr's son—Maren's brother—who was missing.

"Perhaps thirty minutes."

An entire half hour. "We'll be expected, then."

His eyebrows lifted. "Biscuits? Butter?"

She could almost hear the growl of his hopeful stomach over the wind. Their last few meals resembled soldier's rations, confined to crusty bread resembling hardtack and the few tinned items—mutton, apricots and condensed milk—that Aron had not consumed while piloting her boat back to Glasgow. "Sausage and black pudding," she promised with a smile. "But only if you can manage to convince my mother that I'm not your mistress. We need her to focus on the situation, not our relationship." Nor could they afford to burn any bridges.

"Understood."

Was it her imagination, or did his voice hold a regretful note?

Soon their booted feet crunched over the gravel of the path that led to her mother's home, a squat, thatched blackhouse on a hillside beside the sea. A curl of peat smoke rose from its chimney, one that was quickly snatched away by the ever-present wind.

Before she could knock, the door flew open. "Isa!" Her mother's relieved smile turned stiff and starchy—held in place by sheer will—when her eyes fell on the man who stood beside her daughter. Easy to tell from Alec's height that he was anything but Finn. "And who is this... gentleman you've brought with you?" Her mother's voice rose to a piercing pitch as she struggled with civility. As always, her focus was on the man, on controlling her daughter's "future" as a wife and mother.

Isa quickly performed introductions. "Dr. McCullough and I are colleagues. He graciously agreed to accompany me to see what can be done to help Nina."

"Colleagues." The word was spoken with extreme doubt as her mother crossed her arms and glowered. A firm believer in the Finn tradition of arranged marriages, she'd long ago dismissed any contributions Isa might make to society as a woman of medicine, and Isa had long ago stopped trying to convince her otherwise. "Would this be same doctor who assisted you with your examination of Larsa?"

Hands balled at her sides, Isa stepped forward so quickly her mother had no choice but to step backward into her cottage. "Yes." The word exited between clenched teeth. "And he's trying to help, no thanks to Mr. or Mrs. Carr." She dragged in a breath. "Nina's husband—their missing son—might be the next to wash up on shore. Dr. McCullough is here to help. Me. Her. You."

"No need." Her mother lifted her chin.

Isa bit her tongue so hard it nearly bled. It took her far longer than it once had to unlock her jaw and reply in a civil manner. "I'm told Nina is asking for me. I came to see her. Now."

"Well, of course," her mother huffed. "You *are* her sister."

Her mother turned on her heel and led Isa through the blackhouse—past the peat fire and a dresser laden with crockery and through the narrow door that led into the bedroom. A single candle burned upon a low chest that was pushed beside the box bed. Her sister lay on the straw mattress with a foot propped up on a pillow, eyes closed and face sallow. Alec followed.

"They found her like this." Her mother dipped a rag in a bucket of cold water, wringing it out before draping it over Nina's forehead. "She's been delirious for two days. Mostly she sleeps. But when she wakes she's raving about your uncle and Jona and a giant shark. And you." The last two words were grudgingly spoken. "Your brother is out with the men looking for Jona."

"What happened?" Isa focused on drawing forth the facts. Worry needed to wait.

"They took Jona's boat and were on their way to Glasgow, to visit family. A day later, Mr. Wilson spotted Nina on the beach." Her mother peeled back the sleeve of Nina's nightgown, and Isa gasped, reaching out to touch the hot, swollen flesh. "Her skin is scraped and bruised all over, like she was tossed against the cliffs."

Alec's gaze caught hers briefly, but he said nothing as he shifted silently in the corner, his black wool coat buttoned to his chin.

Her mother frowned. "Nina needs her sister, not a stranger. You'd best come with me. I suppose you'll want something to eat."

"That would be lovely, Mrs. Guthrie." His voice low yet firm. "But I'll stay for now."

"Hrmph." Her mother turned and left.

"Nina?" Isa sat on the edge of the bed beside her sister and smoothed long, brown strands of hair from her face while Alec stayed hidden in the shadows. "It's me, Isa. I've come."

"Isa?" Her sister's gray eyes slitted open, her voice fogged with fever as she struggled to speak. "No one would believe... you were right... all that time... our uncle not to be trusted... or Maren... only you understand."

She did. "Can you tell me what happened, Nina?"

"Hates me. Hates you. Hated Da."

Their father? What had this to do with anything? A few years ago, her father hadn't returned from the harbor. His body had been found nearby, badly beaten. His pockets had been turned out, every last shilling gone. His murderer was never caught.

After that, everything had changed. With her brother Danel already in Glasgow with a wife and infant, he'd willingly handed the reins to Uncle Gregor after the funeral. In her grief, her mother had been grateful to let her brother take control, an abdication of responsibility that had ended in Isa's arranged marriage.

Mother of Pearl. Was their uncle that Machiavellian? Had he murdered their father? Her blood ran cold.

Nina lifted a hand and spread her fingers wide. "Maren tested my blood. Said scars are lies. Not Finn enough. Never was a good swimmer." Her eyes closed again. "Uncle is fixing. Wants pure blood only."

Her sister not Finn enough? Utter nonsense. But if her uncle—and Maren—were screening members of their community for factor Q, they would uncover outliers, men and women who possessed the physical characteristics of Finn, but did not express the glycoprotein in their blood. Alas, blood levels of factor Q *did* determine a Finn's ability to dive. And her uncle's obsession with attaching a biomech octopus meant that blood levels of factor Q would prejudice his opinion as to what traits defined a Finn.

"Nina, wake up." She patted her sister's burning cheek. "Please, try to focus. You were on a boat..."

"A shark... yellow, glowing eyes." Nina reached out and latched onto Isa's wrist. "We were attacked. Carried into its belly. I woke up on a ledge inside a sea cave."

"Where?"

"Not certain." She rocked her head back and forth on the pillow. "North of Traigh Ghearadha."

"How did you manage to escape?"

"A woman chained to the rock pushed me back into the water. Told me to go, that they were distracted. That I needed to swim for help. That the octopus would kill my husband if I didn't hurry." Nina struggled onto her elbows, but fell back, weeping. "I have to go back for Jona."

She blotted the tears from her sister's eyes. "We're going to bring Jona home as soon as we can, as soon as we can find the cave." A promise she would keep. Or die trying. A decided possibility. "Is there anything more you can tell me?"

"The cliffs were tall and the opening to the cave was under the water."

Isa wanted to scream in frustration. If the opening to the sea cave wasn't visible, how were they to find it?

"How long were you in the water?" Alec prompted from his dark corner.

"Who's there?" Nina's eyes flew wide open, recoiling and drawing breath as if to scream.

"A friend," Isa said hastily. "A doctor who's here to help. Please, Nina, how long did you swim down the coastline?"

"An hour? Maybe two." Nina's fingers worried the edge of her blanket, her voice tight with anguish and uncertainty. "I'm not sure."

"It's something," Alec said. "If we take that information, account for weather, currents and tides—"

"We can narrow the location of cave," Isa finished. "But finding the opening..." Impossible to search that stretch of the coastline by swimming underwater along its length.

"Recall that my brother found the castle all but empty. I overheard plans to consolidate their work in the sea cave. Though your mother sent for your uncle, he will first wish to unload cargo and his associates. To move them into the cave, the megalodon will need to surface." He straightened. "Sea caves tend to form in specific locations. Do you have any topographical or nautical charts?"

"We have both."

After calming Nina and tucking her beneath the covers, Isa led Alec back into the main room—where the smell of breakfast frying in a pan made her own stomach growl—and pulled a number of rolled maps from a drawer. Together they stretched them out upon the table while her mother watched with pursed lips. "This is where they found Nina," she said, pointing.

"If you'll mix the bannocks," her mother from beside the fire, "we can feed our guest."

It wasn't a request. A woman's place was in the kitchen, beside her mother, where words could be exchanged under one's breath in relative privacy.

Which was why Isa hastened to wind the clockwork mixer. But though its grinding sounds discouraged conversation, it didn't stop her mother from dropping a daguerreotype onto the counter. Metallic and monochromatic, one Mr. Reid stared up at her without so much as a smile.

"No," Isa said, skipping the usual preliminaries and cutting straight to the quick. She measured and poured oat and barley flour, butter and milk into the mixer's bowl, then stood watching the paddles beat the dough into submission. Satisfied with the ratio, she brushed flour from hands and turned toward the fire to check the heat of the griddle that hung above it.

"Mr. Reid is most keen," her mother said. "And he doesn't mind small imperfections."

Meaning her red hair or her presumed infertility. Hers. Even dead, Anton's masculinity would not be called into question.

"Because he has three children under the age of five. He does not wish for a wife, he wishes for a housekeeper and a nanny but has no means to hire one." No doubt he also wished to find someone to hold still while he *eased* his male needs upon her body as well, but she kept that thought to herself. She turned away, flipping the switch to turn off the clockwork mixer. She ripped pieces of dough free, shaping them and dropping them onto the griddle.

"Enough!" her mother hissed. "It's time to put aside your unconventional, unfeminine lifestyle and marry. Already the village matchmaker warns me that her network buzzes with speculation and rumors about your suitability. You are a widow, no longer fresh and untouched."

"I'm only twenty-five!"

Her mother crossed her arms. "Old. I had three children by that age. Mr. Reid owns five fishing boats. He has employees. He is an unqualified catch. You say you want to help our people. Marry him. Help him and, yes, his three children. I'm only looking out for you, Isa."

Alec cleared his throat. "As a surgeon, Mrs. McQuiston's profession touches many lives—"

Isa's mother stiffened. "My daughter is no such thing."

"Not officially, no. But she trained at Dr. McQuiston's side for years. Longer than some surgeons who touch scalpel to skin. Tethering her to a hearth with apron strings would deprive far too many people of her help."

"Alec." Isa tugged at his sleeve. No one ever won this battle.

"Her uncle was wrong to marry her to a Glasgow physician, but at least her husband kept his promise." Her mother planted her hands on her hips. "And who does she bring home? Another doctor. You're only encouraging her delusions. She risks her future, traveling about with you—unchaperoned—a man who is not even a Finn."

"Promise?" Dread trickled down her spine. "What promise did Anton make you?"

"That he would keep you out of medical school and in the home. Where a woman belongs."

Isa staggered backward from the blow of her mother's words. There was a faint scent of something burning. The memories of her marriage turning to ash. Her mother cried out and pushed past her, rushing to the hearth.

Her entire marriage had been one lie after the other. Could any man in her life be trusted? *Alec.* Not only did he treat her as an equal, he didn't shield her from difficult or unpleasant truths. Impossible for the matchmakers to ever unearth a man who could compare.

Chapter Twenty-Six

Alec followed Isa outside and down to the rocky shore. The wind spit water at them, and dark clouds collecting overhead promised a more thorough soaking in the near future. When he'd met her, he'd assumed that a widow of independent means would be free to enjoy his attentions. Instead, he'd learned she faced an intense pressure to remarry on nearly all fronts.

Uncertain what to say, he stood beside her, silent.

"My mother is right about one thing," she said, wrapping her arms about herself. "If the University of Glasgow once again denies my application, my choices are limited. Apply further abroad. Pursue my current life as an itinerant healer. Or marry."

They'd promised each other an affair, but his presence here, working with her as a physician negatively impacted her reputation within the Finn community. A continued association would cause potential patients to turn her away, possibly ending her career among the Finn. He wasn't even certain marrying her would help.

Marriage had never been something he'd seriously considered, tainted as his view was by his parents' bad example. If he were being brutally honest, he had to admit there was a certain appeal to the idea of marrying a woman with a strong mind, one driven to pursue interests that overlapped with his own. He would miss Isa when their lives pulled them in opposite directions, for he was rather enjoying their liaison, both in and out of bed.

Chair.

Alec grinned. Then sobered. Had he actually just considered proposing? His heart gave a great thud. Marriage wasn't what she wanted. Nor him. Not now.

But maybe he could peel back a cloud?

"There are always alternatives," he said. There *had* to be. "We will catch two madmen and put an end to whatever nefarious plan they have in mind, thereby preventing further deaths of British citizens. The Queen will be indebted. With a wave of her royal scepter, she will offer to grant you one wish. And you will say..."

A hint of a smile tugged at her lips. "I wish to attend medical school, Your Highness."

"And that will be that. You'll remain in Glasgow." He closed the gap between them, tracing the edge of her jaw with his finger. "And whenever I'm on base, I will make clandestine calls, dragging you away from dry textbooks for practical exercises in human anatomy that will have you screaming in delight."

Isa's eyes fluttered closed. "Promises, promises. No sooner made than they are broken."

He couldn't fix them, but he would endeavor not to add to her list. "Not all men are afraid of a woman's intelligence," Alec murmured as he ran his thumb over her mouth. He pressed a quick kiss to her lips and deliberately took a long step backward. "Time to hunt for a secret, underwater cave. I expect your uncle will return at dusk, after the fishing boats have put into harbor when any unusual vessels or activities are unlikely to be remarked upon. I've plotted likely locations for caves in the area and would like to narrow down the possibilities. Shall we say goodbye to your mother and take to the sea?"

~~~

They returned for a brief silent and tense meal—for which his stomach was eternally grateful—then parted ways. As they descended the narrow roadway that led back to the main road, they passed a handful of individuals who declined to return Isa's greeting, including one Mrs. Carr who stood in the doorway of her blackhouse scowling. Though she uttered not a word, Alec could swear he heard her growl.

Back stiff and chin held high, Isa insisted they make a brief stop at The Dragon and the Flea. "It's impossible
~~~

to know how many men—or women—my uncle is holding inside that cave or how many biomech octopuses may be attached."

"We can't manage a full-scale rescue operation," Alec argued, growing increasingly worried as he eyed the supplies the shopkeeper piled upon the counter at Isa's behest. Not only did a number of amber glass bottles containing usual anesthetic compounds rest upon the counter, she'd decimated the man's supply of sharksilk and severely depleted his store of bandages before sending him hunting for every last hemostatic clamp—excellent for clamping a bleeding vessel—he could locate. "This is only a sneak and peek."

"I'm aware." She pointed her chin at the message Alec now printed on a long strip of paper. "Neither can we assume there will be time to return to Stornoway should your men arrive to assist."

"True." He blew at the ink—impatient to be on their way—and rolled it up before inserting it into a brass canister and affixing it to the leg of a skeet pigeon. He slid the punch card into the bird's cipher cartridge and wound the clockwork mechanism.

Minutes later they emerged, laden with brown paper-wrapped packages tied up with string, and he threw the skeet pigeon aloft. By the time they arrived at the pier, the bird was no more than a black dot in the eastern sky.

~~~
~~~

Isa's boat rose and fell upon the waves. After dropping anchor near one potential sea cave after another, daylight was now fading fast. Alec unhooked the boat's Lucifer lamp and stowed it in a cabinet, lest its glow attract unwanted attention. The blue paint upon their hull would allow them to blend into the vast expanse of night-dark water.

Much hung upon his supposition that Isa's uncle would visit this secret, underwater cave. Doubt crept in. They were bobbing on the waves beside Hebridean cliffs, acting upon the assertions of a feverish woman. Her story rang true, but could they truly trust the accuracy of her report?

Perhaps he should have insisted upon bringing Isa's sister with them, despite her fever. What if Commodore Drummond returned to Stornoway and learned of their proximity? Would he harm Nina? Come hunting them in turn?

Aether, he missed his team. With a few more pairs of eyes, all possibilities could be covered. The meager selection of weapons and ammunition he had on hand—an air rifle and pistol fitted with TTX darts, both useless under water—put them at a disadvantage. He thought of the skeet pigeon, winging its way to Glasgow. He'd even be grateful for his brother's assistance, but ever since his promotion this past fall, Logan was more distracted than ever.

Returning to the deck, he glanced at his time piece. This would be Isa's fifth and final dive for the day. She'd been underwater sixteen minutes and was due to surface momentarily.

Though a blow to his pride, he'd been forced to admit that sending her—a Finn—below water to make a preliminary survey of the rock face was the only feasible approach. Not only would swimming tire his still-sore knee, but his aquaspira breather could absorb carbon dioxide for a sum total of only three hours without replacing the scrubber canister filled with soda lime. He'd already expended thirty minutes of breathing time crossing the loch and wanted to save every last minute for the moment Isa found an underwater cave entrance that held promise.

Wearing his dive suit—knife strapped to his thigh—wasn't mere readiness or optimism, it was necessary protection against the cold wind that lashed across the deck. Still, he kept his swim fins and his aquaspira breather easily accessible.

He lifted his spyglass again, scanning the water for the hundredth time. So far only a few innocent fishing boats had ventured near the coast, but even those had departed for harbor now. There was nothing more he could do at the moment save watch and wait. It made his skin itch.

A faint sound alerted him to Isa's return, and he set aside the spyglass, reaching for a woolen blanket to hand her as she climbed onto the deck and stood, wearing nothing but a dive knife strapped to her thigh. With her skin made golden by the setting sun, it was impossible not to stare. A twist of crimson-wet hair. Rosy-peaked breasts. The gentle flare of hips. He gaped, unable to imagine being ready to let this woman leave his life any time soon.

She blushed at his open admiration and wrapped the blanket about her shoulders. "No luck. A promising beginning, but the channel only cut into the cliff a dozen feet or so."

He placed a hand over his heart. "We may hunt a monster, but I'll never grow tired of this sight."

It baffled him how no one in her community fully appreciated the gem in their midst. Scorned for the color of her hair, tolerated for her healing skills, all of them—particularly her relatives—sought to anchor her to a small fishing village, to wall her away, cutting her off from the world and all it had to offer.

Isa sauntered forward to rise onto the bare tips of her toes and plant a kiss on the edge of his jaw. "Careful," she teased. "You might start wanting to keep me."

"And if I did?" His heart gave an approving thud at the thought.

"Consider the ramifications. The sight of your very own selkie has enchanted you to the point of distraction."

She tipped her head, and he followed her gaze. There, on the distant horizon, the dark silhouette of an approaching vessel. He grabbed his spyglass.

A steamboat chugged slowly in their direction. For several long minutes they watched, passing the spyglass back and forth. And then he saw it. As the sun sank behind the Isle of Lewis, a few last rays of light glinted off a dorsal fin. Water poured off the back of a gray, metal cylinder that rose from the sea, its eyes glowing a faint yellow. Shadows shifted behind the odd window as those within ran about at their various tasks.

"The megalodon has surfaced."

Isa snatched the spyglass from his hands, looked, then set it aside. "Its snout is pointed away from the cliffs." She pointed at the dark shadow of the sea cliffs. "Mark that formation in your memory."

"The megalodon has never been glimpsed by the Navy," Alec mused aloud. "As Commodore Drummond, your uncle would not want anyone to connect him to such a unique and deadly submersible."

"You think he travels aboard the boat. That the megalodon rises to meet him."

Alec nodded. "To transport him into the sea cave along with anything deemed worthy of salvaging from the castle."

"We need to get closer." She threw aside her blanket. "Let's go."

"Isa, wait." He caught her wrist. "They're more than half a mile distant. The water is frigid. You've been swimming all day."

She smiled, but waved a hand, dismissing his concern. "The cold doesn't bother me. Besides, there's no choice."

He nodded, then pulled on his swim fins and reached for his goggles. "Be careful not to alert them to our presence."

Together, they slid into the water. Isa set a blistering pace and, by the time they reached the megalodon, he was so impressed he would have declared his undying devotion. Except his lungs were filled with fire. His oxygen-starved muscles were bathed in lactic acid. And he'd swallowed enough seawater to pickle his last meal. His arthroflex knee—thank aether—was the only part of his body that didn't throb or burn.

They held onto the megalodon's pectoral fin, beside what might have been termed gill slits, were they not covered with metal screening and serving to take on water to cool the internal combustion engine. Yet there was genuine sharkskin covering a yielding sort of flesh beneath his hands. The biotechnology involved in this creature's construction was at once both fascinating and horrifying.

Alec stared at the small steam-powered boat that now approached. As the captain reversed its engines, bringing the boat to a stop, the submersible's jaw opened with a faint metallic creak. A glowing Lucifer lamp hung from the roof of its mouth as several armed men jogged up a kind of staircase, spreading out behind jagged, metal teeth upon a grated platform. A vaguely familiar woman followed, fashionably attired but—oddly—barefoot.

"Maren!" Isa hissed beside him. "And those beside her holding harpoons were gathered around my sister's wedding bonfire."

An entire assortment of traitorous guests, loyal to one particular Finn.

Commodore Drummond himself stepped out onto the bow of the ship. Men rushed forward to drop a gangway between the two vessels so that he might cross to his wife.

Rather than greeting her with any kind of fondness, he cut to the quick. “Nina escaped, and you’ve allowed her to live. Why?”

Alec strained, listening for the answer.

“Simple expediency,” Maren answered her husband. “Whisper a few well-chosen threats in her ear, and Nina will clamp her lips together to save her husband. Though she tested negative for factor Q and is, therefore, expendable, my brother’s blood has proven most pure. As predicted by our biochemist, the increased level of factor Q allowed the bypass octopus to attach to Jona exceptionally well. Provided Nina remains unharmed, he is prepared to cooperate with our demands. I thought perhaps such a reprieve might be a useful policy, subject to your agreement, of course.”

“I see.” The commodore stroked his chin. “The family of any Finn that turn traitor are subject to extermination, unless a full-blooded male submits to attachment.”

The answering smile Maren displayed contained far too many teeth. “After all you have invested in the future of the Finn culture, why waste precious natural resources?”

Pureness of blood. Future of a people. Drummond had a lofty vision for the future. A Finn could assist his quest or be sacrificed to the cause.

"Brilliant, as always." Drummond drew his hand down the side of Maren's face, his eyes gleaming with prideful possession. "Now turn your mind to the problem of my other niece. She and that Scot need to be eliminated."

"She still lives?" Maren's lips twisted. "I thought—"

"Aye, a problem we shall take steps to correct. Soon. Tonight, however, we have a collection to make. I've received word that several Finn men—likely pure bloods—are at sea this evening. We'll return to the cave and collect a volunteer to help us fetch them."

Maren nodded. "As you wish."

"A moment..." He turned toward the armed men and snapped his fingers. "Send over the passengers and begin offloading the materials."

Lord Roideach crossed the bridge to the megalodon's mandible first, his hand wrapped tightly about his son's wrist. Miss Russel followed, a small bag in hand, her every step cautious, her wide-eyed gaze darting about. Behind her, men began to carry wooden crates from the boat onto the megalodon and down its throat.

Thomas, jumping and leaping with excitement, tugged at his father's restraint. "Mother?"

Maren bent low and opened her arms, her expression now one of warm, maternal welcome. "Thomas! I do believe you've grown another inch!"

The boy slipped his father's grip to throw himself into Maren's arms. "Do you have my seal skin ready?"

"Of course, darling." Her smile faltered as she looked at her Finn husband, sparing not a glance to the man who—in British eyes—had made her Lady Roideach.

"Keep the children close," Drummond said. "With a BURR team member involved, we need to increase security."

Maren nodded. "We'll be below."

Roideach moved to follow, but the commodore lifted his hand. Several weapons pointed directly at the lord's chest.

"I've done everything you asked," Roideach said. "She's mine. You agreed. A woman can have only one husband."

"You misunderstood." Drummond shook his head. "I promised to let her choose. And her choice is clear." He unholstered his own pistol and pointed it at Roideach. "She has chosen her own people, and I will see her crowned a queen."

"Sir!" Miss Russel exclaimed.

"You need me!" Roideach yelled, fisting his hands at his side.

Without taking his eyes from his quarry, Drummond spoke. "Do I? Miss Russel, need him? Or, without the constant threat of his wandering hands, might you prove an exceptional scientist?"

"I—" Miss Russel stammered, glancing between the men.

"Let's find out, shall we?"

Bang!

Roideach fell, clutching his abdomen and howling in pain.

Beside Alec, Isa sucked in a breath of salty sea spray.

"No harm will befall your son," Drummond said, bending over the lord. "He is, after all, a valued member of the peerage and a Finn. We mean to make good use of him." He placed the sole of his boot against the dying man's shoulder and shoved.

Splash.

"We've new volunteers to collect," Drummond announced. "We leave in two hours."

"Yes, sir!"

The small boat departed, leaving Roideach floating in the water, already forgotten.

Deep within the megalodon engines roared to life. The great mandible began to close, and the fin shuddered beneath his hands.

~~~

"I'm going with it," Isa announced. Discussion of the disturbing conversation they'd overheard would have to wait.

"With the megalodon?" Alec said, his blue eyes large behind the lenses of his swim goggles.

The Frankenstein fish shuddered and began to move. "I'll track its path. Meet you back at the boat."

"I need to find Roideach. Try to save him. I have questions." He grabbed her hand and squeezed before letting go, calling as the vessel picked up speed, dragging her away. "Please don't go inside the cave without me!"

Waves washed over her head, and she tightened her grip on the pectoral fin as the biomech creature turned. As it surged forward and began to submerge, she took
~~~

a deep breath. Pressure rose in her ears, in her lungs, across her body. Her endurance would not be tested by temperature or oxygen depletion, but by the strength found in her fingertips. She was tired and no match for a submersible moving at full speed.

The gleam of the megalodon's eyes cast a glow over the dark, gneiss cliffs that plunged deep into the water, revealing an even darker shadow inside the cliff. An underwater opening, ragged and rough. A mouth that waited to swallow the shark—her—whole.

Where Alec would never find her. And she needed him, needed his help.

Not a moment too soon, Isa released the pectoral fin. As the megalodon sped past, jets of water swirled about her, tossing her against rough rocks, knocking free what little air was left in her lungs and sending flashes of light across her vision. She couldn't lose consciousness. Not underwater. That meant death, even for a Finn.

Kicking furiously, she stroked upward, breaking the surface and dragging in great lungfuls of air. Waves crashed over her, flinging her at the sheer cliff. She scrabbled at the rough wall, seeking a handhold, but was dragged backward.

That's when she saw it. A crevice.

As the next wave pitched her forward, Isa angled her body, catching at the gap and wedging herself into its relative safety. Naked, cold, bruised and afraid for the lives of her sister and her brother-in-law, she forced herself to study the surrounding cliffs.

The opening through which the megalodon had passed was far enough beneath the water's surface that it was invisible. This stretch of cliffs was so sheer, so tall and treacherous, that there were no nearby villages, no natural harbors.

A perfect location for a mad Finn to ferment his delusions of grandeur while subjecting his own people to inhuman treatment.

~~~

Had Roideach resigned himself to a quiet death, Alec never would have found him midst the choppy waves. As it was, however, the man never stopped screeching for help, not even after the boat's engines faded away to nothing.

This frantic, the lord would drown them both long before his stomach wound would end him. Alec punched his UP bag, tied it to a length of rope and swam in the man's direction, careful to hold the buoy far in front. Shipwrecked men were rarely rational. The moment it hit Roideach on the shoulder, the man thrashed wildly, grabbing onto the float and clutching it to his chest.

"A simple thank you will suffice," Alec yelled, swimming backward until the rope drew taut, drawing the man in the direction of Isa's boat even though saving this particular man's life was about as appealing as dining on pufferfish prepared by an untrained chef.

"You!" Roideach sputtered, the whites of his eyes flashing.
~~~

"Me," Alec agreed. "We might make it back to my boat. Or we may not. Depends on your rate of blood loss, the speed at which I swim, and whether or not you answer my questions."

"Please," the lord begged. "I can't feel my feet anymore."

Cold or blood loss, impossible to say in these frigid waters. "CEAP. Name the committee members."

"Impossible. There are several subdivisions, divided by anthropomorphic curiosity. For security purposes. I served only on the Selkie Committee."

Aether, how many existed? He was willing to bet Logan knew. "Names!"

"Me. Lord Dankworth." A wave hit Roideach, and his grip slipped.

Hard to tell beneath a starlit sky, but Alec could swear the man spat bloody seawater from his mouth. The bullet had penetrated near the man's liver but appeared to also have caught a portion of his lung. In which case this would be a short interrogation.

"Dankworth is dead," Alec called. "Poisoned."

"Necessary. I had no choice." The man drew a ragged breath and started coughing again. More blood. "He discovered Drummond's true nature and threatened to expose him. Us."

Bilge rats had more personal honor. "Names! Or I stop swimming." Alec slowed.

"Commander Norgrove." Roideach's hands slipped again. He wasn't much longer for this earth.

Another traitor within the Royal Navy. Lovely. "His role?"

But a wave washed over Roideach's head, across the UP bag, and when the water receded, the lord's fingers no longer clutched the gas-filled float. *Dammit.*

This was an unwanted complication. Not the justice he'd planned for Roideach. Moreover, this would leave two extremely amoral Finn now in control of the unfortunate child's future. Treading water, Alec waited several long minutes. Waited until it was clear young Thomas had inherited the title.

Chapter Twenty-Seven

Alec pulled himself onto the deck of Isa's boat. He could no longer feel his fingers. Or toes. Or other body parts he rather valued. He fumbled open the latch on her door and staggered into the dim cabin, pulling the goggles from his face.

"Alec! Thank the tides, I'd begun to worry."

She was back? Already? They could use a few good Finn men on the BURR team. Wait, there were. Well, at least one. Heck, they should form an all-female team.

Isa—wearing nothing but her dressing gown—helped him to a chair set beside her small cookstove. Inside, a stack of peat bricks smoldered in anticipation of his arrival. Grateful, he leaned into the radiating warmth and let her yank the swim fins from his feet.

"Your lips are purple!" She pressed a hot cup of tea into his hands. "Drink. It's fortified."

His teeth chattered too hard to reply, but he drank. More whisky than tea, it cauterized his esophagus on the way down. Internal icicles began to thaw.

"Roideach?" she asked.

He shook his head.

"Dead?"

"Yes," he whispered.

"I found it." She fairly vibrated with the news. "The cave. It's not far. But there's a reason it's not on any map." Alec listened, amazed and horrified as she described a near-fatal adventure. Any woman but her would have been dashed against the rocks. "The entrance to the cave was twelve feet below the water. Perhaps thirteen. But the tide has turned and it will soon be less."

She spoke as if it would be no task at all to enter the sea cave. She was Finn and, from what he'd seen, she had every right to such confidence. But a ten-foot depth was the lower limit of established safety for his aquaspira breather.

Davis's death flashed to mind, and Alec's heart rate jumped. But his teammate's death had been a factor of the drug, of the high concentration of factor Q pumped into his bloodstream. Chances were Alec's aquaspira would function satisfactorily, and it wasn't as if he had a choice. There was no knowing how long the channel was—ten feet? Seventy? All with nothing but water and rock above him until they reached the central cavern.

As if it mattered. They needed to know what lay inside, and he would not send her in alone. "Let me send a skeet pigeon to my team. Inform them of recent developments. Then we can go."

~~~

With the boat anchored as close to the cliffs as she deemed safe, Isa joined Alec aboard the deck. His spyglass was trained upon the dark expanse of water, waiting for the megalodon to exit. Meeting it head on within the channel would mean certain death for them both.

"Norway." She stood beside him, wrapped in a thick blanket against the cold wind. The water didn't sap her body heat, but a cold night wind would. "When I was a child, I remember Mrs. Carr—Maren's mother—speaking about emigrating, of building a community of Finn. If my uncle held such a vision, why not merely gather those who share the same dream and emigrate?" She shook her head. "Why go to so much trouble to build a biomech shark? Or—worse—the biomech octopus."

Without lowering his spyglass, Alec answered. "He's a naval officer. I've no doubt both chimeras are part and parcel of his plans to protect his... settlers. Though Norway wouldn't take kindly to such an invasion, the subtle, quiet occupation of a small Shetland island or two might not make much of a splash. Unless they caused trouble, I doubt the Crown would be inclined to fuss."

"Perhaps." Isa frowned. "But whatever my uncle is up to, I doubt it's peaceful or benign." Far too many
~~~

bodies had been left in his wake. Though the most recent casualty, one Lord Roideach, was hard to regret.

A sudden and large displacement of water shifted the boat beneath their feet, and the tip of an iron fin broke the surface.

Alec tossed the spyglass aside. "Let's go."

Minutes later they descended, dropping deeper into the water that churned above the base of the cliff. Amidst a tumble of scree, a wide, jagged hole opened. Alec, garbed in his dive suit and unrecognizable behind goggles and the aquaspira breather in his mouth, motioned for her to take the lead.

She swam into the passageway. Some sixteen feet in, a faint green light began to illuminate the water above her head. Careful to keep close to the rough gneiss wall, she ascended and broke the surface.

A giant cavern arched overhead. A stone shelf ran alongside the edge of the water, a portion of it widening and lengthening into another chamber that extended into the cliff.

Her stomach tightened. Her own sister had lain on this very ledge where chains bolted into the rough, rock walls ended in metal cuffs clasped about the wrists of five women. They huddled against the cave walls, shivering and clutching wool blankets about their shoulders. Their faces were bleak with hopelessness, captive witnesses to the horror that had befallen their spouses.

For along the edge of the pool, iron-barred cages—she counted six—hung in the water, suspended by long chains that stretched upward to pulleys embedded in the cave's ceiling. Inside the cages were men, their husbands. Some floated listlessly, some gripped the iron bars. All had the same horrible octopus attached to their upper back. In a decided contrast to their pale, glistening white undersides, the upper surface of each creature's body pulsed a reddish-brown, as if human blood coursed through its body. It most likely did.

Each octopus wrapped tentacles about its host's neck and shoulders, twining others down the victim's arms and legs. Half-submerged as the Finn men were, it was impossible to trace insertion points.

Alec caught her elbow and tipped his head, and she followed his direction. The chains from which the cages hung descended again at an angle, all anchoring to a winch powered by a motor that rattled and hummed and sputtered in readiness. A guard holding a rifle was positioned beside the machine and stood all of an arm's length from a single lever designed to raise—or lower—all six cages at once.

Bored, the guard slouched against the rock wall and picked at his fingernails while throwing irritated glances at his colleagues—four armed men—who sat about a small table, enjoying an engrossing game of cards.

Keeping only their eyes above water, Isa and Alec swam along the rock wall of the cave until the interior of the secondary chamber came into view: a laboratory.

Miss Russel gesticulated wildly at a man who frowned at the onslaught of her heated words, his knuckles growing white with anger as he gripped a long, pointed stick. He growled back an answer, and Miss Russel's mouth dropped. But whatever they argued about was lost to the acoustics of the cave.

Scattered throughout the space were tables laden with all manner of bottles, flasks and test tubes. Equipment of all kinds littered the room, including a long, metal gurney complete with leather straps to hold a patient against his will. But her eyes were drawn to the agonizingly familiar tank that stood in its center. Within, a man floated, his arms bound by buckled, leather manacles, the water tinged red with his own blood.

An octopus crouched upon his back, gripping his neck and shoulders and tapping two tentacles upon the man's legs and arms and shoulders as if unable to locate the precise blood vessel it desired. Then, one tentacle drew back and plunged into the man's thigh. The man screamed, every muscle in his body straining against the painful attack.

She looked to Alec, her eyes wide. "We have to stop this," she mouthed. But Alec shook his head slowly, reminding her this was a reconnaissance mission only. Too many people. Too many weapons—and none of them theirs. There could be no wholesale rescue. Not today.

But they still needed information.

Isa pointed at the nearest cage, one furthest from the guards, indicating that she was going to contact the prisoner. From his silhouette, she was almost certain it was Jona. They could at least speak with him, reassure him of Nina's safety and find out what—if anything—he might know about her uncle's plans.

Alec frowned and jerked his head back toward the tunnel.

But Isa took a deep breath and submerged. Swimming underwater, she stopped beside the cage and tapped on the knee of the man held within. His leg jerked away, but a moment later, his face appeared beneath the water and behind the bars.

It *was* Jona. Eyes wide with recognition, they stared at each other. Isa pressed a finger to her lips, then pointed upward. Quietly, they both broke the surface. The octopus that griped his back pulsed and whirred. It shifted, staring at her over Jona's shoulder through its strange, horizontally-slitted eye. She shuddered. What went through the creature's mind? Would it cry out if it were able, alert the guards to her presence?

"Nina?" Jona whispered across the water.

Feverish. Sick with worry. And not particularly safe from their uncle. "At home with our mother."

Relief washed over his face. "Don't let the others see you," he warned, glancing at the other caged Finn. "The winch adjusts for the tide, but if anyone makes trouble of any kind, a guard raises the cages. It makes it... difficult to breathe."

The water stirred beside her as Alec approached. "I've a companion with me," she whispered as his head broke the surface. He tugged his mouthpiece free, and Isa made hasty introductions. "We can't free you just yet, not with so many armed guards, but Alec has a whole BURR team on its way." His eyes slid sideways, and she knew she'd promised too much.

"Soon, I hope." Jona said. "I'm not sure how much longer I have." He shifted in his cage, planting his feet on the lower bars. Ever so slightly, he lifted his shoulder above the water's surface. “If this grows worse, they’ll feed me to the hyena fish.”

Alec swore under his breath, and Isa clamped a hand over her mouth.

The creature’s beak was sunk deeply into the base of Jona’s neck. Nearby, its tentacle had inserted in his shoulder and, though the sight of blood pumping through some internal vessel just beneath the creature's translucent skin was stomach-turning, the skin surrounding the insertion point was red and throbbing. Infected.

Unhappy, the octopus tightened its grip, strangling Jona, and her brother-in-law dropped back into the water. "That empty cage?” He jerked his chin. “That man didn't make it. They've left on an acquisition trip. My sister and your uncle loaded him onto the megalodon to... dispose of."

"Hyena fish," she whispered.

Alec frowned. "And to conscript more Finn men?"

Jona nodded. "Those that pass the blood test. They'll need more free cages when they return. My sister and your uncle have come unhinged."

"Family." Isa twisted her lips, wondering why her uncle bothered to pretend it mattered.

"Change of plans," Alec breathed. Unhooking a strange tool from his dive belt, he shifted, inserting a long metal rod into the cage's padlock. "Does the infection affect the octopus?"

"Hard to say," Jona answered. "It's not alive. Not entirely. Part machine, part animal. And there are design flaws. For every successful attachment, five Finn men die. All too often, the tentacle burrows into the skin and misses. A bad attachment drains the blood before it can circulate back. Or—like me—infection sets in. With so many half-blooded Finn conveniently at hand, the scientists find it easier to discard the body than to attempt to save the man."

"Half-blooded," Isa repeated. Alec was entirely focused on his task.

Jona glanced away. "Your uncle, he has this dream about restoring the purity of our people. About establishing a homeland. Something to do with our blood and our ability to swim. He approached us about joining his colony. We were to visit the Orkneys and speak with the others. But your sister failed the blood test." His eyes grew wide. "I tested pure, and your uncle suggested a divorce. I objected, loudly, and... well, that's how we ended up in here."

"A colony in Norway?"

"No," Jona said. "On the Faroe Islands."

"Tell me about this octopus," Alec asked. "We'll have to surgically remove it, and the more you can tell us, the better. I gather it's filtering your blood, oxygenating it using gills as a secondary air source?"

Jona swallowed hard and nodded. "Blood flows out from my leg, through the creature, then back into my shoulder. With this thing attached, I can stay underwater indefinitely. But out of the water," he shook his head, "it's hard to breathe. Not only because the beast objects, but because so much blood is diverted."

There was a soft, wet thud as the lock popped open.

"Me next," a man hissed from the next cage over.

"Shh!" Eyes wide, Isa lifted a finger to her lips. "We'll be back."

The guard's head snapped up. He barked something out in a strange language that echoed off the stone walls and pulled the lever. Overhead, chains clanged. His colleagues snapped to attention, searching the water while lifting their rifles to their shoulders. Alec yanked her under the water as Jona's cage—as all the cages—began to rise.

Jona shoved at the door of his, desperate to escape, but the hinges must have been rusty. He—like all the men—gasped for air, his rib cage straining to drag more oxygen, but no matter how deeply they drew breath, it wasn't enough. The women cried out, pleading with the guards, but to no avail.

At last, Jona's door swung free with a loud creak, and he leapt. But not before the guards took aim all firing at once. Alec grabbed Isa, spinning her away, pinning her between his body and the cave wall as bullets struck stone. When the gunfire ceased, the screaming and yelling and weeping continued, all voices muffled by the water.

"Stop!" It was Miss Russel.

"Orders were to prevent any and all escape," the guard answered. "It's our neck on the block."

"Don't hurt them, you idiots," she countered. "We don't have time to create more OctoFinn. Get the hook. Launch the raft and drag the water."

"Where is he?" another guard yelled. He swept a bioluminescent torch over the surface of the water, hunting for Jona. Her heart pounded. The guards stood on the ledge, ignoring Miss Russel's continued cries of outrage and aiming their rifles at the water, waiting. If Jona surfaced again, he would not survive.

Alec tugged her to the surface beneath a dark shadow cast by an overhanging rock. "Dive," he ordered in a harsh whisper. "Head out. I'll grab Jona." He shoved in his mouthpiece and submerged without waiting for comment.

Taking a deep breath, Isa dove deep. Heart pounding, she followed a shadow that slid through the water. She drew closer. Alec dragged a limp and unconscious Jona. A dark stream of blood flowed from a bullet wound to his shoulder. With baleful eyes, the octopus stared upward at her, but it made no move to prevent their exit.

Swallowing her disgust for the creature, Isa reached out and caught Jona under his other arm. They needed to hurry. An unconscious Finn reflexively drawing a breath could drown before they reached the other end of the tunnel, in which case this abhorrent biomech octopus might—for once—save a Finn's life.

Chapter Twenty-Eight

Alec heaved the unconscious man onto the deck of Isa's boat, and together they dragged him into the cabin. Isa grabbed a cloth and pressed it to Jona's shoulder, but the gunshot wound wasn't an immediate crisis. He was struggling to breathe, dragging in deep and unnerving lungfuls of air. The biomech octopus drew so much blood from his circulatory system that his lungs couldn't compensate out of the water. And, true to its nature, the beast slowly tightened its grip about Jona's throat. His breaths were horrible, tortured affairs. Unsustainable.

Wave after wave rocked the boat. He'd performed surgeries aboard ships, but detaching this creature would require vascular surgery and a steady hand. Not to mention a live patient. He pulled a knife from his dive belt and reached for the tentacle that strangled Jona.

"Wait!" Isa cried. "We don't know how it's connected to his circulatory system. We need to stabilize him first." She grabbed a bucket and ran from the cabin. "I have an idea."

A few minutes later, they'd cobbled together an odd sort of platform from a chair, a sea chest and two long, wooden planks. Jona lay on his back beneath a blanket—lashed in place with a length of rope—while the body of the creature passed through a gap between the two boards, suspended beneath him in a bucket of water.

The octopus released its stranglehold.

Alec sagged against the cabin wall, exhausted and—if he were being honest with himself—unreasonably distracted by Isa's naked form as she bent over Jona, examining the bullet wound.

A straightforward, easy affair with an attractive, young widow who wanted him in her bed, not on bended knee, wasn't progressing at all as he'd planned. Isa was different somehow. And not in a Finn-Selkie kind of way.

He struggled to shape unfamiliar feelings into a coherent thought. While the cruel machinations of mad men threw obstacles in their paths, his attraction to her had deepened. Lust had become... not love, but something more.

Not that he was about to consult with a jeweler.

But Alec had a feeling that "quick" and "tumble" wasn't going to be enough to slake his thirst. Whatever currents flowed between them were too deep. He was caught in her net, but was she equally ensnared?

"A clean exit," she announced, yanking him out of his thoughts. "But he's bleeding far more than normal."

"Hirudin." What he wouldn't give for a few quiet hours alone with her, without some fresh disaster pressing down upon them. "Remember the blood I analyzed." Only a week had passed, though it felt longer. "There were traces of an anticoagulant produced by leeches."

"I'd forgotten." She grimaced, packing and binding Jona's shoulder. "Disgusting, yet along with a ceramic blood filter, it's an effective way to ensure a smooth circulation between Finn and octopus." Straightening, she unhooked a simple woolen gown from the wall and dressed, forgoing the usual undergarments in her haste. "The nearest harbor is twenty minutes north. I'll get us there."

She turned to go, but he caught her by the waist. "You're an amazing woman." He traced a finger down the side of her face. "Don't ever let anyone convince you otherwise."

He thought of how she'd held on to the megalodon, riding it to the very cliff's edge, determined to save one family member and stop another. Dragging a wounded, sick man from an underwater cave under threat of gunfire. The quicksilver in her eyes flashed and swirled as he stared in awe. *Aether*, he was falling for this woman.

Curving her hand around the back of his neck, Isa pulled him down until her face was mere inches from his own. "You're the first to think so," she murmured, pressing her warm lips to his.

The taste of her flooded his system with adrenaline, waking every nerve ending. He yanked her against his chest, delighting in the press of her soft breasts against him as he spread his fingers wide over her arse. A mere layer of soft wool kept her skin from his palms. A dangerous thought.

He pushed her away with a groan. "Go. Find us a safe harbor. We need to rid Jona of that creature."

With a sly smile, she departed. A moment later, the boat—much like his heart—lurched back into motion.

~~~

Isa took a deep breath of the cool, salty air that whipped her hair about her face. Such admiration had shone in Alec's eyes that she'd been unable to stop herself from reaching for him, reaching for everything in her life that was solid and dependable. Then the rough scrape of his beard had sent flames licking across her skin, nearly emptying her mind of all thoughts. Another moment, stolen in the midst of disaster.

What would it be like to have a man like this to call her own? Foolishness, such thoughts. A man fueled by adrenaline would never fall for the likes of her, a woman who—until recently—had lived a dull, staid life, content to follow her calling in medicine.

She needed to focus on the immediate task before her. Only once, at her brother's insistence, had she practiced running this boat aground. She steered toward the harbor ahead of her, plotting a ninety-degree approach.
~~~

Jona would live. She'd see to that.

Much as she wanted to pry the parasite from his back and dash it upon the rocky beach, extricating his circulatory system from that of the octopus's would be a delicate process. For that, they needed stable ground. The smallest of waves could cause a fatal slip of the knife.

Flipping a switch, she activated the landing gear—four wheels built into the bottom of the boat. A technological feature her brother had insisted upon installing for an emergency in which the boat needed to be removed from the water. No doubt he'd been imagining gale-force winds and ten-foot waves, but Jona's deteriorating condition certainly counted as a crisis.

The dark shoreline rushed at her. She gripped the handles of the wheel tightly, aiming for a narrow stretch of rocky beach. As the front tires bounced onto rocks, rushing through the surf zone, Alec yelled below. Perhaps she should have warned him.

The back tires hit, and Isa pushed the throttle forward. The tide was on its way out, and she wanted to make certain they were firmly lodged on the beach when it returned.

She hurried back into the cabin.

~~~

"You might have warned me you were going to run us aground." Alec grumbled, but in truth he was grateful
~~~

the wild rocking had stopped. Every large wave had sloshed water from the bucket housing the octopus, and he'd had to rush to the side of the boat to fetch more.

"My apologies," she said. "Someone distracted me as I left the cabin."

"Flattery accepted." He held out a canvas apron that she dutifully tied on. "We need to begin. I'm not certain the octopus is managing to oxygenate Jona's blood very well while confined to this bucket. He's barely stirred. Once we begin, however, we'll need to work quickly. I've no idea how a cephalopod will react to anesthesia, standard or otherwise."

"A quick, but complete external exam before we begin," Isa agreed. "Have you been able to examine the creature?"

"Some. It appears the octopus is using one tentacle to extract blood from Jona's venous system—from the femoral vein. The blood is oxygenated via its gills, then returns the blood to his arterial circulation. Possibly into his axillary artery."

With the faintest of cringes, Isa wrapped a hand gently about the tentacle impaled in Jona's leg. "No pulse." Then tested the tentacle that plunged into Jona's shoulder. "Faint, but I can sense an odd kind of pulse."

Together, they crouched while Alec pointed a decilamp to illuminate the creature inhabiting the bucket.

"Eyeballing the size of this octopus," he said, "I'd estimate that—at any given moment—the biomech octopus draws about one-third of Jona's total blood volume."

They could not simply tourniquet both tentacles; the blood within the beast belonged to Jona and needed to be returned to him. He had lost quite a bit of blood volume to the gunshot wound and was in shock. His skin was cool and unnaturally pale, his pulse elevated and his breaths irregular.

Isa moved her hands over Jona, checking his pulse, his respiratory rate, and the temperature of his skin, which judging from the pallid color, was dropping at an alarming rate.

Beneath its reddish-orange and semi-translucent skin, dark—unoxygenated—blood flowed into the creature's body, flushed a brighter red, then surged forth, out the other tentacle into Jona's shoulder with every contraction of its body—the muscular mantle. That very same movement also drew water in and out of its siphon, a long, rubber-like tube at the side of its head. That water would pass over its gills, oxygenating blood before returning it to Jona's circulation.

"The ceramic filter?" Isa asked.

"Must lay within its head," he answered. "Hirudin to reduce the chance of blood clots forming combined with a simple mechanical device to prevent any blood clots that do form from re-entering circulation."

But in a living creature, could such a filter be changed? Or did a clock begin to tick the moment a biomech octopus attached to a Finn?

Bulging eyes rolled in their direction. Strange horizontal and rectangular pupils narrowed in the bright light. The creature closed its eyes until he pointed the beam elsewhere, whereupon an unattached tentacle listlessly draped over the edge of the bucket lifted, reaching toward the decilamp, curling the suckered end of its leg about the small cylinder.

Alec released his hold, watching in amazement as it pointed the light back at him, as if the creature conducted its own examination.

Isa gasped. "Just how alive is it?"

He met her eyes. "An excellent question."

Could it possibly be sentient? Without a human attachment, would it survive? "Not that it matters. We need to sever its connection to Jona."

Alec nodded.

"Anesthesia," Isa ticked off the steps on her fingers. "An application of two tourniquets, one after the other allowing blood to return to his system. Then we sever the tentacles."

"We'll also need to pry the beak free from his neck. Some cephalopods have poisonous saliva, making that gland the logical place to bioengineer a continuous source of hirudin."

"The anticoagulant." She cringed. "I suppose we need to take a closer look before we begin."

He nodded. "If you can lift his shoulder slightly..."

While Isa held Jona, Alec used a long-handled, wooden spoon to gently shift the circular buccal mass—fleshy tissue—that surrounded the creature's mouth. A chitinous beak was indeed partially embedded into the neck muscles.

The octopus tightened its grip about Jona's throat, rolled its eyes toward Alec and bit down. Isa squeaked in distress as a thin, watery rivulet of blood trickled down Jona's back and dripped into the bucket.

Alec swore. "It knows we're up to something." He dropped the spoon and stood. Any hope of coaxing the creature to voluntarily release its victim evaporated. "There'll be no removing the octopus while it's awake. Time to prep for surgery."

Lucifer lamps were fed, shaken and—using ropes and pulleys—positioned over each of the tentacle attachments. Surgical instruments were laid out upon a tray. Curved suture needles were threaded with sharksilk. Bandages were stacked an arm's reach away, and bottles of anesthetic agents were placed upon the table.

At last she lifted a leather and rubber anesthesia mask from its case, and he paused. All patients needed to be carefully monitored during surgery as anesthetic drugs suppressed a number of autonomic functions. Heart rate, blood pressure, and breathing to name the basics. Any or all might be affected.

"The presence of factor Q in a Finn's blood complicates the procedure," she reminded him. "No need to test his blood levels. As noted by my uncle, Jona is full-blooded—and therefore extremely sensitive to the volatile gasses. The mixture I prepare rarely triggers a dive reflex, but we'll need to closely monitor his gas levels, body temperature and heart rate."

He leaned close to examine the embedded brass gauges upon the mask's surface. He tapped the two attached dials. "It monitors levels of oxygen intake *and* carbon dioxide output?"

"It does that and more. See the markings on the dials?"

He nodded. Two lines of different colors were inscribed.

"At optimum levels, the indicator needles ought to point to red for standard humans, blue for Finn. In-between if their family lineage is intertwined with that of the Scots. But, no matter who the mask is used on, I've designed it to ensure an even delivery of anesthesia without compromising normal blood gas levels."

Beyond impressive. "It's a work of pure genius."

Flushing with pride, Isa tucked a ball of cotton wool into a chamber of the mask. She plucked a vial of ether from the collection of bottles and uncapped it. A faint, sweet smell wafted through the air. After carefully measuring and mixing together a variety of volatile liquids, she used a glass eyedropper to drip the combined anesthetic onto the cotton, then held the mask over Jona's face. "Ready?"

While they'd been making preparations, the biomech octopus had kept a close eye on their activities in an unsettling and worrisome manner. Its bulbous eyes now stared at him as if pleading for mercy, while tentacles that had relaxed into the seawater-filled bucket began to writhe and twist. The one holding the decilamp uncurled, dropping the device on the floor in favor of threading upward to wrap about Jona's neck.

"Expect resistance," Alec warned, keeping a wary eye on the creature. "Take Jona under slowly. The octopus knows we're up to something, and I've no idea how a cephalopod reacts to anesthetic agents." He clenched and unclenched his hands, hoping he wouldn't need to reach for his knife.

She lowered the mask onto Jona's face. Nothing happened. He glanced at the dials. Oxygen and carbon dioxide exhalation levels were low—for human or Finn. But perhaps that was to be expected, what with the octopus in the bucket responsible for oxygenating a full third of the man's blood.

"It knows!" Isa yelled, dancing sideways to avoid the reach of an undulating tentacle.

A tentacle whipped out, curling about Alec's wrist and squeezing with vicious force. Suckers latched onto his skin, and the muscular arm twisted, yanking him to the floor. Alec brought his fist down upon the creature's tense flesh, striking again and again until it loosened its grip. He leapt to his feet, backing away to grab a scalpel from the instrument tray.

She slid her dive knife from its sheath. Dodging thrashing tentacles, they tried to advance while two tentacles rippled as they wrapped tighter about Jona's neck, squeezing. His back arched, his arms and legs tensed. The octopus bit down with its beak, hard. Blood poured from Jona's neck and his eyes flew open, bulging from their sockets. His lips pulled back, exposing teeth in a silent, screaming rictus of pain.

Praying pain wouldn't further enrage the octopus, Alec positioned his scalpel above the first tentacle—ready to slice it free—when Jona suddenly slumped upon the wooden planks, silent and limp. Tentacles loosened and fell slack, sliding from his neck and flopping with a soft *plop* onto the wooden floor.

Mouth open, hand still fisted about her knife, Isa stared at him.

Swearing, Alec threw the scalpel onto the tray with a clatter. "Enough. Tie off the venous tentacle. I'll pry off the beak." He snatched up a self-retaining Weitlaner retractor. Shaped like blunt-tipped scissors, they had a uni-directional ratchet mechanism that—when locked in place—allowed movement in one direction only: open.

He crouched beside Jona, shoved aside the mass of buccal tissue and inserted the tool into the octopus's beak, forcing the sharp halves apart. Limp, the bulk of the octopus fell and sank to the bottom of the bucket. Without a constant flow of hirudin, the blood soaking Jona's bandages should taper and stop.

"Alec," Isa said.

He looked up to see her holding the raw, severed end of a tentacle, tightly tied off with cording. A few inches of tentacle—also securely tied—protruded from Jona's leg.

"I need your assistance. If you'll lift the octopus above his shoulder, that should drain most of the blood back into his system."

A few minutes later, the second tentacle had been severed. Isa checked Jona's vitals in preparation for vascular surgery, and Alec dropped the octopus in the bucket. He rubbed the edge of his jawline as he studied the creature. It lay there, its body still pulsing, but with a gentler, softer rhythm.

"Cephalopods can regenerate a lost limb," he mused aloud. "Most cephalopods have copper-based blood—hemocyanin. It's why I used the Ichor machine to test for copper in the first victim's wounds, but I found no traces of elevated copper. *If* the octopus possesses its own, separate circulatory system, unconnected to the one it shared with Jona, there's no reason to think it won't live."

Isa wiped her hands on a towel, giving him a long, unamused look. "You want to save it. As evidence."

"My brother wanted me to find proof." He waved a hand. "Here it is." He imagined dropping this bucket at Logan's feet and smiled. Payback for all the years of bugs and lizards he'd found beneath his pillow. "We need say nothing of Finn."

"That boat has long since sailed." She tossed aside the towel and scanned the gleaming array of surgical tools. "If your BURR team arrives to successfully raid that cave, there'll be no hiding the Finn."

"When," he answered. "They'll come. And as you've admitted, Aron Moray is Finn. He'll have an opinion on how this ought to be handled." He moved toward the basin of soapy water to scrub his own hands before joining her at their makeshift surgical table. "Have you performed vascular surgery before?"

"I've assisted," she said, handing him his surgical glasses, the very ones she'd won from him the day they met. "The tentacle appears to pass between two muscles, the sartorius and the adductor longus, on its way to the femoral vein. From what I could see, octopus-human vessel fusion isn't quite complete. Separating the two tissues ought not be too difficult."

He bent over Jona's thigh. The retractor Isa had inserted gently opened the wound, allowing him to trace the path of the tentacle using a blunt probe. "Agreed." A glint of light caught on the braided wire. "Can you spread the tissue more?" The barbed tip was not at all where he'd predicted. He traced its path to the tip. "Shit," he muttered.

This explained the drilling pain Jona described. Another diabolical feature of the engineered tentacle. The Finn who'd been attacked by the biomech octopus hadn't had a chance of removing the tentacle once it attached to them. Not without surgical intervention.

Someone willing to risk death by severe and sudden blood loss might attempt to break free by yanking on the tentacle. Attempt. There was little chance that they would be able to overcome this.

"What is it?" Isa asked.

"The braided wire, remember the barb?"

"Of course."

"More than a simple fish hook function. It's lodged not in muscle or connective tissue, but has actively drilled into bone."

Isa lifted a handheld magnifying lens and leaned closer. "And deeply. You'll need my burr saw. Extraction and irrigation. But I'd close the vein first."

"Agreed."

They bent to the task.

An hour later, they were done. Both Jona's vein and artery had been separated from the tentacles, and the barbed wire extracted from bone. All with minimal tissue damage. Still, he would have a lengthy and painful recovery. For now, all they could do was close and dress the wounds while hoping his immune system could overcome the worrisome infection.

Alec pulled the suture needle through skin, repairing the inflamed tissue of Jona's shoulder as best he could.

Thud.

Isa screamed.

He dropped the needle and reached for his TTX pistol.

Chapter Twenty-Nine

Thud.

Thud.

Thud thud thud.

Black-booted feet dropped from the air onto the boat's deck. A rope dangled outside the window. Alec started to laugh. Isa—plastered to the wall—cried out a protest as he holstered his weapon.

"It's my team dropping from a dirigible," he said. *Thank aether.* His muscles had tied themselves into Gordian knots guarding against the next—seemingly inevitable—disaster. But now his team was here, and they always had his back. He could finally relax.

Shaw's face appeared in the doorway. "Got a bird telling us we were needed? Something about raiding an underwater cave?"

a woman who wasn't Alec's wife—or even a fiancée—warranted punching a team member in the nose.

Isa placed her hand on his arm. "It's the way of things out here on the islands. Let it go."

Moray's face grew serious. "Is that Jona?" He pushed past Alec to stand beside Isa. "He looks like shit."

"Loss of blood will do that to a man." Isa slapped at Moray, then picked up the needle Alec had dropped. "You've caused enough trouble. Stand back. I need to finish closing his wound."

Pale, Moray shot the BURR team a pointed glance. "Mind you all keep your mouths shut. This is why we don't share the details of our particular heritage."

"Lips tighter than a clam," Rowan said.

Isa tied a knot, packed Jona's shoulder with a poultice, then wrapped it with a final bandage. With that, there wasn't much more to do save wait and hope his fever passed. She drew the blanket over his chest, busying herself with restoring order to her cabin and avoiding the curious glances of his team.

"About that cave," Shaw nudged.

"We've already been," Alec said. "But Jona is the only man we were able to rescue." The first note he'd sent—the one they'd received—had been brief, focused more on ensuring his team arrived quickly and with the right equipment in tow. He'd omitted names, not knowing the extent of Drummond's reach within the Navy. "Commodore Drummond and his wife are the masterminds behind the disappearance of Finn. The megalodon, hyena fish, biomech octopus? All his."

Jaws fell slack as he and Isa detailed what they'd found, from her own imprisonment to the discoveries they'd made in the sea cave.

Moray swore.

Rowan shook his head. "Mad scientists and their freaking inventions."

Shaw nudged the bucket with his toe, jostling the subdued creature awake. "This thing here's what's been attacking Finn?"

An eye rolled in his direction as an octopus tentacle lazily lifted into the air, snaking toward Moray's leg, tapping on his thigh. Hungry.

Alec yanked Moray away. "You're welcome. This particular creature thinks you're food. It's been engineered to find Finn extra tasty."

Isa spoke up. "What we don't fully understand is what my uncle intends to accomplish using this biomech octopus. He's on a quest to purify the bloodline, to establish a Finn homeland."

"A kingdom," Alec said. "He specifically promised to crown his wife queen."

"Did he promise her a castle too?" Rowan asked. "Denmark is floating one across the North Sea to Iceland on giant pontoons. We're supposed to help guard it during the wedding ceremony."

"Not Iceland," Rip spoke up. "Didn't you pay attention to the briefing? The plan is to run it aground on the Faroe Islands. Establish a royal residence between the two countries."

"A whole castle?" Alec's eyebrows drew together. He could see from the various expressions of his team that they also didn't find this a coincidence. Drummond had plans for that castle. They merely needed to determine what, exactly, those were. "Wouldn't it tip or something?" he asked, envisioning the building canted upon a beach, its floors approaching a forty-five-degree angle.

Rowan shrugged. "Not my department, but the engineers were all aflutter with plans. *If* the BURR team is sent, we're to function as no more than glorified bouncers keeping unwanted guests off the castle grounds."

"Icelandic radicals would happily side with a powerful man—no matter how crazy—willing to storm that castle and stop the wedding." Shaw tapped his chin. "We thought Commander Norgrove was on our side, ordering us to stop using aquaspira to exit submersibles, but now it turns out he's in Drummond's pocket. He's already objected—vociferously—to Britain's participation in the security detail for this royal wedding. Keeping the BURR team away would clear the way for Drummond to send in his OctoFinn."

"An island kingdom could make good use of an underwater security force," Alec mused aloud. He turned a considering eye on Moray. "If that creature was attached to the likes of you..." His voice trailed off as everyone stared at the pulsing creature, whose legs—arms?—now spilled over the edge of the bucket, some gently curling in the air, others skimming along the floor boards.

“I could stay under water indefinitely,” Moray admitted. “But there’s not a chance in hell I’d ever volunteer to let that thing touch me." Tentacles contracted, hoisting the octopus's head above the edge of the container. Two bulging, slit-like eyes stared out at them.

Shaw slid his knife free. “It looks like it might make a run for the door."

"Keep it alive," Alec ordered. "I want to study it."

Isa poked the creature with a wooden spoon, and it fell backward into the bucket with a splash. She grabbed a bottle and poured a good bit of whisky into the seawater, then decanted a bit into a glass for herself, slugging it back.

Rip laughed. Laughed!

Alec's own mouth twitched at her choice of sedative. It was the first crack of stress he’d witnessed in her demeanor; she’d held out far longer than he thought possible. “So, hypothetically speaking,” he ventured. “If a Finn attached to this creature was coerced to do Drummond’s bidding, he could exit a submersible at a significant depth, swim a great distance, then board a designated ship to, say, assassinate someone?”

Moray’s eyes narrowed. “With ease.”

Alec ran both hands through his hair. “Commander Norgrove reversed his position just last week.”

“The same day the royal wedding plans were announced,” Moray said.

“What wedding?” Isa asked.

All heads swiveled in her direction. All amazed that there was a single female in all of the British Isles that didn't know. But then, Isa was a unique woman. Her intense focus on saving lives left her no time for the foibles and fancies of fashion and society.

"The wedding between the Crown Prince of Iceland and the Princess of Denmark," Alec told her. "One to end the many disputes between their countries, a step toward unification, and so on and so forth." He waved a hand about, then summed it up in one word. "Politics."

"I see," Isa said, tilting her head in thought.

"The wedding takes place in two weeks," Shaw added.

"Drummond has gone to a lot of trouble to develop this biomech octopus." Alec frowned, wondering if it was possible to convince her not to be directly involved. Unlikely. Besides, he'd promised her equal standing, insofar as that was possible. "He's going to use it. If he's not above killing and enslaving Finn men to perfect his technology, he's certainly not above disrupting a wedding."

"Grab your gear, Mac," Shaw said. "Time to clean out a cave."

~~~

"Mrs. McQuiston, this is Jasper Sinclair," Alec said. "Newest member of our team. Like all the men, he's trained as a medic."
~~~

And would function as her guardian and assistant while the other men raided the underwater cave. This man had slid down the rope that hung from the dirigible, landing on her deck with a heavy sack of first aid equipment slung across his shoulder. The BURR definition of "first aid" consisted of enough supplies to open a small hospital.

"Call me Sinclair," he said, flashing her a grin before executing a quick bow. "I'm told we need to prepare for up to four more tentacle-entangled men."

She might hate being left behind, but this man was BURR, trained and capable of participating in the raid. If he could set aside such feelings to deal with the situation at hand, so could she. They were armed to the teeth and diving with the intent to put an end to all activities within the cave. She'd only be at risk and in the way. Besides, she couldn't leave her brother-in-law.

Isa nodded. "And for any injuries your men might incur during the raid. For now, we need to move this man to a more comfortable location. There are extra blankets in that chest." She pointed across the room. "The operating table was improvised. I'm certain we can improve upon its design and stability."

"So noted." Mr. Sinclair nodded. He quickly evaluated Jona's condition, then began to roam through her cabin, taking stock of its contents so that they might assemble a temporary field hospital while ignoring Isa and Alec completely.

Thus granted an illusion of privacy, Isa crossed to Alec. "Your knee?" she asked softly. Her chest was tight with a mix of fear and pride as Alec gathered his equipment and prepared to head back into the cave.

"No longer crunches or grinds," he reassured her. "Whatever Dr. Morgan installed fixed the problem."

"But you're wearing the brace?" Did all paramours fret so over their lovers?

"Of course." He ran the back of a finger across her cheek. A movement so tender, she half-expected a declaration of love.

She blinked back a tear and closed her eyes. It seemed she was not immune to childish dreams of romance after all. The ties that bound them together were stretching. Whatever happened in the next few hours could strengthen them, or snap them irrevocably. She chose them carefully. "Come back to me, Alec. I'm not done with you yet."

"I will," he whispered. "Stay safe. With luck, we'll return in an hour."

As much as she wanted to see her uncle—and Maren—locked away in a dry prison without so much as a view of the ocean, Alec's presence brought an excitement into her life and she did her best to embrace it.

After Aron's comments impugning her character, Isa no longer cared who watched. She threaded her fingers into Alec's hair and dragged his rough face down to hers. "I've grown rather more attached to you than I expected."

His strong arms wrapped about her waist and drew her close. "Likewise." His eyes glittered. "Perhaps we ought to reevaluate the terms of our affair?"

Excitement fluttered in her stomach. "Perhaps." But certainly not in the presence of his team.

Pressing her lips to his, she claimed him openly with a kiss that was laced with an emotion that felt startlingly close to love.

Chapter Thirty

Isa paced out onto the deck of her boat, lifting the spyglass to fix a nervous eye upon the aether-filled silver envelope that floated the BURR team's dirigible a few miles distant. The cliffs that rose on either side of the small, rocky beach upon which her boat rested might provide a comforting sense of isolation, but they blocked her view of the water in front of the underwater passage to the sea cave.

Here, several miles away in this secluded harbor, nothing seemed out of the ordinary. She scanned the stretch of water before her. Seabirds soaring, diving for food. Sunlight reflecting off waves. The occasional steamer passing on the horizon.

How much longer?

Inside the cabin, Jona rested. He was still feverish, but the infection showed no sign of growing worse. The biomech octopus's attempts at escape had subsided with the application of more whisky. And Sinclair prepared for a full-scale disaster.

But the BURR dirigible showed no signed of returning. *Wait.* The balloon shifted, swinging in their direction, growing larger with each passing second. She pressed a shaking hand to her chest, praying that Alec and his team would return unhurt, that the raid was successful, that they had found enough evidence to convict her uncle so that no further disasters would befall the Finn people.

With blood stains and hours of surgery occupying the forefront of her mind, she'd selected an old, drab dress to pull over her linen shift. A corset had no place in a surgical suite regardless of its location. While Sinclair kept his gaze respectfully averted, she'd strapped her dive knife to her thigh, bound her hair tightly, and pulled on thick wool socks to wear beneath sturdy shoes. BURR boots were exceptionally thick-soled and, with luck, they'd soon be pounding across her deck carrying in octopus-laden Finn.

Boots, as it turned out, were a mistake.

A hand wrapped about her arm and pulled. One second she was on deck, the next falling through the air.

Splash.

She hit the surface of the water on her back. Not once had she ever entered the sea in such a manner. Never had she swum wearing so much clothing. Reflexes made her gasp at the air before she was dragged—a tangle of wet wool and linen—downward into a murky swirl of current and out to sea.

She thrashed, trying to yank free from the hand that held her, kicking and punching wildly, managing a few glancing blows to whomever—whatever—gripped her. An overwhelming urge to scream seized her, but it would be a silent and fatal breath. She needed to hold onto what little oxygen she'd managed to drag in.

A tentacle snaked about her waist. She clawed at it, but it was hopeless. Bare fingers couldn't break the creature's ever-tightening grasp.

Twisting, she turned and found herself face to face with the octopus's host Finn. Two unfamiliar eyes as dark as wet slate locked onto her. Pitiless. Ruthless. A black pit of despair. She would find no mercy at his hands.

Heart pounding, lungs burning, Isa stopped resisting lest the creature wrap more tentacles about her limbs. It was the only way to save herself. The host Finn's mouth flattened into a grim line, but he nodded. Releasing his hand from her arm, he swam with greater speed, swiftly descending. Bound to him by the parasitic tentacles, she was dragged along, ever deeper into the ocean toward a yellow, glowing disc. The eye of the megalodon.

She had interfered with her uncle's plans—again—and this time she doubted he would show much mercy. But the OctoFinn he'd sent hadn't killed her, a task he could have accomplished easily given the harpoon gun strapped to his bare thigh. Yet it was too much to hope

Uncle Gregor might merely use her as an experimental subject; she expected torture would precede a gruesome death.

Dragging sodden skirts upward, Isa reached for her dive knife. She yanked it from its sheath and slashed at the tentacle buried in the man's shoulder. The serrated blade edge caught at the braided wire within, tearing apart the twisted iron fibers. Bright blood gushed from the severed limb, and the Finn man stopped swimming.

The octopus rolled its slitted eyes in her direction, squeezing the tentacle about her waist. A new tentacle threaded itself through her hair—torn loose from its knot in her struggles—and yanked her head back as a third tentacle twisted about her neck. She cut her hair free, then sliced through the tentacle that gripped her throat.

Watery clouds of blood billowed around her. Through the haze, she saw the Finn man clutching at the creature's severed limbs. With conjoined circulatory systems, the creature's blood loss was his own. Fear faded, replaced by an ache in her chest. Who did he protect? Himself? A wife or child?

The scene above her grew ever more distant, as if lead sinkers had been sewn to the hem of her skirts. She blinked. Leather boots and wet wool dragged her downward. Not the death her uncle planned for her, but effective nonetheless.

Her heart raced and her lungs burned with an indescribable and unfamiliar pain as her body demanded oxygen, demanded she inhale. Now. If she didn't reach the surface immediately, she would learn what it was like to drown.

Forcing herself into action, Isa cut at her skirts, at the laces that bound boots to her feet. Kicking away their burden, she swam upward. Her face broke the surface, and she gasped for air, dragging in great lungfuls. Flopping onto her back—as only a desperate Finn would swim—she kicked for shore, searching the sky for the dirigible. Closer. But not close enough.

Nearing the boat, she heard a sharp yell. A crash. Then a dreadful silence.

Limp and drained, she staggered through the surf and onto the rocky beach. Dare she call out to Sinclair? Or would she alert another desperate OctoFinn to her presence? Covered in wet and grit, Isa staggered to the boat's ladder and pulled herself upward slowly, warily eyeing the deck.

A smear of blood. A dropped harpoon gun. A drag mark to where the smear became a pool. In its midst lay another Finn. Blood oozed from a severed tentacle protruding from the naked man's leg, but he was still bound to a parasitic octopus by a single tentacle inserted in his shoulder. The man was dead—his chest no longer rose or fell—but the octopus lived. Thrashing its tentacles, the creature heaved its gelatinous body left and right, trying to pry itself free from its host, trying to save itself. But it was dying. With every passing second, its efforts ebbed.

A shout echoed from her cabin.

Knife in hand, she peered around the door jamb.

"Thank aether," Sinclair gasped, taking in her half-drowned appearance with obvious relief. "If anything had happened to you, Mac would have seen me keelhauled."

As if the man could have saved her. He was slumped against the wall, pinned in place by the shaft of an iron harpoon. White-faced with pain, he clutched at his shoulder, his palm cupping the entry wound. Blood oozed from between his fingers. At his feet was a bloody knife. Across the room, Jona lay upon his pallet, untouched and unconscious.

With a hand clapped to her mouth, Isa rushed to Sinclair's side. She examined the exit wound with a wince.

"I'll be fine." Sinclair spoke through gritted teeth.

She wasn't inclined to agree. "Your clavicle is broken." Possibly shattered with a very real chance of significant nerve damage. "The harpoon tore muscle, flesh, but appears to have missed any significant blood vessels." It would take a bolt cutter to separate the barbed head of the harpoon from the shaft. She didn't have one. "Hang in there. Your team is minutes away."

~~~

They touched down on base just outside Glasgow in the dead of night. Not that time of day ever mattered on a military base. This time Isa climbed down from
~~~

the gondola under her own power, though Alec held her hand to be certain. She, her mother, her brother, her sister and brother-in-law were a bit green about the gills—buckets had become a necessity—and needed time to absorb the enormity of a family member's betrayal, but were otherwise fine.

Moray took charge of these Finn passengers, loading them into a steam carriage to transport them to Mr. Guthrie's home where he and his wife would care for them. All but Isa. Her brother had protested, arguing about propriety, but Alec refused to let her out of his sight. Lust? Love? Who knew. His feelings were such a primitive, tangled mess they felt as if they originated directly from his brainstem. His mother might also throw a fit, but he was taking her home. Hell, he was contemplating keeping her, if she'd have him.

Sinclair was dispatched posthaste to the Fifth Ward. If anyone could patch his shoulder together again, it was Dr. Morgan.

It bothered him, that unpredicted attack on Sinclair and Isa. Though he'd expected Drummond's minions to send out an alert, what Alec hadn't expected was such swift pursuit. An attempt to catch the escaped prisoner? Of course. But he and Isa had turned north, away from civilization. A small—but unfortunately bright—boat on a vast coastline.

The sea cave had been emptied with uncanny speed, stripped of anything portable. Empty of all but the tank, the cages and a few odds and ends. Had the OctoFinn succeeded, all biological material—victim and biomech octopus—would have been destroyed. Alec could think of only one man in Drummond's pocket, one man who might have sent word that BURR had launched a dirigible without Naval approval. Commander Norgrove. A leak that needed to be plugged.

But for the moment, Isa was his first priority. Not once had he ever placed a woman above the job. That the decision had been easy and instinctive brought him peace. He wanted her for himself. Though she'd claimed to not aspire to marriage, her words aboard her houseboat suggested her feelings had also shifted, that she too might want more.

“I killed him,” Isa had sobbed into his shoulder when he'd gathered her into his arms. “All that blood. His family—wife, child—whomever is held hostage will be devastated. I can't...”

“Shh,” he'd murmured, brushing away her tears. No words could console her, and there was no way to reassure her that everything would be fine. Her uncle's actions made his next move an easy decision. He and his team had gathered her relatives—wide-eyed and in shock—from Stornoway and insisted they travel under their escort to Glasgow where his men would set guards upon her brother's house. He could at least keep her family safe.

What little they'd manage to disassemble, crate and drag through the water-filled tunnel from the cave was now being carried off to the BURR staging room. Including the water-logged, rock-battered, barely recognizable body of Lord Roideach that they'd scooped from the sea.

"Sir!" A young officer stood before him. "Mr. Black has arranged for a temporary laboratory on base staffed by one Miss Lourney." He hefted the buckets containing two half-dead biomech octopuses. "I'm to collect and transport any biological materials directly into her care."

Excellent. Alec doubted it had taken much effort on Logan's behalf to turn yet another disgruntled employee against their former employer. If anyone could save the creatures, it would be Miss Lourney. "See she receives the box of laboratory notations as well."

With the biomech octopuses in her care, the technician would—with luck—spend the next few hours advancing their understanding of these creatures. It was a relief to pass the responsibility—however briefly—to another.

His brother waited at the side of the airstrip, leaning against a carriage hitched to two clockwork horses. Relief was mixed with the certain knowledge that Logan himself never appeared merely for the pleasure of his brother's company. Alec let out a long sigh, resigning himself to the necessity of listening to Logan's report. So long as his brother drove them home. He was in desperate need of sleep, and he wanted Isa in his bed beside him.

Shaw held out a carpet bag containing a few items Isa had stashed within before they'd abandoned her boat upon the shore. "You'll be at home?"

He nodded, accepting the bag. “Keep me updated.”

“Will do.”

With his arm about Isa—damp, bedraggled, her hair and dress in tatters—he performed introductions. “Mrs. McQuiston meet Mr. Logan Black, my brother, who is never anywhere convenient when you really need him.”

Logan snorted. “Who bypassed all the red tape and sent your team to raid a cave? I doubt you’d have chosen my presence over theirs.” He turned toward Isa and inclined his head as if she were the belle of the ball. “A pleasure to finally meet the woman who has tied my brother in such knots.”

“I’ve heard much about you.” Isa offered him a small smile.

Logan grinned. “That’s unfortunate.” He tipped his head toward the carriage door and held out a hand. “While I’d love to return the favor by sharing embarrassing stories from Alec’s childhood, those must wait. There is a new development we need to discuss.”

They climbed into the carriage and, with a tap on the roof, the driver set the clockwork horses in motion.

His brother wasted no time. “Lady Roideach has returned to Glasgow with two children in tow and is making much of her husband’s disappearance. Legally, no evidence exists that would allow us to take her into custody.”

“Yet,” Alec grumbled. "Give me time. I’ll find it.”

"No need."

Isa's mouth fell open, then snapped shut. "She intends to abandon my uncle, to establish herself in Glasgow society as a widow, mother of the young Lord Roideach. With her legal husband dead, she'll finally have access to all his funds."

His brother lifted a finger. "Unless her husband's body is never found, in which case the estate will enter probate for a period of seven years."

"You would threaten to bury him in a pauper's grave? That's blackmail."

"Exactly." Logan's eyes were bright with approval. "Moreover, by taking a second husband in an irregular marriage, she has committed bigamy. Their daughter is irrefutable proof of consummation. But we shall hold that card close to our chests to play at a later date." He paused, making it clear that Lady Roideach would not enjoy her deceased husband's fortune for long. "Your next task is to meet with her and collect all necessary information to stop Commodore Drummond."

"Me?" Isa pressed a hand to her chest.

"Both of you. Who better to verify any information she has to share?" Logan said. "Lady Roideach is wary of meeting privately. Because an afternoon social call lasting no longer than the prescribed fifteen minutes will raise no red flags, Cait has extended her an invitation to tea. Where better to hold a polite interrogation than right under your mother's nose?"

"Perfect Patsy is certain to be in attendance. She will cling to my arm tighter than any octopus ever would." Alec groaned.

"Already anticipated." Logan tossed a familiar box on his lap. "A solution. Arrive home with a fiancée on your arm. Your mother will refuse to speak to you both, and the ladies will be too busy sobbing into their teacups to interrupt your conversation with Lady Roideach."

Alec frowned. He might have been contemplating a more permanent future with Isa, but this wasn't at all how he'd envisioned proposing.

"Open it," Isa whispered.

He cracked open the box to reveal his grandmother's pearl ring. One she'd worn for decades and passed directly into his hands, telling him to keep it safe for his future bride. He'd locked it away in a safe intending to do exactly that if such a day ever arrived. His free hand curled into a fist. That Logan was able to crack that safe surprised him not one bit, that he would do so without permission made him want to relieve his brother of a few teeth.

"You need to be convincing," Logan said, leaning forward. Smart of him to close the distance so Alec's swing couldn't gather too much momentum. "Need more help?" His voice lowered to a comical growl. "Mrs. McQuiston, will you do me the great honor of—"

Alec grabbed his brother's cravat and dragged him close. He found himself incapable of anything but a low growl. Perhaps a quick butt to the head instead.

"Don't." Isa snatched the box from Alec's hands and slid the ring onto her finger. "It's nothing but a brief charade." She threw Logan a dark look. "No need to come to blows. We'll do whatever is necessary to stop my uncle."

He stared at the pearl ring upon her hand. It was exactly where he wanted it, where it belonged. But his brother had deprived him—them both—of a heartfelt and true proposal. He glared at Logan. Perhaps tonight he'd strangle his brother in his sleep.

Chapter Thirty-One

Isa gaped out the window as the carriage rattled into a neighborhood built by Glasgow's entrepreneurs. The streets were wide and clean, the paving stones smooth and perfectly horizontal. Lined with an abundance of bright, gas-lit lamps, few shadows remained, allowing residents to rest, assured of their safety. The houses themselves stood quite proud with their ornately carved stone façades, with tall windows stretching upward to peaked roofs where private dirigibles languished on roof pads. All the luxury made her a touch lightheaded.

"Our mutual grandfather made his fortune in shipping," Mr. Black said, answering her unasked question. "Allowing our father, also a talented merchant, to indulge himself in many things, including travel. He's rarely home."

"Thank aether," Alec grumbled. "The fighting becomes unbearable."

His lips had flattened into a thin, bloodless line when his brother produced the ring upon her finger. It hadn't been hard to imagine Mr. Black sporting a black eye by the time they rolled to a stop before their family home. His teasing tone had set her own teeth on edge. She'd already endured one engineered proposal. The humiliation of listening to such false words fall from Alec's lips might break her. She'd snatched the ring from the box before he could pry his mouth open. Yet it made her stomach twist itself into knots. If only they'd arrived at this moment without any pretense.

The carriage turned down a narrow street and came to a halt beside the service entrance. The door cracked open, spilling light into a small garden. A beautiful, dark-haired woman stood in the doorway, waiting.

"My sister," Alec said. "I expect you'll take to each other like flames to coal." He drew a deep breath.

"But if you don't, steer clear of any food she offers you." Mr. Black laughed, then excused himself to speak to the driver, leaving her alone with Alec.

"My brother presumes much. If—"

"It's nothing but a small white lie," Isa cut him off. "A quick, easy solution. If we cause a bit of social unrest, the company will shun us. All the better to speak with Maren." She was rather looking forward to the confrontation. Better this than to be carted off to her brother's home where her sister-in-law would wrap her up in a warm blanket and tuck her into a chair before the fireplace, an easy target for the matchmakers. Safe, perhaps, but no longer involved in stopping her uncle.

He nodded. “My sister will whisk you away the moment we reach the door. If there’s anything you need, you’ve only to ask.”

Need. She needed him.

“Will you come to me tonight?” She held her breath. The beds in a house such as this would be wide and soft. Unfamiliar—a welcome prospect for there would be no memories to crowd in the moment she closed her eyes. If he joined her, for a few hours they could push the nightmares of the past few days into dark corners and make new memories. The possibilities sent a shiver across her skin.

His eyes flashed with interest. “Are you certain you’re up for it?” he asked, his voice a low rumble.

With the situation diffused, she let her lips curve upward. “Are you?”

A spark flared in Alec's eyes. "It wouldn't be proper."

Catching his hand, she pressed his palm to her flaming cheek. "Why start now?"

He grinned. “Try not to fall asleep again before I arise.”

“If I do, it’ll be your turn to wake me.” She winked, then climbed from the carriage.

“Aether!” Cait stepped forward, pressing a hand to her chest as she took in Isa's appearance. “What on earth happened?"

Isa swept her hands down the front of her still-damp and bloodstained dress. Its skirts ended in tatters above her knees. Her hair fell in ragged, uneven lengths and her feet were bare. Her appearance certainly warranted an explanation, though the truth strained credibility.

She glanced at Alec, and he shrugged. "Easier to tell her than to wonder if she's developed a truth serum."

Cait swatted her brother's arm. "If only." She grinned at Isa. "You were saying..."

Why prevaricate? "An octopus attacked and dragged me into the ocean. I was forced to cut myself free from its grip."

Alec—dressed in salt-crusted clothing, his face unshaven with ever-deepening dark shadows beneath his eyes—nodded, his voice weary. "It's a long and convoluted tale."

"I see." Cait blinked. "In short, my brothers happened." She caught one of Isa's hands. "Come. Tell me while you soak in the tub. I want to know everything. Spare no detail about Lady Roideach's involvement. Were you friends?"

"No." A bitter taste rose to the back of Isa's throat as her mind replayed Maren's suggestion that any Finn men daring to challenge her husband be tossed in a tank with a biomech octopus. "We are, unfortunately, acquaintances of some duration."

Cait led her up the servant's stairs, down a long hall, through a large room with a four-poster bed, and into a grand bathroom. Water steamed from a clawfoot tub. French-milled soap rested on its narrow ledge. A stack of clean, white towels waited nearby upon a chair. A tall mirror—

"Don't look. It's nothing that can't be fixed. If you want, I'll trim your hair."

Relief flooded her. “Please. I submit to any and all repairs.”

Cait spun Isa about and unfastened the hooks and ribbons that held the remnants of her bodice in place, before tugging the whole sodden mass loose from her skin and over her head. "Impressive scars," she commented. "What happened to your legs?”

"Corpse fish." Bruised and battered, Isa sighed with relief as she sank into the hot water, reaching for the bar of sweet-smelling soap.

"Really?" Cait's voice rose with her eyebrows. She dropped the towels to the floor and dragged the chair close. "Start talking. Begin with why you're wearing Alec's grandmother's ring. I never thought to see it on another woman's finger."

"A temporary ruse to unsettle your mother and a woman named Patsy." Tiny hairs on the back of her neck lifted. She hadn’t thought to ask. “Alec never led her to believe—”

"Never." Cait laughed. "But Mother has schemed for years, thrown them together at every opportunity. Logan's instincts are unerring. This will be most entertaining. Now, begin at the beginning. How did you meet Alec?"

Isa told her everything—leaving out the attraction that drew her to Alec as certain as the moon pulled on the sea. Eyes wide, Cait leaned forward, propping her elbows on her knees and her chin on her fists, interrupting only for clarification.

Nearly an hour later, as the water grew cold, Isa ran her fingers through her hair, tugging ruefully on the uneven ends. "Can you even them?" she asked.

"Of course. I nearly forgot." Cait lifted a pair of scissors, and snippets of red hair began to fall, floating on the surface of the bathwater. "Such a beautiful color, a golden red."

Isa twisted her lips. "It irks my mother to no end that I refuse to dye it brown like a proper Finn."

"What?" Cait shook her head in disbelief. "I'd kill for such hair."

She snorted. "And I for yours. My grandfather was Scottish, and red hair marks my bloodline as polluted."

"Polluted." Cait's laugh was bitter. "That I understand. I am a child of spite. When Mother learned of Logan's existence, she took a lover." She waved a hand at her face. "Society disapproves of my complexion, one that whispers of the Indian subcontinent. But that's neither here nor there."

Isa reached out and squeezed Cait's free hand. She could only offer sympathy, not solutions. "I struggle daily to accept that I needn't fix what's not broken."

"A most excellent position to take." Cait set aside the scissors. "Now, tell me more about this Lady Roideach we're to interrogate."

Discovering a fast friend in Alec's sister was unexpected, but so very welcome. For once, Isa did not feel judged and found wanting. "I knew her as Maren, the only daughter of the town's matriarch. Every inch of her is Finn perfection. An excellent swimmer. Bright. Beautiful. Spoiled. But nothing was ever enough..."

~~~

A rusty "coo" echoed through his bedchamber. Giving his wet hair a final rub, he wrapped the towel about his waist and padded barefoot across the floor. Stepping over the salty, sweaty clothes he'd peeled from his aching body and dropped to the floor, he nabbed the bird perched in his window.

He unrolled the message attached to the skeet pigeon's foot and scanned the words of Shaw's report before crumbling the paper in his hand.

Jona was stable, but still unconscious. Nina's fever had abated. Sinclair was out of surgery and expected to make a full recovery. After confirming that Mr. Black had set every water skimmer on high alert for the megalodon, Shaw had made his way to the makeshift BURR marine biology laboratory where Miss Lourney had stabilized the biomech octopuses. Not only were they no longer showing signs of distress, but—after polishing off a meal of several lobsters—they had become rather intent on climbing out of the tanks in which they'd been imprisoned.

In short, there were no pressing emergencies. He could finally rest. Catch a few hours of sleep. But not here, not in his own bed alone. Not when Isa's invitation beckoned.
~~~

Why then did he hesitate? She was everything he looked for when selecting a lover. A stunning woman, a widow who professed no interest in marriage, a woman who could heat his blood with a single glance. Except she was more. Intelligent. Loyal. Brave. What he felt for her was far, far stronger than lust. He wanted more. Was it really too soon to contemplate a future with her in it? Permanently.

Dragonflies slammed into the walls of his stomach. His parents were miserable together, happier apart, and their poor example had rather soured his opinion of marriage. But Alec no longer felt complete without Isa by his side. Their bond strengthened daily, as feelings between them shifted and changed. Was this how it felt to fall in love? He rather thought the answer was yes. If he wanted her, he had to renegotiate the terms of their affair. He needed to propose.

Fiancée. The term touched a match to his heart. It pounded, sending warmth rushing through his veins. He slapped on the hated knee brace, buckling it in place. Dressing quickly, he strode from his room with purpose. Not a soul caught him walking down the hallway, save Munro, whose wire eyebrows lifted with disapproval as he cracked open Isa's door.

Legs curled beneath her, she sat in a wingback chair set before the fireplace. Firelight flickered, setting the soft copper waves of her stunning hair aglow, hair that now brushed the tops of her shoulders. She wore nothing but a dressing gown and, as she smiled her welcome, its lace edges parted, caressing the inside curves of her breasts. A clear invitation.

But instead of scooping her into his arms, he hesitated. Resting on the table beside her was his grandmother's ring. They weren't truly engaged, he hadn't spoken the words, so why the ache in his chest?

He picked it up. Holding the worn gold band between this thumb and forefinger, he dropped into the chair across from her and met her gaze.

"It felt wrong," Isa admitted. "No worries. I'll wear it for tea tomorrow."

Damn his brother and his meddling ways.

"Too big? Too small?"

"Too presumptuous." She lifted her shoulder and the silken sleeve slid down her arm, exposing the delightful and distracting curves of her collarbone. "I invited a lover to my bedchamber, not a suitor."

The smoldering heat in her eyes nearly made him abandon his plans in favor of the suggested activities. No. Not yet. He wanted to make his intent clear. "We agreed to renegotiate the terms of our affair."

Pain rippled across her face. "Not tonight. Not now."

"Why not? For once there is no pressing crisis." A deep sense of rightness settled over him as he lowered himself onto his good knee. "Marriage to a Navy man is never easy. BURR assignments *will* drag me away." A fact he'd once relished, the better to keep grasping, social-climbing women at an arm's length. He couldn't be caught and trapped if he wasn't around. Couldn't be forced into a marriage of convenience wherein he would risk repeating his parents' many mistakes. Pledging himself to Isa was not at all the same thing. She would complicate his life in all the best ways. "As will your own work, your own career. But never before have I met a woman with whom I wished to build a life. Will you—"

Her quicksilver eyes flashed, and she leapt to her feet. "Stop. Please."

~~~

Heartache tore through her as she turned and walked across the room. Away from Alec. Hand pressed to her stomach, she tried to still an upwelling of doubt and uncertainty. Silk slid over her skin and her bare feet sank into the thick pile of the carpet beneath her. Luxury surrounded her. It defined the room. A soft down-filled mattress. A mirrored dressing table. Brocade curtains. A marble mantle. The list went on and on. They might be merely things but, nonetheless, they reminded Isa of all that separated them.

"We come from such different worlds," she said, tracing the flocked pattern of the wallpaper with a fingertip. "Finn and Scot. Merging our lives might prove impossible."

The pearl ring clinked as he set it down upon the table, and then his warm body pressed against her back with firm evidence of his growing physical desire. "Even though we share so much? A love of the sea. An interest
~~~

in medicine. Equally messy families." He swept her hair aside and kissed the top of her ear. "An array of scars." He tugged at the collar of her robe and brushed warm lips over the curve of her neck. "A fierce attraction."

"All true." She wanted him, there was no denying that. Did she love him? She rather thought she might. But marriage? The thought scared her. How much of her hard-won independence was she willing to surrender? How much would he expect her to bend and shape her life to fit his?

His hot, wet mouth trailed down the column of her spine, peeling the dressing gown from her shoulders, from her arms, until she was bare to the waist. She tugged the bow at her midriff free and let the silk pool on the ground. Alec growled his approval.

Good. Let his primal instincts take over. She didn't wish to discuss a wedding. Not now.

He swept strong, rough hands over the curves of her hips and nipped at the rise of her arse. "So pretty," he whispered.

His words made her flush. She glanced over her shoulder, and his eyes flashed such heat that her blood began to simmer. What would happen when it boiled?

With one large hand, he caught her wrists, lifting her arms over her head and pressing her palms to the papered wall. Nibbling at her neck, he cupped her breast, brushing the rough pad of his thumb over her nipple. Only his touch could set her skin on fire, only he had ever sent ripples of pure pleasure from her head to her toes, until every nerve quivered with need. She was in danger of losing herself to this man.

"Please, Alec," she begged, wanting him inside her. "More." The bed was only a few feet away.

Instead of sweeping her off her feet, he nudged his knee between hers. "Open for me."

Here? Against the wall? She let her legs part, and he slid his hand downward over her stomach. A soft moan escaped her lips when his fingers found her damp curls, parting her folds to stroke and tease the small, sensitive nub at her core.

"Aether," she breathed, her knees growing weak as he slid one finger, then another into her wet channel. Her hips bucked against his hand as he stoked her, driving her to a dizzying height of pleasure. She threw her head backward onto his shoulder and cried out as she climaxed, her body convulsing with pleasure. If he'd pressed her for an answer now, she would be unable to deny him.

Hands on her waist, he turned her around and pushed her back against the wall. Her heart pounded. Would he ask again? But his eyes held an entirely different question than the one he'd begun to ask earlier. *This* she knew how to answer.

"Yes," she whispered. She plucked the buttons of his shirt free and shoved the garment from his broad shoulders. "Don't stop."

Leaning forward, her still-sensitive breasts rubbed against his chest as she dealt with the problem of the trousers that hung on his narrow hips. With them unfastened, a most impressive erection stood proud. Hastily, she pushed at the material until they fell away. He kicked them aside, standing before her in all his glory. *Such a magnificent physique.* He hesitated a moment, then caught at her hand, tugging her forward. Toward the bed.

But she'd seen a certain desire in his eyes. She crooked her finger. "I rather thought you wanted to stay."

His grin took on a devilish glint. "Are you sure?" he breathed, nuzzling her neck. "Here?"

So it *could* be done. "If you think you can manage it," she teased.

"Oh, I certainly can." His hands cupped her thighs, spreading them as he lifted her. With her back pressed to the wall, Alec bent down and caught her lips with a hungry mouth. She welcomed his tongue, giving herself over to the desire that stirred anew and coursed through her veins. But it wasn't enough.

Hooking a leg behind his thigh, she yanked him flush to her body. Their bodies met in a firestorm of heat and need, and she writhed against his hot, hard erection, her own arousal growing more insistent by the second.

She wrapped her arms about his neck and nipped the edge of his jaw, desperate to feel his thick length buried inside her. "Now!" she demanded, lifting her gaze to his and staring into such blue depths she feared she might drown. "Take me."

~~~
~~~

Exactly what he'd hoped to hear. Alec notched himself against her wet opening. Before, he'd been afraid of hurting her, but remembering what made her scream, he plunged into her with a single, deep thrust.

She cried out with pleasure as he pinned her to the wall, as she squirmed against him.

But he didn't move. Instead, he nipped at her jaw, letting her desire swell. He wanted her to beg, to plead, to realize how very right they were for each other. What she'd be giving up if she didn't say yes. Gently, he kissed the edge of her mouth, brushing his lips softly over hers until she fisted her hands in his hair and dragged his mouth to hers, thrusting her tongue deep.

Still—though heat gathered and coiled at the base of his spine with an intensity he'd never before experienced—he did no more than kiss her. The woman he would always want to find in his bed. He nibbled her lower lip. Against his wall. Above his chair.

"Alec!" She tore her face away with a gasp. Wild passion flared in her eyes. She flexed her hips and his will shattered. With a growl, he pulled back, then gave her what she wanted, driving into her.

"Aether!" Her legs wrapped about his hips, and she dug her heels into his arse, driving him mad as she urged him deeper still. "More!"

Need built to dizzying heights. The coiled tension at the base of his spine grew tighter with each thrust. Over and over, he drove into her burying himself to the hilt.

With a cry, she bent forward and sank her teeth into his shoulder as yet another climax ripped through her, squeezing his length. Blood roaring in his ears, he battered into her, slamming their bodies together. With a shout, he spilled his seed inside her, hot and wet.

Alec dropped his forehead against the wall. Heart pounding, chest heaving, he held her, unable to find the words to express how very right she felt in his arms. He could have stayed like this forever, but gravity and his knee insisted otherwise. Reluctantly, he pulled free and carried her to bed.

Beneath the covers, he wrapped an arm about her waist and dragged her soft, naked form close. She was everything he ever wanted, everything he needed, and he was lucky to have found her. Damned if he intended to let her go without a fight.

"Think about it," he whispered. For now, he would let his interrupted proposal stand, let her contemplate the possibility of a real future together.

"Alec, I don't—"

"Shh," he murmured. "Don't make any decisions yet. Answer me when this is over. Until then, wear my ring, stand beside me as my intended. Will you promise me that much?"

"Very well." She snuggled closer, planting a seed of hope. "Provided you honor your original vow."

Passion seemed to have addled his brain. "Remind me?"

"I was promised a torrid affair." She sighed with mock disappointment. "It's possible I'm wrong, but I'm fairly confident two such encounters don't meet the minimum requirements."

He laughed softly into her hair. No woman was her match. He could be patient. Wait for her to grasp how perfect they were for each other, both in and out of bed. "Sleep, Isa. If you insist upon keeping count, we'll work at remedying that problem as soon as I'm able. At a minimum, I anticipate doubling our numbers before dawn."

"Only twice more?" She turned her head upon the pillow, throwing him a sultry look over her shoulder. "That's disappointing. I thought you might be up for more."

His groin stirred. "Strike that." He slid his hand to palm the weight of her breast. "Challenge accepted. Sleep can wait."

Chapter Thirty-Two

"I ought to mention my bedroom wall shares one with yours." Cait dropped the statement into their conversation casually, while her steam maid fussed with Isa's hair, pinning strands with quick and calculated precision.

Isa's face grew hot. Her mouth fell open, then snapped shut. "I—" She swallowed. It didn't help that she and Alec had slept past noon. In the same bed. Worse, he'd been caught leaving her room. "I'm so sorry."

Except she wasn't. Alec tore down walls she'd built around her heart and threw open doors she'd thought forever closed to her. Including the possibility of wedded bliss.

Cait laughed as the steam maid jabbed in another hair pin. "As you should be." She eyed the pearl ring on Isa's finger. "Unless my brother proposed in truth and you accepted. I can't think of anyone I'd rather have as my sister-in-law."

Isa bit her lip. The sight of Alec kneeling before her had made her hands shake, her head spin and her heart pound. She'd had to stop him. She wanted too badly to say yes, to leap into his arms with abandon. But she'd leapt into marriage before without thinking clearly, without considering the consequences. Never again.

She caught Cait's eyes in the mirror. "I'd like nothing more. But marriage is an enormous commitment."

"Is it his career?"

"Partly." There were so many questions to consider and no easy answers.

Once this mission was complete, when her uncle was stopped, Alec would still be a member of BURR. Could she cope, not knowing where he was, what dangers he faced or when he might come home? *If* he would come home? Men sometimes died. Sinclair—pinned to the wall of her boat by a harpoon—had come close.

"I also have my own career to consider."

Joining their lives together would be a complicated affair. If the University of Glasgow refused to accept a woman into their medical program, would she need to travel to London? Or perhaps further? The *Université de Paris* accepted women and, though she spoke no French, she could learn. Regardless, she could no more ask Alec to accompany her than she could ask a fish to sprout legs and walk upon the ground. Her heart grew heavy at the thought of leaving him behind, but he belonged here, in Scotland, working with his team.

"Mostly it's too soon," Isa finished. Why had he felt the need to push, to complicate everything between them? "We've known each other all of perhaps two weeks."

"But you're still considering it?" Cait brightened. "I'll take that as a maybe." She held up a hand. "No, don't disillusion me further. I've a role to play at tea, same as you. Mother is already huffing like a steam engine. The only thing keeping her tongue civil is the hope that your 'friendship' with Lady Roideach will translate into social connections. Her ambition is to find me a marriageable gentleman with a title."

The steam maid rolled backward and whistled in appreciation while Isa stared at her reflection in the mirror. The steambot's jointed fingers had struggled to apply the pattern of the punch card Cait had inserted but, in the end, Isa's cropped hair had been twisted and pinned into a delightfully whimsical upsweep.

Smiling, Isa lifted a hand, then thought the better of touching her hair. "I've never looked so grand. So much like a lady."

"One must look her best when confronting the enemy," Cait agreed, already garbed in a navy silk gown, its bodice and bustle trimmed with copper-striped ribbon. Her dark eyes flashed. "Now for your armor."

She held up Isa's best corset—the one embroidered with silver swirls—rescued from her houseboat moments before the evacuation began. Cleaned and aired, it looked as new as the day she'd purchased it. Excellent. Such fitted garments were difficult to obtain on short notice.

While the steam maid applied her nimble fingers once more to the laces—pulling so tight Isa could barely breathe—Cait plunged into her wardrobe, emerging over and over to hold swaths of silk and satin beneath Isa's face, before tossing gown after gown onto the bed with exclamations of disgust.

"Aha!" Cait burst from her wardrobe, holding a beautiful green gown aloft in her hands. "Perfect! It will set off both your silver eyes *and* your lovely copper hair. My brother will gape and Perfect Patsy will despair. Lift your arms and don't move.""

Though the sleeves were long and the neck high, the dress was anything but demure. Black lace dripped from her wrists and framed her face. Seafoam silk cascaded from her hips, bustled behind her in giant poofs. Beneath the overskirt, layer upon layer of black ruffles fell to the floor. The heeled slippers she wore almost made up for their difference in heights, but she would need to be careful while walking to avoid tripping.

"You look absolutely beautiful," Cait declared, sliding thin gold wires through the holes in Isa's earlobes. From each dangled a single pearl, their luster glowing in the gaslight. "My brother would be a fool not to do anything he can to make this a permanent arrangement."

~~~

His brother and sister were both evil. Their individual plans merging to perfection.
~~~

Isa swept into the parlor, a fiery-haired goddess in green. His not-quite-a-fiancée. All conversation stopped. Alec wanted to admire the curve of her neck, the bow of her full lips, her quicksilver eyes. Alas, her neck was stiff, and her lips were pressed into a thin line. Everyone stared openly, but no one greeted her. Not even the roving tea table.

Perfect Patsy, whose fingertips had pressed lightly against the back of his hand, then fluttered away, over and over, like a fly briefly alighting on an uncovered tart, desperately wanting a taste, but afraid of being swatted, stepped aside. For Isa's gray eyes had darkened, promising an approaching storm.

"Mother." Alec tugged at his over-tight cravat and prepared to force the issue. He stepped forward to lead Isa into the fray. Tea. An afternoon social ritual of sophisticated and highly refined torture. "Allow me to introduce Mrs. Isa McQuiston, my future bride."

"It's true," a woman hissed, before slapping her hand to her mouth, eyes wide, shocked by her own outcry.

"Welcome," his mother said at last. One could almost hear the ice in her voice crack and shatter with the effort it took her to speak politely. "I understand you are friend to Lady Roideach."

"We've known each other since we were children," Isa equivocated with finesse.

"Please. Sit." His mother indicated a seat beside her, her smile stiff. "I see you wear my mother's ring. Lovely, if perhaps old-fashioned."

His mother meant *cheap*, an attempt to suggest to her friends that this alliance couldn't possibly last, that an old circlet of gold holding a lump of sand coated in the secretions of a bivalve cemented nothing.

Still, humiliation stained Perfect Patsy's face bright red, and her own mother's face was a mask of outrage. The two women had been whispering about arranging the marriage of their children from the moment they both lay in bassinets.

"It suits me perfectly," Isa replied, her chin held high. "I'm quite fond of the ocean."

Her words were a breeze—tinged with salt—that cleared the dreary miasma from the room. Pride filled his lungs.

Cait's eyes darted warily toward her mother, then defiantly handed Isa a cup of tea. "Would you care for some cream cake?"

"Please." Isa lifted her teacup, but paused at the distinctive sound of canvas wings flapping.

Alec turned.

A skeet pigeon flew down the length of the room, then beat its wings backward as it stretched orange-painted feet forward. Startled to find its landing pathway covered with silver and china, it attempted a course correction. Hopping and skidding across the roving table, it came to a sudden and sodden stop.

Plop.

Cake, cream and raspberry jam flew everywhere.

Patsy's mother squealed and jumped to her feet, dropping her teacup in her haste to rush to her daughter's aid. A number of ladies dabbed ineffectively at their bodices and gowns with bereft moans. Cait and Isa glanced at each other. Isa covered her mouth, but Cait giggled. Mother sucked in a horrified gasp before turning a furious gaze upon him.

He snorted. If only he could enjoy the moment of chaos. Alas, the skeet pigeon's eyes flashed red—an indication the bird carried time sensitive communication. At the thought of some new fresh hell, a ball of ice formed in his stomach.

Alec plunged his hand into the dessert, his fingers searching for the message canister. Success. Dragging it forth, he wiped it clean, unscrewed the end cap, and pulled out the rolled message within.

"Alec!" his mother exclaimed, her face suffused with an angry glow. "Must you?"

He didn't answer. He was too busy reading the message his brother had sent. The ice in his stomach thawed—everyone was fine. Still, the situation was once again conspiring against them, ruining his plans to spend another night in Isa's bed convincing her to never leave him.

With a heavy sigh, he looked across the table and caught Isa's gaze. "There's been a development. We're wanted—"

A familiar *chuff* of exhaust gas—akin to the clearing of a throat—sounded at the doorway. "Lady Roideach," Burton intoned.

In a froth of black silk and crow feathers, the woman in question swept into the parlor. Introductions were made.

Bowing and scraping began. Would knowing this woman had callously arranged for her brother to participate in a ghastly experiment dampen their admiration?

Patsy's mother pushed her forward, launching into an exhaustive list of her daughter's many talents. Alec had the decided impression the woman was panicking, frantically attempting to market a child who—for too long—had made assumptions that weren't hers to make. His engagement must be convincing.

"I'm afraid I must make this brief," Lady Roideach interrupted, her voice bored but her eyes piercing. "Uncouth as it may be to appear in public at such a distressing time, I couldn't pass on the chance to welcome Mrs. McQuiston back to Glasgow." She glanced at the ring on Isa's finger and lifted an eyebrow. "Perhaps there's a library where we might catch up? Where we might privately discuss Miss McCullough's social future?"

"Ladies?" Alec bowed, then swept his hand outward. "Allow me to escort you?" Leaving the bird where it lay, he lowered his voice and murmured into Isa's ear. "No worries. Good news for a change. But we'll need to leave immediately after your... visit."

~~~

Injecting steel into her spine, Isa laid her hand on Alec's proffered arm and allowed herself to be led away.

Though she rather preferred the rough, devil-may-care, Navy man she'd come to know, this clean-shaven,
~~~

polished version of Alec standing in the parlor took her breath away. Not that her warrior was gone, for beneath the fine wool, she felt the iron of his muscle flex as he clenched his fist. Such strength. Thoughts of the wall he'd held her against made the breath in her throat catch.

"Mr. Black's hopes are inordinately high," she murmured as they walked the length of the hallway. "Maren is no fool. So long as there's a possibility he'll survive, she won't reveal my uncle's location." A point she'd meant to make last night before he... distracted her.

"Which is why my brother handed us a trump card," Alec said, calm but determined.

She pursed her lips. Distasteful as it might be, their possession of Lord Roideach's body might prove critical.

Peripheral vision absorbed what it could of her surroundings—heavy curtains, a dark mahogany desk, books lining the walls, a ladder set upon wheels leaning against a track—as Maren enthroned herself upon an overstuffed armchair placed beside an unlit fireplace.

Cait, escorting a roving table bearing a fresh tea tray, took the chair opposite and began to pour. She held out a teacup to the traitorous wife and widow.

Instead of reaching for the teacup, Maren narrowed her eyes. "I've been warned about you." Her gaze fixed upon an overly large ring Cait wore. "A bit of advice. Find a protector who will give you a long leash, or you're going to find yourself locked in a cage."

Cait's face paled. Isa had never despised Maren more and could only wonder at the source of the woman's bitterness.

A retort was pointless. Anyone who would sacrifice her own brother to please her husband had long ago cast aside all integrity.

"He's fine, your brother." Isa stepped forward to stand behind Cait's chair, her fingers gripping its back as she drew Maren's attention upon herself. "Both he and my sister are expected to make a full recovery."

"How unfortunate." Maren fixed her dull, pewter eyes on Isa, answering in the old language. "But as I've no intention of returning to the islands, how Jona chooses to pollute the family blood is no longer my concern. I will remain here in Glasgow. However, a missive from one Mr. Black informs me that should I wish to retain my freedom, I must first betray my remaining husband. I'm not at all convinced such an action would be in my best interest."

Something inside her snapped. "Must everything always be about you? A title wasn't enough?"

Alec frowned, no doubt unhappy at being cut out of the conversation, but he held his tongue when most men would have sought to interfere.

"An impoverished lord is no prize," Maren sneered. "But I am indebted to your uncle for helping my son come into a sudden inheritance, one I will ensure is carefully managed."

"The trail of bodies in your wake is most impressive." Isa struggled to maintain an appearance of calm detachment, but her body begin to vibrate with anger. "Years of effort only to abandon my uncle at this critical juncture. You return to Glasgow and propose to remain. Why? My uncle has promised you a crown. As queen you could stand upon a castle balcony and peer down your nose upon your subjects."

Maren leaned forward. "Lessons both of us should take to heart. Men promise much, and deliver only if and when it suits them. A title was supposed to come with money. A queen should be treated like royalty. Your marriage was supposed to provide a medical career, a chance for your brilliance to shine. We were both used."

Isa gaped at the open admission of Maren's involvement.

"My first husband wished to make a name for himself studying selkies, but was regretfully unfaithful." Maren curled her lip. "My second husband wishes to purify our bloodline at any cost. I offered him suggestions, possibilities, in return for certain... favors. How else would he have learned about factor Q, the blood protein that defines a Finn?"

"*You* told my uncle about Anton's work!"

"Dr. McQuiston was struggling despite my husband's mentorship." Maren smirked. "Your bright mind was all he needed. No sooner were you married than the breakthroughs began."

An icy rivulet of distress trickled down her spine. This was all her fault. Isa purposefully switched back to

English. "He means for pure blood lineages to rule. For half-bloods to serve."

"Of course." Maren arched an eyebrow but answered in kind. "But what advantage is a pure blood line if one is forced to live on a wind-blown, rocky island in the North Atlantic? Which circles us back around to the purpose of this meeting. What does Mr. Black offer to entice the betrayal of my remaining husband?"

Time for negotiations. "If you intend to remain in Glasgow, to establish yourself here, widow's weeds might not be an appropriate fashion choice." Isa crossed her arms. "Establishing death *in absentia* can involve lengthy legal proceedings. Without Lord Roideach's body, you won't officially become a widow for another seven years."

"You have his corpse." Maren's lips twisted.

"Conveniently collected from the water beside a certain underwater sea cave," Alec answered, his shoulders relaxing now that he could once again follow their conversation. "Provide us with accurate information leading to the capture of Commodore Drummond, and Lord Roideach's body will be discovered and ruled an accidental death. Then, you may schedule a funeral without any further interference."

"Understood," Maren said. "We have an agreement." Her harsh laugh grated. "The fool intends to sink that bloody castle."

"What?" Isa, Alec and Cait all spoke at once. "Why?"

Maren huffed. "Without consulting me, he has decided that Denmark would stop at nothing to reclaim a structure built by their country at great expense and effort. He does not wish to engage any country in direct battle. Instead, your uncle intends to build his own palace 'from the stone of our new homeland' while consolidating and expanding his influence. It will take decades, and I do not wish to live in a smoky blackhouse while he spends my son's inheritance."

Not when she could live the life of a wealthy peer in Scotland.

Face tight, Maren rose. "Our fifteen minutes of social discourse are nearly over. Details will have to wait. In short, there will be no royal wedding. Drummond intends to transport his OctoFinn—and other hostages—to the North Sea. From a safe and undetectable position, they will rise from the depths to disable the structure upon which the castle floats."

"When?" Alec demanded.

Maren smirked. "Produce a death certificate, and I will provide you with a detailed timeline." She swept from the room without a backward glance.

Chapter Thirty-Three

Dressed in all their afternoon finery, Alec and Isa burst into the BURR operations room. Logan—dressed in his well-tailored but unimaginative dark suit—stood alongside Shaw, Moray, Rowan, and Rip. Joining them was one Mr. Danel Guthrie, Isa's brother. All of them bent over the large, wooden table at its center. Several brightly lit Lucifer lamps hung overhead, illuminating sheaves of paper covered in line drawings: the detailed plans for a submersible.

Shaw's head snapped up. "A top hat to a mission briefing." He grinned. "Classy."

"Is it, though?" Moray's lips twitched as he tapped his chin. "I think the brocade waistcoat takes it a touch too far."

"But the lady looks lovely." Rowan swept a bow. "Silk sets a refined tone our team sadly lacks."

Isa caught at her skirts and curtsied. "Standards, gentlemen, must be raised."

The men snickered.

"Is that a ring I spy upon your finger, milady?" Shaw's eyes sparked with unabashed interest.

The mood in room shifted. All humor evaporated.

"Isa?" Her brother frowned.

In their haste to leave, they'd not thought to tuck away his grandmother's pearl ring for safekeeping. No need to maintain the charade before his team. Alec pried open his mouth to say something flippant, to deny the significance of the adornment.

But Moray's eyebrows slammed together, and he took a step in Isa's direction. "Tell me you didn't. I'd hoped—" He bit off the rest of his sentence with a guilty glance at Alec. He'd lied. Moray was not at all over his infatuation with his childhood sweetheart.

"What I have or haven't done is none of your concern." Isa lifted her chin, honoring her promise to consider his offer, to make her decision when the danger was past and her uncle behind bars. Or dead. Alec rather preferred the second option. His mind flashed to the empty cave and the certainty that there were women, possibly children, aboard the man's submersible. Dead, provided it didn't come at the cost of innocent lives.

In any case, he certainly wouldn't be allaying any of Moray's romantic concerns, not when he hoped to convince Isa to say yes, to accept his suit. Instead, he stared stonily at Moray, sending a clear message as he slid his arm about her waist and drew her tight to his side.

Mine.

There was a moment of stunned silence. Then Shaw threw his head back and roared with laughter. Rip stared in disbelief. Rowan hooted. Moray paled.

Holding up his hand, Alec caught his brother's eyes. "Lady Roideach arrived as planned. In exchange for a death certificate, she'll provide the details of her husband's plans. For now, all we know is that he intends to have his OctoFinn sink the castle before the wedding."

"Sink? We'd not considered that possibility. We'll have to table this discussion for now." Logan's eyes glimmered with plans and backup plans and who knew what else. "Suffice it to say, Mr. Guthrie was good enough to share what he knows of the megalodon's interior layout."

Isa gaped at her brother, then swept forward. She scanned the diagrammatic sketches strewn across the surface of the table. "*You* built a submersible for Uncle Gregor?" Distress laced her voice.

"No," Mr. Guthrie said. Yet shame hunched his shoulders. "But I may have accidentally helped design its mechanics, though I've no idea when or how the biomech aspects were incorporated." His eyes were downcast. "Uncle Gregor came to me a year ago, wanting to discuss hypotheticals. I produced a few drawings." He waved his hands at the papers. "A submersible modeled upon the side-to-side swing of a shark's tail. To generate lift, the top portion of the so-called tail has to slant backward and extend past that of the bottom—"

Logan cleared his throat. "Thank you, Mr. Guthrie, for all your assistance. The information is invaluable. I'll fill them in later. I wish I could allow you time with your sister, but I'm afraid there are now other pressing matters to which I must attend."

A corpse, for example.

"A moment." Isa's brother crossed to stand before her and spoke in a low voice. "Though Mr. Black informs me you are a valued, if temporary, member of this team, I have serious doubts about allowing you to remain in their custody, particularly given this Scot appears to have asked for your hand in marriage."

Isa sucked in a breath. "I will marry whomever I choose, Danel. And I'm here of my own free will. I'm not going anywhere."

Alec met her brother's stony stare. "I'll do everything I can to keep her safe."

"Very well." Though Mr. Guthrie didn't look the least bit convinced, he recognized defeat. Pressing an awkward kiss to Isa's cheek, he said his goodbyes. "Send a pigeon if you change your mind." The heavy iron door clanged shut behind him.

"Follow me." Logan turned on his heel.

They marched down the long hallway to the BURR indoor training facility. Without stopping, Logan passed through the gymnasium, ignoring the curious stares of a handful of new recruits, to another hallway—this one tiled. He shoved open the door and waved them all through.

The indoor swimming pool itself was empty, a rarity. Easy to understand why men were foregoing its use. At the side of the pool sat two large, cylindrical glass tanks. A band of iron encircled the rim of each, allowing metal mesh lids to be locked in place. Each tank held a convalescing biomech octopus attended to by Roideach's former laboratory technician.

"Welcome!" Bright-faced, Miss Lourney greeted them. Hands clasped tightly at her waist, she rocked onto her toes. "The creatures healed remarkably fast once I repaired the tips of the braided wires incorporated within their attachment appendages." She glanced over her shoulder at the tanks. "So much so that I've sedated them. Catching an escaped octopus sporting two barbed legs is remarkably tricky."

"Legs?" Shaw asked. "I thought octopuses had arms."

"Not incorrect," she answered. "Though it's generally accepted that two appendages function as legs to propel them along the sea floor. In this case, those two limbs have been modified to insert and fuse with the vasculature of a Finn host expressing a blood protein designated factor Q."

Beside him, Isa shuddered. He caught her hand in his and gave her fingers a gentle squeeze.

"Excuse me, Miss Lourney." Logan interrupted the biology discussion, drawing everyone's attention. "Time is of the essence. Listen closely. Regardless of how you arrived here, your participation is not mandatory. In fact, it's probably ill-advised. Major Fernsby is on extended leave. This is a joint operation between BURR and the Queen's agents involving two civilians. However, you will be working for me, under my command, and Queen's agents work strictly off the record."

The BURR team exchanged wary glances.

Logan continued, "If this operation goes bad, we're buggered. The Queen will disavow all knowledge of our activities. We may well face criminal charges, possibly in the courts of a foreign government. If all goes well, her Majesty will look upon us fondly, but nothing will be committed to paper or placed in our files. Ever."

The men shifted on their feet. Miss Lourney's posture grew rigid. Isa, however, lifted her chin. Pride swelled in his chest. Like all his team members, little could make her back down.

"If we do nothing, an attempt will be made to sink a floating castle—along with all its guests and residents—into the North Sea. In our territorial waters. Under our watch. I do not have time to list the political ramifications of such an event." Logan scanned the room. "If anyone wishes to leave, now is the time."

The chaos resulting from such death and destruction would keep countries at each other's throats for months, possibly years. A diplomatic nightmare. Drummond might not wish his fledgling would-be country to become *involved* in a war, but he might well *start* one.

No one moved.

"Good." Logan nodded. "To sum up the situation. A high-ranking man in the British Navy is Finn. He—and those who have aligned themselves with him—regard themselves as a people separate from that of the general Scottish population. For several years, he has fostered a small but growing group of Finn situated on the Faroe Islands. We know his ultimate goal was to wrest control of the islands from Denmark and establish an independent kingdom."

Isa frowned. "A goal he has been working toward for quite some time."

"Until the royal wedding upset his plans." Moray crossed his arms and frowned.

"Exactly. As a wedding gift, the King of Denmark promised Iceland control of the Faroe Islands. To provide his daughter with an appropriate wedding venue and later a residence, he commissioned a floating castle, currently en route to the islands as we speak. The intent is to affix the castle—via complicated engineering techniques—to the Tinganes peninsula adjacent to the capital of Tórshavn."

"And you collected this information how?" Alec needled his brother.

"As if I would compromise my sources." Logan fixed his intense gaze upon Isa. "Thank you, Mrs. McQuiston, for meeting with his chosen queen. I'm almost certain it was unpleasant."

She nodded. In the warm, humid air of the natatorium, tendrils of hair that had escaped Isa's upsweep began to curl, much like the heat in his loins. Tonight he would twist his finger through its coils and—

"I will inform my superiors of this latest development, but the Queen has indicated that Iceland and Denmark are both dismissive of her concerns." Logan cleared his throat. "Our basic mission consists of two goals. One, board and take control of the megalodon. Two, prevent Drummond's OctoFinn from scuttling the floating castle."

His teammates all swore at once. It might be spring, but it wouldn't feel like that in the waters of North Sea.

"Do we have any schematics for the castle?" Shaw asked.

"A rough approximation," Logan answered. "With the help of whisky, one of my men contrived to coax one of the project engineers into boasting about the construction. He wrote down all such details in a notebook. I'll have it in your hands by morning. Alec, Shaw, Rowan, and Rip. You will function at approved aquaspira breather depths beneath the pontoons that keep the castle afloat. Plan to intercept and disable any OctoFinn and/or explosive devices. Moray and Isa will attempt to board the megalodon."

His brother glanced at him, and Alec *knew*. "No," he said, his voice low and threatening.

"It's the only chance of rescuing those aboard Drummond's submersible," Logan replied, his expression implacable. "No one else can dive that deep. Mr. Guthrie indicated that there are two underwater ports located on the—"

"You want to fuse a biomech octopus to Moray," Alec concluded. It wasn't a *bad* idea, but—

"Hell no!" Moray shouted, backing away.

Alec had expected exactly that reaction. What he hadn't expected was to watch Logan's gaze once again fall upon Isa.

She paled.

"You can't be serious," he said. Fury filled his chest as fratricide became a real possibility. His brother did nothing impulsively. Like a game of chess, he always thought several moves ahead, and that was why the BURR team was assembled in the natatorium beside the tanks of *two* rescued and repaired biomech octopuses.

His heart slammed against his sternum. Sending Isa into the icy depths of the ocean wasn't protecting her, it was deliberately placing her in harm's way. He could feel an artery at his temple begin to throb. He wanted to forbid her participation. The words were on the tip of his tongue when he bit them back. He'd promised to treat her as an equal, but how could he possibly view her as such? Her natural skills were breathtaking, but she lacked any military training.

"Finn men attached to an octopus can easily function at great depths with no worries of equipment failure or decompression sickness." Logan pressed onward, seemingly unaware of his brother's skyrocketing blood pressure. "There's no reason to think a Finn woman less capable. The megalodon need never surface near the castle. How else do you propose we board the submersible?"

Isa placed a hand on Alec's arm and took a deep, shuddering breath as she stared at the two tanks. "I want to help," she said in a low voice. "Cold doesn't affect me, nor will the depth. You've seen me swim. I can do this." Stiffening her back, she faced Logan. "I'm in."

Shaw and Rowan jostled Moray with their elbows, taunting him under their breath.

Moray's response blistered even Alec's ears. "Fine," he spat out, his face red.

"There is a reason only men serve on the BURR teams." Alec had to raise his voice to be heard over the ruckus. "In case your keen observational skills missed it, my fiancée is a woman. She lacks the physical strength to open a submersible port from the outside. She has no weapons training."

"I escaped that OctoFinn, did I not, wielding nothing more than a dive knife?" Isa threw him a glare, then huffed. "I can learn to fire a pistol. Moray can open the hatch and steer. That megalodon is filled with my people, with women and children, hostages to make the men cooperate. There's not a chance in the world I'm staying behind." Frowning, she stepped away from him. "If you can't handle working with a civilian female, I'll work with Aron. He knows the full value of a Finn woman's abilities."

Oh, hell no. There was not the faintest chance of that happening. Crossing his arms over his chest, he blew out a long, rough breath as he struggled to reconcile himself. It didn't work. Still, he had no choice. "Fine. I'll support you. But only if you agree to an intensive training session wherein you learn the bare basics about how to pilot a submersible."

Chapter Thirty-Four

The moment of insertion was upon them.

Wearing nothing but a flimsy, sleeveless chemise beneath a dressing gown, Isa curled her bare toes over the rough cement edge of the BURR training pool and stared at the two biomech octopuses slinking about beneath the water. Under Miss Lourney's close supervision, buckets of salt and a large, noisy aerator had turned the pool into an enormous aquarium.

"They seem hungry," she murmured, watching the way they paced back and forth upon their tentacles, their eyes constantly scanning. One stopped moving, fixing its slitty-eyed gaze on her.

"They are," Miss Lourney agreed. "Lobster—and other offerings—failed to satisfy them. Sausage casings filled with sheep's blood settled them some but—" Her sideways glance held a note of apology. "I expect they've developed a taste for Finn."

Isa's stomach flipped and sank to her knees. She didn't relish being thought of as a food source. The thought of letting that horrid creature touch her, of allowing it to fuse with her cardiovascular system gave her nightmares.

She glanced at Alec who stood beside her. And she worried harboring this parasite would drive the wedge between them even deeper. He'd grown distant and tense, all while imparting a barrage of details concerning submersible operations. Somewhere in the fifth hour of lectures her brain had all but shut down, refusing to absorb any additional material. A fact that Alec discovered while quizzing her.

A few feet away, Aron swore. "The things I do for my country. For my people."

From the moment he'd agreed to raid the megalodon, every other word from his mouth had been profane, and she concurred with every sentiment.

"You don't have to do this." Alec squeezed her hand. "We'll catch Drummond another way. Or Moray can handle it alone."

"Moray prefers backup." Aron slanted him a look. "Finn are not infallible."

Too true. "I'm going," she said simply. There was no need to say more. Repeated discussion had exhausted the topic. Besides, fear had all but stolen her ability to speak.

Pouring for hours over pages upon pages of schematics, the BURR men had drawn a number of conclusions. One, that despite being a marvel of Danish engineering, the floating castle could easily be scuttled with the detonation of a number of well-placed explosives attached to the pontoons that held it aloft. Two, releasing the OctoFinn from the megalodon would be best accomplished by positioning the submersible directly beneath the castle at a depth of one hundred and fifty feet—fifty meters—well below aquaspira depths.

The exit of the OctoFinn would provide an infinitesimally narrow window of opportunity for Aron and her to board the megalodon. While they attempted this daring feat, the remaining BURR men would patrol the pontoons, disabling explosives and OctoFinn.

Individual assignments were given, plans were drawn up, reports were issued—only to be shredded and tossed aside for a better scheme, the process repeating itself until everyone was satisfied. Except Alec. There were dark circles under his eyes, ones she'd put there. Isa hated that she was the cause, but she was determined to see this through.

She felt responsible for the entire situation. Without her research into Finn blood factors, biomech octopuses wouldn't exist. There would be no OctoFinn, no captive women and children aboard a megalodon. An international alliance would have no reason to fear an underwater attack.

Not that Iceland or Denmark had taken Mr. Black's warnings seriously. *Selkies were mythological creatures. No, they would not evacuate the floating castle or delay the wedding. Had Queen Victoria lost her mind?*

Aron tugged off his dressing gown and, wearing nothing but a pair of drawstring drawers, beckoned to Miss Lourney. "Do it."

Miss Lourney flushed bright pink at his near nudity—or was it appreciation for Aron's muscular form?—but she bent close, applying scalpel to skin. She made tiny nicks above his axillary artery and femoral vein. Aron barely flinched. The hope was that the scent of blood would guide the biomech octopus, helping it to attach quickly and accurately.

With a final string of searing expletives, he dove into the pool. The octopuses immediately moved in his direction.

Isa quickly shed her robe, lifting the hem of her chemise. Aron did not need two octopuses simultaneously attempting to attach to him.

Miss Lourney made two shallow cuts. "Good luck."

“Opposite ends of the pool,” Alec growled, clearly unhappy with the thought of anyone else glimpsing her nearly naked form, especially Aron.

Some dark, primitive part of her relished Alec's absurd, simmering jealousy.

He had insisted upon bathing suits, and Moray had laughed so hard he almost stopped breathing. Isa pointed out that clothing would impede the attachment process.

Prudish, Scottish morals were finally satisfied with a bare minimum of underclothes.

She pulled the pearl ring from her finger and pressed it into Alec's palm, curling his fingers about it. "Keep it safe for me," she whispered, finding it impossible to say more. If only they'd had more time to sort out their feelings without the constant weight of everyone's eyes upon them.

He frowned. "Don't do this. Please. Too many things can go wrong. I want—"

Raising onto the tips of her toes, she stopped his words with the gentle press of her lips. She wanted too. Wanted to promise him everything. Love. A future. A family. But she wouldn't promise him a future she wasn't certain she had.

Perhaps there were other, more qualified Finn men in the Navy who could take her place, to risk their lives in her stead. But time was limited—it was impossible to know who might be allied with her uncle or under the scrutiny of Commander Norgrove—and this was personal. Her uncle had stolen her life, her research, even her husband. Everything. She intended to wrest back whatever she could manage, to fight for a future on her own terms.

She ran her palm slowly down the side of Alec's rough, bristled cheek as he returned her kiss. Did she dare hope love was the motivation behind his almost-proposal? Did she dare place the care of her heart in another man's hands? Searching out those answers would have to wait, but when this was over she would do her best to find out.

Taking a deep breath, she plunged into the pool. Hanging in the water fully submerged, Isa opened her eyes. A biomech octopus turned on his tentacle tips and began to slink in her direction. Surfacing, she swam to the side of the pool and grabbed hold of the ladder, gripping its rungs and bracing for the first tentative touch that would signal its arrival. She gritted her teeth against the bad memories of being held captive in Lord Roideach's tank, of Thomas's stick.

Hungry for blood, the creature wasted no time. Within minutes, its heavy weight settled upon her back, wrapping cold, suckered tentacles about her neck and waist. A tentacle twined about her thigh, tapping. Isa closed her eyes, fighting a desire to flee.

"One word," Alec said through gritted teeth as he crouched beside the pool. "And I will end it."

"No." Her voice quivered. "This is something I have to do."

On the far side of the room, Moray howled. And then she too felt a piercing pain, as the barbed tip of the braided wire pierced the skin of her thigh. Muscles in the octopus's tentacle twisted and writhed, pushing the barb deeper, anchoring itself within her flesh.

She whimpered as another tentacle twined about her shoulder. Gritted her way through another piercing pain. One more time. The beak. The hirudin. She could do this. But when the octopus bit down on her shoulder, sinking its beak into her trapezius, she could hold back no longer. She screamed.

Through it all, Alec stayed beside her, steadfast and supporting, though she saw in his eyes the pain it brought him to be able to do nothing to ease her suffering.

Panting, she struggled to keep her breathing even, waiting, dreading the final stage: blood vessel fusion. There it was... a curious kind of lightheadedness. The room about her wavered and shifted as her blood pressure plummeted, as the creature siphoned off a full third of her blood volume.

"Isa?"

She couldn't answer.

Alec called to Miss Lourney. A needle pierced her arm. An intravenous saline line. But not fast enough, for stars twinkled and winked before her eyes a moment before blackness swallowed her whole.

~~~

Floating. Rocking. Drifting.

"That's the one-hour mark," Shaw called. "Tell him to come up and give us a report."

Isa peeled her eyes open. Some ten feet away, the BURR man stood on the pool deck, stopwatch in hand. Another man—impossible to name as he was suited up much like Alec had been when he'd attempted to rescue her after the megalodon attack—pushed the mouthpiece of his aquaspira into place and sank beneath the water.

Aron surfaced a moment later, shaking water from his hair. "Amazing. Almost worth the pain."
~~~

“Might turn off the women,” Shaw quipped.

"Might.” Aron’s gaze flicked in her direction. "Unless she was wearing one too."

"Watch it," Alec growled.

"What—?” Isa lifted her head from his shoulder.

Warm, solid and fully dressed, Alec floated in the pool beside her. Despite the biomech octopus latched onto her back—a nightmare of a dowager's hump—his arm was wrapped about her waist, holding her tight against his side. The other gripped the pool’s edge.

“You passed out from temporary blood loss," he reminded her.

And he’d leapt into the water to hold her head above water. Warmth spread through her. “How long have you—?”

"Two hours.” Worry filled the depths of his eyes. He pushed aside a lock of her wet hair. “How do you feel?"

“Sore.” Her shoulder throbbed, and there was a sharp pain in her thigh. She shifted. So did the octopus. Its pliant flesh brushed over hers, sending a ripple of nausea from her stomach into her throat. But it was too late for regrets; it was done. She swallowed her disgust. “Uncomfortable. But otherwise fine.”

“I hate to say it, but Moray's results are impressive. The biomech octopus has an innate intelligence that anticipates his actions. It moves to assist him with every task. Your own octopus has kept a slitted eye on me this entire time, as if it remembers me. I’ve the uncanny feeling that with the slightest questionable move on my part, it would reach out to strangle me." Alec's hand slipped from her hip, trailing over the wet cotton of her chemise as he loosened his grip. "Moray has come full circle. At first he hated the creature, now he's named it Rupert."

Isa rolled her eyes.

"I know." He flashed her a grin even as his arm fell away, leaving her bobbing in the water. "It's time for you to trial any new superpowers you now possess. We've only a few more hours here in the pool."

"Hours?" The schedule drawn up last night involved a full day of training exercises.

Alec's mouth flattened into a grim and worried line. "Keeping this room on lockdown is proving difficult. A number of high-ranking Naval officers have made inquiries. One even attempted to personally gain access. My brother is worried your uncle covertly alerted Commander Norgrove. In any case, we're being watched, and no one can be allowed to know Finn—or the biomech octopuses—exist."

"Agreed."

"While my brother arranged for Lady Roideach to claim her husband's body, Miss Lourney worked with the engineers to assemble a container to transport you both to the submersible. Sea loch training maneuvers begin tomorrow." He glanced over her shoulder, past the creature, and frowned. Isa turned. At the far end of the pool, Rip and Rowan—wearing dive suits and aquaspira breathers—slid into the water.

Ah, he was needed elsewhere. "You should be with them, training." She gave him a light push. "Go." The octopus perched upon her back reached out with one tentacle and poked Alec's shoulder.

For an awkward moment, they gaped at the creature.

"I'm not certain if it agrees with you, or remembers how I brutally separated it from Jona." He squinted. "Is it the same one?"

"Impossible to tell." She forced a smile onto her face, not wanting to keep him from necessary tasks. Besides, he would still be in the pool, a short swim away. "I wonder what would happen if I were to kiss your cheek?"

His eyes widened.

"Go." She laughed. "Train with Aron. There are at least half a dozen OctoFinn you will meet beneath the floating castle."

All humor drained from around his eyes. "When this is over, we talk."

Before she could respond, he turned, planted his hands on the edge of the pool and vaulted onto the deck. Folding her arms, she propped her chin on her hands and watched—unabashed—as he stripped away every last inch of his wet clothing, reminding her of all she'd yet to explore. Soon. The very minute this was over and her body was once again her own. He winked, then pulled on loose, linen trousers that—given the rough stubble of his dark beard and tousled damp hair—made him look like a shipwrecked pirate. On went his heavy rubber suit and the aquaspira breathing device. With a final wave, he grabbed a long stick and leapt into the deep end of the pool, ready to battle Aron and Rupert.

She dropped beneath the water's surface and swam the perimeter of the pool, adjusting to the feel of the octopus that gripped her back. With each kick, with each stroke, the creature assisted, propelling her almost effortlessly along the bottom of the pool. Four times she circled without the slightest urge to surface for a breath of air.

Irritatingly impressive.

Sinking to the deepest portion of the pool, Isa sat. As her red hair fanned out about her in a coppery cloud, the octopus adjusted its buoyancy, coiling its tentacles loosely about her arms and shoulders. Unable to bring herself to touch it any more than so-compelled, she folded her hands in her lap as the BURR men executed training maneuvers.

Married to a military man.

She tried to envision it. Never before had she had time for romance. Perhaps there had been a brief moment of possibility with Aron years ago. Standing in the moonlight on the beach when she'd received her first real kiss. But any chance they'd had was doomed long before he had petitioned her uncle for her hand. Not with a certified, licensed Finn physician living in Glasgow pressing his suit. With the slightest nudge, she'd rushed headlong into marriage, grasping at an opportunity that promised her so much, but delivered only disappointment and heartbreak.

Marriage was a commitment she'd not intended to repeat, unable to believe that any man could possibly be worth taking such a risk again. She'd been content to live alone, carving out a new life one day at a time.

Until Alec swept into her life, taking her by storm with his easy smile and his charming, flirtatious ways. Appearing at a Finn wedding, demanding escort to examine a dead body, swimming to her boat injured, but determined to unravel the mystery. A burst of bubbles escaped her lips. How long had she managed to resist him? A few days?

Beneath the water in front of her a mock battle raged. Aron played the role of an enemy combatant. Hand-to-hand—or rather hand to tentacle—combat as the BURR team tested a variety of techniques and weapons for fighting a man hosting a parasitic biomech octopus. The creature—Rupert—had bonded with Aron, observing and responding to his body language without delay. Between Aron's BURR training and the octopus's assistance, he had the decided advantage.

From the very beginning, Alec had made it clear he had no interest in marriage. As had she. The sparks between them were to be fanned into a torrid affair, one that would eventually end. But somehow, despite being doused repeatedly by treachery, a stronger bond had been forged between them.

What would it be like to be married to one Captain Alec McCullough? The very moment an engagement ring appeared in his hands, her heart had begun to pound with misplaced hope.

A false engagement. A brief ruse to inject a touch of discord into a social event, just enough to ensure an overly persistent mother and daughter would allow them a few moment's peace. She'd not expected for him to offer for her in truth, hardly dared hope that he would want more than the torrid affair he'd promised, but now she was the one who hesitated.

These past weeks had been filled with excitement and terror. When this mission was over, what then? She would never ask him to leave BURR or the Navy, but could she handle being left on shore while he disappeared on secret missions for days, weeks, possibly even months? Would the worry wear her down? Would regrets surface?

And what of *her* future? If she were willing to adjust to his life, would he extend her the same consideration? Standing together on the beach, he'd encouraged her dream of attending medical school. Would he do the same if she was his wife? She rather thought he might. Her heart flipped with joy. Was she a fool to hope she could have it all?

Wrapped in rubber and an alarming face mask, Alec finned to her side, pointing upward.

With a kick of her feet, she and her creature swam to the surface and joined Aron at the pool's edge. Her octopus reached out with one arm to grip the side of the pool, holding her steady. *Uncannily impressive.*

The clock hanging upon the wall indicated that, though she'd spent more than two hours completely submerged, not once had she felt a need—or even an urge—to breathe. *Terrifyingly impressive.*

Alec peeled the mask from his face and caught her gaze. "It's time," he said, clasping her hand as he nodded toward the door.

With a great clanking and rattling, several men pushed forth two cast iron bathtubs with wheels affixed to their claw feet. Attached to the side of each was an aerator, frothing and churning the water within.

Mouths hanging open in shock and amazement, the men glanced at each other but said nothing, not daring to inquire about the odd, slitty-eyed octopuses that stared at them from the shoulders of a nearly naked man and woman.

"Ready for your bubble bath, Moray?" Rowan laughed.

With a smirk, Aron pointed at his teammate and a tentacle reached out to grab Rowan by the ankle and dunk him. He glanced at Alec. "That's the solution to transporting us, tubs on wheels?"

"Parasitic octopuses are rather outside the realm of Navy preparation and experience," Alec answered. "This will be a short—if interesting—trip to the harbor."

Chapter Thirty-Five

With a whistle, the train pulled away from the depot. As the wheels clacked over the rails, Alec set his baggage on the floor of a cargo car beside crates of clucking chickens that were stacked from floor to ceiling. Shaw, Rowan and Rip did the same. A combination of steam trains, crank carts and coal carriages would carry them to points north.

He lowered himself to the floor. A slight creak emanated from his knee. A frown tugged at his lips. Dr. Morgan had fixed it. He wore the brace religiously, and it had been fine for days. He muttered a curse under his breath. One more day. He just needed his knee to last one more day.

Traveling with Isa and Moray via submersible had been the original plan, but was foiled by one Commander Norgrove who summoned Alec and the rest of the BURR team from the sea loch back to Glasgow on the very day the submersible needed to depart.

Alec had sworn until he was blue in the face.

Lord Roideach's final words had been to name Commander Norgrove as a member of the CEAP Selkie Committee, to admit that the commander answered to Isa's uncle, Commodore Drummond. Plans to sink the castle complex had been in place for months, plans that risked being exposed by CEAP inquiries into Davis's death. Commander Norgrove had not been protecting the BURR team by objecting to unsafe use of aquaspira breathers, he'd been acting on Drummond's orders to ensure that the BURR team never took their aquaspira breathers to depths that might interfere with any OctoFinn missions.

But words gasped out by a dying man weren't proof. Logan had been working around the clock—judging by the dark circles beneath his brother's eyes—without time to search for definitive evidence of the man's involvement.

"He's suspicious and rightly so," Logan grumbled, rubbing the back of his neck. "If you fail to appear, he might manage to alert Drummond, and we've no way of adjusting to any changes made to the timeline."

Resigned, they hastily cobbled together plan B. Not remotely ideal, but they had little choice.

"Go," Logan said. "But see Miss Lourney first to pick up your new weapons and supplies. She's been hard at work devising methods to ensure we don't harm any Finn hosts. In particular, she has designed a contraption—a mechanical ring—that incorporates cephalopod stunning powder and physical pressure to clamp down on the biomech octopus tentacles."

The two dozen devices that Alec collected from Miss Lourney wouldn't physically remove the creature from a Finn, but they would subdue the octopus while isolating the two circulatory systems. True separation—requiring vascular surgery—could then be performed at a time and location more conducive to surgery.

"Use these only if the Finn are capable of keeping their heads above the water's surface," Miss Lourney warned, then pointed. "At lower depths, your team should use these spears. The tips are loaded with cephalopod stunning powder. Jab the creature to render it unconscious but still capable of oxygenating Finn blood."

He was impressed. The restrictions of working under Lord Roideach's supervision had smothered her ingenuity and innovation. If this mission was successful, the Glaister Institute really ought to offer her directorship of her own laboratory.

Isa and Moray planned to employ the experimental ring clamps—impossible to test them—immediately upon boarding the megalodon. He hated the very thought of them depending so heavily upon an unproven device, but there was little choice. To seize control of the megalodon, Isa and Moray would need to function in dry conditions. He hated *everything* about their plan but, most specifically, he hated her involvement. The risks were astronomical. Were this a true BURR mission, her participation would have been prohibited. Again his concerns had been noted, then overruled.

Teeth gritted to the point of molar-cracking forces, Alec gathered his teammates and reported to headquarters.

"You are on convalescent leave, are you not, Captain McCullough?" Seated behind a large oak desk, Commander Norgrove twisted his lips, unhappy at being informed that Sinclair and Moray were hospitalized, consoled only by forcing the majority of the team to stand at attention before him, a captive audience.

"I am."

"Yet it has been brought to my attention that you have been involved in at least two BURR missions during this time period." Commander Norgrove steepled his fingers, and Alec took note of a network of faint, white scars that ran along their inside edges.

Finn. The missing connection that explained much. What position had Drummond promised the man? Military command of his fledgling nation? A young, pure-blooded Finn bride? He frowned. With luck, they'd never know.

"Training missions, sir," Shaw lied. "And only in a supervisory capacity."

Not the answer Commander Norgrove wished. He frowned. "That falls under the category of restricted duty. Has Dr. Morgan authorized your return to work?"

Not a chance.

"Has the appropriate paperwork been filed?"

Given Logan was in charge? Unlikely.

"I assume so, sir," Alec equivocated.

"Until such documentation crosses my desk, you are still on convalescent leave. No. More. Missions. Of any kind." He looked at each BURR team member in turn, his expression pinched. "Your assignment to guard the royal wedding is cancelled so that you might attend to paperwork. Consider this a friendly warning to all of you." Commander Norgrove tapped the top of his desk, uncertain they would follow orders. "I'll be keeping a close eye on your activities."

"Yes, sir." But they worked for the Queen now, if indirectly. Norgrove's warning altered nothing, save their travel accommodations.

"Dismissed."

Now, hours later, Alec leaned against the rough panel of the freight car's wall and stared at his dinner rations—tinned beef. He missed her, Isa. That first night, he'd laid out a bed roll beside her tub, unable to sleep as an aching loneliness settled deep inside his chest, as if he could feel her drifting away from him. With the creature attached, he could barely hold her in his arms. Still, despite his many apprehensions, he was proud of her. At the sea loch—though she lacked the strength and aim of a BURR man—she'd impressed everyone but Moray with her aquatic skills, learning to exit and enter a submersible with relative ease.

Without him, Isa and Moray would complete their mission by submersible, traveling in modified, aerated clawfoot tubs positioned mere feet from the exit hatch. The only way to accommodate their needs, what with the biomech octopuses attached.

Leaving her in the care of another man—even if he trusted Moray with his life—left a permanent lump of lead in his stomach. He had to force himself to eat; the upcoming operation would sap his every last calorie. Tossing aside the tin can, he leaned against his rucksack and passed a hand over his eyes, forcing himself to sleep. A restless slumber, filled with dreams of Isa hovering just beyond his reach.

They reached a small, remote fishing village on the northeast coast of Scotland the day before the royal wedding. In exchange for an ungodly sum, a local agreed to take them aboard his rusty, decrepit fishing boat, to steer past precise and defined coordinates, and not wonder when his passengers disappeared overboard.

While the fisherman kept his eyes pointed at the horizon, the BURR men geared up. Rip and Rowan flipped two flat rubber packages into the water and yanked on the inflation cord. With a hiss, the portable canoes inflated. Compressed gas canisters were attached to the stern of each, permitting a limited degree of steering capability. Two to a canoe, they boarded the inflatables and hunkered down to wait.

~~~
~~~

Though Isa had originally laughed at Alec's insistence that she and Aron wear clothing, she'd rapidly reversed her position. Not a single sailor was able to pass them without, at the very least, taking a peek. Many openly stared. Not that she could blame them. How many humans regularly wore tightly attached octopuses upon their backs and floated leisurely in a large, bubbling tub of water aboard a submersible?

"It's the only way to travel the north seas, mate," Aron quipped when they ogled. "Embraced by a cephalopod, soaking alongside a beautiful woman."

Aron joked constantly as sailors passed, drawing the attention away from her and onto himself. But no matter how funny or clever his witticisms, not a single sailor could untie their tongues or close their gaping mouths long enough to offer a rejoinder.

"There's no need," Isa said, "to take on the role of court jester. I'm fine, relatively speaking."

"I'm not." Aron closed his eyes and tipped his head back against the edge of the tank. "It's a bad idea to marry a BURR man. We're often away for undetermined lengths for inexplicable reasons. If I'd thought you open to the idea—"

"Don't." They'd cobbled together a comradery these past few days, though she'd not been blind to the extra effort he expended in an attempt to impress her. She refused to let him ruin his relationship with Alec with unwanted advances. "We're not suited, you and I. I told you as much the night you asked me to run away with you. I thought we could be—"

"Friends?" Aron sighed. "Fine. But I expect an invitation to the wedding."

Isa bit her lip. Would there be one, a wedding? She wasn't at all sure it was wise. But any decisions she reached would be her own, uninfluenced by Scot *or* Finn expectations. It certainly wasn't a topic she wished to discuss with a disappointed suitor.

For several long moments the only sounds came from the submersible's engines, a soft thumping and clunking, an ever-present noise. But another faint sound added to the rhythm. Footsteps. Crepe soles upon the floor. A head poked through the doorway but not, this time, to gawk.

"We're beneath the floating complex." The midshipman assigned to assist them with the escape hatch handed Moray a pair of scissors. He cleared his throat and two spots of color rose high on his cheekbones. "I'm told you wish to enter the water—"

"Stark naked. Wearing nothing but a tool belt." Aron twirled his finger. "Avert your eyes, sailor."

~~~

The sun hung low on the horizon. A few feet away in the other canoe, Rip and Rowan rocked on the waves. Kneeling for hours in the same position made his knee ache, but Alec did his best to ignore it. Cold water splashing into the inflatable combined with a relentless, icy wind made the dull pain manageable. As if it mattered. He'd see this mission completed at any cost.
~~~

"Time until we begin deep-sea fishing?" Alec asked Shaw, wanting a more precise reckoning.

"Eighteen minutes."

Submersibles usually arrived late. Occasionally, however, they were early. "Time to string the line."

Shaw clipped the end of the wire cable to the nose of their canoe, testing its strength. Satisfied, he handed the roll of wire to Rip who had brought his canoe closer and held out a hand. Fifty yards of steel cable spun off the reel as they paddled their canoes apart, stretching the line taut between the two vessels.

Five minutes before the scheduled hooking, Shaw and Rip each snapped a chemical stick and touched its tip to the wire. As the bioluminescent bacteria flowed along the steel cable, it fluoresced a deep red, alerting the approaching submersible to their orientation.

Every minute passed like ten as they scanned the surface of the water, searching for an approaching periscope. The critical moment had arrived. If the periscope missed the cable, even by so much as an inch, they would miss their ride. Alec didn't relish the idea of bobbing on the North Sea, hoping the captain would see fit to turn the submersible about for another try. It was a strong possibility that he wouldn't.

"Incoming!" Shaw called.

A blinking red light rose from the sea on the end of a gray, steel periscope that rushed toward them at high speed. Alec and his teammates gripped the sides of their canoes as the periscope snagged the middle of the cable, jerking the front ends of their canoes from the water, skipping them across the crests of choppy waves on a wild ride that shook every bone of every joint. Icy salt spray stung his face and his knee protested, but Alec couldn't stop the grin that stretched across his face.

His smile faltered. He'd miss this. The adrenaline rush of speed and danger. But the surgeries were mounting. Eventually, Dr. Morgan might not be able to repair his knee. It was a bitter pill to swallow, but his time on the BURR team was limited. Better to accept a promotion than to risk compromising a mission and being tossed out on his ear.

On the horizon, the last rays of the sun reflected off vast sheets of metal held together with great rivets. Steel, copper, and iron—the mélange of materials that comprised the floating castle.

As they drew closer, the multi-storied structure seemed to rise from the waves. Its base, the outer perimeter, mimicked an ancient medieval wall. A ship had no choice but to dock beside a single entrance flanked by tall watchtowers. Inside the walls upon an artificial hillside, a small village crouched at the base of the castle.

Curling through the town and leading upward to the castle's barbican—complete with a portcullis—was a road illuminated with the blue-white light of gas flames. A number of towers and turrets clustered together about a courtyard. Bright light gleamed from every window and joyful music filled the air.

A single patrol boat bobbed in the water beside the entrance to the complex, though several guardsmen marched back and forth upon its walls, bearing weapons and scanning the dark waters, ready to cut down any intruders. Not that the BURR team would venture close to test them. The greatest—and unseen—threat to the princess and the prince—along with their many guests—lurked below.

"Cut!" Alec yelled into the wind.

Shaw pulled a serrated knife from his hip and sliced through the cable connecting them to the other canoe, freeing them from the periscope as it sank back into the dark waters. Their ride was at an end. Some fifty feet below, Isa and Moray would be preparing to exit the submersible. Time to get to work.

His teammates inserted the mouthpieces of their aquaspira breathers, then slid into the cold waters of the North Sea. Cold didn't begin to cover it. Bone-chilling came close. The vulcanized rubber suit prevented them from reaching frozen and hypothermic, but just barely. They quickly disassembled their canoes, allowing the pieces to float away, nothing more than random bits of debris on the waves.

Submerging, they stayed close as they slipped beneath the waves. Time to inspect the many pontoons, scaffolding and platforms that held the floating complex at the ocean's surface.

Chapter Thirty-Six

As Isa stepped from the tub, she felt a shift in the rhythm of clanking beneath her feat. The Navy submersible slowing. The midshipman helped her buckle a kind of utility belt about her waist. Numerous items hung from its grommets including ring clamps, a novel device that she and Aron were counting upon to isolate their circulatory systems once they boarded the megalodon.

She climbed into the airlock escape chamber beside Aron. The biomech octopus gripped her tightly, unhappy that water no longer bathed its gills. Her head spun. Her heart pounded. And she was short of breath. Fear? Lack of sufficient oxygenation? Impossible to tell where one left off and the other began.

"Ready?" Aron asked.

As if I can change my mind now.

They'd practiced this in the sea loch, over and over, exiting smoothly with every iteration. With almost no equipment to check, and only the controls to monitor, this was a relatively simple exit. Yet her mind raced with "what ifs." What if the outside hatch door slammed closed during their exit? What if she missed the steel handholds on the outside surface of the submersible and was swept away into the giant propellers that drove the vessel forward?

She pulled the bioactive nocturnal goggles over her eyes. "Ready," she said. But she wasn't. Not at all. Even the biomech octopuses were apprehensive, clutching at each other's tentacles as if they sensed that this time something was different. It was. Impossible not to feel tinges of guilt, but she would do whatever was necessary to save the women and children aboard that megalodon.

Aron flipped a lever. Pipes rattled and creaked as water gushed into the chamber about her ankles. Frothing and churning, the level rose quickly. Calves. Knees. Thighs—in seconds she was fully submerged, the pressure of one hundred and fifty feet of water bearing down on her skin, her chest. The biomech octopus hunched between her shoulder blades seemed to sigh with relief.

Aron kicked past her, his arms extending toward the crank wheel that would open the exterior hatch. His octopus also reached for the wheel, at the same time tugging her octopus—and thus her—upward.

The moment was upon them. Isa gripped the ladder as tightly as possible and was relieved to see her octopus do the same. The hatch flipped open. Aron disappeared, leaving them connected only by their octopuses, by the two tentacles that gripped each other. Hand over hand, careful never to let go—lest the current sweep her away—Isa slowly made her way out and into the depths of the North Sea. Together, she and her octopus clutched the steel rungs of an exterior ladder welded to the outside surface of the submersible while Aron closed the hatch.

For what felt like hours, but was more likely mere minutes, they scanned the waters, seeing nothing but darkness. The North Sea was cold, so frigid that even a Finn would begin to feel a chill after prolonged submergence.

There. She could see it, the megalodon. Or rather its glowing, yellow eyes. As people moved about the control center in the vessel's "eye", the pupil seemed to shift—as if searching the depths for an unwelcome approach.

With a tap on her shoulder—tentacle or finger she knew not—Aron indicated it was time to move. She crouched on the side of the submersible, and her octopus extended its tentacles, ready to propel her out into the water just as it had done during countless practices in the sea loch. A second tap. She shoved off the submersible into the dark water, kicking furiously away from the submersible's wake.

An eerie stillness settled over her as they neared the mechanical fish, careful to avoid its bifurcated, jointed tail as it sliced through the water, aiming for the backside of its iron pectoral fin. Arriving before the

OctoFinn departed was their best chance for entry. They planned to slip into the mechanical beast via the airlock escape chamber before the external door was resealed. If they missed this opportunity, they might find the escape hatch drained of water, making entry impossible.

According to Maren, captive host Finn—six of them—would be ejected from the escape hatch as the evening activities aboard the floating castle complex commenced. Not that they ever intended to surface. Underwater explosives—mussel mines—were another dreadful invention to emerge from her uncle's efforts aimed at developing a Finn militia. Carefully placed for maximum effect, they would be attached to the giant pontoons that held the iron castle aloft and would, at the stroke of midnight, detonate.

Water would rush into the now-exposed hollows of the pontoons, and the entire castle would rapidly sink into the icy waters. Dressed in their evening finery and gathered together in the great hall, guests—lords and ladies, princes and princesses, the occasional king and queen—would rush from the castle gates in shock and horror, desperate to board the lifeboats. Of which there were not enough.

Her octopus caught the side of the megalodon, landing beside Aron. Ten feet away, on the other side of the pectoral fin, shadowy figures bearing sacks of mussel mines emerged from the escape hatch, rising quickly. One, two... Aron held up a hand, indicating that she should stay where she was while he crept beneath the surface of the pectoral fin. Three, four, five—

He nabbed the sixth and final departing OctoFinn, bringing his fist down on the side of the man's head rendering him unconscious. The octopus on his back jerked with alarm, until it sighted the octopus on Aron's own back. The two octopuses tangled their tentacles, as if speaking by secret hand signals.

With practiced efficiency, Aron snapped a belt about the man's waist, a belt attached to an UP bag and a sounding beacon. No ring clamps for this octopus. Not yet. The creature's gills were still very necessary. With the biomech octopus breathing for him, the OctoFinn would rise to the surface. Once the BURR team had the situation beneath the castle under control, they would enlist the aid of the castle's patrol boat to retrieve any and all reclaimed Finn.

That left four BURR agents handling five conscious and motivated OctoFinn.

Much discussion had revolved around an attempt on Aron's part to render all six OctoFinn unconscious, but starting a fight one hundred and fifty feet below the water's surface was deemed ill-advised and likely to fail. They were to focus on incapacitating the megalodon engine and securing the safety of the prisoners before raising the submersible to the surface.

Aron waved her into the escape hatch. Feet first, she slid into the narrow tube. He followed, closing the door and draining the water from the chamber. Her bare feet met the iron floor, and she staggered upright, pushing the goggles upward onto her forehead.

With his face a mask of determination fixed in place to avoid upsetting the two biomech octopuses, Aron unhooked two ring clamps from his belt. She did the same. With a nod, they worked in tandem to clamp the tentacles that drew blood from their legs. A faint chemical tingle rushed across her thigh. On her back, the octopus squirmed in objection, then subsided, calmed by the cephalopod stunning powder now flowing through its system. She counted to ten, then clamped the tentacle attached to her shoulder.

Mentally apologizing to the creature, she drew her dive knife and cut through the tentacles, through the braided wires. Cringing against the pain, she pried its beak from her shoulder and let the octopus fall to the floor with a wet thud. Free. Rupert, however, was allowed to ride on Aron's back. Plans had been made to return with the creature still attached for further study. Isa shuddered.

Silently, Aron unsealed a wet bag and reached inside to withdraw two TTX pistols. He slapped one into her hand with a look of warning. Aim had not proved to be a skill she possessed; a mere three darts not nearly enough ammunition for her to hit a target.

Weapon drawn, he darted from the chamber, making a sharp left toward the stern. Priority was to incapacitate the engine. With luck, he'd find the kill switch with ease.

Isa turned right, wending her way down hallways, moving deeper into the belly of the beast as blood trickled from her neck. She started to turn right when she heard the angry shout of a man. Women and children whimpered and cried. Drawing the TTX pistol, she breathed a silent prayer to an ancient sea goddess and turned the corner. Aiming for his stomach, she pulled the trigger.

Whoosh. Whoosh. Whoosh.

She fired all three darts. A single one hit the guard.

For a moment, the man clutched his thigh, then dropped like a stone to the floor in front of a series of cages that held six women and three small, crying children.

"Mrs. McQuiston?"

She blinked. "Avra?" Not three weeks ago, she'd removed the webbing between this girl's fingers and toes. "Your father?"

With tears in her eyes, Avra sobbed. "Mr. Drummond sent him to the surface. There's this octopus creature—" Her mouth fell open. "Your leg... shoulder... you had an octopus..."

Holstering her empty weapon, Isa bent over the fallen guard, pulling a set of keys from his belt, grateful she wouldn't need to pick the locks. "All for the purpose of rescuing prisoners." She pushed a key into the lock, trying one after the other until the barred door fell open. "Is... Mr. Drummond aboard?"

"At the helm." Avra took the keys Isa pressed into her hands. "Five men, including our guard, should be left on board. Be careful. The woman in charge of caring for the octopuses has aspirations that have made her blindly loyal."

There was a loud *thunk*. The megalodon shuddered, then fell silent. Men yelled. Loud thuds and bangs—sounds of fighting—echoed through the vessel.

"What's happening?" a woman cried, her children stood behind her, their eyes wide.

"We're taking this submersible to the surface where help waits." That was the plan, but the grunts and cries issuing from the hallway weren't promising. "Stay calm," she said. To herself as much as to the prisoners. "Free the others." With a rueful look at the empty TTX pistol, she slid her dive knife free. "Then stay here. Hang on to something. The naval officer with me is unfamiliar with this particular vessel and its controls. It could be a rough ride."

Stomach churning, heart pounding, she stepped into the hallway and began to make her way toward the brains of the mechanical shark.

Bodies littered the floor. She counted three. That left her uncle and—

"Aron!" she cried. Then clamped her hands to her mouth. He had eliminated a number of the guards, but now found himself locked in a multi-armed struggle to subdue Rupert.

"Stay back!"

The octopus upon his back had woken and was convulsing, its tentacles frantically thrashing. Aron fought to stay upright as it heaved its bulbous body from left to right, then backhanded him with a tentacle sideswipe to the head. Blinking, he attempted to control the many tentacles, but the creature was intent upon escape, yanking at the clamped tentacles still fused to Aron's shoulder and thigh.

He hissed in pain as dark blood ran in a steady stream down his leg. The creature's movements calmed for a moment as it peered at her over Aron's shoulder, and she could swear its eyes narrowed as it fixed her in its sights.

"Enough." Cursing, he pulled the TTX pistol from his holster and shot the creature between its bulging eyes. With a brief look of shock, it slumped in a gelatinous heap as Aron slid to the floor, leaning heavily against the wall. "Rupert woke," he mumbled. "Tried to pull free. Cut it off?"

With her dive knife, she obliged. But dark blood flowed from his thigh where the tentacle connected. Yanking a length of cord from her belt and fashioning a tourniquet Isa pushed his hands—and a limp tentacle—aside.

"The ring clamps won't help. The tentacle has pulled away from your femoral vein. The damage is deep inside your leg." As she twisted, the seeping blood stopped, but his face was far too pale. Between the injury and the hirudin that had flowed from the octopus's beak into his circulatory system, thinning his blood, he'd lost a significant amount of blood. He needed more help than she could provide here.

An alarm began to blare. Red lights began to flash. And the floor of the submersible tipped. They were rising.

Isa gently slapped Aron on the cheek. "Wake up," she begged. "What do I do?"

No response. But she knew the answer: stop her uncle.

"Avra!" she yelled, waving to the girl when she peeked about the corner. "Come. Hold the tourniquet. Don't release the pressure on his leg, or he'll bleed to death."

Wide-eyed, Avra complied.

Isa loaded more darts into her pistol, slid Aron's own loaded weapon into her holster, and began to creep down—or rather up—the slanted hallway. Heart pounding, she peered around each corner before moving forward, trying to imitate the way she'd seen the BURR team move. At the end of the hallway was a room. She could see a periscope, a control panel—its expanse covered with buttons and dials—and an empty captain's chair. She was about to step forward when a familiar form rushed from a room into the hall and skidded to a halt.

Miss Russel stared at Isa, her jaw slack. "You!" Her eyes narrowed. "I should have left you to die from that amoeba infection."

"But you didn't." Isa lifted the TTX pistol and—doing her best not to close her eyes—fired at the woman's heart. *Thunk.* The dart struck her midsection. Good enough.

"What!" Miss Russel yanked the projectile from her abdomen as she staggered sideways. "Commodore Drummond!" she yelled, lifting her skirts and turning on unsteady feet to lurch down the hallway.

Ice flowing through Isa's veins at the memory of the torment she'd suffered at this woman's hands, she followed, firing again. *Whoosh.* The second dart skewered Miss Russel's gastrocnemius just above her Achilles tendon. Screeching, she fell to the floor and clutched her calf. "Please!"

Isa recalled Alec's words. "One bullet slows a man down. Two will drop him. Three will kill." Mr. Black and the BURR team would want to question Miss Russel. Extensively. Resisting the temptation to end Miss Russel's life, she lowered the pistol.

Her mistake.

A fist struck her wrist, knocking the TTX pistol from her grip. She glanced sideways in time to see fury contort her uncle's face a moment before his arm lashed out again. He wrapped his fingers about her neck and pushed her backward against the wall, cutting off her air. He yanked the other pistol from her holster and threw it away. It clattered as it skittered across the floor. Her dive knife followed.

"Unexpected visitors." Her uncle's chiding voice held a dark note. "How very rude. I presume you have arrived to inform me that Maren divulged my plans and all is lost?" He released the pressure on her throat ever so slightly.

"How could you?" she rasped, clawing at his chest, her fingernails catching at his leather waistcoat. "You betrayed your own family, your own people!"

"I beg to differ, *niece.*" He leaned closer, his nostrils flaring, his voice edged with blades. "I work—tirelessly—to steer the Finn people back onto the path from which they should have never strayed. My sister, you—all those who are the product of interbreeding with Scots—are impure and unworthy. Some of you are, however, useful and will be allowed to live, should you agree to serve."

"Not a chance! It's you who should surrender." She kicked at his legs, but without enough oxygen, her blows did little but inconvenience him. "You'll regret this!"

He barked a laugh. "Unlikely. If reliable, *capable* help was available, they wouldn't have sent *you*." He glanced at her shoulder, at her leg where stubs of tentacles protruded from raw and bloody entry wounds. "Stealing my creation. Boarding my vessel. Attacking my men. You have an overinflated opinion of yourself. Barely worth keeping alive. After all that effort I went to marry you to a man who would use your talent for the greater good of Finnfolk." He shook his head. "Anton was forever complaining about his infertile wife, so upset his laboratory work suffered, but I tolerated it all because *you* were brilliant."

He pushed harder against her neck and spots began to dance in her vision. She tried to fight back, but her kicks, her punches were feeble protests in the face of his anger.

"Look at you now, martyr to a lost cause." Her uncle's lips twisted. "Same as your husband. He had the gall to defy me, to refuse to hand over the results of your work—work I enabled—citing ethical concerns. He was warned not to defy my orders."

Anton had taken a stand against her uncle? That would explain why her husband had been so anxious the last weeks of his life, pacing in his study, restless and uncommunicative.

Her uncle snarled, his eyes filled with pewter ice. "Yet someone had to be the first to trial the attachment procedure. Torturous and prolonged, that groundbreaking experiment generated a plethora of data, even if it was, ultimately, a failure. I'd rather hoped he would survive."

Stars flickered on a field of black velvet as a tear ran down her cheek. Poor Anton. Their marriage might have failed, but he'd been a decent man. He didn't deserve such a death, alone and in pain. Had her uncle not shoved such a wedge between them, might they have found their way to a happy marriage? Might they have eventually grown to love each other? But they'd never had a chance, not with her uncle manipulating their lives.

Beneath her feet, the megalodon shuddered. Metal rivets creaked and groaned as the submersible shot its way toward the surface. Her uncle grabbed hold of a metal handle bolted to the wall, the only warning she received before they were airborne, lifted off their feet for the briefest of moments before the vessel slammed back onto its stomach.

She crumpled to the floor, gasping for air. Her uncle crossed the room to a metal box mounted to the wall. He opened a small door in its side, exposing a glowing white-blue orb within. Coiled wire connected it to a dial. To a timer. His fingers flew over a tiny control panel, flicking a series of levers.

"What are you doing?" she gasped.

"Do you think I'd let my ship fall into the hands of the Royal Navy? I'd rather see this vessel sink to the bottom of the sea."

A bomb? Heart racing, she forced herself onto her hands and knees. Did he intend to go down with his submersible? No. Otherwise he'd not have brought it to the surface. He planned to escape.

Her uncle slammed the door shut, then strode in her direction as she scrambled across the floor, grabbing her dive knife, slashing him as he drew close. Her blade caught at the cloth of his trousers, slicing through his flesh beneath.

With a roar, he struck the side of her head. Blackness exploded and the world disappeared.

Chapter Thirty-Seven

Wearing bioactive nocturnal goggles, Alec and his swim partner, Shaw, completed their circuit beneath the floating castle complex, sweeping the faint light of a red decilamp over its underwater framework as they hunted for any signs of mussel mine clusters and found nothing.

The giant pontoons were the most obvious targets. But a determined man—and Drummond had gone to great trouble—might also see value in destroying the giant, caged propellers that constantly turned on and off, forcing seawater downward as they spun, an essential system that helped to stabilize the complex above. The propellers kept everyone standing upright. If they stopped working, everyone aboard, from kings to kitchen boys, would land on their arses. This event was so politically charged that any number of high-ranking gentlemen might take offense at having their billiard balls rearranged or their cards scattered. And the ladies could not withstand the social trauma of having their unmentionables exposed or their finery ruined by a sudden upending of the punch bowl.

Amusement hitched up the corner of his mouth.

Alec and Shaw were joined by Rip and Rowen. There was a quick exchange of hand signals. Neither had found any sign of tampering. As planned, they'd arrived before the OctoFinn.

Nothing to do but begin another circuit.

Beneath the third pontoon, Alec tapped Shaw on the shoulder and pointed. Faint blue lights trained over a distant pontoon. A classic mistake. Blue light—though it illuminated surfaces nicely—was all too easily detected by the human eye. Following protocol, Alec and Shaw extinguished their red decilamps. Red light didn't travel as far into the dark water, making it far more difficult for enemies to detect.

As the OctoFinn utilized a tube of bissel thread glue to attach a mussel mine to the pontoon, he and Shaw swam closer. The OctoFinn never saw them coming. A blow to the side of the head. A quick jab with the spearhead to the body of the biomech octopus, and the creature fell limp.

Shaw flipped on his lamp and swept a red decilamp overhead. Several mussel mines hung from bissel threads at regular intervals from pontoons and propellers. Quickly removing them, Alec and Shaw attached UP bags and blue locater beacons to both the OctoFinn and the bag of explosives, dragged them from beneath the castle and sent them to the surface. If Moray had done his job—eliminating one of the six OctoFinn Lady Roideach insisted would be sent—four remained.

They found a second OctoFinn easily enough and repeated the procedure, sending him and his parasite to the surface. While doing so, they passed Rip and Rowan with their own limp OctoFinn in tow.

A quick conference via hand signals told Alec that five of the presumed six OctoFinn had been dispatched. He and Shaw had snagged two, Rip and Rowan another pair. Rowan had sighted a fifth unconscious OctoFinn floating at the water's surface, his UP bag flashing a green light.

Relief washed over him. Moray had been assigned the green beacon. That meant he and Isa had successfully intercepted the final OctoFinn to exit the megalodon. Alec hoped their entry and the rest of their tasks had met with equal success.

One sole OctoFinn remained to be captured.

A decision was reached. Rip and Rowan swam for the surface, intent on commandeering the patrol boat attached to the castle guard. Alec and Shaw headed back beneath the castle.

Long, cold minutes passed as they swam, searching for a glimmer of faint blue light.

There.

Alec tapped Shaw's shoulder and pointed. The final OctoFinn, a sack of mussel mines suspended from the belt about his waist. Not enough explosives to collapse the structure entirely, though there would be significant damage.

Finning for all he was worth and ignoring a growing pain in his knee, he surged forward, keeping pace with his swim partner. Shaw hoisted his spear into position, jabbed the creature's body. But this time, the cephalopod stunning chemical failed to subdue the biomech octopus.

Instead of falling limp, it began to thrash. Those four tentacles not occupied with holding onto the Finn man—who glanced over his shoulder with alarm and drew his dive knife—whipped through the water, reaching for them. A tentacle lashed Alec's arm, striking the rubber of his suit with a force that was certain to leave a bruise. Shaw wasn't as lucky. One of the flailing tentacles ripped the aquaspira from his mouth, snapping a return valve and flooding the breathing loop. Another tentacle wrapped about his ankle as he finned away.

Alec's mind flashed to Davis's death. But Shaw was conscious, even now grabbing the bailout bag breather from his chest harness and shoving the mouthpiece into place. Drawing his own dive knife, Alec sliced through the creature's tentacle, freeing Shaw from its grip. *Go!* he signaled. With just enough oxygen in reserve to make the surface, Shaw kicked away.

Blue octopus blood gushed from the severed tentacle into the sea water, and Alec jabbed his own spear into the body of the octopus, hoping that a second dose might subdue—but not kill—the creature. Or exert an undue effect upon the Finn man to which it was attached. Either way, he needed to place a ring clamp about the injured octopus's limb so that it might continue to breathe as Alec dragged its host to the surface.

The Finn man moved with startling agility, lunging at him with his serrated knife. Nor was the biomech octopus through fighting. Dodging both tentacles and the man's blade proved impossible. The creature caught Alec by the wrist, squeezing tight, attempting to force him to drop his knife. The Finn man slashed through Alec's rubber suit, and a deadly cold trickle of water flowed across his skin. He was on borrowed time.

He maneuvered away. But the creature lashed out, its eyes glinting in the white-blue light the Finn still held, and wrapped another tentacle around Alec's knee. His mechanical knee. With an effortless flex of its muscles, the octopus squeezed, and Alec felt a vague pop—then excruciating pain.

One of the bolts holding the artificial knee joint in place had snapped.

Agony made every movement a struggle. Alec rammed his elbow into the man's jaw with a bone-jarring crunch then—ignoring the cold icicles piercing his skin—punched the octopus directly in the eye.

Biting on his mouth piece, gritting against the pain, Alec forced himself to take several long, deep breaths. Hyperventilation would lead only to death. His and the OctoFinn's, for the creature had finally fallen limp.

Quickly, Alec clipped an UP bag and an active beacon to the man. He clamped a clotting cuff around the bleeding tentacle. He reached for the sack of remaining mussel mines—

Gone.

During the fight, it must have been jarred loose. Currents would have carried the sack of explosives away. No telling if they were beneath the castle complex, lodged in the blades of a stabilizing propeller, or lost to the sea. Either way, they were irretrievable.

He grabbed the unconscious OctoFinn and began to swim. Progress was slow with only one leg fully functional and the frigid water creeping into his suit, but at last he cleared the castle complex. Punching the UP bag, he let it haul them to the surface.

Shouts rang out. An engine roared. Moments later he was dragged from the water onto the deck of the patrol boat. Alec ripped his goggles from his face and found himself staring up at Shaw. "Situation report?"

Shaw tipped his head toward the cabin. "All OctoFinn retrieved, the attached creatures cuffed with ring clamps. No deaths. All mussel mines recovered, save any this last one carried." An eyebrow lifted.

"Gone." Alec sat up and—with a grimace—yanked the swim fins from his feet. His knee throbbed. "There might be damage. Probably not enough to compromise the structure. I wouldn't risk ordering an evacuation." Particularly given the paucity of life boats and the panic such an order would create. "But I'd advise we move some distance away from the structure."

Shaw swore. "Better to leave them in their palace."

"Isa and Moray?" Alec asked.

"Sent up the expected OctoFinn, so contact was made. No sign yet of the megalodon."

"I'll speak to the captain." Shaw started to move away, when his eyes dropped to Alec's leg. Only the brace had saved it from total destruction. "Shit. The octopus?"

"A minor inconvenience." It was a trick to relax his jaw enough to speak as bolts of lightning shot through his leg with the slightest movement. He waved a hand. "I just need a few minutes. Go. Move us out of range."

The minute Shaw's back was turned, he pulled a medic bag toward him. Fished out a syringe and rummaged through vials of medications, searching. He pulled a glass vial of a local painkiller from the supply box and filled the syringe. He jabbed the needle into his leg, shoving the plunger home. Blessed numbness overtook his knee.

Pain faded, only to be replaced by growing worry.

Who was he kidding? With each beat his heart whomped its dread against his rib cage. The woman he loved was on her insane uncle's submersible, hundreds of feet below icy waves. Far from where he could do anything to help her.

Or Moray.

The boat began to pull away, moving a safe distance from the castle. Impossible to calculate the damage the mussel mines might cause.

"Bad plan," Rowan said, frowning down at the syringe he still held. *Caught.* "If I thought for one second you intended to stay off your feet, I'd approve. But from the moon eyes you've been making at that woman and the way you're staring off into the dark..."

"I need to be ready." Alec lifted a hand. "Help me up."

Rowan sighed, but helped him struggle to his feet. "Dr. Morgan is going to tie your arms and legs to a bed. Good luck convincing him to fix your knee again. Last time he was muttering about amputation."

He leaned against the railing, shifting most of his weight to his good leg. This was it. His last mission. "I'm thinking I'd better accept that offer of promotion."

He'd miss working as part of the BURR team, but the promotion would ensure he didn't leave this world entirely behind. Passing on all he'd learned, strategizing with his team and its future members. With Isa at his side, they'd carve out a new and exciting life. Together. He had to convince her that they belonged together.

Light from the castle windows poured out across the rough sea. Inside nobility danced, unaware—or uncaring—of the potential threat beneath their feet. But his thoughts lay deeper, with Isa and the megalodon. Any number of things could have gone wrong. He tried not to list them in his head. And failed.

Muffled thuds—felt as a pressure wave rather than heard—reverberated beneath his feet. He closed his eyes briefly, praying that the explosion originated beneath the castle, not within the megalodon.

Feet pounded as Rip and Shaw jogged across the deck to stand beside him. Rip raised a spyglass to his eye, scanning the base of the castle complex. They'd stopped six OctoFinn, confiscating all but one twelfth of the explosives. Would it be enough?

"The structure appears intact," Rip reported. "Wait. It's beginning to tilt. At least one pontoon has sustained significant damage. Possibly two."

Lights flickered in the castle window. A few blinked out. Not hard to imagine the screams and chaos within. Crowns and tiaras toppling. Silk skirts and coattails doused with punch. Steambots scattering nuts and bolts as they crashed into walls. The BURR men held their collective breath as they watched, then exhaled with relief as the structure rebounded and settled—so much as was possible on the North Sea—but with a tilt of approximately ten degrees. A definitive end to the festivities.

Still, there was no sign of the megalodon.

"Time to move in," Shaw announced. "We need access to their infirmary. These OctoFinn need care." He frowned at Alec. "You need a cot as well."

Alec shook his head. "Not until—"

The megalodon breached the surface, water streaming down its nose in great rivulets as it leapt from the ocean. Its chest slammed back down onto rough waves with a great crash that reverberated across the waves.

That was not the plan. *That* was an emergency blow. Something had gone wrong. That Moray and Isa had managed to take control of the boat was now in serious doubt. They needed to board the vessel—weapons drawn—and assess the situation.

Rip and Rowan ran for the helm, ordering the captain to turn about. The patrol boat's engine roared to life. As it bounced across the crests of the waves, shooting toward the submersible, Alec wrapped his hand around the nearby railing and hauled himself along the gunwale, ignoring the ominous crunching of his knee, gritting his teeth against a fresh pain uncontrolled by the numbing agent.

The great metal jaws of the megalodon opened, baring jagged iron teeth illuminated by the Lucifer lamp that hung from the roof of the submersible's mouth.

Silence. The submersible's engine had stopped. Moray—and he prayed—Isa had boarded the vessel and stopped the submersible's engine, forcing it to surface. But the eerie silence wasn't promising. Icy fear gripped his heart.

His teammates seized weapons and prepared to board. Alec grabbed hold of a nearby weapon, one likely provided to the castle's guards—basic, but effective. A single shot was loaded. Shaw frowned at him, but said nothing. He understood.

Their boat bumped against the megalodon, and Alec's world narrowed to a single focus: Isa.

They swarmed over the jagged teeth as one, but soon left Alec in their wake, much as he tried to scramble behind them. By the time he descended the stairs that led directly into the helm, his teammates were already rushing down a long corridor without him.

Leaving a weeping Isa behind. He growled as he limped to her side. She was tied to the captain's chair—naked—her arms bound to her sides with rough rope. Drummond, formerly of the Royal Navy, knew his knots.

Cries and shouts echoed back to him as the BURR team took possession of the submersible. He pressed a quick kiss to her damp hair, then set his weapon down and applied his fingers to the knots. "It's over. We saved the castle. Mostly."

"Stop," she said, her voice choked and panicked. "Moray is hurt. Bleeding badly. I've no idea where my uncle went, but he has no intention of letting the Navy confiscate his megalodon. There's a bomb." She tipped her head at a strange metal box bolted to the wall.

He threw open the door in its side and swore. Four dials—each designed to accept a number between zero and nine—were mounted inside; a means to activate—or deactivate—the bomb. Copper wire wove and coiled across the surface of a glass sphere. Occasional swirls of faint light flashed through its fluid-filled interior. A single wire passed through the glass surface, threading its way to a gray, metallic cube suspended within.

"A Lucifer lamp detonator." Clipping the wire or breaking the glass would cause it to immediately explode. "There's no feeding portal. Judging by the occasional flicker of the bioluminescent organisms, the creatures are running low on nutrients." When the glow faded below a predetermined luminosity, it would trigger the bomb. He scanned the device. Inputting a four-digit code was the only way to save this submersible.

But without knowing the code, stumbling upon the correct combination was unlikely in the time left to them. Still, he would try.

“Shaw!” Alec bellowed. Drawing his knife, he quickly cut through the ropes that bound Isa. “We need to evacuate!”

He turned back to the bomb.

Chapter Thirty-Eight

At Alec's cry, chaos erupted. Shaw appeared with Aron flung over his shoulder, still unconscious and bleeding, followed closely by Rip who shepherded the terrified captive women and their children up the metal staircase and outward to where the boat waited with their loved ones. In his arms was a limp Miss Russel, the TTX dart still protruding from her lower leg. He raised his eyebrows, a silent inquiry as to whether she was friend or foe.

"Tie her up," Isa said. "She works for my uncle."

A muscle jumped in his jaw, and he nodded. There would be no escape for Miss Russel.

"Here." Avra broke away from the group, stepping sideways to hold out a simple chemise, which she gratefully accepted.

"Thank you." Naked in front of Finn was one thing but standing nude among the BURR team felt wrong. Isa pulled the garment over her head while Avra rushed up the metal stairs as Shaw urged them all to hurry.

Anger, worry and relief washed over her. Once everyone was safely evacuated, she'd like nothing better than to see this submersible sink to the bottom of the sea. The Royal Navy, however, would want to keep this extraordinary technology within its grip.

Alec bent over the four small dials, frantically working through different sequences of numbers. "Do you know of any combination that might mean something special to your uncle?"

None came to mind, though she rattled off the year of his birth—he was rather self-important—along with those of a few family members. But not a single combination worked. Her mind raced. Four digits, possibly random, though she doubted it. Her uncle always planned and schemed.

"Go," he said. "Follow the others. Please."

"Not without you." She didn't like the way he was favoring his knee, and there was not the slightest chance she would leave the man she loved behind on a ship rigged with a bomb.

"Caught the bastard trying to use the escape hatch." Gripping her uncle by the collar, Rowan shoved the traitor into the room. Arms tied behind his back, his lip was split and an eye was rapidly swelling. His trousers were wet from the knees down, and a steady trickle of blood flowed from beneath their hem over his bare feet. A grim satisfaction pulled at her lips.

Alec's jaw dropped, then snapped shut. He glared at their prisoner. "The code." Expectant, he lifted his hand again to the dial. The Lucifer lamp flickered and dimmed.

"Not a chance." Her uncle lifted his chin. "I'd rather go down with my ship."

"Tempting," Alec said. "But I rather think the Crown would prefer an extended interrogation followed by lifetime imprisonment, though I won't rule out execution."

Defiant, he lifted his chin. "They will learn nothing."

"Martyr to a lost cause?" she parroted.

"Another will rise." Pragmatism drained away as a fervent look burned in her uncle's eyes. There would be no reasoning with such a zealot.

Beside them, the Lucifer lamp dimmed. The crystalline structure within the glass sphere began to release tiny bubbles of gas.

"We're down to mere minutes," Alec warned, continuing to work at the dials.

Her uncle took a deep breath and closed his eyes.

Isa narrowed hers. "A number. You're a navy man, through and through. Committed to the ocean. What do you value? Your work. Latitude and longitude?"

Her uncle started, the slightest jerk of his shoulder. That was it. A location on a map.

"Stornoway?" She strode to the chart cabinet and slid open one of the three drawers and began to leaf through the maps. Nothing was marked. Her stomach churned. Could she guess it in time? She looked back at her uncle. "The location of your cave?" Nothing. What did he value more than anything? Becoming a king. "The Faroe Islands?" The skin about his eyes twitched.

"That's it!" She dug through the maps, dragging out one that included her uncle's would-be kingdom, and called their geographic coordinates. "Sixty-two degrees north latitude and seven degrees west longitude. Six-Two-Zero-Seven."

Alec spun the dials into position. A loud *thunk* sounded in the wall behind them. He looked up at her, his eyes bright with pride. "It worked!"

With a roar, her uncle twisted. Breaking free from Rowan's grasp, he ran up the stairs with the kind of speed only achieved by those with nothing to lose.

Rowan chased after him, and Isa followed. She ran as fast as her feet would carry her, arriving at the megalodon's mouth the moment her uncle leapt over its jagged iron teeth, flinging himself into the sea—arms tied behind his back.

He might make it. He might not. Either way they would lose any information he possessed.

"Keep an eye out," Isa yelled. "Be ready to catch him if he surfaces!" She darted back down the stairs. "He jumped!" she yelled to Alec. Running to the control panel, she scanned the many levers and buttons. It had to be here somewhere.

"Drummond?" Alec limped to her side. "The man is insane."

"Agreed. But he might manage to survive. Might. But if we activate the hyena fish, there's a chance we could drive him back to the surface. Help me figure out how to release them!"

Alec blinked at her. "You're a most vengeful enemy." But he too began to search the instruments. "My brother will want him alive." He paused, then—as if there was some doubt—added, "For questioning."

Isa didn't much care what happened to him, provided that from this point forward his life was wretchedly unpleasant and preferably spent behind bars. "Mr. Black will have a few hours at the very least. Longer, if my uncle consents to reveal the cure for a *caeruleus* amoeba infection in order to save his own skin. This one?" She pointed at an unusual button.

"Possibly. It's not anything critical to the submarine, so push it and see what happens."

Without hesitation—but with quite a bit malice aforethought—she jammed her finger down on the blue button.

Nothing happened.

"Try whatever button lies beneath that odd, orange flip cover."

Desperate and willing to push any button that would not send them on a nose dive to the sea floor, she lifted the guard cover and pushed.

Beneath their feet, something mechanical ground to life. The metal floor vibrated. There was a shout from above. They looked at each other with wide eyes. Without asking, she ducked beneath his arm. "Lean on me," she said, offering what support she could as they made their way—together—up the metal stairs and out onto the strange balcony formed by the shark's mandible.

Rowan—using a large metal hook on a pole—was busy fishing her bloody, bitten and screaming uncle from the water. They hauled him onto the patrol boat's deck where he flopped about, cursing while Rowan flipped hyena fish back into the water.

Evil of her, perhaps, but his pain and suffering were gratifying. She hoped he suffered at least one bite for every single Finn he'd ever injured or killed.

Rip held out a hand, assisting her onto the patrol boat. Alec followed, his landing accompanied with a long slow hiss escaping from between his clenched teeth.

"How bad is it?" she asked, about to bend over to examine his knee, despite the thick rubber dive suit he still wore.

"Don't." He caught her by the waist, tugging her close. "It's been better. Dr. Morgan will need to fix it. Again. But our mission was accomplished. You're safe. For the moment, nothing else matters."

She stared at the floating castle and raised an eyebrow. It tipped at a rather precarious angle. Impossible to imagine those within would agree.

"Mostly accomplished," he amended. "We averted an international catastrophe. Well, mitigated it at the very least. The Queen will be able to lift her eyebrows and remind the other monarchs that they *were* warned." His voice grew soft. “You have no idea how much I love you. I have never been so much in awe of a woman. Words fail me.” He lowered his mouth to hers for a soul-wrenching kiss that left her in no doubt of how he felt.

Of how *she* felt. She shook as emotion overwhelmed her. For the first time, a man had well and truly swept her off her feet. “I love you,” she whispered as he pulled away.

“You have no idea how much I’ve hoped to hear those words.” This time, his kiss held enough heat to make her skin steam.

The boat’s engine roared to life. It leapt across the waves toward the floating castle, yanking them. Alec brushed his knuckles over her cheek and leaned forward, intent on claiming another kiss.

A loud whistle pierced the air. They looked up to find Shaw staring and shaking his head, exasperated.

“Enough of that, lovebirds,” Shaw barked. “Moray and the Finn men need medical care, and they need it now.” Assessing eyes swept over them. “As do the both of you.” He pointed at a bench with a pistol. “Sit. Try to take another step on that knee, Mac, and we’ll find out exactly how many TTX darts it takes to drop a BURR man.”

Chapter Thirty-Nine

Purple. A reasonable compromise between somber and celebratory. A deep shade appropriate for a widow, Isa's dress was trimmed with ruffles and black lace that swept backward into a bustle. Slight puffs of silk capped her shoulders, quickly tapering into tight sleeves that ended at her wrists. The neckline revealed a hint of her clavicle but no cleavage. Demure, yet not dull. A gown fitting for Alec's promotion ceremony.

She pinned a matching hat with a scattering of feathers to her upswept hair, snatched up a pair of black, lace gloves, and descended the stairs to wait at the window of her townhome. Outside, the Glasgow sky was overcast. A fine mist of water collected upon the window, gathering itself into drops before slipping down the glass in streaming rivulets.

A month had passed since that near disastrous night on the North Sea. The immediate days following the megalodon's capture and the castle explosions had been a blur.

With the BURR team dismissed from security detail and instead working beneath the aegis of the Queen's agents, the Royal Marines had no official presence and therefore no right to make demands upon those who staffed the floating castle. Fortunately, the resulting chaos had thrown the castle guards into such a confusion that not one man had questioned the BURR team's authority as they transported a small company of wounded Finn men and their families to the castle complex's infirmary.

Nor had the castle physician in charge objected. The appearance of several men and one woman—herself—with a number of severed octopus tentacles sprouting from their bodies had rendered him momentarily speechless. But he was a man of science, easily intrigued, and the moment he finished treating assorted minor injuries the guests had sustained during the explosion—burns from toppling candles, cuts from shattered chandeliers, blows from tumbling potted palms—he joined Alec and Isa in the surgical suite, his interest captured.

Aron was the Finn in most need of surgical attention, having lost much blood during his struggle with the biomech octopus. She immediately set about prepping him for surgery. Alec struggled to repair the damage done to his leg, commenting that further operations would likely be needed once they returned to Glasgow.

With Aron at last stable, they moved on to the next Finn patient, working steadily but quickly, removing tentacle after tentacle before infection could take hold.

Performing vascular surgery was a challenge what with the castle's floor tilted at a ten-degree angle, making every step feel like a drunken stagger. Alec—his knee kept numb with a strong, local-acting anesthetic—propped himself on a stool beside the operating table, avoiding any unnecessary steps. Isa stood at the patient's head, monitoring oxygen levels of each Finn, taking extreme care with their anesthesia. The castle physician listened and watched carefully—albeit with wide eyes—as she explained the finer details of Finn physiology.

Convinced of the Danish physician's capabilities and reassured by Alec's oversight, she'd climbed onto the operating table, the final patient.

Almost.

Her uncle had refused to reveal the full treatment for the *caeruleus* amoeba. Though his infected leg wound was forcibly submerged in cold saline water and subjected to deep debridement, the organism continued to spread, engulfing his lower leg and creeping proximally up his thigh. Treatment options were under debate when Mr. Black arrived and ordered a swift and conclusive amputation, followed by immediate dirigible evacuation. The former navy commodore was delivered directly to a secure underground cell where he would recover. Or not.

Though Mr. Black's frown carved deep lines about his mouth when he caught sight of his brother's knee, Alec refused to accompany him on the dirigible, insisting he would remain with his BURR team while they piloted the captured megalodon submersible back to Glasgow. All Finn—patients and family—elected to reboard the submersible for a return trip rather than set foot in a dirigible's gondola. Including Aron, who insisted he would not survive a dirigible ride in his current condition.

Isa worried for him. Not only had he lost a lot of blood, the octopus's attempt to wrench free had done some serious tissue damage. Alec too was in agony, his lips white with pain. By the time they reached Glasgow, the drug he'd injected had long since lost its effectiveness. Their care had taken immediate priority upon docking on the River Clyde.

She'd left the organization and care of the Finn in the hands of Avra, who had proven to be a remarkable young woman. "Go," Avra had said, waving her off. "I'm quite capable of arranging for their transport back to the islands."

Shrugging away the guilt that tried to wrap itself about her shoulders, she'd followed a grim Dr. Morgan who—after a long-suffering sigh—took Alec into surgery immediately. "Before you do any more damage to the bone vasculature. At this point, you'll be lucky to keep your leg."

Worry churned a hole in her stomach as she paced outside the operating room for hours. From time to time, a nurse or an orderly would zip in and out of the surgical suite—muttering about nerve blocks and bolts and gears—while Dr. Morgan rebuilt Alec's knee.

At last, success was declared, and Alec was wheeled into a recovery room.

"He managed to snap a bolt, slip three gears and rupture two lubricant sacs," Dr. Morgan announced. "I had to resect another inch of femur." He fixed Isa with a stare. "Perhaps he'll listen to you? Try to convince him that he ought to leave the BURR team before he loses a leg."

Sage advice. But who was she to order Alec about? Time and again she'd been told to abandon her dreams of medical school, yet she persisted. The BURR team meant everything to him, and he knew the risks of returning to active duty.

Time passed and, as yet, neither she nor Alec had broached the topic of marriage. Nor had she caught sight of his grandmother's pearl ring. Though their torrid affair had certainly continued apace. Her cheeks heated. Not that Alec had neglected to court her. They'd spent hours talking, speaking about anything and everything. Save their futures—separate or together.

He'd sent flowers, escorted her on long walks quayside, visited with her mother—where flattery won him every regard—and spent time with the rest of her extended family along with many other members of the small Finn Glasgow community. Much heated debate surrounded the marriages of Mrs. Drummond, also known as Lady Roideach. Scottish law decreed her actions bigamous, but not all Finn people agreed. Regardless, Maren sat inside a cell, awaiting trial for her misdeeds. Mr. and Mrs. Carr had custody of Thomas and their granddaughter, with Nina and Jona's supervision.

For her own part, Isa had braved Alec's mother's disdain and accepted a grudgingly offered invitation to tea. Mrs. McCullough—her back stiff with disapproval—had offered a few comments about the weather. Conversation had been difficult until Cait introduced the topic of pharmacobotany.

Heads bent together in the parlor, they'd sipped tea and discussed journal articles detailing recent discoveries of bioactive substances extracted from unusual plants found growing in the Amazonian rainforest, ones that scientists now struggled to fabricate in laboratories. One substance in particular held much promise. Added to the mix of substances already present in Finn anesthesia, it might completely eliminate the risk of induced dive reflex during surgical procedures. Alas, the compound was experimental and beyond her reach. Much, it seemed, like medical school.

And marriage.

Though it appeared Alec had finally reached a decision concerning his career. Yesterday, a skeet pigeon had landed on her windowsill, pecking at a pane of glass. She'd unfurled a message from him.

You are cordially invited to attend a promotion ceremony. Tomorrow, I become Major McCullough. I'll send a carriage for you at three o'clock in the afternoon. It's a formal event. Still, please say you'll come.

Hence her formal attire.

At exactly three o'clock, a familiar carriage drawn by clockwork horses stopped before her townhome. But it was Mr. Black, not Alec, who knocked at her door. She tried hard to suppress her disappointment.

"I requested a few moments alone with you, Mrs. McQuiston," he said, once they were settled and underway. He reached inside his coat and drew forth an envelope. "The Queen sends her regards."

With trembling fingers, she opened it. Drew forth the thick, heavy paper within. And read its contents. Mouth agape, she looked up. "You, Mr. Black, are a miracle worker."

"So it's been said." He grinned. "But I find myself compelled to mention that it was Alec who ensured your medical school application was brought to the attention of the Queen. Furthermore, because it was held against you in the past, my brother asked me to make it clear that the offer of enrollment stands, regardless of your marital state."

She nodded, her chest tight. This was a moment she'd rather hoped to share with Alec, not his brother. "Thank you."

Mr. Black sighed. "Don't look so crestfallen, Mrs. McQuiston. I am but the squire, performing a few last official tasks so that your knight might present a final token of his regard."

Her eyebrows drew together and she peppered him with many questions, but Mr. Black refused to elaborate.

Not even—after weaving their way through the busy streets of Glasgow—when the carriage stopped before a small building near the Glaister Institute. A single guard snapped to attention, and a fevered memory of passing through its door once before swam to the surface.

Could this be an entrée to the famed Glaister Institute? A tremor of excitement ran through her. Dare she hope she was to be granted access? They descended a spiral staircase, arriving at a broad iron door. A red light glowed steadily in an odd box affixed to the multi-toothed and geared lock.

"If you'll place your finger there." Mr. Black indicated a touch sensor.

Heart pounding, she complied. A cool gel oozed out, as if the lock tasted her fingertip. There was a faint buzz of electricity, the light blinked green and the lock popped open.

"First door on your left."

"Will you be at your brother's ceremony?" she asked, beginning to wonder if she herself would be in attendance. All too easy to be lost and forgotten in a dusty corridor such as this.

He laughed. "Not a chance. The Royal Navy would prefer to forget I exist. No worries," he said when she frowned. "I prefer it that way. Alec and I have already toasted to his success."

With a clang, the door closed behind her. Turning about in amazement, she took in the narrow hall and the high ceilings where various conduits ran in all directions, some emitting steam, some dripping with condensation. Throughout the network of pipes and wires, spiders had spun cobwebs. This was not a heavily trafficked area.

"I did make an effort to dust our laboratory." Alec stood in a doorway, grinning. He was dressed in all his military splendor. Quite a different image than the one he'd first presented all those weeks ago out on the island.

"*Our* laboratory?" She lifted an eyebrow, walking closer. Drawing a fingertip across one of the many medals pinned to his chest. "Is this a tryst? Or has something unusual and unexplained turned up on a distant beach?"

Grabbing her about the waist, Alec spun her around into an... airshaft? "All of the above, though I've been told selkies are nothing but myth." He kicked the door shut behind them and stared down at her. "I've an inclination to share my underground lair, if you'll have me."

"Have you?" She bit her lip, fighting a smile. "In exactly what manner?"

"You do look ravishing." Grinning, he pulled her close. "But business first. Despite the trauma of earlier weeks, the ingenuity of the science behind the biomech octopus, the megalodon draws me. Interrogation of your uncle, Lady Roideach and Miss Russel has produced an Icelandic name—albeit an alias—of the evil genius who succeeded in fusing mechanical components with living organisms. The Queen's agents are already at work tracking down this scientist. Meanwhile, I wish to study the techniques used to create these biomech creatures, to be involved in any decisions as to the wisdom of applying them." He paused. "And there is the issue of my mechanical knee. Though I don't wish to leave my BURR team, I can no longer actively participate in their missions."

She nodded, waiting.

"A joint position both in the Glaister Institute and with my team has been arranged. I may occasionally deploy, but my involvement will be limited to oversight only. Leaving me more time for a wife and, eventually, a family."

"Children?" Worry tinged her voice.

"In a few years. When we're ready. As suits *both* our careers." The corner of his mouth hitched up. "We'll have plenty of time to work—and play—in this laboratory. Together. I've arranged for you to have full access to the resources of the Glaister Institute. If you wish to explore the possibilities of newly discovered pharmacobotanicals, we'll fill out the paperwork—maybe lean a bit on my brother—until you have your way."

Isa tugged off a lace glove and pressed her palm to his freshly shaven face, enjoying the rare sensation. She grinned. "Have my way..."

With a laugh, Alec lowered himself onto his good knee and tugged a familiar ring from his pocket. "I love you, Isa, and I don't want to wait any longer. I've given you about as much time to reach a decision as I can bear. Please. Attend my promotion ceremony as my fiancée. Say you'll marry me."

Emotions hit her like a tidal wave, strongest among them was love. Marriage wasn't a risk she'd wanted to take again. Until she'd met Alec. With him at her side, she no longer felt hollow, empty of all but her goals. He offered her everything she'd ever wanted and more. Time to stop doubting herself and her feelings.

"Yes," she said. "Yes, I'll marry you... according to the Finn tradition while standing barefoot on the sand."

He slid the ring onto her finger and stood. "Please tell me there's no tradition of an extended engagement among the Finn?" He caught her by the waist as he stepped closer. Then closer still, backing her up until her rear bumped into a sturdy—if old—wooden desk that stood against the wall.

Did they have time for investigating the thoughts that fueled the bright gleam in Alec's eyes?

"None." She swallowed, dropping her gaze to the cravat tied so expertly about his neck. "It's only a matter of gathering family and enlisting an elder to perform the ceremony."

"Excellent." He caught her lips in long, tender kiss. "Now that our future is arranged, perhaps we might explore the benefits of matrimony? I *am* cleared for desk work." He lifted her, depositing her on its surface and delving into the froth of ruffles about her ankles without waiting for her answer. He nipped at her earlobe. "And today's ceremony isn't for another hour."

She pushed half-heartedly at his beribboned chest as he spread her knees apart. "I spent half the morning primping. These are my only pair of silk stockings."

"Oh?" His fingers brushed upward over the surface of her thinly-clad legs until they found the bare skin of her thighs. He nuzzled at her neck, whispering into her ear, "And still you managed to overlook a certain undergarment. Am I meant to think that an accident?"

Hooking her legs about his, she drew him close. "No."

"I promise not to ruffle a single feather." Love shown is his eyes and echoed in her heart. "Trust me?"

"I do." With that she gave herself over to the sheer pleasure of his touch, and the outside world vanished, leaving only the love and heat that sparked to life whenever they were together.

Epilogue

Barefoot upon the sand, her skirts whipping about her knees, Cait stood as a witness to her brother's marriage, one of which she heartily approved. Not only was Isa beautiful, she was brilliant and unconventional and... other. Unlike her, Isa was completely at home in her own skin. Cait had learned much about the Finn world these past weeks and, though this world wasn't truly hers, the fact that such a people existed? That gave her hope.

Her gaze drifted over the water. Too long she'd wondered about her own unusual origins. It was long past time she set about finding—demanding—answers.

The couple stood in the surf as it surged, swirling and frothing about their ankles, staring into each other's eyes, as if someone had slipped a love potion into their afternoon tea. An old woman—the Finn elder—cleared her throat and began the ceremony by joining the bride and groom's hands together. She spoke in a strange, old language, one that was apparently rarely spoken, even among the Finn.

"Beneath the moon, where the land meets the sea," Nina spoke softly beside her, translating for her benefit, "we join together a daughter of the seal and," the elder paused, adjusting for her brother's Scottish heritage, "her chosen one."

Nicely done.

A small girl stepped forward, lifting a crown that looked to be woven of dried seaweed and wildflowers. The woman placed it upon the bride's head, chanting more words about the duality of a life lived both on land and in the sea.

The bride's mother looked proud, even if Cait's mother looked somewhat pained. After all, years of matchmaking, of throwing Perfect Patsy in Alec's path, had failed.

Alec's BURR team members were all present and in their element. Informal, wet and wind-swept suited them. Her brother Quinn had proved unreachable, but Logan was here. Barefoot and in his shirtsleeves, she was reminded of the boy he'd been when his gypsy mother had first dropped him off on their doorstep. Wild and carefree. A side of himself he'd long ago stuffed into a suit and tied off with a starched cravat.

He caught her glance and frowned, shaking his head. But he'd promised. She'd done all he asked and more.

Tipping her face upward, she let the wind whip the long, dark locks of her unbound hair about her face and smiled. She'd already accepted a position at Lister Laboratories in London where—despite her brothers—she *would* find adventure.

~~~~~
~~~~~